The Book Shelf
920 Memorial Ave. Thunder Bay (behind Mr. Sub)
(807) 343-7323 or 1-877-854-7323
www.thunderbay.com

Dear Reader,

The night is a time for danger, mystery—and romance. Silhouette Books is thrilled to offer you the last of three special volumes containing the final title in the award-winning Night Tales series, in addition to a bonus story, all by bestselling author Nora Roberts.

In *Night Shield,* Allison Fletcher refused to be seduced by Jonah Blackhawk's smooth charm while she worked undercover at his nightclub. She was too much a cop to fall for a shady renegade like him. But the more she learned about Jonah, the stronger her attraction to this bad boy grew. If only she could start trusting him...and stop wanting him!

In *Night Moves,* widow Maggie Fitzgerald has moved to a small town tucked away in the Blue Ridge to put her grief behind her. Meeting sexy landscaper Cliff Delaney was an unexpected surprise! But her newfound happiness is threatened when a body is uncovered on her land—and the man she is falling for might be the prime suspect!

Under the cover of night, danger lurks in the shadows...can love triumph over the dark?

Enjoy!

The Editors
Silhouette Books

NORA ROBERTS

Night Tales:
Night Shield & Night Moves

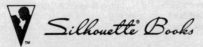
Silhouette® Books

Published by Silhouette Books

America's Publisher of Contemporary Romance

SILHOUETTE BOOKS

NIGHT TALES: NIGHT SHIELD & NIGHT MOVES

Recycling programs for this product may not exist in your area.

ISBN-13: 978-0-373-28588-4

Copyright © 2010 by Harlequin Books S.A.

The publisher acknowledges the copyright holder of the individual works as follows:

NIGHT SHIELD
Copyright © 2000 by Nora Roberts

NIGHT MOVES
Copyright © 1985 by Nora Roberts

Visit Silhouette Books at www.eHarlequin.com

Printed in U.S.A.

CONTENTS

NIGHT SHIELD

Chapter 1

He didn't like cops.

His attitude had deep roots, and stemmed from spending his formative years dodging them, outrunning them—usually—or being hassled by them when his feet weren't fast enough.

He'd picked his share of pockets by the time he'd turned twelve and knew the best and most lucrative channels for turning a hot watch into cold cash.

He'd learned back then that knowing what time it was couldn't buy happiness, but the twenty bucks the watch brought in paid for a nice slice of the happiness pie. And twenty bucks cannily wagered swelled into sixty at three-to-one.

The same year he'd turned twelve, he'd invested his carefully hoarded takes and winnings in a small gambling enterprise that centered around point spreads and indulged his interest in sports.

He was a businessman at heart.

He hadn't run with gangs. First of all he'd never had the urge to join groups, and more importantly he didn't care for the pecking order such organizations required. Someone had to be in charge—and he preferred it to be himself.

Some people might say Jonah Blackhawk had a problem with authority.

They would be right.

He supposed the tide had turned right after he'd turned thirteen. His gambling interests had grown nicely—a little too nicely to suit certain more established syndicates.

He'd been warned off in the accepted way—he'd had the hell beat out of him. Jonah acknowledged the bruised kidneys, split lip and blackened eyes as a business risk. But before he could make his decision to move territories or dig in, he'd been busted. And busted solid.

Cops were a great deal more of an annoyance than business rivals.

But the cop who'd hauled his arrogant butt in had been different. Jonah had never pinned down what exactly separated this cop from the others in the line of shields and rule books. So, instead of being tossed into juvie—to which he was no stranger—he'd found himself yanked into programs, youth centers, counseling.

Oh, he'd squirmed and snapped in his own cold-blooded way, but this cop had a grip like a bear trap and hadn't let go. The sheer tenacity had been a shock. No one had held on to him before. Jonah had found himself rehabilitated almost despite himself, at least enough to see there were certain advantages to, if not working in the system, at least working the system.

Now, at thirty, no one would call him a pillar of Denver's community, but he was a legitimate businessman whose enterprises turned a solid profit and allowed him a lifestyle the hustling street kid couldn't have dreamed of.

He owed the cop, and he always paid his debts.

Otherwise, he'd have chosen to be chained naked and honey-smeared to a hill of fire ants rather than sit tamely in the outer office of the commissioner of police of Denver.

Even if the commissioner was Boyd Fletcher.

Jonah didn't pace. Nervous motion was wasted motion and gave too much away. The woman manning the station outside the commissioner's double doors was young, attractive with a very interesting and wanton mass of curling red hair. But he didn't flirt. It wasn't the wedding ring on her finger that stopped him as much as her proximity to Boyd, and through him, the long blue line.

He sat, patient and still, in one of the hunter-green chairs in the waiting area, a tall man with a long-legged, tough build wearing a three thousand dollar jacket over a twenty-dollar T-shirt. His hair was raven-black, rain straight and thick. That and the pale gold of his skin, the whiplash of cheekbones were gifts from his great-grandfather, an Apache.

The cool, clear green eyes might have been a legacy from his Irish great-grandmother, who'd been stolen from her family by the Apache and had given the brave who'd claimed her three sons.

Jonah knew little of his family history. His own parents had been more interested in fighting with each other over the last beer in the six-pack than tucking their only son in with bedtime stories. Occasionally Jonah's father had boasted about his lineage, but Jonah had never been sure what was fact and what was convenient fiction.

And didn't really give a damn.

You were what you made yourself.

That was a lesson Boyd Fletcher had taught him. For that alone, Jonah would have walked on hot coals for him.

"Mr. Blackhawk? The commissioner will see you now."

She offered a polite smile as she rose to get the door. And she'd taken a good, long look at the commissioner's ten o'clock appointment—a wedding ring didn't strike a woman blind, after all. Something about him made her tongue want to hang out, and at the same time made her want to run for cover.

His eyes warned a woman he'd be dangerous. He had a dangerous way of moving as well, she mused. Graceful and sleek as a cat. A woman could weave some very interesting fantasies about a man like that—and fantasies were probably the safest way to be involved with him.

Then he flicked her a smile, so full of power and charm she wanted to sigh like a teenager.

"Thanks."

She rolled her eyes as she shut the door behind him. "Oh boy, are you welcome."

"Jonah." Boyd was already up and coming around his desk. One hand gripped Jonah's while the other gave Jonah's shoulder a hard squeeze in a kind of male hug. "Thanks for coming."

"Hard to refuse a request from the commissioner."

The first time Jonah had met Boyd, Boyd had been a lieutenant. His hair had been a dark, streaked gold, and his office small, cramped and glass walled.

Now Boyd's hair was deep, solid silver, and his office spacious. The glass wall was a wide window that looked out on Denver and the mountains that ringed it.

Some things change, Jonah thought, then looked into Boyd's steady bottle-green eyes. And some don't.

"Black coffee suit you?"

"Always did."

"Have a seat." Boyd gestured to a chair then walked over to his coffee machine. He'd insisted on one of his own to save himself the annoyance of buzzing an assistant every time he wanted a hit. "Sorry I kept you waiting. I had a call to finish up. Politics," he muttered as he poured two mugs with rich black coffee. "Can't stand them."

Jonah said nothing, but the corner of his lips quirked.

"And no smart remarks about me being a damn politician at this stage of my game."

"Never crossed my mind." Jonah accepted the coffee. "To say it."

"You always were a sharp kid." Boyd sat on a chair beside Jonah's rather than behind the desk. He let out a long sigh. "Never used to think I'd ride a desk."

"Miss the streets?"

"Every day. But you do what you do, then you do the next thing. How's the new club?"

"It's good. We draw a respectable crowd. Lots of gold cards. They need them," Jonah added as he sipped his coffee. "We hose them on the designer drinks."

"That so? And here I was thinking of bringing Cilla by for an evening out."

"You bring your wife, you get drinks and dinner on the house—is that allowed?"

Boyd hesitated, tapped his finger against his mug. "We'll see. I have a little problem, Jonah, I think you might be able to help me with."

"If I can."

"We've had a series of burglaries the last couple of months. Mostly high dollar, easily liquidated stuff. Jewelry, small electronics, cash."

"Same area?"

"No, across the board. Single family homes out in the burbs, downtown apartments, condos. We've had six hits in just under eight weeks. Very slick, very clean."

"Well, what can I do for you?" Jonah rested his mug on his knee. "B and E was never my thing." His smile flashed. "According to my record."

"I always wondered about that." But Boyd lifted a hand, waved it away. "The marks are as varied as the locations of the hits. Young couples, older couples, singles. But they all have one thing in common. They were all at a club on the night of the burglary."

Jonah's eyes narrowed, the only change of expression. "One of mine?"

"In five out of the six, yours."

Jonah drank his coffee, looked out the wide window at the hard blue sky. The tone of his voice remained pleasant, casual. But his eyes had gone cold. "Are you asking me if I'm involved?"

"No, Jonah, I'm not asking you if you're involved. We've been beyond that for a long time." Boyd waited a beat. The boy was—always had been—touchy. "Or I have."

With a nod, Jonah rose. He walked back to the coffeemaker, set down his cup. There weren't many people who mattered enough to him that he cared what they thought of him. Boyd mattered.

"Someone's using my place to scope marks," he said with his back to Boyd. "I don't like it."

"I didn't think you would."

"Which place?"

"The new one. Blackhawk's."

He nodded again. "Higher end clientele. Likely a bigger disposable income than the crowd at a sports bar like Fast Break." He turned back. "What do you want from me, Fletch?"

"I'd like your cooperation. And I'd like you to agree to work with the investigating team. Most specifically with the detective in charge."

Jonah swore, and in a rare show of agitation, raked his fingers through his hair. "You want me to rub shoulders with cops, set them loose in my place?"

Boyd didn't bother to hide his amusement. "Jonah, they've already been in your place."

"Not while I was there." Of that, he could be sure. He could sense cop at half a mile, while he was running in the other direction in the dark.

And had.

"No, apparently not. Some of us work during daylight hours."

"Why?"

With a half laugh, Boyd stretched out his legs. "Did I ever tell you I met Cilla when we were both on night shift?"

"No more than twenty or thirty times."

"Same smart mouth. I always liked that about you."

"That's not what you said when you threatened to staple it shut."

"Nothing wrong with your memory, either. I could use your help, Jonah." Boyd's voice went soft, serious. "I'd appreciate it."

He'd avoided prisons all his life, Jonah thought. Until Boyd. The man had built a prison around him of loyalty and trust and affection. "You've got it—for what it's worth."

"It's worth a great deal to me." He rose, offered his hand to Jonah again. "Right on time," he said as his phone rang. "Get yourself some more coffee. I want you to meet the detective in charge of the case."

He rounded the desk, picked up the receiver. "Yes,

Paula. Good. We're ready." This time he sat at the desk.
"I have a lot of faith in this particular cop. The detective
shield's fairly new, but it was well earned."

"A rookie detective. Perfect." Resigned, Jonah poured
more coffee. He didn't bobble the pot when the door
opened, but his mind jumped. He supposed it was a
pleasant thing to realize he could still be surprised.

She was a long-legged, lanky blonde with eyes like
prime whiskey. She wore her hair in a straight, sleek tail
down the middle of her back over a trim, well-cut jacket
the color of steel.

When she flicked those eyes over him, her wide,
pretty mouth stayed serious and unsmiling.

Jonah realized he'd have noticed the face first, so classy
and fine-boned, then he'd have noticed the cop. The
package might have been distracting, but he'd have made
her.

"Commissioner." She had a voice like her eyes, deep
and dark and potent.

"Detective. You're prompt. Jonah, this is—"

"You don't have to introduce her." Casually Jonah
sipped fresh coffee. "She has your wife's eyes and your
jaw. Nice to meet you, Detective Fletcher."

"Mr. Blackhawk."

She'd seen him before. Once, she recalled, when her
father had gone to one of his high school baseball games
and she'd tagged along. She remembered being impressed by his gutsy, nearly violent, base running.

She also knew his history and wasn't quite as trusting
of former delinquents as her father. And, though she hated
to admit it, she was a little jealous of their relationship.

"Do you want some coffee, Ally?"

"No, sir." He was her father, but she didn't sit until the
commissioner gestured to a chair.

Boyd spread his hands. "I thought we'd be more comfortable having this meeting here. Ally, Jonah's agreed to cooperate with the investigation. I've given him the overview. I leave it to you to fill in the necessary details."

"Six burglaries in a period of under eight weeks. Estimated cumulative loss in the ballpark of eight hundred thousand dollars. They go for easily fenced items, heavy on the jewelry. However, in one case a victim's Porsche was stolen from the garage. Three of the homes had security systems. They were disengaged. There have been no signs of break-in. In each case the residence was empty at the time of the burglary."

Jonah crossed the room, sat. "I've already got that much—except for the Porsche. So, you've got someone who can boost cars as well as lift locks, and likely has a channel to turn over a variety of merchandise."

"None of the goods have turned up through any of the known channels in Denver. The operation's well organized and efficient. We suspect there are at least two, probably three or more people involved. Your club's been the main source."

"And?"

"Two of your employees at Blackhawk's have criminal records. William Sloan and Frances Cummings."

Jonah's eyes went cold, but didn't flicker. "Will ran numbers, and did his time. He's been out and clean for five years. Frannie worked the stroll, and it's her business why. Now she tends bar instead of johns. Don't you believe in rehabilitation, Detective Fletcher?"

"I believe your club is being used as a pool to hook fish, and I intend to check all the lines. Logic indicates someone on the inside's baiting the hook."

"I know the people who work for me." He shot Boyd a furious look. "Damn it, Fletch."

"Jonah, hear us out."

"I don't want my people hassled because they tripped over the law at some point in their lives."

"No one's going to hassle your people. Or you," Ally added. Though you did plenty of tripping of your own, she thought. "If we'd wanted to interview them, we would have. We don't need your permission or your cooperation to question potential suspects."

"You move them from my people to suspects very smoothly."

"If you believe they're innocent, why worry?"

"Okay, simmer down." Boyd stayed behind the desk, rubbed the back of his neck. "You're in an awkward and difficult position, Jonah. We appreciate that," he said pointedly with a subtle lift of his eyebrows for his daughter. "The goal is to root out whoever's in charge of this organization and put an end to it. They're using you."

"I don't want Will and Frannie yanked down into interrogation."

"That's not our intention." So he had a hot button, Ally mused. Friendship? Loyalty? Or maybe he had a thing going with the ex-hooker. It would be part of the job to find out. "We don't want to alert anyone on the inside to the investigation. We need to find out who's targeting the marks, and how. We want you to put a cop on the inside."

"I'm on the inside," he reminded her.

"Then you should be able to make room for another waitress. I can start tonight."

Jonah let out a short laugh, turned to Boyd. "You want your daughter working tables in my club?"

Ally got to her feet, slowly. "The commissioner wants one of his detectives undercover at your club. And this is my case."

Jonah rose, as well. "Let's clear this up. I don't give a

damn whose case it is. Your father asked me to cooperate, so I will. Is this what you want me to do?" he asked Boyd.

"It is, for now."

"Fine. She can start tonight. Five o'clock, my office at Blackhawk's. We'll go over what you need to know."

"I owe you for this, Jonah."

"You'll never owe me for anything." He walked to the door, stopped, shot a glance over his shoulder. "Oh, Detective? Waitresses at Blackhawk's wear black. Black shirt or sweater, black skirt. Short black skirt," he added, then let himself out.

Ally pursed her lips, and for the first time since she'd come into the room relaxed enough to slip her hands casually into her pockets. "I don't think I like your friend, Dad."

"He'll grow on you."

"What, like mold? No," she corrected. "He's too cool for that. I might end up with a little skin of ice, though. You're sure of him?"

"As sure as I am of you."

And that, she thought, said it all. "Whoever's set up these B and E's has brains, connections and guts. I'd say your pal there has all three." She lifted her shoulders. "Still, if I can't trust your judgment, whose can I trust?"

Boyd grinned. "Your mother always liked him."

"Well then, I'm half in love already." That wiped the grin off his face, she noted with amusement. "I'm still going to have a couple of men under as customers."

"That's your call."

"It's been five days since the last hit. They're working too well not to want to move again soon."

She strode toward the coffeepot, changed her mind and strode away again. "They might not use his club next time, it's not a given. We can't cover every damn club in the city."

"So, you focus your energy on Blackhawk's. That's smart, and it's logical. One step at a time, Allison."

"I know. I learned that from the best. I guess the first step is to go dig up a short black skirt."

Boyd winced as she walked to the door. "Not too short."

Ally had the eight-to-four shift at the precinct, and even if she left on the dot and sprinted the four blocks from the station to her apartment, she couldn't get home before 4:10 p.m.

She knew. She'd timed it.

And leaving at exactly four was as rare as finding diamonds in the mud. But damned if she wanted to be late for her next meeting with Blackhawk.

It was a matter of pride and principle.

She slammed into her apartment at 4:11 p.m.—thanks to the delay of a last-minute briefing by her lieutenant—and peeled off her jacket as she raced to the bedroom.

Blackhawk's was a good twenty minutes away at a brisk jog—and half again that much if she attempted to drive in rush-hour traffic.

It was only her second undercover assignment behind her detective's shield. She had no intention of screwing it up.

She released her shoulder harness and tossed it onto the bed. Her apartment was simple and uncluttered, mostly because she wasn't there long enough for it to be otherwise. The house where she'd grown up was still home, the station house was second on that list of priorities, and the apartment where she slept, occasionally ate and even more rarely loitered, was a far down third.

She'd always wanted to be a cop. She hadn't made a big deal of it. It simply was her dream.

She yanked open her closet door and pushed through a selection of clothes—designer dresses, tailored jackets and basketball jerseys—in search of a suitable black skirt.

If she could manage a quick change, she might actually have time to slap together a sandwich or stuff a handful of cookies into her mouth before she raced out again.

She pulled out a skirt, winced at the length when she held it up, then tossed that on the bed as well to dig through her dresser for a pair of black hose.

If she was going to wear a skirt that barely covered her butt, she would damn well cover the rest with solid, opaque black.

Tonight could be the night, she thought as she stripped off her trousers. She had to stay calm about it, cool, controlled.

She would use Jonah Blackhawk, but she would not be distracted by him.

She knew a great deal about him through her father, and she'd made it her business to find out more. As a kid he'd had light fingers, quick feet and a nimble brain. She could almost admire a boy with barely twelve years under his belt who'd managed to organize a sports' betting syndicate. Almost.

And she supposed she could come close to admiring someone who'd turned those beginnings around—at least on the surface—and made himself into a successful businessman.

The fact was she'd been in his sports' bar and had enjoyed the atmosphere, the service and the truly superior margaritas Fast Break provided.

The place had a terrific selection of pinball machines, she recalled. Unless someone had broken her record in the last six months, her initials were still in the number one slot on Double Play.

She really should make time to get back there and defend her championship status.

But that was beside the point, she reminded herself. Right now the point was Jonah Blackhawk.

Maybe his feathers were ruffled because she'd made it clear that two of his employees were on her short list of suspects. Well, that was too bad. Her father wanted her to trust the man, so she'd do her best to trust him.

As far as she could throw him.

By 4:20 p.m., she was dressed in black—turtleneck, skirt, hose. She shoved through the shoes on the floor of her closet and found a suitable pair of low heels.

With a nod to vanity, she dragged the clip out of her hair, brushed it, clipped it back again. Then she closed her eyes and tried to think like a waitress in an upscale club.

Lipstick, perfume, earrings. An attractive waitress made more tips, and tips had to be a goal. She took the time for them, then studied the results in the mirror.

Sexy, she supposed, certainly feminine and in a satisfactory way, practical. And there was no place to hide her weapon.

Damn it. She hissed out a breath, and settled on stuffing her nine millimeter in an oversize shoulder bag. She tossed on a black leather jacket as a concession to the brisk spring evening, then bolted for the door.

There was enough time to drive to the club if she got straight down to the garage and hit all the lights on green.

She pulled open the door. Swore.

"Dennis, what are you doing?"

Dennis Overton held up a bottle of California Chardonnay and offered a big, cheerful smile. "Just in the neighborhood. Thought we could have a drink."

"I'm on my way out."

"Fine." He shifted the bottle, tried to take her hand. "I'll go with you."

"Dennis." She didn't want to hurt him. Not again. He'd been so devastated when she'd broken things off two months before. And all his phone calls, pop-ins, run-intos since then had ended badly. "We've been through all this."

"Come on, Ally. Just a couple of hours. I miss you."

He had that sad, basset hound look in his eyes, that pleading smile on his lips. It had worked once, she reminded herself. More than once. But she remembered how those same eyes could blaze with wild and misplaced jealousy, snap with barely controlled fury.

She'd cared for him once, enough to forgive him his accusations, to try to work through his mood swings, enough to feel guilty over ending it.

She cared enough now to strap her temper at this last invasion of her time and her space. "I'm sorry, Dennis. I'm in a hurry."

Still smiling, he blocked her way. "Give me five minutes. One drink for old times' sake, Ally?"

"I don't have five minutes."

The smile vanished, and that old, dark gleam leaped into his eyes. "You never had time for me when I needed it. It was always what you wanted and when you wanted it."

"That's right. You're well rid of me."

"You're going to see someone else, aren't you? Brushing me off so you can run off to be with another man."

"What if I am." Enough, she thought, was way past

enough. "It's no business of yours where I go, what I do, whom I see. That's what you can't seem to get straight. But you're going to have to work harder at it, Dennis, because I'm sick of this. Stop coming here."

He grabbed her arm before she could walk by. "I want to talk to you."

She didn't jerk free, only stared down at his hand, then shifted her gaze, icy as February, to his eyes. "Don't push it. Now step back."

"What're you going to do? Shoot me? Arrest me? Call your daddy, the saint of the police, to lock me up?"

"I'm going to ask you, one more time, to step back. Step way back, Dennis, and do it now."

His mood swung again, fast and smooth as a revolving door. "I'm sorry. Ally, I'm sorry." His eyes went damp and his mouth trembled. "I'm upset, that's all. Just give me another chance. I just need another chance. I'll make it work this time."

She pried his fingers off her arm. "It never worked. Go home, Dennis. I've got nothing for you."

She walked away without looking back, bleeding inside because she had to. Bleeding inside because she could.

Chapter 2

Ally hit the doors of Blackhawk's at 5:05 p.m. One strike against her, she thought and took an extra minute to smooth down her hair, catch her breath. She'd decided against the drive after all and had run the ten blocks. Not such a distance, she thought, but the heels she wore were a far cry from track shoes.

She stepped inside, took stock.

The bar was a long, gleaming black slab that curved into a snug semicircle and offered plenty of room for a troop of chrome stools with thick, black leather cushions. Mirrored panels of black and silver ran down the rear wall, tossed back reflections and shapes.

Comfort, she decided, as well as style. It said, sit down, relax and plunk down your money.

There were plenty of people to do so. Apparently happy hour was under way, and every stool was occupied. Those who sat at the bar, or kicked back at the chrome tables, drank and nibbled to the tune of recorded music kept low enough to encourage conversation.

Most of the patrons were the suit-and-tie crowd with briefcases dumped at their feet. The business brigade, she concluded, who'd managed to slip out of the office a little early, or were using the club as a meeting arena to discuss deals or close them.

Two waitresses worked the tables. Both wore black, but she noted with a hiss through her teeth that they wore slacks rather than skirts.

A man was working the bar—young, handsome and openly flirting with the trio of women on stools at the far end. She wondered when Frances Cummings came on shift. She'd need to get work schedules from Blackhawk.

"You look a little lost."

Ally shifted her gaze and studied the man who approached her with an easy smile. Brown hair, brown eyes, trim beard. Five-ten, maybe one-fifty. His dark suit was well cut, his gray tie neatly knotted.

William Sloan looked a great deal more presentable tonight than he had for his last mug shot.

"I hope not." Deciding a little agitation fit the role, Ally shifted her shoulder bag and offered a nervous smile. "I'm Allison. I'm supposed to see Mr. Blackhawk at five. I guess I'm late."

"Couple of minutes. Don't worry about it. Will Sloan." He offered a hand, gave hers a quick, brotherly squeeze. "The man told me to keep an eye out for you. I'll take you up."

"Thanks. Great place," she commented.

"You bet. The man's in charge, and he wants the best. I'll give you a quick go-through." With a hand on her back, Will led her through the bar area, into a wide room with more tables, a two-level stage and a dance floor.

Silver ceilings, she mused, glancing up, set with pinpoint lights that blinked and shimmered. The tables were black squares on pedestals that rose out of a smoky silver floor with those same little lights twinkling under the surface, like stars behind clouds.

The art was modern, towering canvases splashed or streaked with wild colors, odd, intriguing wall sculptures fashioned from metals or textiles.

The tables were bare but for a slim metal cylindrical lamp with cut-outs in the shape of crescent moons.

Deco meets the third millennium, she decided. Jonah Blackhawk had built himself a very classy joint.

"You work clubs before?"

She'd already decided how to play it and rolled her eyes. "Nothing like this. Pretty fancy."

"The man wanted class. The man gets class." He turned down a corridor, then punched a code into a control panel. "Watch this."

When a panel in the wall slid open, he wiggled his eyebrows. "Cool, huh?"

"Major." She stepped in with him, watched him reenter the code.

"Any of us who've got to do business on the second level get a code. You won't have to worry about it. So, you new in Denver?"

"No, actually I grew up here."

"No bull? Me, too. I've been hanging with the man since we were kids. Life sure was different then."

The door opened again, directly into Jonah's office. It was a large space, split into business and pleasure with an area to one side devoted to a long leather sofa in his signature color, two sink-into-me armchairs and a wide-screen TV where a night baseball game was being battled out in silence.

Automatically she checked the stats in the top corner of the screen. Yankees at home against Toronto. Bottom of the first. Two out, one on. No score.

The focus on sports didn't surprise her, but the floor-to-ceiling shelves of books did.

She shifted her attention to the business area. It appeared to be as ruthlessly efficient as the rest of the room was indulgent. The workstation held a computer and phone. Across from it stood a monitor that showed the club area. The single window was shielded with blinds, and the blinds were tightly shut. The carpet was cozily thick and stone-gray.

Jonah sat at the desk, his back to the wall, and held up a hand as he completed a call. "I'll get back to you on that. No, not before tomorrow." He lifted a brow as if amused by what was said to him. "You'll just have to wait."

He hung up, sat back in his chair. "Hello, Allison. Thanks, Will."

"No problem. Catch you later, Allison."

"Thanks a lot."

Jonah waited until the elevator door shut. "You're late."

"I know. It was unavoidable." She turned to the monitor giving him an opportunity to skim his gaze down her back, over those long legs.

Very nice, he thought. Very nice indeed.

"You have security cameras throughout the public areas?"

"I like to know what's going on in my place."

She just bet he did. "Do you keep the tapes?"

"We turn them over every three days."

"I'd like to see what you've got." Because her back was to him, she allowed her gaze to slide over and check the action in Yankee Stadium. Toronto brought one home on a line drive bullet. "It'll help to study the tapes."

"For that you'll need a warrant."

She glanced back over her shoulder. He'd changed into a suit—black and, to her expert eye, of Italian cut. "I thought you'd agreed to cooperate."

"To a point. You're here, aren't you?" His phone rang and was ignored. "Why don't you sit down? We'll work out a game plan."

"The game plan's simple." And she didn't sit. "I pose as a waitress, talk to customers and staff. I keep my eyes open and do my job. You keep out of my way and do yours."

"Wrong plan. I don't have to keep out of anyone's way in my place. Now, ever worked a club?"

"No."

"Ever waited tables?"

"No." His cool, patient look irked. "What's the big deal. You take the order, you put in the order, you serve the order. I'm not a moron."

He smiled now, that quick, powerful strike. "I imagine it seems that way when you've spent your life on the other side of it. You're about to get an education, Detective. Head waitress on your shift is Beth. She'll help train you. Until you've got a handle on it, you'll bus tables. That means—"

"I know what busing tables involves."

"Fine, I've put you on six to two. You get a fifteen minute break every two hours. No drinking during shift. Any of the customers get overly friendly or out of line, you report to me or to Will."

"I can handle myself."

"You're not a cop here. Somebody puts hands on you in an inappropriate way, you report to me or to Will."

"You get a lot of that?"

"Only from the women. They can't keep their hands off me."

"Ha-ha."

Out of the corner of his eye, he noted the Yankees ended the inning on a strikeout. "No, we don't get a lot of it, but it happens. Some guys cross lines when they drink. They only cross them in my place once. The crowd starts getting thick after eight. Entertainment starts at nine. You'll be busy."

He got to his feet, walked to her, walked around her. "You've got a nice cover over the cop in you. You have to look hard to see it. I like the skirt."

She waited until he'd come around and they were face-to-face. "I'll need work schedules for all employees. Or do I need a warrant?"

"No, I can help you out there." He liked the scent of her. Cool and clearly female. "I'll have printouts for you by closing. Anyone I hire who I don't know personally—and even some I do—goes through a full background check. Not everyone here's been lucky enough to come from a nice, tidy family and live a nice, tidy life."

Jonah picked up a remote, switched the angle of the cameras so the bar area popped on screen. "Kid just coming off shift at the bar? Grew up with his grandparents when his mother ran off. Got into a little trouble when he was fifteen."

"And what kind of trouble was that?"

"Got tagged with a joint in his pocket. He straightened out, they sealed the records, but he was up front with me when he wanted the job. He's putting himself through night school."

At the moment she wasn't interested in the young man going off shift at the bar. She kept her eyes on Jonah. "Is everyone up front with you?"

"The smart ones are. That's Beth." He tapped the screen.

Ally saw a little brunette, about thirty, come in through a door behind the bar.

"Bastard she was married to used to kick her around. She can't weigh a hundred pounds. She's got three kids at home. Sixteen, twelve and ten. She's been working for me on and off about five years, used to come in every couple weeks with a black eye or split lip. She took the kids and left him two years ago."

"Is he leaving her alone?"

Jonah shifted his gaze to Ally's. "He was persuaded to relocate."

"I see." And she did. Jonah Blackhawk looked after his own. She couldn't fault him for it. "Did he relocate in one piece?"

"Mostly. I'll take you down. You can leave your bag up here if you want."

"No, thanks."

He pushed the button for the elevator. "I assume you've got your gun in there. Keep it in there. There's a secure employee area off the bar. You can lock it up in there. This shift Beth and Frannie have keys. Will and I have keys or codes for all areas at all times."

"Tight ship, Blackhawk."

"That's right. What's the cover?" he asked as they stepped into the elevator. "How'd I meet you?"

"I needed a job, you gave me a job." She shrugged. "Keep it simple. I caught you at your sports bar."

"Know anything about sports?"

She sent him a smile. "Anything that takes place off a field, a court or outside an arena is just marking time."

"Where have you been all my life?" He took her arm as they stepped out on the main floor. "So, Jays or Yankees?"

"Yankees have stronger bats this season and rule the

long ball, but their gloves are sloppy. The Jays chip away
with reliable base hits, and their infield's a ballet of guts
and efficiency. I go for guts and efficiency over the power
stroke every time."

"Is that a baseball statement, or a life statement?"

"Blackhawk, baseball is life."

"Now you've done it. We have to get married."

"My heart's all aflutter," she said dryly and turned to
scan the bar area. The noise level had bumped up several
notches. They were two and three deep at the curved
black slab now, the after-work, before-dinner crowd.

For some it was unwind time, she thought, for others
a casual mating ritual. But for someone, it was a hunt.

People were so careless, she mused. She saw men
leaning on the bar, back pockets ripe for picking. More
than one handbag hung vulnerable on the back of a stool
or chair. Coats and jackets, some likely to have car or
house keys in their pockets, were tossed aside.

"Nobody ever thinks it can happen to them," Ally
murmured, then tapped Jonah's arm, inclined her head.
"Check out the guy at the bar—six down, with the news
anchor hair and teeth."

Amused, Jonah tagged the guy from Ally's description
and watched him flash his wallet, choked with bills and
credit cards.

"He's trying to lure the redhead there, or her pretty
blond friend. Doesn't matter which. Odds are he hits
with the blonde," Jonah concluded.

"Why?"

"Call it a hunch." He looked down at Ally. "Wanna bet?"

"You don't have a license for gambling on the
premises." As she watched, the blonde sidled over and
batted her lashes at the man with the wallet. "Good call."

"It was easy. And so's the blonde." He steered Ally

back toward the club area where Beth and Will huddled over the reservation book at a black podium.

"Hey, boss." Beth plucked the pencil out of her thick curls and made a note in the book. "Looks like we're turning most tables over twice tonight. Big dinner crowd for midweek."

"Good thing I brought you some help. Beth Dickerman, Allison Fletcher. She needs training."

"Ah, another victim." Beth shot out a hand. "Nice to meet you, Allison."

"Ally. Thanks."

"You show her the ropes, Beth. She'll bus tables until you figure she can wait them."

"We'll whip her into shape. Come on with me, Ally. I'll get you set up. Got any experience in food services?" she asked as she plowed through the crowd.

"Well, I eat."

Beth let out a bright cackle of a laugh. "Welcome to my world. Frannie, this is Ally, new waitress in training. Frannie's captain of the bar here."

"Nice to meetcha," Frannie called out, flipped a smile, dumping ice into a blender with one hand and shooting soda into a glass with the other.

"And that gorgeous specimen down the other end of the bar's Pete."

The big shouldered black man sent them a wink as he measured Kahlúa into a short glass.

"Now, no flirting with Pete, 'cause he's my man and nobody else's. That right, Pete?"

"You're the one for me, sugar lips."

With another laugh, Beth unlocked a door marked Employees Only. "Pete's got a beautiful wife and a baby on the way. We just tease. Now, if you need to get in here for any reason—hey, Jan."

"Hey, Beth." The curvy brunette on the other side of the door had her waist-length hair pulled back with combs from a lovely, heart-shaped face. Ally gauged her as mid-twenties, and a fashion plate. She'd gone for a skirt the approximate size of a table napkin, and a clingy shirt with small silver buttons. Silver winked at her wrists, ears and throat as she freshened her lipstick in a mirror.

"This is Ally. Fresh meat."

"Oh, yeah." The smile when she turned was friendly enough, but there was a measuring gleam in her eye. One female sizing up another, and the competition.

"Jan works the bar area," Beth explained. "But she'll pinch hit in the club if we need her." There was a wild burst of laughter from outside the door. "Tom-toms are beating."

"I'd better get out there." Jan tied a short, many-pocketed black apron at her waist. "Good luck, Ally, and welcome aboard."

"Thanks. Everybody's so friendly," Ally said to Beth when Jan strolled out.

"You get to be kind of a family when you work for Jonah. He's a good boss." She pulled an apron out of a closet. "You work your butt off for him, but he lets you know he notices and that he appreciates. Makes a difference. Here, you'll need this."

"Have you worked for him long?"

"About six years, give or take. I handled tables at Fast Break, his sports bar. And when he opened the club here, he asked me if I wanted to switch. It's a classy place, and closer to home. You can leave your purse in here." She opened a narrow locker. "You reset the combination by spinning around zero twice."

"Great." Ally set her purse inside, palming her beeper

out of it and hooking it on the waist of her skirt under the apron. She shut the locker, set the combination. "I guess that's it."

"You want to freshen up or anything?"

"No, I'm fine. A little nervous, I guess."

"Don't worry. In a few hours your feet are going to ache so bad you won't think about nerves."

Beth was right. About the feet anyway. By ten, Ally felt she'd hiked twenty miles in the wrong shoes, and lifted approximately three tons of trays loaded with dirty dishes.

She could have marched the trail from table to kitchen in her sleep.

The live band was considerably louder than the recorded music that had played until just after nine. The crowd shouted above it, crammed the dance floor and jammed together at the tables.

Ally piled dishes on trays and watched the crowd. There were plenty of designer clothes, expensive watches, cell phones and leather briefcases. She saw a woman flash a lightning bolt diamond engagement ring for three friends.

Plenty of money here, she noted. And plenty of marks.

Hefting the loaded tray, she headed off for the kitchen, detouring toward an attractive couple when the man signaled her.

"Sweetheart, can you get me and my lovely companion a refill here?"

She leaned closer, pasted on her sweetest smile and made a quiet and crude suggestion.

The man only grinned. "Cops have such filthy mouths."

"Next case I'm going to be the one sitting on my butt,

Hickman, while you work out," Ally replied. "See anything I should know about?"

"Nothing's popped yet." He grabbed the hand of the woman sitting next to him. "But Carson and I are in love."

Lydia Carson gave Hickman's hand a vicious squeeze. "In your dreams."

"Just keep your eyes open." She aimed a stare at Hickman's glass. "And that'd better be club soda."

"She's so strict," she heard Hickman murmur as she walked away.

"Beth, table…ah, sixteen's looking for a refill."

"I'm on it. You're doing good, Ally. Go dump those and take your break."

"You don't have to tell me twice."

The kitchen was a madhouse, full of noise and shouted orders and heat. Gratefully Ally set down her tray, then lifted her eyebrows as she spotted Frannie slipping out the back door.

Ally stalled for ten seconds, then followed.

Frannie was already leaning against the outside wall and taking her first drag from a cigarette. She blew out smoke with a long, relieved sigh. "Break time?"

"Yeah. I thought I'd grab some air."

"Zoo in there tonight. Blackhawk's really packs them in." She pulled the cigarettes out of her pocket, offered them.

"No, thanks. I don't smoke."

"Good for you. I can't kick it. No smoking in the employee lounge. Jonah gives me a break and lets me use his office if the weather's lousy. So how's your first night?"

"My feet are killing me."

"Occupational hazard. First paycheck you buy yourself one of those bubbling footbath things. Put some eucalyptus in it and go straight to heaven."

"I'll do that."

An attractive woman, Ally noted, though the lines around Frannie's eyes made her look older than twenty-eight. She kept her dark red hair cut short and the makeup subtle. Her nails were short and unpainted, her hands ringless. Like the rest of the staff, she wore black, and finished off the simple shirt and slacks with sturdy yet trendy black shoes.

The only touch of flash was the silver hoops that swung at her ears.

"How'd you get into tending bar?" Ally asked her.

Frannie hesitated, then puffed on her cigarette. "I guess I hung out at bars a lot, and when there came a time I was looking for what you could call gainful employment, Jonah asked me if I wanted a job. Trained me over at Fast Break. It's good work. You need a decent memory and people skills. You interested?"

"I'd better see if I make it through one shift busing before I start raising my sights."

"You look like you can handle whatever comes along."

Ally smiled into Frannie's considering eyes. "You think so?"

"Observation's one of those people skills. And on short observation you don't strike me as the type who expects to make waiting tables her life's work."

"Gotta start somewhere. And paying the rent's a priority."

"Don't I know it." Though Frannie had already calculated that Ally's shoes equaled half a month's rent on her own apartment. "Well, if you want to climb the ladder, Jonah's the one to give you a boost. You'd have figured that."

Frannie dropped the cigarette, crushed out the butt. "Gotta get back. Pete pouts if I go over break."

The ex-hooker, Ally decided, was proprietary when it came to Jonah. They were probably lovers, she thought as she went back inside. When you factored in his defensive attitude toward her, it added up.

As lover, as trusted employee, Frannie was in a prime position to cull out marks, to pass the information along. The bar faced the entrance. Whoever went in or out passed by her station.

People handed her credit cards, and the name and account number led to addresses.

It would pay to look at her most closely.

Jonah was doing his own looking. From his office, from the floor. He knew enough about cons, short and long, to calculate who the targets might be. He pegged three possibilities that would have topped his list if he'd been running the game. And since he'd also spotted the cops at table sixteen, he wandered over.

"Everything all right tonight?"

The woman beamed up at him, swept back her short swing of streaky blond hair with one hand. "Everything's terrific. It's the first night on the town Bob and I have managed in weeks with work keeping both of us so busy."

"I'm glad you picked my place." Jonah laid a friendly hand on Bob's shoulder, leaned down. "Next time ditch the cop shoes. Dead giveaway. Enjoy your evening."

He thought he heard the woman snort out a laugh as he walked away.

He headed for the table Ally was busy cleaning. "How you holding up?"

"I haven't broken any of your dishes yet."

"And now you want a raise?"

"I'm going to stick with my day job, thanks all the

same. I'd rather clean up the streets than tables." Absently she pressed a hand to the ache in the small of her back.

"We go back to bar food at eleven, so the busing slows down."

"Hallelujah."

He laid a hand on her arm before she could lift the tray. "You corner Frannie outside?"

"Excuse me?"

"She went out, you went out, she came in, you came in."

"I'm doing my job. However, I resisted shining a light in her eyes and smacking her in the face with my rubber hose. Now let me get on with it."

She hefted the tray, shoved past him.

"By the way, Allison."

She stopped, a snarl working up her throat. "What?"

"The power ball trounced your guts and efficiency. Eight to two."

"One game doesn't a season make." She jerked up her chin and strode off. On her way by the dance floor, a man reached out and gave her butt a hopeful pat. As Jonah watched she stopped dead in her tracks, turned slowly and gave him one, long icy look. The man stepped back, lifted his hands in apology and quickly melted into the dancers.

"Handles herself," Beth said from beside him.

"Yeah. Yeah, she does."

"Pulls her weight, too, and doesn't whine about it. I like your girlfriend, Jonah."

He was too surprised to comment and only stared when Beth hustled away.

He let out a short laugh and shook his head. Oh, that one had slipped by him. Right on by him.

Last call was enough to make Ally all but weep with gratitude. She'd been on her feet since eight that

morning. Her fondest wish was to go home, fall into bed
and sleep for the precious five hours she had before
starting it all over again.

"Go on home," Beth ordered. "We'll go over closing
tomorrow night. You did fine."

"Thanks. I mean it."

"Will, let Ally into the lounge, will you?"

"No problem. Nice crowd tonight. Nothing I like
better than a crowded club. Want a drink before you head
out?"

"Not unless I can stick my feet in it."

He chuckled, patted her back. "Frannie, pour me one,
will you?"

"Already on it."

"I like a brandy at the end of a shift. One glass of the
good stuff. You change your mind," he said as he
unlocked the door. "Just pull up a stool. The man, he
doesn't charge employees for an end of shift drink."

He went off, whistling through his teeth.

Ally shoved her apron into her locker, pulled out her
bag and jacket. She was just putting the jacket on when
Jan breezed in. "Heading out? You look beat. Me, I'm
just hitting stride this time of night."

"My stride hit me about an hour ago." Ally paused at
the door. "Don't your feet hurt?"

"Nah. I got arches of steel. And most guys tip better
if you walk around on skinny heels." She bent to run a
hand up her leg. "I believe in using what works."

"Yeah. Well, good night."

Ally stepped out of the lounge, shutting the door
behind her, and bumped solidly into Jonah.

"Where'd you park?" he asked her.

"I didn't. I walked." Ran, she remembered, but it came
to the same thing.

"I'll drive you home."

"I can walk. It's not far."

"It's two in the morning. A block is too far."

"For heaven's sake, Blackhawk, I'm a cop."

"So naturally, bullets bounce off you."

Before she could argue, he caught her chin in his hand. The gesture, the firm grip of his fingers, shocked her to silence. "You're not a cop at the moment," he murmured. "You're a female employee and the daughter of a friend. I'll drive you home."

"Fine. Dandy. My feet hurt anyway."

She started to shove his hand away, but he beat her to it and shifted his grip to her arm.

"Night, boss." Beth called out, grinning at them as they passed. "Get that girl off her feet."

"That's my plan. Later, Will. Night, Frannie."

Suspicion was buzzing in Ally's brain as Will lifted his brandy snifter and Frannie watched her with quiet and serious eyes.

"What was that?" Ally demanded when they stepped out in the cool air. "What exactly was that?"

"That was me saying good-night to friends and employees. I'm parked across the street."

"Excuse me, my feet have gone numb, not my brain. You gave those people the very distinct impression that we have a thing here."

"That's right. I didn't consider it, either, until Beth made some remark earlier. It simplifies things."

She stopped beside a sleek black Jaguar. "Just how do you figure that having people think there's a personal thing between us simplifies anything?"

"And you call yourself a detective." He unlocked the passenger door, opened it. "You're a beautiful blonde with legs up to your ears. I hire you, out of the blue, when you have basically no experience. The first assumption from people who know me is I'm attracted to you. The second would be you're attracted to me. Add all those together and you end up with romance. Or at least sex. Are you going to get in?"

"You haven't explained how those deductions equal simple."

"If people think we're involved they won't think twice if I give you a little leeway, if you come up to my office. They'll be friendlier."

Ally said nothing while she let it run through her head. Then she nodded. "All right. There's an advantage to it."

Going with impulse he shifted, boxed her in between his body and the car door. There was a light breeze, just enough to stir her scent. There was a three-quarter moon, bright enough to sprinkle silver into her eyes. The moment, he decided, seemed to call for it.

"Could be more than one advantage to it."

The thrill that sprinted straight up her spine irritated her. "Oh, you're going to want to step back, Blackhawk."

"Beth's at the window of the bar, and she's got a romantic heart despite everything that's happened to her. She's hoping for a moment here. A long, slow kiss, the kind that slides over melting sighs and heats the blood."

His hands came to her hips as he spoke, rode up to just under her breasts. Her mouth went dry and the ache in her belly was a wide stretch of longing.

"You're going to have to disappoint her."

Jonah skimmed his gaze down to her mouth. "She's not the only one." But he released her, stepped back. "Don't worry, Detective. I never hit on cops, or daughters of friends."

"Then I guess I've got a double shield against your wild and irresistible charms."

"Good thing for both of us, because I sure as hell like the look of you. You getting in?"

"Yeah, I'm getting in." She got into the car and waited until the door shut before letting out the long, painful breath she'd been holding.

Wherever that spurt of lust inside her had come from, it would just have to go away again. Cool off, she ordered herself, but her heart was bumping madly against her rib cage. Cool off and focus on the job.

Jonah slid in beside her, annoyed that his pulse wasn't quite steady. "Where to?" When she rattled off the address, he shoved the key into the ignition and aimed one hot look at her. "That's a damn mile. Why the hell did you walk?"

"Because it was rush hour. It's quicker. And it's ten blocks."

"That's just stupid."

She had a response for that. The venom of it scalded her tongue as she rounded on him. She didn't even recognize the vibration of her beeper for several seconds, mistaking it for the vibration of rage.

She yanked it from her skirt, checked the number. "Damn it. Damn it." From her purse she pulled out her cell phone and quickly dialed. "Detective Fletcher. Yeah, I got it. I'm on my way."

Calming herself, she shoved the phone back into her purse. "Since you're determined to play cabdriver, let's get going. I've got another B and E."

"Give me the address."

"Just take me home so I can get my car."

"Give me the address, Allison. Why waste time?"

Chapter 3

Jonah dropped her off in front of an attractive, ranch-style home in an upscale development convenient to the freeway. In reasonable traffic, the commute to downtown would take under twenty minutes.

The Chamberses, Ally discovered, were an attractive, upscale couple, both lawyers in their early thirties, child-less professionals, who spent their comfortable income on the good life.

Wine, wardrobe, jewelry, art and music.

"They got my diamond earrings, and my Cartier tank watch." Maggie Chambers rubbed her eyes as she sat in what was left of her sprawling great room. "We haven't gone through everything, but there were Dalí and Picasso lithographs on that wall there. And in that niche there was an Erté sculpture we bought at an auction two years ago. Joe collected cuff links. I don't know how many pairs he had offhand, but he had diamond ones, and ruby for his birthstone and several antique pairs."

"They're insured." Her husband reached out to take her hand, squeeze it.

"It doesn't matter. It's not the same. Those thugs were in our house. In our house, Joe, and they've taken our things. Damn it, they stole my car. My brand-new BMW, and it didn't have five thousand miles on it. I loved that stupid car."

"Mrs. Chambers, I know it's hard."

Maggie Chambers whipped her gaze toward Ally. "Have you ever been robbed, Detective?"

"No." Ally set her notebook on her knee a moment. "But I've worked plenty of burglaries, robberies, muggings."

"It's not the same."

"Maggie, she's just doing her job."

"I know. I'm sorry. I know." She covered her face with her hands, drew air in, slowly let it out. "I've got the shakes, that's all. I don't want to stay here tonight."

"We don't have to. We'll go to a hotel. How much more do you need, Detective…was it Fletcher?"

"Yes. Just a few more questions. You said both of you were out all evening."

"Yeah, Maggie won a case today, and we decided to go out and celebrate. She's been piled under for more than a month. We went to the Starfire club with some friends." As he spoke, he rubbed soothing circles over his wife's back. "Drinks, dinner, a little dancing. Like we told the other policeman, we didn't get home until nearly two."

"Does anyone other than the two of you have a key?"

"Our housekeeper."

"Would she also have the security code?"

"Sure." Joe started to speak, then blinked, stuttered.

"Oh, listen, Carol's been cleaning for us for nearly ten years. She's practically family."

"It's just procedure, Mr. Chambers. Could I have her full name and address, for the record?"

She took them through the entire evening, looking for a connection, a contact, anything that struck a chord. But for the Chamberses it had been nothing more than an entertaining evening out, until they'd walked back in their own front door.

When Ally left them, she had a partial list of stolen items, with a promise for the complete as well as the insurance information. The crime scene unit was still working, but she'd gone over the scene herself. She didn't expect the miracle of fingerprints or dropped clues.

The moon had set, but the stars were out and brilliant. The wind had picked up to dance down the street in little whirls and gusts. The neighborhood was hushed, the houses dark. Those who lived here had long since been tucked in for the night.

She doubted the canvass was going to turn up any handy eyewitnesses.

Jonah was leaning against the hood of his car, drinking what appeared to be a cup of takeout coffee with one of the uniforms.

When she approached the car, Jonah held out the half cup he had left. "Thanks."

"You can have a whole one. There's a twenty-four-hour place a few blocks down."

"This is fine," she replied, taking the cup. "Officer, you and your partner were first on scene?"

"Yes, ma'am."

"I'll need your report on my desk by eleven hundred." With a brisk nod, the officer headed for his car. Ally sipped the coffee, then turned to Jonah and handed him the cup. "You didn't have to wait. I can get a ride home in one of the radio cars."

"I have a stake here." He opened the car door. "Were they at my place?"

"Now why would you ask me when we both know you just got finished pumping that uniform?"

"Hey, I bought the coffee." He handed it back to her, then walked around to the driver's side. "So, the perps picked their marks at the Starfire tonight. Have they hit there before?"

"No, you're still the only repeater. They'll come back to you." She shut her exhausted eyes. "It's just a matter of time."

"Well, that makes me feel lots better. What kind of take did they get?"

"BMW roadster out of the garage, some art, high-end electronics and heavy on the jewelry."

"Don't these people have safes?"

"These did, a small one in the walk-in closet of the master suite. Of course they had the combination for it written down on a piece of paper in the desk."

"That'll discourage the criminal element."

"They had a security system, which they swear they engaged when they left—though the wife didn't look quite so sure of that. Anyway, the point is they felt secure. Nice house, nice neighborhood. People get sloppy." Eyes still closed, she circled her head, cracking out the tension. "They're both lawyers."

"Well, hell then, what do we care?"

She was tired enough to laugh. "Watch it, ace. My aunt is district attorney in Urbana."

"You going to drink that coffee or just hold on to it?"

"What? Oh, no, here, I don't want anymore. It'll just keep me awake."

He doubted a tanker truck of coffee could keep her awake much longer. Her voice was going thick, adding, he thought, to the in-the-gut sexiness of it. Fatigue had her unguarded enough to tilt her face toward him as she tried to find a comfortable resting spot. Her eyes were shut, her lips soft and just parted.

He had a feeling he knew exactly how they'd taste. Warm and soft. Ripe with sleep.

At a stop sign, he put the car in neutral, engaged the emergency brake, then leaned over her to press the mechanism that lowered her seat back.

She jerked up, rapped her head smartly against his. Even as he swore she slapped a hand on his chest.

"Back off!"

"Relax, Fletcher, I'm not jumping you. I like my women awake when we make love. I'm putting your seat back. If you're going to sleep, you might as well get as close to horizontal as we can manage."

"I'm all right." Mortified, but all right, she thought. "I wasn't sleeping."

He put a hand on her forehead, shoved her back. "Shut up, Allison."

"I wasn't sleeping. I was thinking."

"Think tomorrow. You're brain-dead." He glanced over at her as he started to drive again. "How many hours have you been on duty?"

"That's math, I can't do math if I'm brain-dead." She gave up and yawned. "I'm on eight to fours."

"It's closing in on 4:00 a.m., that gives you twenty hours. Why don't you put in for night shift until this is over, or do you have a death wish?"

"It's not my only case." She'd already decided to talk to her lieutenant. She couldn't give her best to the job on a couple of hours sleep a night. But it wasn't any of Jonah's business how she ran her life.

"I guess Denver's not safe without you on the job."

She might have been tired, but she still had a pretty good ear for sarcasm. "That's right, Blackhawk. Without my watchful eye, the city's in chaos. It's a heavy burden but, well, somebody's got to shoulder it. Just pull up at the corner. My building's only a half a block down."

He ignored her, drove through the light and pulled smoothly to the curb in front of her building. "Okay. Thanks." She reached down to retrieve her bag from the floor.

He was already out of the car, skirting around the hood. Maybe it was fatigue that had her reacting so slowly, as if she were moving through syrup instead of air. But he had the outside handle of the door seconds before she had the inside handle.

For about five seconds they battled for control. Then with a halfhearted snarl, Ally let him open the door for her. "What are you, from another century? Do I look incapable of operating the complex mechanism of a car door?"

"No. You look tired."

"Well, I am. So good night."

"I'll walk you up."

"Get a grip."

But he fell into step beside her, and damn him, reached the door one pace ahead of her. Saying nothing, merely watching her with those impossibly clear green eyes, he held it open for her.

"I'll have to curtsy in a minute," she muttered under her breath.

He grinned at her back, then crossed to the lobby elevators with her, sliding his hands into his pockets.

"I can make it from here."

"I'll take you to your door."

"It's not a damn date."

"Lack of sleep's making you irritable." He stepped into the elevator with her. "No, wait, you're always irritable. My mistake."

"I don't like you." She jabbed the button for the fourth floor.

"Thank God you cleared that up. I was afraid you were falling for me."

The movement of the elevator tipped her already shaky balance. She swayed, and he closed a hand over her arm.

"Cut it out."

"No."

She jerked at her arm. He tightened his grip. "Don't embarrass yourself, Fletcher. You're asleep on your feet. What's your apartment number?"

He was right, and it was stupid to pretend otherwise, and foolish to take it out on him. "Four-oh-nine. Let me go, will you? I'll be all right after a couple hours' sleep."

"I don't doubt it." But he held on to her when the elevator opened.

"You're not coming in."

"Well, there go my plans to toss you over my shoulder, dump you in bed and have my wicked way with you. Next time. Key?"

"What?"

Her burnt-honey eyes were blurry, the delicate skin beneath them bruised. The wave of tenderness that swept inside him was a complete surprise, and far from comfortable. "Honey, give me your key."

"Oh. I'm punchy." She dug it out of her jacket pocket. "And don't call me honey."

"I meant Detective Honey." He heard her snicker as he unlocked her door. He pulled the key back out of the lock, took her hand, dropped it in and closed her fingers around it. "Good night."

"Yeah. Thanks for the lift." Because it seemed the thing to do, she closed the door in his face.

Hell of a face, she thought as she stumbled toward the bedroom. Face that dangerous ought to be registered as a weapon. A woman who trusted a face like that got exactly what she deserved.

And probably enjoyed every minute of it.

Ally stripped off her jacket, whimpering a little as she pried off her shoes. She set her alarm, then fell facedown and fully clothed on the bed. And was instantly asleep.

Four and a half hours later, she was finishing up her morning meeting in the conference room at her station house. And her fourth cup of coffee.

"We'll canvass the neighborhood," Ally said, "We could get lucky. In that kind of development, people tend to look out for each other. Some sort of vehicle was necessary to get the perpetrators to the Chamberses', and to transport at least some of the stolen goods. The sports car they boosted wouldn't hold that much. We have a full description of the car, and the APB's out on it."

Lieutenant Kiniki nodded. He was a toughly built man in his mid-forties who enjoyed the way command sat on his shoulders. "The Starfire's a new pool for them. I want two men over there to check out the setup. Soft clothes," he added, indicating he wanted his detectives to dress casually rather than in suit jackets. "Let's keep it low-key."

"Hickman and Carson are canvassing pawn shops, pressuring known fences." Ally glanced toward her two associates.

"Nothing there." Hickman lifted his hands. "Lydia and I've got a couple of good sources, and we've put the heat on. Nobody knows anything. My take is that whoever's running this has an outside channel."

"Keep the heat on," Kiniki ordered. "What about the insurance angle."

"It doesn't play out," Ally told him. "We've got nine hits and five different insurance companies. We're still trying to find a connection, but so far that's a dead end. We've got no common links between the victims that carry through," she went on. "Out of the nine, we've got four different banks, three different brokerage houses, nine different doctors, nine different places of employment."

She rubbed the ache at the back of her neck and went down her list. "Two of the women go to the same hair salon—different operators, different schedules. They use different cleaning services, different mechanics. Now two of the targets used the same caterer in the last six months, and we're running that. But it doesn't look like a hook. The only common link so far is a night on the town."

"Give me the rundown on Blackhawk's," Kiniki ordered.

"The place does a hell of a business," Ally began. "Pulls in a big crowd, and the crowd varies, though it's heavy on the upwardly mobile. Couples, singles on the prowl, groups. He's got good security."

Absently Ally rubbed her eyes, then remembered herself and lowered them. "He's got cameras, and I'm working on getting the security tapes. Sloan is the floater. He works the public areas, has access to everything. There are six tables in the bar area and thirty-two in the club. People push them together if they get friendly. There's a coat check but not everybody bothers with it.

I couldn't count the number of handbags left on tables when the dancing started."

"People mill," Lydia added. "Especially the younger customers. It's a regular meeting ground for them, and they tend to table hop. Lots of sex vibes." She gave Hickman a bland look when he chortled. "It's a sexy place. People get careless when their blood's hot. There's a ripple when Blackhawk comes through."

"A ripple?" Hickman repeated. "Is that a technical term?"

"The women watch him. They don't watch their bags."

"That's accurate." Ally walked over to the board where the list of victims and stolen items were posted. "Every hit involved a woman. There are no single men on the list. The female's the prime target. What's a woman carry in her purse?"

"That," Hickman said, "is one of life's most complex mysteries."

"Her keys," Ally continued. "Her wallet—with ID, credit cards. Pictures of her kids if she has them. None of the victims had children at home. If we break this down to its basic element, we're looking first for a pickpocket. Somebody with good fingers who can get what he needs out of a bag, then put it back before the victim knows she's been hit. Do an imprint of the key, make a copy."

"If you pick the pocket, why put the stuff back?" Hickman asked.

"Keep the victim unaware, buy more time. A woman goes into the bathroom, she takes her purse. If she reaches in for her lipstick and doesn't find her wallet, she's going to send up an alarm. This way, the house is hit and the perpetrators are out before the victims get home. Whatever time they get home."

She turned back to the board. "Twelve-thirty, one-fifteen, twelve-ten, and so on. Somebody at the club alerts the burglars when the victims call for their check. Somebody's on the inside, or a regular and repeat customer. At Blackhawk's the average time between calling for the check and leaving the club was about twenty minutes."

"We have two other clubs involved now, besides Blackhawk's." Kiniki's brow furrowed. "We'll need stakeouts on all of them."

"Yes, sir. But Blackhawk's is where they'll come back. That's the money tree."

"Find a way to cut down the tree, Fletcher." He got to his feet. "And take some personal time today. Get some sleep."

She took him up on it and curled up on the small sofa in the coffee room, leaving word that she was to be notified when the reports she was waiting for came in.

She got ninety minutes and felt very close to human when Hickman shook her shoulder.

"Did you steal my cheese bagel?"

"What?" She pushed herself up, shoved back her hair.

"You like cheese bagels. I had one. It's gone. I'm detecting."

Shaking off sleep, she dug her clip out of her pocket and pulled back her hair. "It didn't have your name on it."

"Did, too."

She circled her shoulders. "Is your name Pineview Bakery? Besides I only ate half of it." She checked her watch. "The first-on-scene reports in yet?"

"Yeah, and so's your warrant."

"Great." She swung to her feet, adjusted her weapon harness. "I'll be in the field."

"I want a cheese bagel back in that box by end of shift."

"I only ate half of it," she called out and stopped by her desk for the paperwork. Scanning it, ignoring the backwash of noise from the detectives' bull pen, she hitched her harness into a more comfortable position, then shrugged into her jacket.

She glanced up when the noise became a murmur, and watched her father walk in. Like Blackhawk, she thought, this was a man who created ripples.

She knew a few of her fellow officers harbored some resentment over her rapid rise to detective. There were mutters now and then, just loud enough for her to hear, about favoritism and oiling the ranks.

She'd earned her badge and knew it. Ally was too proud of her father and too secure in her own abilities to let mutters worry her.

"Commissioner."

"Detective. Got a minute?"

"A couple." She pulled her shoulder bag from her bottom desk drawer. "Can we walk and talk? I'm on my way out. Got a warrant to serve on Jonah Blackhawk."

"Ah." He stepped back to let her pass, and his eyes scanned the room. If there were any mutters, they would wait until he was well out of range.

"Stairs okay with you?" she asked. "I didn't have time to work out this morning."

"I think I can keep up with you. What's the warrant?"

"To confiscate and view Blackhawk's security tapes. He got pissy about it yesterday. I seem to put his back up."

Boyd pushed open the door to the stairwell, then angled his head to study his daughter's back as she passed through. "I seem to detect a few ruffled feathers on yours."

"Okay, good eye. We put each other's backs up."

"I figured you would. You both like to do things your own way."

"Why would I want to do them someone else's way?"

"Exactly." Boyd skimmed a hand down the long, sleek tail of her hair. His little girl had always had a mind of her own, and a very hard head around it. "Speaking of ruffled feathers, I have a meeting with the mayor in an hour."

"Better you than me," Ally said cheerfully as she jogged down the stairs.

"What can you tell me about last night's break-in?"

"Same M.O. They hit a real treasure trove with the Chamberses. Mrs. Chambers got me the loss list this morning. The woman's efficient. They were fully insured—value of stolen items comes to a solid two hundred and twenty-five thousand."

"That's the biggest haul so far."

"Yeah. I'm hoping it makes them cocky. They took some art this time. I don't know if it was dumb luck or somebody knew what they had when they saw it. They have to have somewhere to keep the goods before they turn them. Big enough for a car."

"A decent chop shop could have a car dismantled and turned in a couple hours."

"Yeah, but…" She started to push open the next door herself, but her father beat her to it. It reminded her oddly, and not entirely happily, of Jonah.

"But?" he prompted as they crossed the lobby.

"I don't think that's the route. Somebody likes nice things. Somebody has really good taste. At the second hit, they took a collection of rare books, but they left an antique clock. It was appraised at five thousand, but it was dead ugly. It's like they said, please, don't insult us. There've been other cars at other scenes, but they've only taken two. Cool cars."

"Burglars with standards."

"Yeah, I think so." When they stepped outside she blinked against the brilliant sunlight until she pulled out her shaded glasses. "And a kind of arrogance. Arrogance is a mistake. That's going to turn it my way."

"I hope so. The pressure's on, Ally." He walked her to her car, opened the door for her in a way that made her frown and think of Jonah again. "We're getting press, the kind that makes the mayor uncomfortable."

"In my best judgment they won't wait more than a week. They're rolling now. They'll come back to Blackhawk's."

"They got a bigger slice of pie from the new place."

"Blackhawk's is reliable. Once I spend a few nights under there, I'll start recognizing faces. I'll pin him, Dad."

"I believe it." He bent down to kiss her cheek. "And I'll handle the mayor."

"I believe it." She slid behind the wheel. "Question."

"Ask it."

"You've known Jonah Blackhawk for what, like fifteen years?"

"Seventeen."

"How come you never had him over to the house? You know, for dinner or football afternoons or one of your world-famous cookouts?"

"He wouldn't come. Always acknowledged the invitation, thanked me and said he was busy."

"Seventeen years." Idly she tapped her fingers on the steering wheel. "That's a lot of busy. Well, some people don't like socializing with cops."

"Some people," Boyd told her, "draw lines and never believe they have the right to cross them. He'd meet me at the station house." The memory made Boyd grin. "He didn't like it, but he'd do it. He'd meet me for coffee or a beer, at the gym. But he'd never come to my home. He'd consider that crossing the line. I've never convinced him otherwise."

"Funny, he strikes me as being a man who considers himself good enough for anything, or anyone."

"There are a lot of twists and pockets in Jonah. And very little about him that's simple."

Chapter 4

She called ahead, and had to admit she was surprised when Jonah answered the phone in his office.

"It's Fletcher. I didn't think you were much on daylight hours."

"I'm not. Some days are exceptions. What can I do for you, Detective?"

"You can come downstairs and let me in. I'll be there in ten minutes."

"I'm not going anywhere." He waited a beat. "So, what are you wearing?"

She hated herself for laughing, and hoped she managed to smother most of it. "My badge," she told him and flicked the phone off.

Jonah hung up, sat back and entertained himself by imagining Allison Fletcher wearing her badge, and nothing else. The image came through, entirely too clear, entirely too appealing, and had him shoving back from the desk.

He had no business imagining Boyd's daughter naked. No business, he reminded himself, fantasizing about Boyd's daughter in any way whatsoever. Or wondering how her mouth would taste. Or what scent he'd find on the flesh just under the line of that very stubborn jaw.

God, he wanted to sink his teeth there, right there. Just once.

Forbidden fruit, he told himself and paced since there was no one to see. She was forbidden fruit and therefore all the more alluring. She wasn't even his type. Maybe he liked leggy blondes. Maybe he liked leggy blondes with brains and a strong backbone. But he preferred friendlier women.

Friendlier, unarmed women, he thought, amusing himself.

He hadn't been able to get her out of his head, and the clearest most compelling picture had been the yielding and temporary, he was certain, fragility of her when she'd fallen asleep in his car.

Well, he'd always been a sucker for the needy, he reminded himself, as he pulled up the blinds on his office window. Which should solve his problem over Allison. Despite that short interlude of vulnerability early that morning, needy was one thing the gorgeous detective wasn't.

She had a use for him, again temporary. And when the job was done, they'd both go back to their separate corners in their separate worlds. And that would be the end of that.

He saw her pull up in front of the club. At least she'd had the sense to drive, he noted, and wasn't hiking all over Denver today.

He took his time going down to let her in.

"Good morning, Detective." He looked around her,

studied the flashy lines of the classic red-and-white Stingray. "Nice car. Is that the new police issue? Oh wait, what was I thinking? Your daddy's loaded."

"If you think you can razz me over a car, you're going to be disappointed. Nobody razzes like a precinct full of cops."

"I'll practice. Nice threads," he commented and rubbed the lapel of her subtly patterned brown jacket between his thumb and forefinger. "Very nice."

"So we both like Italian designers. We can compare wardrobes later."

Because he knew it would irritate her, because he enjoyed the way the gold highlighted her eyes when he irritated her, he shifted, blocking her before she could step inside. "Let me see the badge."

"Come off it, Blackhawk."

"No. Let's see it."

Eyes narrowed behind her sunglasses, she pulled her badge out of her pocket, pushed it close to his face. "See it?"

"Yes. Badge number 31628. I'll buy myself a lottery ticket and play your numbers."

"Here's something else you might want to look at." She took out the warrant, held it up.

"Fast work." He'd expected no less. "Come on up. I've been reviewing the tapes. You look rested," he said as they walked to his elevator.

"I am."

"Any progress?"

"The investigation is ongoing."

"Hmm, policy line." He gestured her into the elevator. "We seem to be spending a lot of time in these. Close quarters."

"You could do your heart a favor and take the stairs."

"My heart's never caused me any problems. How about yours?"

"Whole and healthy, thanks." She walked out when the doors opened. "Wow, you actually let the sunlight in here. I'm shocked. Let's have the tapes. I'll give a receipt."

She wasn't wearing perfume today, he noted. Just soap and skin. Odd how erotic that simplicity could be. "In a hurry?"

"Clock's ticking."

He strolled into an adjoining room. After a small internal battle, Ally walked over to the doorway. It was a small bedroom. Small, she noted, because it was two-thirds bed. A black pool of bed, unframed and on a raised platform.

Curious, she looked up and was mildly disappointed there wasn't a mirror on the ceiling.

"It would be too obvious," Jonah told her when her gaze skimmed back to his.

"The bed's already a statement. An obvious one."

"But not vain."

"Hmm." To amuse herself she poked around the room. On the walls were a number of framed black-and-white photographs. Arty, interesting, and all stark or shadowy night scenes.

She recognized a couple of the artists, pursed her lips. So the man had a good eye for art, and decent taste, she admitted.

"I've got this print." She tapped a finger against a study of an ancient man in a ragged straw hat sleeping on a cracked concrete stoop, a paper bag still clutched in his hand. "Shade Colby. I like his work."

"So do I. And his wife's. Bryan Mitchell. That's one of hers beside it. The old couple holding hands on the bench at the bus stop."

"Quite a contrast, despair and hope."

"Life's full of both."

"Apparently."

She wandered. There was a closet, closed, an exit door, securely locked, and what she assumed was a bath or washroom just beyond. She thought of the sex vibes Lydia Carson had referred to. Oh, yeah, this room had plenty of them. It all but smoked with them.

"So, what's through there?" She jerked a thumb at another door. Instead of answering he gestured, inviting her to see for herself.

She opened the door, let out a long sigh of pleasure. "Now we're talking." The fully equipped gym was a great deal more appealing to her than a lake-size bed.

He watched as she trailed her fingers over machines, picked up free weights, doing a few absent curls as she roamed. Very telling, he thought, that she'd given the bed a sneer, and was all but dewy-eyed over his Nautilus.

"You got a sauna?" Envy curled inside her as she pressed her nose to a little window of a wooden door and peered into the room beyond.

"Want to try it out?"

She turned her head enough to slide her gaze in his direction. And the sneer was back. "This is pretty elaborate when you could be at a full-service health club in two minutes."

"Health clubs have members—that's the first strike. They also have regular hours. Strike two. And I don't like using someone else's equipment."

"Strike three. You're a very particular man, Blackhawk."

"That's right." He took a bottle of water out of a clear-fronted bar fridge. "Want one?"

"No." She replaced the free weight, moved back to the

doorway. "Well, thanks for the tour. Now, the tapes, Blackhawk."

"Yeah, clock's ticking." He unscrewed the top of the bottle, took a casual sip. "You know what I like about night work, Detective Fletcher?"

She looked deliberately toward the bed, then back at him. "Oh, I think I can figure it out."

"Well, there's that, but what I really like about night work is that it's always whatever time you want it to be. My favorite's the three o'clock hour. For most people, that's the hard time. If they don't sleep through it, that's the time the mind wakes up and starts worrying about what they did or didn't do that day, or what they'll do or not do the next. And the next, and right up until life's over."

"And you don't worry about yesterday or tomorrow."

"You miss a lot of the now doing that. There's only so much now to go around."

"I don't have a lot of the now to stand around philosophizing with you."

"Take a minute." He crossed to her, leaning on one jamb as she leaned on the other. "A lot of people who come into my place are night people—or those who want to remember when they were. Most have jobs now, the kind of jobs that pay well and make them responsible citizens."

She took the water bottle from his hand, drank. "Your job pays well."

He grinned. That quick jab was just one of the things that attracted him to her. "You saying I'm not a responsible citizen? My lawyers and accountants would disagree. However, my point is that people come in here to forget about their responsibilities for a while. To forget the clock's ticking and they have to punch in at 9:00 a.m. I give them a place without clocks—at least till last call."

"And this means?" She passed the bottle back to him.

"Forget about the facts a minute. Look at the shadows. You're hunting night people."

And he was one of them, she thought. Very much one of the night people, with his black mane of hair and cool, cat's eyes. "I'm not arguing with that."

"But are you thinking like them? They've picked their prey, and when they move, they move fast. It would be less risky, give them more time to study the lay of the land, if they waited to make the hit during the day. Stake out the mark, learn their patterns—when do they leave for the office, when do they get back? These guys could probably nail it down in a couple of days."

He lifted the bottle, drank. "That would be more efficient. Why don't they play it that way?"

"Because they're arrogant."

"Yeah, but that's only the top layer. Go down."

"They like the kick, the rush."

"Exactly. They're hungry, and they like the thrill of working in the dark."

It irked almost as much as it intrigued her that his thought process so closely followed her own. "You think that hasn't occurred to me before?"

"I figure it has, but I wonder if you've factored in that people who live at night are always more dangerous than people who live during the day."

"Does that include you?"

"Damn right."

"So warned." She started to turn away, then stopped, stared down at the hand he'd shot out to grip her arm. "What's your problem, Blackhawk?"

"I haven't figured it out yet. Why didn't you send a uniform over here to pick up the tapes?"

"Because it's my case."

"No."

"No, it's not my case?"

"No, that's not the reason. I'm crowding you." He edged forward to prove it. "Why haven't you decked me?"

"I don't make a habit of punching out civilians." She angled her chin when he nudged her back against the doorjamb. "But I can make an exception."

"Your pulse is jumping."

"It tends to when I'm irritated." Aroused, she'd nearly said aroused because that was the word that came into her head. That was the sensation sliding through her body. And enough was enough.

She shifted, a smooth move that should have planted her elbow in his gut and moved him aside. But he countered, just as smoothly, and changed his grip so that his fingers wrapped tight around her wrist. Instinctively she pivoted, started to hook her foot behind his to take him down.

He adjusted his weight, used it to plaster her back against the door. She told herself it was annoyance that quickened her breathing, and not the way the lines of his body pressed against the lines of hers.

She bunched the hand at her side into a fist, calculated the wisdom of using it for one short-armed punch to the face, and decided sarcasm was a more potent weapon against him.

"Next time, ask me if I want to dance. I'm not in the mood to—" She broke off when she saw something sharp come into his eyes, something reckless that had her already rapid pulse tripping to a faster rate.

She forgot self-defense, forgot the fist she still held ready. "Damn it, Blackhawk, back off. What do you want from me?"

"The hell with it." He forgot the rules, forgot the consequences of breaking them. All he could see was her. "The hell with it, let's find out."

He let the bottle drop, and the water that remained in it spilled unnoticed on the bedroom rug. He wanted his hands on her, both his hands, and used them to hold her arms over her head as his mouth came down on hers.

He felt her body jerk against his. Protest or invitation, he didn't care. One way or the other, he was bound to be damned for this single outrageous act. So he might as well make the most of it.

He used his teeth on her, the way he'd already imagined, scraping them along the long line of her lower lip. Freeing the warmth, the softness of it to him, then absorbing it. She made some sound, something that seemed to claw up from her throat and was every bit as primitive as the need that raged through him.

The scent of her—cool soap and skin—the flavor of her, such a contrast of ripeness and heat, overwhelmed him, stirred every hunger he'd ever known.

When his hands took her, fingers sliding down, gripping her hips, he was ready to feed those hungers, to take what he craved without a second thought.

Then his hand bumped over her weapon.

He jerked back as if she'd drawn it and shot him.

What was he doing? What in God's name was he doing?

She said nothing, only stared at him with eyes that had gone blurry at the edges. Her arms remained over her head, as if his hands still pinned them there.

Her body quaked.

"That was a mistake," she managed to say.

"I know it."

"A really serious mistake."

With her eyes open, she fisted her hands in his hair and dragged his mouth back to hers.

This time it was his body that jerked, and the shock of it vibrated through her, down to the bone. He'd savaged her mouth with that first mad kiss, and she wanted him to do it again. He would damn well do it again until her system stopped screaming.

She couldn't breathe without breathing him, and every desperate gulp of air was like the pump of a drug. The power of it charged through her while their lips and tongues warred.

With one violent move, he yanked her shirt out of the waistband of her slacks, then snaked his hand beneath until it closed over her breast.

The groan came from both of them.

"The minute I saw you." He tore his mouth from hers to feast on her throat. "The first minute I saw you."

"I know." She wanted his mouth again, had to have it. "I know."

He started to drag her jacket off, had it halfway down her arms when sanity began to pound against madness. The madness urged him to take her—why shouldn't he?—fast and hard. To take what he needed, the way he needed it, and please himself.

"Ally." He said her name, and the old-fashioned sweetness of it clicked reality back into place.

She saw him step back—though he didn't move, she saw the deliberate distance he built between them by the change in his eyes. Those fascinating and clear green eyes.

"Okay." She sucked in a breath. "Okay, okay." In an almost absent move she patted his shoulder until he did indeed step back. "That was…whoa." She sidestepped, paced away into his office. "Okay, that was…something."

"Something or other."

"I need a minute for my mind to clear." She'd never had passion slam into her with a force that blanked the mind. But she'd have to worry about that, deal with that later. Right now it was essential she find her balance.

"We probably both knew that was in there. And it's probably best we got it out," she said.

To give himself a moment he bent down, picked up the empty water bottle, set it aside. Then he dipped his hands into his pockets because they weren't altogether steady, and followed her into the office.

"I'll agree with the first part and reserve judgment on the second. What do we do now?"

"Now we…get over it."

Just like that? he thought. She'd cut him off at the knees, and now he was supposed to just hobble away and get over it?

"Fine." Pride iced his voice. He walked over, took three tapes out of his desk drawer. "I believe these satisfy your warrant."

Her palms were sweaty, but she couldn't sacrifice the dignity she was trying to rebuild by wiping them off. She took the tapes, slipped them into her shoulder bag. "I'll give you a receipt."

"Forget it."

"I'll give you a receipt," she repeated, and took out a pad. "It's procedure."

"We wouldn't want to tamper with procedure." He held out his hand, accepting the copy she offered. "Don't let me keep you, Fletcher. Clock's ticking."

She strode to the door, yanked it open. Dignity be damned, she decided and spun back. "You can save the attitude. You made the first move, I made the second. That's an even slate to me, and now it's done."

"Honey—make that Detective Honey, if we were done, we'd both be feeling a lot better right now."

"Yeah, well. We'll live with it," she muttered and sacrificed dignity for satisfaction by slamming the door.

Ally wasn't cut out to be a waitress. She was sure of it when, during her second shift at Blackhawk's, she poured the drink Beth had allowed her to serve over the head of the idiot customer who grabbed her butt and invited her to engage in a sexual act that was illegal in several states.

The customer had objected, rather strongly, to her response, but before she could flatten him, Will had appeared like smoke between them. She'd had to stand passively and be rescued.

It had grated for hours.

But if she was sure of her lack of waitress potential after her second shift, she was desperate to shed her cover by the third.

She wanted action. And not the kind that required her to serve wild wings in demon sauce and take orders for drinks called tornadoes to young executives on the make.

Twenty minutes into her third night at Blackhawk's had given her a profound respect for those who served and cleared and tolerated impatience, lousy tips and lewd propositions.

"I hate people." Ally waited for her drink order at the bar while Pete drew a beer off tap.

"Ah, no, you don't."

"Yes. Yes, I do. I really do. They're rude, annoying, oblivious. And all of them are jammed into Blackhawk's."

"And it's only six-thirty."

"Please. Six thirty-five. Every minute counts." She glanced back at Jan who worked the bar area, all but dancing between tables as she cleared, served and played up her assets. "How does she do it?"

"Some are born for it, Blondie. You'll excuse my saying so, but you're not. Not that you don't do the job, but you don't have the passion."

She rolled her eyes. "I don't have the arches, either." She started to lift the tray, eyes tracking the room as always, then she let it drop again when she spotted the man coming in the front door.

"Oh, hell. Pete, ask Jan to get this order to table eight club side. I have to do something."

"Ally, what're you doing here?"

It was all Dennis got out of his mouth before Ally grabbed his arm and hauled him through the bar, into the kitchen and out the back door. "Damn it, Dennis. Damn it!"

"What's the matter? What did you drag me out here for?" He put on his best baffled look, but she'd seen it before. She'd seen the whole routine before.

"I'm on the job. You'll blow my cover, for God's sake. I told you what would happen if you started following me again."

"I don't know what you're talking about." His injured air had worked on her once. More than once.

"You listen to me." She stepped close, jabbed a finger in his chest. "Listen hard, Dennis. We're done. We have been done for months. There's no chance that's going to change, and every chance, if you keep hassling me, I'll slap a restraining order on your butt and make your life a living hell."

His mouth thinned, his eyebrows lowered, the way she knew they did when he was backed into a corner. "This is a public place. All I did was walk into a public place. I'm entitled to buy a drink in a bar when I'm in the mood."

"You're not entitled to follow me, or to jeopardize my cover in a police investigation. You crossed the line, and I'm calling the D.A.'s office in the morning."

"You don't have to do that. Come on, Ally. How was I supposed to know you were on the job here? I just happened to pass by and—"

"Don't lie to me." She balled her hand into a fist, then in frustration tapped it against her own temple as she turned away. "Don't lie."

"I just miss you so much. I think about you all the time. I can't help it. I know I shouldn't have followed you. I didn't mean to. I was just hoping we could talk, that's all. Come on, baby." He took her shoulders, buried his face in her hair in a way that made her skin crawl. "If we could just talk."

"Don't...touch me." She hunched her shoulders, started to pull away, but he wrapped his arms around her, one hard squeeze of possession.

"Don't pull away. You know it makes me crazy when you go cold like that."

She could have had him flat on his back with her foot on his throat in two moves. She didn't want it to come to that. "Dennis, don't make me hurt you. Just leave me alone. Take your hands off me and leave me alone or it's going to be so much worse than it already is."

"No. It'll be better. I swear, it'll be better. You just have to take me back, and things'll be the way they used to be."

"No. They won't." She stiffened, braced to break the hold. "Let me go."

Light spilled out of the kitchen door as it opened. "I'd advise you to do what the lady asked," Jonah warned. "And do it fast."

She closed her eyes, felt temper and embarrassment rise up under the frustration. "I can handle this."

"Maybe, but you won't. This is my place. Take your hands off her."

"We're having a private conversation." Dennis turned, but pulled Ally with him.

"Not anymore. Go inside, Ally."

"This is none of your business." Dennis's voice rose, cracked. It was a tenor she'd heard before. "Just butt out."

"That wasn't the right response."

She moved now, breaking free and stepping between the men when Jonah moved forward. There was a gleam in his eye that worried her, like a flash of lightning against thin ice. "Don't. Please."

Anger wouldn't have stopped him, nor would an order. But the plea in her eyes, the weariness in them, did. "Go back inside," he said again, but quietly as he laid a hand on her shoulder.

"So that's the way it is." Dennis lifted bunched fists. "There's nobody else. That's what you told me. No, there was nobody else. Just another lie. Just one more of your lies. You've been sleeping with him all along, haven't you? Lying bitch."

Jonah moved like a snake. She'd seen street fights before. Had broken up her share while in uniform. She only had time to swear and leap forward, but Jonah already had Dennis up against the wall.

"Stop it," she said again and grabbed his arm to try to pull him off. She might as well have tried to shove aside a mountain.

He shot her one steely look. "No." He said it casually, like a shrug. Then he plowed his fist into Dennis's belly. "I don't like men who push women around or call them names." His voice stayed cool and steady as he delivered a second blow. "I won't tolerate it in my place. You got that?"

He let go, stepped back, and Dennis collapsed in a heap at his feet. "I think he got it."

"Great. Wonderful." While Dennis moaned, Ally pressed her fingers to her eyes. "You just gut-punched an assistant district attorney."

"And your point would be?"

"Help me get him up."

"No." Before she could try to haul Dennis to his feet, Jonah took her arm. "He walked in on his own, he'll walk away on his own."

"I can't leave him here, curled up like a damn shrimp on the pavement."

"He'll get up. Right, Dennis?" Elegant and unruffled in black, Jonah crouched down beside the groaning man. "You're going to get up, you're going to walk away. And you're not going to come back here in this lifetime. You're going to stay very far away from Allison. In fact, if you find out that by some mischance you're breathing the same air, you'll hold your breath and run in the opposite direction."

Dennis struggled to his hands and knees, retched. Tears swam in his eyes, but behind them was a rage that drilled in his head like a diamond bit. "You're welcome to her." Pain radiated through him as he stumbled to his feet. "She'll use you, then toss you aside. Just like she did me. You're welcome to her," he repeated, then limped away.

"Looks like you're all mine now." Jonah straightened, flicked fingers down his shirt as if removing some pesky lint. "But if you're going to start using me, I'd prefer we do it inside."

"It's not funny."

"No." He studied her face, the shadowed eyes and the pity in them. "I can see that. I'm sorry. Why don't you come inside, take a few minutes up in my office until you're feeling steadier."

"I'm okay." But she turned away, dragged the clip out of her hair as if it were suddenly too tight. "I don't want to talk about it now."

"All right." He put his hands on her shoulders, used his thumbs to press at the tension. "Take a minute anyway."

"I hate having him touch me, and I feel lousy because I hate it. I don't think it jeopardized the cover."

"No. According to Pete, some dude walked in, you flipped and dragged him out."

"Anybody asks, I'll keep it close to the truth. Ex-boyfriend who's hassling me."

"Then stop worrying." He turned her around. "And stop feeling guilty. You're not responsible for other people's feelings."

"Sure you are, when you help make them. Anyway." She lifted a hand to the one he still rested on her shoulder, patted it. "Thanks. I could have handled him, but thanks."

"You're welcome."

He couldn't stop himself from leaning into her, drawing her close. He watched her lashes lower, her mouth lift to his. And was a breath away from tasting her when the light spilled over them.

"Oh. Sorry." Frannie stood, framed in the door where kitchen noise clattered, a lighter in one hand, a cigarette at the ready in the other.

"No." Ally broke away, furious with herself for forgetting her priorities. "I was just going back in. I'm already late." She flicked one look at Jonah then hurried back inside.

Frannie waited until the door swung shut, then stepped over to lean back against the wall. She flicked on her lighter. "Well," she said.

"Well."

She blew out smoke on a sigh. "She's beautiful."

"Yes, she is."

"Smart, too. It comes across."

"Yeah."

"Just your type."

This time he angled his head. "You think so?"

"Sure." The tip of her cigarette glowed as she lifted it to her lips. "Classy. Class shows. She suits you."

It troubled him, more than he'd imagined it would, to dance around the truth with an old friend. "We'll see how well we fit."

Frannie moved a shoulder. But she'd already seen. They fit like lock and key. "Was there trouble with that suit?"

Jonah glanced in the direction Dennis had taken. "Nothing major. An ex who doesn't like being an ex."

"Figured it was something like that. Well, if it matters, I like her."

"It matters, Frannie." He walked to her, touched a hand to her cheek. "You matter, and always have."

Chapter 5

Six days after the Chamberses' burglary, Ally stood in her lieutenant's office. To save time, she'd already changed into her waitress gear for the evening. She had her badge in the pocket of her trousers and her clutch piece strapped just above her ankle.

"We haven't been able to trace one single piece of stolen property." She knew it wasn't what he wanted to hear. "There's no news on the street. Even Hickman's bottomless sources are dry. Whoever's pushing the buttons on this is smart, private and patient."

"You've been inside Blackhawk's for a week."

"Yes, sir. I can't tell you any more than I could the first day. Between the security tapes and my own in-the-field observations I've tagged several regulars. But nobody pops. On the upside, my cover's secure."

"Fortunately. Shut the door, Detective."

Her stomach sank a little, but she did so and stood in

the glass box of his office with the noise from the bull pen humming behind the clear wall.

"On the matter of Dennis Overton."

She'd known it was coming. Once she'd made the complaint to the D.A.'s office, it was inevitable that some of the flak would scatter into her own house.

"I regret the incident, Lieutenant. However, the way it ultimately played out added to my cover rather than detracting from it."

"That's not my concern. Why didn't you report his behavior previously to the D.A.? To me?"

They both heard the unspoken *To your father.*

"It was personal business, and until this last incident, on my personal time. I believed I could handle it without involving my superiors or Dennis's."

He understood the defensive stance, because he understood her. "I've spoken with the district attorney. In your complaint to him you state that Overton has, over a period of time beginning the first week of April, harassed you with phone calls both here and at home, has staked out your apartment, followed you on and off duty."

"He didn't interfere with the job," she began, then wisely closed her mouth when her lieutenant stared at her.

Kiniki set aside a copy of her written statement, folded his hands on it. "Contacting you against your stated wishes when you're on duty, as well as when you're off, interferes. Are you unaware of the stalking laws, Detective?"

"No, sir. When it became apparent that the subject would not desist in his behavior, could not be discouraged and could potentially interfere with this investigation, I reported his behavior to his superior."

"You haven't filed charges."

"No, sir."

"Nor have you, as yet, requested a restraining order."

"I believe a reprimand from his superior is sufficient."

"That, or being knocked back by Jonah Blackhawk?"

She opened her mouth, closed it again. She hadn't mentioned that part of the incident to the D.A.

"Overton claims that Blackhawk attacked him, unprovoked, in a fit of jealous rage."

"Oh, for God's sake." The words, and the disgust in them, were out before she could stop them. She yanked at her hair once, then bit down on control. "That is completely inaccurate. I didn't detail the incident, Lieutenant. It didn't seem necessary. But if Dennis insists on making trouble here, I'll write out a full report."

"Do it. I want a copy on my desk by tomorrow afternoon."

"He could lose his job."

"Is that your problem?"

"No." She blew out a breath. "No, sir. Lieutenant, Dennis and I dated for a period of three months." She hated this, bringing her personal life into her superior's office. "We were…intimate, briefly. He began to display—hell."

She dropped the copspeak, approached the desk. "He got possessive, jealous, irrational. If I was late or had to cancel, he'd accuse me of being with another man. It got way out of hand, and when I broke things off he'd come by or call. Full of apologies and promises to be different. When I didn't go for it, he'd either get nasty or fall apart. Lieutenant, I slept with him. Part of this situation is my doing."

Kiniki waited a moment, pulling on his bottom lip while he studied her. "That's one of the few stupid remarks I've ever heard you make. If a victim came to you describing this situation, would you tell her it was her doing?" When she didn't answer, he nodded. "I didn't think so. You would follow procedure. Follow it now."

"Yes, sir."

"Ally…" He'd known her since she was five. He tried to keep the personal separate as religiously as she. But there were times… "Have you told your father about this?"

"I don't want to bring him into it. Respectfully, sir, I'd prefer you didn't discuss it with him."

"That's your choice. The wrong one, but yours. I'll agree to it if I have your word that if Overton so much as breathes within ten feet of you, you report it to me." He cocked his head when her lips quivered. "That's amusing?"

"No, sir. Yes." She let go of the cop-to-cop stand. "Jonah made nearly the same statement, Uncle Lou. I guess it's… sweet. In a manly sort of way, of course."

"Always had the smartest mouth. Go on, get out of here. And get me something on these burglaries."

Since most waitresses-in-training didn't drive classic Corvettes, Ally was in the habit of parking two blocks away and walking the rest of the distance to Blackhawk's.

It gave her time to shift gears, to appreciate what spring brought to Denver. She'd always loved the city, the way the buildings, silver towers, rode into the sky. She loved seeing the mountains go from winter-white to those steely jags laced by snow and forest.

And though she enjoyed the mountains, had spent many wonderful days in her parents' cabin, she preferred to view them from city streets. Her city.

Her city had scarred-booted cowboys walking down the same streets with Armani-clad executives. It was about cattle and commerce and nightlife. It was about the wild, coated with a sheen or polish but not quite tamed.

The East would never hold the same appeal for her.

And when spring was in full, balmy life, when the sun beamed on the white-tipped peaks that guarded Denver, when the air was thin and bright, there was no place like it in the world.

She stepped out of the city, and into Blackhawk's.

Jonah was at the bar, the far end, leaning casually, sipping what she knew was his habitual sparkling water and listening to one of his regular customers complain about his day.

Those light and beautiful green eyes pinned her the minute she walked in, stayed steady, stayed level and gave away nothing.

He hadn't touched her since the night behind the club, and had said little. It was best that way, she told herself. Mix duty and lust and you end up compromising one and being burnt by the other.

But it was frustrating to see him night after night, to remain just close enough to maintain illusions and not be able to take a complete step forward or back.

And to want him, the way she'd never wanted anyone else.

She shrugged out of her jacket and got to work.

It was killing him, by inches. Jonah knew what it was to want a woman, to have one stir blood and loins and spin images in the mind. It could be a kind of hunger that slowly churned in the belly, gnawing there until it was finally satisfied.

This was a hunger, his desire for Ally. But there was nothing of the slow churning in it. This was sharp, constant and painful.

No other woman had ever caused him pain.

He carried the taste of her inside him. He couldn't rid himself of it. That alone was infuriating. It gave her an advantage he'd never allowed another to have over him. The fact that she didn't appear to know it didn't negate the weakness.

Where you were weak, you were vulnerable.

He wanted the investigation over. He wanted her back in her own life, her own world so he could regain his balance in his.

Then he remembered the way she'd erupted against him, the way her mouth had scorched over his, and her hands fisted in his hair. And he began to worry he'd never find his feet firmly planted again.

"Good thing we don't have a cop around."

Jonah's fingers tightened on his glass, but his eyes were mild as he turned to Frannie. "What?"

She pulled a beer, poured a bump, then served it. "A guy could get arrested for looking at a woman that way. I think it's called intent or something. What you intend is pretty clear, at least when she's not looking."

"Really?" And that, he realized, was another worry. "Then I'd better watch myself."

"She's doing plenty of watching," Frannie murmured as he walked away.

"The man's got trouble on the brain," Will commented. He liked coming over to Frannie's end of the bar so he could get a whiff of her hair or maybe work a smile out of her.

"He's got woman on the brain. And he's not altogether easy with this one." She winked at him and squirted a glass of the soft drink Will drank by the gallon during working hours.

"Women never trouble the man."

"This one does."

"Well." He sipped his drink, scanned the bar crowd. "She's a looker."

"That's not it. Looks are surface stuff. This one's got him down in the gut."

"You think?" Will tugged on his little beard. He didn't understand women, and didn't pretend to. To him they were simply amazing creatures of staggering power and wonderful shapes.

"I know." She patted Will's hand and had his heart throbbing in his throat.

"Two margaritas, frozen with salt, two house drafts and a club soda with lime." Jan set down her tray and walked her fingers up Will's arm in a teasing, tickling motion. "Hey, big guy."

He blushed. He always did. "Hey, Jan. I better do a round in the club."

He hurried off and had Frannie shaking her head at Jan. "You shouldn't tease him like that."

"I can't help it. He's so sweet." She flipped her hair back. "Listen there's this party tonight. I'm going by after closing. Want to tag along?"

"After closing I'm going to be home, in my own little bed, dreaming of Brad Pitt."

"Dreaming never gets you anywhere."

"Don't I know it," Frannie muttered and sent the blender whirling.

Allison carried a full tray of empties, and had two tables worth of drink orders in the pad tucked in her bar apron. Only thirty minutes into shift, she thought. It was going to be a long night. Longer, she realized when she spotted Jonah coming toward her.

"Allison, I'd like to speak with you." About something, anything. Five minutes alone with you might do it. Pitiful. "Would you come up to my office on your break?"

"Problem?"

"No," he lied. "No problem."

"Fine, but you'd better tell Will. He guards your cave like a wolf."

"Take your break now. Come up with me."

"Can't, thirsty people waiting. But I'll shake loose as soon as I can if it's important." She walked away quickly because she'd heard it, that underlying heat that told her what he wanted with her had nothing to do with duty.

She stopped at her station beside Pete and ordered herself to settle down. Since he was in the middle of entertaining three of the stool-sitters with a long, complicated joke, she took the time to rest her feet and study the people scattered at table and bar.

A twentysomething couple who looked like they were on the leading edge of an argument. Three suits with ties loosened arguing baseball. A flirtation, in its early stages, starting to cook between a lone woman and the better-looking of a pair of guys at the bar. Lots of eye contact and smiles.

Another couple at a table laughing together over some private joke, holding hands, she noted, flirting some even though the hands wore wedding rings. Well married, happy and financially secure if the designer handbag on the back of the woman's chair and the matching shoes were any indication.

At the next table another couple sat having a quiet conversation that seemed to please them both. There was an intimacy there as well, Ally noted. Body language, gestures, the smiling looks over sips of wine.

She envied that…comfort, she supposed, of having someone who could sit across the table in a crowded place and focus on her, care about what she said, or what she didn't have to say.

It was what her parents had—that innate rhythm and respect that added real dimension to love and attraction.

If it was lovely to watch, she wondered, how much more lovely must it be to experience?

Brooding over it, she listened to the laughter break out at Pete's punch line. She placed her orders, listening absently to the chatter around her, scanning, always scanning the movements, the faces.

She watched the hand-holding couple signal Jan, and the woman pointing to an item on the bar menu when the waitress moved to the table to take the order. Bending down, Jan waved a hand in front of her mouth, rolled her eyes and made the woman laugh.

"The hotter the better," the woman claimed. "We don't have a club table until eight, so there's plenty of time to cool down."

When Jan had scribbled down the order and moved off, Ally found herself smiling at the way the man brought the woman's hand to his mouth and nipped at her knuckles.

If it hadn't been for that kernel of envy that kept her attention focused on them, she might have missed it. As it was, it took her several seconds to note the picture had changed.

The woman's bag still hung over the back of her chair, but at a different angle, and the outside zipper pocket wasn't quite closed.

Ally came to attention, her first thought to focus on Jan. Then she saw it. The second woman sitting with her back to the first, still smiling at her companion. While under the table, smooth and unhurried, she slipped a set of keys into the purse she held on her lap.

Bingo.

"You gone to the moon, Ally?" Pete tapped a finger on her shoulder. "I don't think anybody's waiting for vodka tonics up there."

"No, I'm right here."

As the woman rose, tucked her purse under her arm, Ally lifted her tray.

Five-four, she thought. A hundred and twenty. Brown hair, brown eyes. Late thirties with an olive complexion and strong features. And just now heading toward the ladies' room.

Rather than break cover, she hurried into the club, spotted Will and shoved the tray at him. "Sorry, table eight's waiting for these. Tell Jonah I need to speak with him. I have to do something."

"But hey."

"I have to do something," she repeated and walked briskly toward the restrooms.

Inside, she scanned the bottom of the stalls, located the right shoes. Making a wax mold of the keys, Ally concluded and turned to one of the sinks. She ran water while she watched the shoes. It would only take a few minutes, but she'd need privacy.

Satisfied, Ally walked out.

"Ally? I got tables filling up here. Where's your tray?"

"Sorry." She shot Beth an apologetic smile. "Little emergency. I'll get on it."

She moved quickly, catching the eye of one of her team members and pausing by the table. "White female, late thirties. Brown and brown. She'll be coming out of the ladies' room in a minute. Navy jacket and slacks. She's sitting in the bar area with a white male, early forties, gray and blue in a green sweater. Keep them in sight, but don't move in. We handle it just like we outlined."

She walked back to the bar to pick up another tray as

a prop. The man in the green sweater was paying the tab. Cash. He looked relaxed, but Ally noted he checked his watch and glanced back toward the restrooms.

The woman came back in, but rather than taking her seat, stood between the tables and reached down for the short, black cape she'd draped over the chair. For a matter of seconds, her body blocked the view, then she straightened, beamed at her companion and handed him the cape.

Smart hands, Ally thought. Very smart hands.

When Jonah turned the corner of the bar, she inclined her head and let her gaze slide over to the couple preparing to leave, then back to him.

Casually she crossed over and ran a hand affectionately up and down Jonah's arm. "I've got two officers to tag them. We want them to get through the setup, all the way through. I want to give it some time before I alert the targets. When I do, I need your office."

"All right."

"We need to keep business as usual down here. If you'll hang around, I can let you know when I want to move. You can tell Beth you need me for something so she can juggle tables. I don't want any alarms going off."

"Just let me know. I'll take care of it."

"Let me have the code for your elevator. In case I need to take them up without you." She leaned in, her face tilted to his.

"Two, seven…" He leaned down, brushed his lips over hers. "Five, eight, five. Got it?"

"Yeah, I got it. See if you can keep attention off me until I move the targets out of the bar."

Her energy was up, but her mind was cool. She waited fifteen minutes. When the female target rose to use the restroom, Ally slipped in with her.

"Excuse me." After a quick check of the stalls, Ally pulled her badge out of her pocket. "I'm Detective Fletcher, Denver P.D."

The woman took a quick, instinctive step in retreat. "What's this about?"

"I need your help with an investigation. I'd like to speak with you and your husband. If you'd come with me."

"I haven't done anything."

"No, ma'am. I'll explain it all to you. There's a private office upstairs. If we could move up there as quietly as possible? I'd appreciate your cooperation."

"I'm not going anywhere without Don."

"I'll get your husband. If you'd walk back out, turn to the left, and wait in the corridor."

"I want to know what this is about."

"I'll explain it to both of you." Ally took the woman's arm to hurry her along. "Please. Just a few moments of your time."

"I don't want any trouble."

"Please wait here. I'll get your husband." Because she didn't trust the woman to stay put long, Ally moved fast. She paused at the couple's table, picked up empty glasses.

"Sir? Your wife's back there. She asked if you could come back for a minute."

"Sure. Is she okay?"

"She's fine."

Ally crossed to the bar, set down the empties. Then ducked quickly back into the corridor.

"Detective Fletcher," she said with a quick flash of her badge as the man joined her. "I need to speak with you and your wife in private." She was already keying in the code.

"She won't say what it's about. Don, I don't see why—"

"I appreciate your cooperation," Ally said again and all but shoved them both into the elevator.

"I don't appreciate being bullied by the police," the woman said with an edge of nerves in her voice.

"Lynn, calm down. It's okay."

"I'm sorry to be abrupt." Ally stepped into Jonah's office, gestured to the chairs. "If you'd have a seat, I'll fill you in."

Lynn crossed her arms, hugged her elbows tight. "I don't want to sit down."

Have it your way, sister, Ally thought. "I'm investigating a series of burglaries in and around Denver during the last several weeks."

The woman sniffed. "Do we look like burglars?"

"No, ma'am. You look like a nice, well-established, upper-class couple. Which has been, to date, the main target of this burglary ring. And less than twenty minutes ago, a woman we suspect is part of that ring lifted your keys out of your purse."

"That's impossible. My purse has been right with me all night." As if to prove it, she started to unzip the pocket. Ally snagged her wrist.

"Please don't touch your keys."

"How can I touch them if they're not there?" the woman argued.

"Lynn, shut up. Come on." He squeezed his wife's shoulder. "What's going on?" he asked Ally.

"We believe molds are made of the keys. They're replaced and the targeted victim remains unaware. Then their house is broken into and their belongings are stolen. We'd like to prevent that from happening to you. Now sit down."

Authority snapped in her voice this time. Visibly shaken, the woman lowered herself into a chair.

"If I could have your names please."

"Don and Lynn—Mr. and Mrs. Barnes."

"Mr. Barnes, would you give me your address?"

He swallowed, sat on the arm of his wife's chair and rattled it off while Ally noted it down. "Do you mean someone's in our house right now? Robbing us right now?"

"I don't believe they can move quite that quickly." In her mind she was calculating the drive time. "Is there anyone at that address right now?"

"No. It's just us. Man." Barnes ran a hand through his hair. "Man, this is weird."

"I'm going to call in your address and begin setting up a stakeout. Give me a second."

She picked up the phone as the elevator doors opened, and Jonah walked it. "I've got it covered here," she told him.

"I'm sure you do. Mr. and Mrs…?"

"Barnes," the man answered. "Don and Lynn Barnes."

"Don, can I offer you and your wife something to drink? I realize this is very inconvenient and upsetting for you."

"I could use a shot. A good stiff bourbon, I think."

"Can't blame you. And Lynn?"

"I…" She lifted a hand, dropped it. "I just can't…I don't understand."

"Maybe a little brandy." Jonah turned away, opened a panel in the wall to reveal a small, well-stocked bar. "You can put yourselves in Detective Fletcher's capable hands," he continued and he chose bottles and glasses. "And meanwhile, we'll try to keep you as comfortable as possible."

"Thanks." Lynn took the brandy from him. "Thank you so much."

"Mr. Barnes." A little miffed at how smoothly Jonah had settled ruffled feathers, she yanked the man's attention back to her. "We have units on the way to your house right now. Can you describe your house for me? The layout, doors, windows?"

"Sure." He laughed, a little shakily. "Hell, I'm an architect."

He gave her a clear picture, which she relayed to the team before she began to set up the coordinates for the stakeout.

"You have dinner reservations here tonight?" Ally asked them.

"Yeah. Eight o'clock. We're making a night of it," he said with a sour smile.

Ally checked her watch. "They'll think they have plenty of time." She wanted them to go back down, to finish their time at the bar, go into dinner and present the appearance of normality. And one look at the woman's face told her it was a long shot.

"Mrs. Barnes. Lynn." Ally came back around the desk, sat on the edge of it. "We're going to stop these people. They won't take your things or damage your home. But I need you to help me out here. I need you and your husband to go back down, to try to get through the evening as if nothing was wrong. If you could hold on for another hour, I think we could wrap this up."

"I want to go home."

"We'll get you there. Give me an hour. It's possible that a member of the organization is assigned to keep an eye on you. You've already been away from your table nearly twenty minutes. We'll cover that, but we can't cover another hour. We don't want to scare these people off."

"If they're scared off, they won't break into my house."

"No, just into someone else's the next time."

"Give me a minute with her, okay." Barnes got up, took his wife's hands. "Come on, Lynn. Hell, it's an adventure. We'll eat out on the story for years. Come on, let's go—let's just go downstairs and get drunk."

"Jonah, go with them. Ah, pass the word that those—what was it—the wild wings you ordered didn't sit too well after all. You're fine now, but you were feeling a little sick. Blackhawk's will cover your bar bill, right?"

"Naturally." Jonah offered Lynn his hand to help her to her feet. "And the dinner tab. I'll take you down. You just needed to stretch out for a few minutes, and I offered to take you and your husband up to my office until you felt better. Good enough?" he asked Ally as he pressed for the elevator.

"Perfect. I need to make a couple more calls, then I'll be down. I'm going to have to cut out before end of shift. I've had a family emergency."

"Good luck with it," he told her, and led the Barneses away.

Chapter 6

She got the key from Jonah and went straight to the employee lounge for her bag. She ran straight out, doing no more than waving a hand when Frannie called out to her from behind the bar.

She was trusting Jonah to answer any questions. No one could do it better, she thought as she raced the blocks to her car. A simple word, a shrug from him and that would be that. No one pumped a man like Jonah Blackhawk.

She had to get to Federal Heights before everything went down.

At first she thought she was seeing things. But the night was clear and cool and her vision excellent. There was no mistaking the fact that all four of her tires were slashed.

She swore, kicked viciously at the mangled rubber. A hell of a time, she thought, one hell of a time for Dennis

Overton to get nasty. Digging into her bag she pulled out her cell phone and called for a radio car.

Time wasted, was all she could think. Two minutes, five minutes ticking away while she paced the sidewalk and waited. She had her badge out and her teeth clenched when the patrol car pulled up.

"Got some trouble, Detective?"

"Yeah. Hit the sirens, head north on 25. I'll tell you when to go silent."

"You got it. What's going down?"

She settled into the back behind the two uniforms, itching to have her hands on the wheel and her foot on the gas. "I'll fill you in." She took her weapon and harness out of her bag, and felt more herself the minute she strapped it on.

"Call for a tow truck, will you? I don't want to leave my car on the street like that."

"Shame about that. Nice car."

"Yeah." She forgot about it as they screamed up the interstate.

A block from the Barneses' address, she hopped out of the car, and arrowed straight to Hickman. "Give me the story."

"They took their time getting here. Balou and Dietz had the first leg of the tail and said they drove like solid citizens, kept under the speed limit, signaled for turns. Woman riding shotgun, made a call on a cell phone. He turned over the tail to me and Carson when they got on 36. They stopped for gas. The woman gets in the back. They're driving a nice, suburban minivan. She's doing something back there, but I couldn't get close enough to see."

"Making the keys. I bet you two weeks' pay she's got the works for it in the van."

"Do I look like I take sucker bets?" He glanced down the quiet street. "Anyhow, we had a unit here, waiting. The suspects were observed parking the van a block down from the target address. They strolled up the street, walked right up to the door, unlocked it and went in like they owned the place."

"Barnes said they have a security system."

"Alarm didn't trip. They've been inside about ten minutes now. Lieutenant's waiting for you. We've got the area blocked off, the house surrounded."

"Then let's move in and wrap this up."

He grinned, handed her a walkie-talkie. "Saddle up."

"God, I love cowboy talk."

They moved fast, kept low. She spotted the cops positioned on the street, behind trees, in shadows, hunched in cars.

"Glad you could join the party, Detective." Kiniki nodded toward the house. "Ballsy, aren't they?"

Lights gleamed, a homey glow against windows on the first and second floor. While Ally watched, she saw a faint shadow move behind the lower window.

"Dietz and Balou are covering the back. We've got them closed in. What's your play?"

Ally reached in her pocket, pulled out keys. "We move in on all sides, and go in the front. When we move, pull one of the radio cars across the driveway. Let's block that route."

"Call it."

She lifted the walkie-talkie, to establish positioning and give the orders. And all hell broke loose.

Three gunshots blasted the air, the return fire slamming into the echoes. Even as Ally drew her own weapon, voices shouted through the walkie-talkies.

"Dietz is down! Officer down! Shooter's male, heading east on foot. Officer down!"

Cops rushed the house. Ally hit the door first, went in low. Blood pounded in her ears as she swept the area with her weapon. Hickman took her back, and at her signal headed up the stairs while she turned right.

Someone was shouting. She heard it like a buzz in the brain. Lights flashed on.

The house opened out like a fan. She brought the layout Barnes had described into her mind as she and the rest of the team spread out. At each doorway she led with eyes and weapon, following training while her breath came short and shallow.

There was more gunfire from outside, muffled pops. She started to turn in that direction and saw the sliding door on what looked like a small solarium wasn't quite shut.

She caught a scent, very female, and following instinct turned away from the shouts and bolted for the door.

She saw the woman, just the silhouette of her, running hard toward a line of ornamental trees. "Police! Stop where you are!"

She would replay it a dozen times. The woman continued to run. Weapon drawn, Ally raced after her, calling out the warning, shouting her position and situation into her hand unit.

She heard calls from behind her, running feet.

They'd cut her off, Ally thought. Cut her off even before she reached the six-foot fence that closed in the property.

Nowhere to go.

She gained ground, caught both the scent of perfume and panic sweat the woman left on the air. Moonlight picked her out of the shadows, the swing of her dark hair, the stream of the short, black cape.

And when, on the run, the woman turned, the moonlight bounced off the chrome plating of the revolver in her hand.

Ally saw her lift it, felt with a kind of detached shock the heat of the bullet that whined past her own head.

"Drop your weapon! Drop it now!"

And as the woman pivoted, and the gun jerked in her hand, Ally fired.

Ally saw the woman stagger, heard the thud as the gun fell from her hand, and heard a kind of sighing gasp. But what she would remember, what seemed to burn on her brain like acid on glass, was the dark stain that bloomed between the woman's breasts even as she dropped.

It was bone-deep training that had her rushing forward, stepping on the woman's gun. "Suspect down," she said into her hand unit as she crouched to check for a pulse. Her voice didn't shake, and neither did she. Not yet.

It was Hickman who got to her first. She heard his voice like something carried on the crest of a wave of churning water. Her head was full of sound, a rushing liquid sound.

"Are you hit? Ally, are you hit?"

His hands were already moving over her, tugging at her jacket to check for injury.

"Call an ambulance." Her lips were stiff, they felt wooden, splintered. She reached forward, crossing her hands over each other, pressing the heels of them on the woman's chest.

"On the way. Come on. Get up."

"She needs pressure on this wound. She needs an ambulance."

"Ally." He holstered his own weapon. "You can't do anything for her. She's dead."

She didn't let herself be sick. She made herself stand and watch as the wounded officer and the woman's partner were loaded into ambulances. She made herself watch when the woman was zipped into a thick black bag.

"Detective Fletcher."

And she made herself turn, face her lieutenant. "Sir. Can you tell me Dietz's condition?"

"I'm on my way to the hospital. We'll know more later."

She rubbed the back of her hand over her mouth. "The suspect?"

"Paramedics said he'll make it. It'll be a couple of hours at least before we can question him."

"Am I...will I be allowed to be in on the interrogation."

"It's still your case." He took her arm to draw her away. "Ally, listen to me. I know what it feels like. Ask yourself now, right now, if you could have done anything differently."

"I don't know."

"Hickman was behind you, and Carson was coming in from the left. I haven't spoken with her as yet, but Hickman's report is you identified yourself, ordered her to stop. She turned and fired. You ordered her to drop her weapon, and she prepared to fire again. You had no choice. That's what I expect to hear from you during the standard inquiry tomorrow morning. Do you want me to call your father?"

"No. Please. I'll talk to him tomorrow, after the inquiry."

"Then go home, get some rest. I'll let you know about Dietz."

"Sir, unless I'm relieved of duty, I'd rather go to the hospital. Stand by for Dietz, and be on hand to question the suspect when we're cleared to do so."

It would be better for her, he thought, to do what came next. "You can ride with me."

Panic was like an animal clawing at his throat. He'd never felt anything like it before. Jonah told himself it was just hospitals that did it to him. He'd always detested them. The smell of them brought back the last hideous months of his father's life, and made him all too aware that a turn here, a turn there in a different direction might have damned him to experience the same fate his father had at fifty years old.

His source had assured him that Ally wasn't hurt. But all he knew for certain was that something had gone very wrong at the bust and she was at the hospital. That had been enough to have him heading straight out. Just to see for himself, he thought.

He found her, slumped in a chair, in the hallway of Intensive Care. The panic digging into his throat released.

She'd taken the clip out of her hair as he knew she did when she was tense or tired. The gilt curtain of hair fanned down the side of her face, concealing it. But the tired slouch, the hands she gripped together on her knees, told him what to expect.

He stepped in front of her, crouched down and saw, as he'd known he would, pale skin and dark, bruised eyes.

"Hey." He gave in to the need to lay his hand over hers. "Bad day?"

"Pretty bad." It seemed like wires were crossed in her brain. She didn't think to wonder why he was there. "One of my team's in critical condition. They don't know if he'll make it till morning."

"I'm sorry."

"Yeah, me, too. The doctors won't let us talk to the

son of a bitch who shot him. Male suspect identified as Richard Fricks. He's sleeping comfortably under a nice haze of drugs while Dietz fights for his life, and his wife's down in the chapel praying for it."

She wanted to close her eyes, to go into the dark, but kept them open and on his. "And for a bonus, I killed a woman tonight. One shot through the heart. Like she was a target I aced at practice."

Her hands trembled once under his, then fisted.

"Yeah, that's a pretty bad day. Come on."

"Come where?"

"Home, I'm taking you home." When she looked at him blankly, he pulled her to her feet. She felt feather-light, her hands fragile as glass. "There's nothing you can do here now, Ally."

She closed her eyes, groped for a breath. "That's what Hickman said at the scene. There's nothing you can do. Looks like you're both right."

She let him lead her to the elevator. There was no point in staying, or arguing or pretending she wanted to be alone. "I can…get a ride."

"You've got one."

No, she thought, no point in arguing, or in resisting the supporting arm he slipped around her waist. "How did you know to come here?"

"A cop came by to take the Barneses home. I got enough out of him to know there'd been trouble, and where you were. Why isn't your father with you?"

"He doesn't know. I'll tell him about it tomorrow."

"What the hell's wrong with you?"

She blinked, like a woman coming out of a dark room into the light. "What?"

He pulled her out of the elevator, across the hospital lobby. "Do you want him to hear about this from someone else? To not hear your voice, hear you tell him you're not hurt? What are you thinking?"

"I…I wasn't thinking. You're right." She fumbled in her purse for her phone as they crossed the lot. "I need a minute. I just need a minute."

She got into the car, steadying herself, steadying her breathing. "Okay," she whispered it to herself as Jonah started the car. She punched in the number, waited through the first ring, then heard her mother's voice.

"Mom." Her breath hitched. She bore down, holding a hand over the phone until she was sure her voice would be normal. "I'm fine. Everything okay there? Uh-huh. Listen, I'm on my way home, and I need to speak to Dad a minute. Yeah, that's right. Cop talk. Thanks."

Now she closed her eyes, listened to her mother call out, heard the warm mix of their laughter before her father's voice sounded in her ear.

"Ally? What's up?"

"Dad." Her voice wanted to crack but she refused to let it. "Don't say anything to upset Mom."

There was a pause. "All right."

"I'm okay. I'm not hurt, and I'm on my way home. It went down tonight, and things went wrong. Ah, one of the team was wounded, and he's in the hospital. One of the suspects is in there, too. We'll know more tomorrow on both."

"You're all right? Allison?"

"Yes, I wasn't hurt. Dad. Dad, I had to fire my weapon. They were armed. Both suspects were armed and opened fire. She wouldn't… I killed her."

"I'll be there in ten minutes."

"No, please. Stay with Mom. You'll have to tell her and she's going to be upset. I need to…I just need to go home and—tomorrow, okay? Can we talk about it tomorrow? I'm so tired now."

"If that's what you want."

"It is. I promise, I'm all right."

"Ally, who went down?"

"Dietz. Len Dietz." She lifted her free hand, pressed her fingers to her lips. They didn't feel stiff now, but soft. Painfully soft. "He's critical. The lieutenant's still at the hospital."

"I'll contact him. Try to get some sleep. But you call, anytime, if you change your mind. I can be there. We both can."

"I know. I'll call you in the morning. I think it'll be easier in the morning. I love you."

She broke the connection, let the phone slide into her purse. She opened her eyes and saw they were already in front of her apartment. "Thanks for…"

Jonah said nothing, simply got out, came around to her door. Opening it, he held out a hand for hers. "I can't seem to get my thoughts lined up. What time is it?"

"It doesn't matter. Give me your key."

"Oh, yeah, the traditionalist." She dug it out, unaware her other hand was clutching his like a lifeline. "I'm going to start expecting flowers next."

She walked through the lobby, to the elevator. "It seems like there's something I have to do. I can't get a rope around what it is, though. There should be something I have to do. We identified her. She had ID anyway. Madeline Fricks. Madeline Ellen Fricks," she murmured, floating like a dream out of the elevator. "Age thirty-seven. She had an address in…Englewood. Somebody's checking it out. I should be checking it out."

He unlocked the door, drew her inside. "Sit down, Ally."

"Yeah, I could sit down." She looked blankly around

the living room. It was just the way she'd left it that morning. Nothing had changed. Why did it seem as if everything had changed?

Jonah solved the matter by picking her up and carrying her toward the bedroom.

"Where are we going?"

"You're going to lie down. Got anything to drink around here?"

"Stuff."

"Fine. I'll go find some stuff." He laid her on the bed.

"I'll be okay."

"That's right." He left her to hunt through the kitchen. In a narrow cupboard he found an unopened bottle of brandy. He broke the seal, poured three fingers. When he brought it back, she was sitting up in the bed, her knees rammed into her chest, her arms roped around them.

"I've got the shakes." She kept her face pressed to her knees. "If I had something to do, I wouldn't have the shakes."

"Here's what you need to do." He sat on the bed, cupped a hand under her chin and lifted it. "Drink this."

She took the first sip obediently when he lifted the glass to her lips. Then she coughed and turned her head away. "I hate brandy. Somebody gave me that last Christmas, God knows why. I meant to…" She trailed off, began to rock.

"Have some more. Come on, Fletcher, take your medicine."

He gave her little choice but to gulp down another swallow. Her eyes watered and color flooded her cheeks. "We had the place closed in, surrounded the house, cordoned off the area in a three-block radius. They couldn't have gotten through. They had no place to run."

She needed to talk through it. Jonah set the brandy aside. "But they ran anyway."

"We were just about to move in, and he—Fricks—came out the back, already firing. He hit Dietz with two rounds. Some of us went around the back, covering both sides. Some of us went in the front. I was first in, Hickman was behind me. We spread out, started the sweep."

She could still see it in her head. Moving through, fast and steady, the lights blazing.

"I could hear more gunfire, and shouting from outside. I nearly turned back, thinking they were both out of the house and running—that they were together. But I saw—there's this bump-out sunroom deal on the house, and the sliding door leading out wasn't closed, not all the way closed. I spotted her as soon as I stepped out. Going in the opposite direction as her partner. Splitting us up, I guess. I called out, told her to stop. I was in pursuit and she fired a round. Sloppy shot. I ordered her to stop, to drop her weapon. I didn't see she had a choice. Where the hell could she go? But she spun around.

"She spun around," Ally repeated. "The moon was very bright, very bright and it was on her face, in her eyes, shining on the gun. And I shot her."

"Did you have a choice?"

Her lips trembled open. "No. In my head that's clear. Jonah, that's so clear. I've gone over it, step after step, a dozen times already. But they don't prepare you for what it's like. They can't. They can't tell you how it feels."

The first tear spilled over and she wiped it impatiently away. "I don't even know what I'm crying for. Or who."

"It doesn't matter." He put his arms around her, drew her head down on his shoulder and held her while she wept.

And while she wept he went back over what she'd told him.

Sloppy shot, she'd said, almost skimming over the fact

that someone had tried to kill her. Yet she wept because she'd had no choice but to take a life.

Cops. He turned his cheek against her hair. He'd never understand cops.

She slept for two hours, dropping into oblivion like a stone in a pool, and staying deep at the bottom. When she woke, she was wrapped around him in the dark.

She lay still a moment, orienting herself, while his heart beat strong and steady under her palm. With her eyes open and her mind clearing she went through a mental checklist. She had a vague headache, but nothing major—just a hangover from the crying jag. There was a stronger feeling of embarrassment, but she thought she could live with that, too.

She wiggled her toes and discovered she was barefoot. And her ankle holster was gone.

So, she realized, was her shoulder harness.

He'd disarmed her, she thought, in more ways than one. She'd blubbered out her story, cried on his shoulder and was now wrapped around him in the dark. Worse than all of that was realizing she wanted to stay there.

Believing him asleep she started to inch away.

"Feel any better?"

She didn't jolt, but it was close. "Yeah. Considerably. I guess I owe you."

"I guess you do."

In the dark he found her mouth with his and sank in.

Soft, unexpectedly soft. Warm, deliciously warm. Yes, she wanted to stay there, and so she opened for him, sliding her hand from his heart to his face, yielding when he turned his body to press hers into the mattress.

The good solid weight of him, the hard lines of his body, the drugging heat of his mouth was exactly what she wanted. Her arms came around him, holding him there as he had held her in tears and in sleep.

He gave himself the moment, the dark taste of her mouth, the sleepy sigh she made, the feminine give of her beneath him. He'd lain beside her, his body alert, his mind restless while hers slept. Wanting her, wanting her so it was like a fever in the blood.

Yet when she woke, he found himself drowning in tenderness.

Yet when she surrendered, he found himself unwilling, unable, to take.

He drew back, skimmed a thumb over the curve of her cheek. "Bad timing," he said and rolled off the bed.

"I…" She cleared her throat. Her body had just started to ache, her mind had just started to float. Now she floundered free. "Look, if you have some weird idea that you were taking advantage, you're wrong."

"Am I?"

"I know how to say yes or no. And while I appreciate you bringing me home, hearing me out and not leaving me alone, I'm not grateful enough for any of that to pay you back with sex. I think too much of myself. Hell, I think too much of sex."

He laughed, sat on the edge of the bed again. "You do feel better."

"I said I did. So." She slid over, tossing her hair back and nuzzling his throat.

His pulse tripped and a fireball burst in his belly. "That's tempting." He was lucky to be able to breathe, and still casually patted her hand and got to his feet. "But no thanks."

Insult came first, and something vile nearly spilled off her tongue. Because it made her think of Dennis, she yanked herself back. "Okay. Mind if I ask why? Under the current circumstances, that seems like a reasonable question."

"Two reasons."

He switched on the bedside light, watched her eyes narrow in defense. And the look of her slammed into him like a fist in the throat.

"God. You're beautiful."

A little thrill jumped up her spine. "And that's why you don't want to make love with me?"

"I want you. Enough that it's starting to hurt. That ticks me off."

Idly he took the ends of her hair, wrapped a length of it around his hand, released it. "You're on my mind, Ally, too often for comfort. I like to be comfortable. So reason one is that I haven't decided if I want to get tangled up with you. If I do half of the very interesting things I have in mind to do with you, I'm going to be tangled."

She sat back on her heels. "I imagine you know how to cut line when you want to."

"I've never had any trouble before. You're trouble. It's that simple."

Insult and annoyance had vanished. "This is fascinating. Here I had you pegged as somebody who took what he wanted when he wanted it, and the hell with the consequences."

"No. I prefer calculating, then eliminating consequences. Then I take what I want."

"In other words, I make you nervous."

"Oh, yeah. Go ahead and grin," he said with a nod. "I can't blame you."

She laughed, lifted her eyebrows. "You said there were two reasons. What's the second?"

"That's easy." He stepped to the bed, bent down and

caught her chin in his hand. "I don't like cops," he said, and brushed his lips lightly over hers.

When he would have leaned away from the kiss, she leaned in, sliding up so that her body rubbed over his. She felt his body quiver, and nothing had ever been more satisfying.

"Yeah, you're trouble," he muttered. "I'm leaving."

"Coward."

"Okay, that stings, but I'll get over it." He walked over to shrug on the jacket he'd tossed onto a chair, slip his feet back into his shoes.

She didn't just feel better, Ally realized. She felt fabulous. Invincible. "Why don't you come on back here and fight like a man."

He glanced at her. She knelt on the side of the bed, her eyes dark and challenging, her hair a tumble of gold around her face and shoulders.

The taste of her was still sizzling on his tongue.

But he shook his head, walked to the door. Tormented himself with one last look. "I'm going to hate both of us in the morning," he told her, then strode away while her laughter followed him.

Chapter 7

Ally was up at six and ready to roll out the door at seven. She nearly rolled right over her parents, who were at her front door.

"Mom." She flicked her eyes up to her father, started to speak, but her mother already had her caught in a hard hug. "Mom," she said again. "I'm all right."

"Indulge me." Cilla held on, tight, heart pressed to heart, cheek pressed to cheek.

Stupid, Cilla thought, so stupid to have kept it together all night and to feel herself falling apart now that her child was in her arms.

She couldn't, wouldn't allow it.

"Okay." She laid her lips on Ally's temple for a moment, then drew back far enough to study her daughter's face.

"I had to see for myself. You're lucky your father held me off this long."

"I didn't want you to worry."

"It's my job to worry. And I believe in doing a job well."

Ally watched her mother's lips curve, saw the tears willed away. And knew it cost her. "You do everything well."

Cilla O'Roarke Fletcher's eyes were the same golden-brown as her daughter's, her short sweep of hair a luxuriant black that suited her angular features and smoky voice.

"But I've got worry down to a science," she said.

Since they were almost of identical heights, Ally had only to shift closer to kiss Cilla's cheek. "Well, you can take a break. I'm fine. Really."

"I suppose you look it."

"Come on inside. I can make some more coffee."

"No, you're on your way out. I just needed to see you." To touch you, Cilla thought. My baby. "I'm heading into work. I'm interviewing a new sales manager at KHIP. Your dad's dropping me off. You can use my car today."

"How did you know I needed a car?"

"I have connections," Boyd told her. "You should have yours back by midafternoon."

"I would've handled it." Ally shut the door behind her, frowned.

"Meaning you would have handled the car, and Overton and the tangle of bureaucracy," Cilla put in. "I hope I didn't raise a daughter who's ungrateful, and who expects her father to stand back with his hands in his pockets when something happens to her." Cilla tilted her head, lifted her brows. "I'd be very disappointed if I had."

Boyd grinned, slipped an arm around Cilla's shoulders and pressed his lips to her hair.

"Good one," Ally muttered, properly chastised. "Thank you, Dad."

"You're welcome, Allison."

"Now, which one of us is going to go beat the tar out of Dennis Overton?" Cilla rubbed her hands together. "Or can we all do it? In which case, I get to go first."

"She has violent tendencies," Ally pointed out.

"Tell me about it. Down girl," he told Cilla. "Let the system work. Now…Detective." Boyd draped his arm around his daughter's shoulders as they walked to the elevator. "You're to report to the hospital first. There's a suspect who needs to be questioned."

"The inquiry into the shooting?"

"Will proceed this morning. You'll need to give your statement and file your report. By ten hundred. Detective Hickman filed his last night, which gives a very clear picture. You don't have anything to worry about."

"I'm not worried. I know I did what I had to do. It gave me some bad moments last night." She blew out a breath. "Some pretty bad ones. But I'm okay with it now. As okay as it gets, I guess."

"You shouldn't have been alone last night," Cilla said.

"Actually I had…a friend with me for a while."

Boyd opened his mouth, shut it again. After Ally's call the night before, he'd contacted Kiniki immediately. He knew that Jonah had driven Ally home from the hospital, so he had a good idea just who the friend was.

But he had no idea how he felt about it.

Ally pulled into the hospital visitors' lot, circled until she found a space. She spotted Hickman as she set the locks and alarm.

"Nice ride," he commented, hands in pockets, eyes

squinted into slits against the brilliant sunshine. "Not every cop's got herself a Mercedes as a backup vehicle."

"It's my mother's."

"You've got some mother." He'd seen Cilla, so he knew it was true. "So, how's it going?"

"Okay." She fell into step beside him. "Look, I know you already filed your report on last night's incident. I appreciate you getting it in so fast and backing me up."

"It happened the way it happened. If it smoothes any edges for you, you should know that you fired about a split hair before I did. If I'd been in the lead instead of you, I'd've been the one to take her out."

"Thanks. Any word on Dietz?"

"Still critical." Hickman's expression darkened. "He made it through the night, so that's hopeful. I want a round with the son of a bitch who put him here."

"Get in line."

"You know how you want to play it?"

"I've been thinking about it." They moved together across the lobby to the bank of elevators. "She made a call from her cell phone—that puts at least one other person in on the deal. I say two. Whoever's inside the club, and somebody pushing the buttons, organizing. Our guy here shot a cop, so he knows he's going down hard. His wife's dead, his operation's broken and he's looking at death row."

"Doesn't give him much incentive to talk. You going to deal him a life sentence?"

"That's the road. Let's make sure he walks it."

She showed her badge to the uniform on guard at Fricks's door, walked through.

Fricks lay in bed, his skin pale, slightly gray. His eyes were blurred, but open. His gaze passed over Ally and Hickman, then returned to contemplate the ceiling.

"I have nothing to say. I want a lawyer."

"Well, that makes our job easier." Hickman walked over to the bed, pursed his lips. "Doesn't look like a cop killer, does he, Fletcher?"

"He's not. Yet. Dietz might make it. Of course, this guy here's still looking at being strapped to a table and being put down like a sick dog. Nighttime B and E, burglary, possession of an unregistered weapon, assault with a deadly, attempted murder of a police officer." She moved her shoulders. "And plenty more where that came from."

"I have nothing to say."

"Then shut up," she suggested. "Why try to help yourself? Trust a lawyer to take care of everything. But…I'm not in the mood to make deals with lawyers. How about you, Hickman?"

"Nope, can't say that's my mood at this time."

"We're not in the mood," Ally repeated. "Not when we have a fellow officer fighting for his life up in Intensive Care. That really puts us off lawyers who look for ways to wiggle cop killers out of the noose. Right, Hickman?"

"Yeah, puts me right off. I don't see any reason we should give this guy any kind of a break. I say let him hang for it all by himself."

"Well, we ought to look at the big picture, though. Show a little compassion. He lost his wife last night." She watched the ripple of pain run over Fricks's face before he closed his eyes.

There, she thought, was the key to him.

"That's rough. His wife's dead, and he's lying here shot up and looking at a death sentence." Ally lifted her shoulders, let them fall. "Maybe he's not thinking how other people, people who helped put him in this situation could walk away clean. Clean, and rich, while he's twisting in the wind on a very short rope. And his wife gets put in the ground."

She leaned over the bed. "But he ought to be thinking about it. Of course maybe he didn't love his wife."

"Don't talk to me about Madeline." His voice wavered. "She was my heart."

"Really. I'm touched. That touches me. Now that might not hold any weight with Hickman here, but me, I've got a soft spot for true love. Since I do, I'm going to tell you you ought to be thinking how you can help yourself now, because if you were her heart, she wouldn't want you to go down for this alone."

His eyes flickered, then closed.

"You ought to be thinking that if you cooperate and tell us what we want to know, we'll go to the D.A. and press for a little leniency. Show some remorse now, Richard, reach out. That'll go a long way toward keeping you off a table in a little room a few years down the road."

"I talk, I'm already dead."

Ally shot Hickman a glance. "You'll get protection."

Fricks's eyes were still closed, but tears began to leak out of them. "I loved my wife."

"I know you did." Ally lowered the bed guard so she could sit beside him.

Intimacy now, she thought. Sympathy. And infused her voice with both. "I saw you together at Blackhawk's. The way you looked at each other tells me you had something special between you."

"She—she's gone."

"But you tried to save her, didn't you, Richard? You ran out of the house first, to cover for her. That's why you're in this jam. She loved you. She'd want you to help yourself. She'd want you to go on living, to do whatever you had to do to go on. Richard, you tried to save her last night, drawing the cops off her so she could get away. You did what you could. Now you've got to save yourself."

"No one was supposed to get hurt. The guns were just a precaution, to scare anybody off if something went wrong."

"That's right. You didn't plan on this. I believe that. That'll make a difference how this all comes out for you. Things just got out of control."

"Nothing ever went wrong before. She panicked. That's all. She just panicked, and I couldn't think of anything else to do."

"You didn't mean to hurt anybody." Ally kept her voice quiet, compassionate, even while the image of Dietz, bleeding on the ground, ran through her mind. "You just wanted to give her time to get away." She took a moment while he wept.

"How'd you get past the alarm systems?"

"I've got a knack for electronics." He took the tissues she handed him, wiped his eyes. "I worked in security. People don't always remember to set their alarms anyway. But when they did, I could usually disarm them. If I couldn't, it was a wash and we walked away. Where have they put Madeline? Where is she?"

"We'll talk about that. Help me out here, and I'll do what I can to arrange for you to see her. Who called you from the club, Richard, to tell you something was wrong with the Barneses? Was it the same person Madeline called from the car?"

He let out a sobbing breath, shook his head. "I want immunity."

Hickman let out a snort, made a move to draw Ally off the bed, make her the protector. "The son of a bitch wants immunity. You're bending over backward to help him out, and he wants a walk. Screw him. Let him hang."

"Hold on. Just hold on. Can't you see the man's upset? Lying here like this, he can't even make arrangements for his wife's funeral."

"She—" Fricks turned his head away, and his chest heaved once. "She wanted to be cremated. It was important to her."

"We can help you arrange that. We can help you give her what she wanted. You have to give us something back."

"Immunity."

"Listen, Richard. You can't ask for the moon and stars on this one. Now I could make you promises, but I'm being straight with you. Best I can do is leniency."

"We don't need him, Ally." Hickman picked up the chart at the foot of the bed, scanned it. "We got him cold, and we'll pick up the rest of the pieces within a couple of days."

"He's right." Ally let out a sigh, looked back at Fricks. "A couple of days, maybe less, we'll have all the answers. But if you save us some time, some trouble, prove you're remorseful over shooting that cop, I can promise to go to bat for you. We know there are other people involved. It's just a matter of time before we get to them. Help me out, I'll help you. I'll help you do what you need to do for Madeline. That's fair."

"It was her brother." He said it between his teeth, then opened his eyes. They were no longer blurry, no longer wet, but burning dry with hate. "He talked her into it. He could talk her into anything. It was going to be an adventure, exciting. He set it up, all of it. He's the reason she's dead."

"Where is he?"

"He has a house down in Littleton. Big house on the

lake. His name's Matthew Lyle, and he'll be coming after me for what happened to Madeline. He's crazy. I tell you he's crazy, and he's obsessed with her. He'll kill me."

"Okay, don't worry. He won't get near you." Ally took out her notebook. "Tell me more about Matthew Lyle."

At four that afternoon, Jonah was settled behind his desk, trying to work. He was furious with himself for calling Ally three times, twice at home, once at the station. And equally furious she'd made no attempt to get back to him.

He'd decided he'd made a very big mistake by walking out of her apartment instead of staying with her in the dark, in the bed, instead of taking what he wanted.

It was a mistake he'd have to live with, and he was certain he could live with it more comfortably than live with the options.

All he wanted now was the simple courtesy of information. Damn it, she owed him that. He'd let her into his life, into his business, let her work side by side with his friends while she deceived them. While he deceived them.

Now, by God, he wanted answers.

He snatched the phone up again just as the elevator doors slid open. And Ally walked through.

"I still had your code."

Saying nothing, he replaced the receiver. She was dressed for work, he noted. Cop work. "I'll make a note to have it changed."

Her eyebrows rose but she continued across the room and dropped comfortably into the chair across from his desk. "I figured you'd want an update."

"You figured correctly."

Something was in his craw, she noted. They'd get to

that later. "Fricks rolled over on his brother-in-law. Matthew Lyle, aka Lyle Matthews, aka Lyle Delaney. Computer crimes mostly, with some assaults. He's got a long sheet, but most of the charges were dumped. Insufficient evidence, deals. Did some psych time, though. He's cleared out. We hit his place a couple of hours ago, and he's gone."

She paused long enough to rub her eyes. "Didn't have time to take everything with him. The house was packed with stolen goods. From what it looks like they've turned very little, if anything. Place looked like an auction house. Oh, and you're going to be short a waitress tonight."

"I didn't think you'd be reporting for work tonight."

"No, I didn't mean me. Jan. According to Fricks, she and Lyle are…" She lifted a hand, crossed two fingers. "Very close. She's the inside man. Scanned for the marks, passed the credit card number to Lyle via beeper. The Frickes move in, she helps cover for them while they lift the keys. Then she alerts them with another code when the targets call for their check. Gives the Fricks time to finish up, clear out. Very smooth all in all."

"Have you got her?"

"No, doesn't look like she went home last night. My guess is she went straight to Lyle, and they went under together. We will get her. We'll get them both."

"I don't doubt it. I suppose that ends your association with Blackhawk's."

"Looks like." She rose, wandered to the window. He had the blinds shut today, so she tapped a slat up, looked out. "I'll need to interview your people. I thought they'd feel more comfortable if I did it here. Do you have any problem with me using your office for it?"

"No."

"Great. I'll start with you. Get it out of the way." She

came back to sit, took out her notepad. "Tell me what you know about Jan."

"She's worked here about a year. She was good at her job, a favorite with a number of the regulars. Had a knack for remembering names. She was reliable and efficient."

"Did you have a personal relationship with her?"

"No."

"But you're aware she lives in the same apartment building as Frannie?"

"Is that against the law?"

"How did you come to hire her?"

"She applied for the job. Frannie has nothing to do with this."

"I didn't say she did." Ally took a photo out of her bag. "Have you ever seen this man in here?"

Jonah glanced at the police photo of a dark-haired man of about thirty. "No."

"See him anywhere else?"

"No. Is this Lyle?"

"That's right. Why are you angry with me?"

"Irritated," he corrected coolly. "I'd classify it as irritated. I don't care to be interrogated by the police."

"I'm a cop, Jonah. That's a fact." She put the photo back into her bag. "I've got a job to finish. That's another fact. And I'm hung up on you, there's fact number three. Now maybe all of that irritates you, but that's the way it is. I'd like to start the interviews now."

He got to his feet as she did. "You're right. It all irritates me."

"There you go. I'd appreciate it if you'd send Will up now. And stay downstairs. I might need to speak with you again."

He came around the desk. Her eyes narrowed, flashed a cold warning as he approached her. They stayed level and cool when he gripped the lapels of her jacket and hauled her to her toes.

A dozen desires, all of them impossible, ran through his mind. "You push too many of my buttons," he muttered, and releasing her, walked away.

"Same goes." But she said it quietly, after he'd gone.

"So…" Frannie lit a cigarette, peered at Ally through the haze of smoke. "You're a cop. I might've figured it if Jonah hadn't been with you. He doesn't like cops any more than I do."

Frannie had put on an attitude, Ally noted, and nodded. "Now, there's breaking news. Listen, let's make this as painless as possible for everyone. You've got the rundown on the burglary ring, how the club was used, Jan's part in it."

"I've got what you've decided to tell me now that you're wearing your badge."

"That's right. And that's all you need. How long have you known her?"

"About a year and a half, I guess. I ran into her in the laundry room of my apartment building. She was waiting tables in a bar. I worked in a bar." Frannie lifted her shoulders. "We hung out together now and again. I liked her well enough. When Jonah opened this place, I helped get her a job. Does that make me an accessory?"

"No, it makes you a jerk for copping an attitude with me. She ever mention a boyfriend?"

"She liked men, and men liked her."

"Frannie." Ally shifted, decided to play another angle. "Maybe you don't like cops, but there's one on the critical list right now, and he's a friend of mine. They're still not sure he'll make it. He's got two kids and a wife who loves him. Another woman's dead. Somebody loved her, too. You want to go a round with me on personal business, fine. Let's just get this done first."

Frannie made a little shrugging movement again. "She talked about this one guy sometimes. Never told me his name. Liked to be mysterious about it. But she said things like pretty soon she wouldn't be hauling trays and bagging tips."

She got up, crossed over to open the panel to the bar in a way that told Ally she was very at home in Jonah's space. She pulled out a soft drink, twisted off the cap. "I figured it was talk. She liked to talk big about men. Conquests, you know?"

"Did you ever see her with this guy?" Ally nudged the photo across the desk.

Sipping from the bottle, Frannie walked back, studied the photo. "Maybe. Yeah." Frannie scratched her jaw. "I saw them come into the building together a couple of times. Didn't seem like her type is what I thought. He's kinda short, a little pudgy. Ordinary. Jan, she went more for flash. Studs with platinum cards was her usual type."

Catching herself, Frannie shook her head, dropped into a chair. "That sounds hard. I liked her. Look, she's young, maybe a little foolish. But she's not mean."

"You might want to keep in mind that she used you, Jonah, and this place. Now, did she ever mention any-place they went together? Any plans?"

"No…well, she might've said something about a place on a lake. I didn't pay much attention when she started bragging. Most of it was just air."

Ally questioned her for another fifteen minutes, but didn't jiggle anything loose.

"Okay. If you think of anything, I'd appreciate a call." Rising, Ally offered Frannie a card.

"Sure." Frannie skimmed her eyes over it. "Detective Fletcher."

"Would you ask Beth to come up, please?"

"Why the hell don't you leave her alone? She doesn't know anything."

"But I have such a good time intimidating and threatening potential witnesses." She came around the desk, sat on the corner. "Okay, there's the bell. Go ahead with your personal round."

"I don't like the way you came in here, the way you used us and spied on us. I know how it works. You did a background check on everybody, pried into all our lives and sat in judgment. I guess you're sorry it turned out to be Jan instead of the former hooker."

"You're wrong. I like you."

Off balance, Frannie sat again. "Bull."

"Why shouldn't I like you? You got yourself out of a spiral that only goes down. You've got a legitimate job, and you're good at it. The only problem I have with you is Jonah."

"What do you mean, Jonah?"

"You've got a relationship with him. I'm attracted to him. That's makes you a personal problem for me."

Baffled now, Frannie took out another cigarette. "I don't get you. You mean it about Jonah?" she said after a minute. "You've got a thing for him?"

"It looks like. But the problem's mine. Like I said, I like you. In fact, I admire the way you turned your life around. I never had to do that, never had to face those kinds of things, make those kind of choices. I'd like to think I'd do as well as you have if I had."

"Damn it." Frannie pushed to her feet, paced the room. "Damn it," she repeated. "Okay, first. I don't have a relationship with Jonah. Not like you mean. Never did. He never bought me when I was for sale, and he never touched me that way when I was free. Even when I offered."

Though a fine sense of relief ran through her, Ally kept her voice mild. "Is he blind or stupid?"

Frannie stopped pacing, took a long, hard look. "I don't want to like you. You're sure making it tough not to. I love him. A long time ago, I loved him…different than I do now. We grew up together, more or less. I mean we've known each other since we were kids. Me and Jonah and Will, we go back."

"I know. It shows."

"When I was working corners, Jonah'd come by sometimes, pay me for the night. Then he'd take me for coffee or something to eat. And that was it." Frannie's eyes softened. "He always was a sucker."

"Are we talking about the same man?"

"If he cares about you, that's it. He'll keep pulling you up no matter how many times you fall down again. Bite his hand, he'll just ignore you and haul you up. You can't fight that. You can't fight that kind of thing for long. I didn't make it easy for him."

With a sigh, she walked over to sit again, picked up the soft drink, finished it off. "A few years ago, I was scraping the bottom of the gutter. I'd been on the stroll since I was fifteen. By the time I hit twenty I was used up. So I figured what the hell, let's just get out of this whole mess. I started to slash my wrists. Seemed just dramatic enough."

She held out a hand, turned it over to expose the scar on the inside of her left wrist. "Only got to the one, and didn't do such a hot job on it."

"What stopped you?"

"First? The blood. Really put me off the idea," she said with a surprisingly cheerful laugh. "Anyway, I'm standing there in this filthy bathroom, stoned, bleeding, and I got scared. Really scared. I called Jonah. I don't know what would've happened if I hadn't reached him, if he hadn't come. He got me to the hospital, then he got me into detox."

She sat back, tracing a finger over the scar as if it brought the memory back with more clarity. "Then he asked me something he'd asked me a hundred times before. He asked me if I wanted a life. This time I said yes. Then he helped me make one.

"Along the way, I thought I should pay him back, and I offered what I was used to offering men. It was the only time he ever really got pissed off." She smiled a little. "He thought more of me than I did of myself. Nobody else ever had. If I knew anything about Jan, or this business, I'd tell you. Because he'd want me to, and there's nothing I wouldn't do for him."

"From where I'm standing, you both got a good deal."

"I've never once had a man look at me the way I've seen him look at you."

"Then you've got your eyes shut." It was Ally's turn to smile. "Keep them open tonight when Will asks for his after-closing brandy."

"Will? Come on."

"Keep your eyes open," Ally said again. "Are we square here?"

"Yeah, sure. I guess." Confused, Frannie got to her feet again.

"Ask Beth to come up. Just give me five minutes to find my brass knuckles."

With a half laugh, Frannie went to the elevator. After pushing the button, she glanced back. "Will knows what I was."

"I guess he knows what you are, too."

* * *

She wrapped up the last interview by seven, circled her shoulders and wondered if there was a possibility of food anytime in her near future.

The clock told her she was officially off duty, and since she had nothing to add to the current status of the case, her reports and follow-ups could wait till morning.

Still, she helped herself to the use of Jonah's phone, checking in, giving updates. She was sitting quietly at his desk when he came in.

"Dietz. The cop who was shot last night. They've upgraded his condition from critical to serious." Closing her eyes, she pressed her fingers against them. "It looks like he's going to make it."

"I'm glad to hear it."

"Yeah." She pulled the clip out of her hair, ran her fingers through it. "It sure fills this big hole in my gut. I appreciate the use of your office. I can tell you that the rest of your people aren't suspects, at this time."

"At this time."

"I can't give you more than that, Blackhawk. All evidence points to the fact that Jan and Jan alone worked the inside. It's the best I can do."

She tossed the clip on his desk. "Now, I've got something else to say."

"Which is?"

"I'm off duty. Can I have a drink?"

"I happen to have a club just downstairs."

"I was thinking of a private drink. From your private bar." She gestured toward the panel. "If you could spare a glass of wine. I noticed a nice sauvignon blanc in there."

He turned toward the panel, opened it, selected the bottle.

"Why don't you join me?"

"I'm still on duty. I don't drink during working hours."

"I noticed that. Don't drink, don't smoke, don't hit on the customers. During working hours," she added.

He turned back, the glass of pale gold wine in his hand. And watched her take off her jacket.

"I hope you don't mind," she said, then shrugged out of her holster. "I find it awkward to seduce men when I'm wearing my weapon."

She laid it on his desk, then walked toward him.

Chapter 8

She might have taken off her gun, Jonah thought, but she wasn't unarmed. A woman with eyes as potent as whiskey and a voice like smoke would never be without a weapon.

Worse, she knew it. That longbow mouth was curved up, just a little, like a cat's when the canary cage was open. He didn't much care for his role as target.

"Your wine." He held out the glass, a deliberate move to keep an arm-span of distance between then. "And though I appreciate the thought, I don't have time for a seduction at the moment."

"Oh, it shouldn't take very long."

She imagined he'd devastated countless women with that careless, almost absent dismissal. For her, it was only a challenge she had every confidence of meeting.

She took the wine, and moved right in, grabbing a fistful of his shirt to hold him in place. "I really like the look of you, Blackhawk. Hot mouth, cool eyes." She took a sip of wine, watching him over the rim. "I want to see more."

His senses went blade sharp. The muscles of his belly tied themselves into a dozen hard and tangled knots. "You get right to it, don't you?"

"You said you were in a hurry." She rose on her toes to nip her teeth into his bottom lip, and sliced a jagged line of need straight through him. "So I'm picking up the pace."

"I don't like sexually aggressive women."

Her laugh was low, mocking. "You don't like cops, either."

"That's exactly right."

"Then this is going to be very unpleasant for you. That's a shame." She leaned in, skimmed her tongue up the side of his neck. "I want you to touch me. I want you to put your hands on me."

He kept them at his sides, but in his mind they were already ripping at her shirt, already taking. "Like I said, it's a nice offer, but—"

"I can feel your heart pounding." She shook her hair back, and the scent of it slithered into his system. "I can feel the way you want me, the same way I want you."

"Some of us learn to shelve certain wants."

She saw the change in his eyes, the faintest deepening of green. Dead giveaway, she thought. "And some of us don't." She took another sip of wine, then moved forward, walking him backward. "I guess I'm going to have to get rough."

Mortified she'd put him in retreat, he stopped short, nearly groaning when her body bumped his. "You're going to embarrass yourself. Drink your wine, Detective Fletcher, and go home."

She imagined he thought his voice was clipped, dismissive. But it was thick and strained. And his heart was a fury under her fist.

"What is that answer you're always giving me? No. Yes, that's it." She drained her glass so the wine pumped in with the reckless power surging through her. "No," she said again and, tossing the glass aside, hooked a hand in the waistband of his trousers.

Aroused and furious, he retreated again. "Cut it out."

"Make me." She threw her head back, then leaped, arms wrapping around his neck, legs vised around his waist. "Come on and make me. You've got plenty of moves."

Her mouth swooped down to tease his, and she tasted a wild, wonderful mix of desire and temper. "Take me down," she whispered, raking her hands through his hair. "Finish it. Finish me."

His blood was raging. The taste of her, hot and female with the faint zip of wine, was on his tongue. "You're asking for trouble."

"So…" She rubbed her lips over his, as if imprinting her flavor on him. "Give it to me."

Control snapped. He could hear it echo in his head like the violent crack of hammer against stone. He gripped her hair, wrapping it around his hand, yanking it back so that she let out a little gasp as her head flew back.

"The line's crossed." His eyes weren't cool now. They simmered, as if a bolt of lightning had struck a pool. "You'll give me everything I want. What you don't give, I'll take. That's the deal."

Her breath was already quickened. "Done."

His gaze lowered to the long, vulnerable curve of her throat. Then he set his teeth on her.

Her body jerked against his as the shock of that threat of pain, that lance of pleasure stabbed into her. Then she was falling, clinging to him as she tumbled into the shadows, into the dark.

She lost her breath when she hit the bed, lost her grip when his body covered hers. Then, for a moment, when he tore her shirt open, she lost her mind.

Floundering for balance, she threw an arm up. Her knuckles thudded against the bedspread, then her fingers dug in. "Wait."

"No."

His mouth was on her breast, ravaging tender flesh with lips and teeth and tongue. She fought for air, fought to find the power that had been hers just moments before. Instead she found herself spinning past control, past reason.

His hands were on her, as she had demanded. And they were hard and fast, ruthlessly exploiting weakness, secrets she hadn't known she'd possessed.

Then his mouth came back to hers, hot and greedy. The low sound in her throat was equal parts terror and triumph. Leaping recklessly toward the heat, she met demand with demand.

She went wild beneath him. Writhing, bucking, reaching. He'd wanted nothing less. If he was to sin, he would sin fully, and reap all the pleasure before the punishment.

Her skin seemed to burn under his hands, his mouth. He craved. The long, clean lines of her. The taut and ready strength. The delicate give of curves.

He rolled with her over the wide pool of the bed, taking what and how he wanted.

She tugged at his shirt, sending buttons flying, then letting out a sound of feral delight when flesh met flesh. When he dragged her to her knees, she trembled. But there was nothing of fear left in her.

She could see his eyes, the predatory gleam of them, from the backwash of light from the office. She let out a ragged breath as she ran her hands up his chest, into his hair.

"More," she told him, and crushed her mouth to his.

And there was more.

Lightning quick flashes of unbearable ecstasy. Gusts of shuddering desperation. And a flood of needs that swamped them both.

He tugged the slacks down her hips, following the path of exposed flesh with his mouth until she was shuddering and mindlessly murmuring his name in that hoarse, erotic voice he couldn't get out of head.

His teeth scraped her inner thigh, sent the strong muscles quivering. When she arched, opened, he feasted on her.

She cried out as the orgasm ripped through her, fisted her hands in the bedclothes and let each glorious aftershock batter her until her system wept with the pleasure of it. Heat swarmed up her body, through her, and she embraced it, reveled in the breathless power of what they made together.

"Now. Jonah."

"No."

He couldn't get enough of her. Each time he thought desperation would overpower him, he found something new to tantalize him. The subtle flare of her hips, the narrow dip of her waist. He wanted to feel the bite of her nails on him again, hear that choked cry of release when he dragged her over the next edge.

Her breath was sobbing, his own so clogged in his lungs he thought they would burst from it. He moved up her again while her hands raced over him and her body bucked.

He could see her eyes, and nothing else. Just the dark

glint of them, watching him as he rose over her. He held back for one quivering instant, then plunged.

Here was everything. The thought stabbed through him then shattered in his brain as she closed hot and tight around him.

She rose to him, fell with him, the slick slide of bodies mating. Sighed with him as pleasure shimmered. Her heart thundered against his, beat for beat. Their breath mixed, drawing him deeper so that his mouth was on hers, another link, as they moved together.

The tempo quickened so that the slide became a slap, and sighs broke into gasps and moans. Her hips pistoned as he pounded into her. As sensations staggered her, she raked her nails down his back, dug them into his hips. Urging him on even as she was swamped by the next crest.

He felt himself slip—a glorious feeling of surrender—and with his face buried in the tumbled mass of her hair, he fell.

It was over for him. He knew it the minute his system leveled and his mind began to work again. He'd never get over her. Never get past her. With one sweep, she'd destroyed a lifetime of careful avoidance.

Now he was stupidly, helplessly, irretrievably in love with her.

Nothing could be more impossible or more dangerous.

She could slice him to pieces. No one had ever been allowed to have that kind of control or power over him. He didn't mean to let that change now.

He needed some sort of defense, and determined to start building it, he rolled away from her.

She simply rolled with him, stretched that long, limber body of hers over his and said, "Mmmmm."

Another time he might have laughed, or at least felt

that knee-jerk of pure male satisfaction. Instead he felt a light trip of panic.

"Well, you got what you wanted, Fletcher."

Instead of being insulted, which would have given him a little room to regroup, she just nuzzled his neck. "Damn right."

To please herself she hooked a leg around him, then shifted to straddle him and slick back her hair. "I like your body, Blackhawk. All tough and rangy and taut." She trailed a finger over his chest, admiring the contrast of her skin against his. "You've got some Native American blood, right?"

"Apache. Very diluted."

"It looks good on you."

He twirled a lock of her hair around his finger. "White bread," he said dryly. "But it looks good on you."

She leaned down until they were nose to nose. "Now that we're all cozy and complimentary, how about doing me a favor?"

"And that would be?"

"Food. I'm starving."

"Want a menu?"

"No. Umm." She tilted her head, teased his mouth with hers. "Just something that's on it. Maybe you could send down for something." She trailed her lips down to his jaw, back up to his mouth. "And we could, you know, fuel up. Mind if I grab a shower?"

"No." He rolled her onto her back. "But you'll have to wait until I'm done with you."

"Oh?" She smiled. "Well, a deal's a deal."

And when he was done with her, she staggered more than walked into the bathroom. She closed the door, leaned back against it and let out a long puff of breath.

She'd never had to work harder to maintain a careless, sophisticated image. Then again, she'd never had anyone turn her inside out and leave her jittering like a mass of jelly before.

Not that she was complaining, Ally told herself as she rubbed the heel of her hand over her heart. But her idea that sex was simply a pleasant occupation between two consenting adults who, hopefully, cared about each other had been forever shattered.

Pleasant didn't begin to describe making love with Jonah Blackhawk.

Waiting for her system to level again, she scanned the bathroom. He'd indulged himself here, she noted, with the deep, why-don't-you-join-me whirlpool tub in his customary jet-black. Though it looked tempting, she thought she'd settle for the separate shower enclosed by seeded glass.

The sink was a wide scoop in a sheer black counter. Nothing stood on it, no pieces of him left out for the casual eye to study. Just as there were no pieces, no odds and ends, memorabilia or personal photographs in his office or bedroom.

She was tempted to poke in the cabinet, rifle through a couple of the drawers—what kind of shaving cream did he use? What brand of toothpaste?—but it seemed so pitifully obvious.

Instead she crossed the white tiles and studied her own face in the mirror. Her eyes were soft, her mouth still swollen from that wonderful assault of his. There were a number of faint bruises shadowing her skin.

All in all, she decided she looked just the way she felt. Like a woman happily used.

But what did he see when he looked at her? she wondered. When he looked at her in that cool, distant way? He wanted her, she could have no doubts about that. But did he feel nothing else?

Did he think she hadn't noticed the way he'd drawn back from her both times, after passion had been spent? As if his need for…separation was as deep as his desire.

And why was she letting it hurt her? It was such a *female* reaction.

"Well, I am a female, damn it," she muttered and turned to switch on the shower.

If he thought he was going to get away with nudging her back whenever he pleased, he was very much mistaken. The man was not going to rock her to her toes then stroll away while she was still teetering.

She stuck her head under the spray, mumbling to herself.

She expected a lot more give-and-take in a relationship. And if he couldn't trouble himself to give her a little affection along with the heat, well then he could…

She trailed off, winced.

She sounded like Dennis, she thought. Or at least close enough.

At least she could stop that before she dug herself a hole too deep to crawl out of.

The only relationship she had with Jonah was a physical one, and she herself had insisted on it. Both of them knew the ground rules and were smart enough not to need them spelled out.

If she needed to mix emotion in with desire, that was fine. That was okay. But it was also her problem.

Satisfied she'd solved the matter in her own mind, she turned off the taps, turned for a towel.

And let out one wild yelp when she saw Jonah holding one out for her.

"Most people sing in the shower," he commented.

"You're the first I've come across who talks to herself in the shower."

"I was not." She snatched the towel.

"Okay, it was more unintelligible mumbling."

"Fine. Most people knock before they come into an occupied bathroom."

"I did, but you couldn't hear me because you were talking to yourself. I thought you might want this." He held up his other hand, and the black silk robe that dangled from his fingers.

"Yeah. Thanks." She wrapped the towel around herself, anchored it with a hand between her breasts.

"Dinner'll be up in a minute." Idly he skimmed a fingertip down her arm, sliding water over flesh.

"Good. I need to get my weapon off your desk."

"I moved it." Frowning now, he traced the curve of her shoulder. "I put it in the bedroom. The door's closed. They'll just leave the tray on my desk."

"Works for me." When she felt the brush of his finger over her collarbone, she released her hold on the towel, let it fall to her feet. "Is this what you're looking for?"

"I shouldn't want you again already." Eyes on hers, he backed her against the wall. "I shouldn't need you again."

"Then walk away." She tugged down the zipper on the trousers he'd pulled on. "Who's stopping you?"

He closed a hand around her throat. Though the pulse under his fingers jumped, she merely lifted her chin and dared him.

"Tell me you want me," he demanded. "Say my name, and that you want me."

"Jonah." She took the first step onto a bridge she knew could burn away under her feet. "I've never wanted anyone the way I want you." Her breath hitched as she drew it in, but her eyes remained steady. "Give it back to me."

"Allison." He lowered his forehead to hers, in a gesture so weary and sweet, she reached out to comfort him. "I can't think for wanting you. Just you," he murmured, then took her mouth, took her body. Desperately.

"I gotta say," Ally commented as she ate like a starving wolf, "you've got a really good kitchen. A lot of clubs, the food's mediocre at best. But yours, um…" She licked barbecue sauce from her thumb. "It's first-class."

She shook her head when he picked up the wine to top off her glass. "No, uh-uh. I'm driving."

"Stay." Another rule broken, he thought. He never asked a woman to stay.

"I would if I could." Smiling she tugged on the lapel of the borrowed robe. "But I don't have a change for tomorrow, and I'm back on eight-to-fours. As it is I'm going to have to borrow a shirt from you to get home. You did a number on mine."

He did no more than pick up his own glass, but she felt him retreat. "Ask me to come back tomorrow and stay."

He looked back at her. "Come back tomorrow and stay."

"Okay. Look at that! Look at that! That runner was safe."

"Out. By a half step," Jonah corrected, amused that she'd nearly come off the sofa when the play on the wide screen caught her eye.

"Bull. You watch the instant replay. They hit the bag at the same time. Tie goes to the runner. See? Manager's coming out. Give him hell. Anyway—"

Satisfied the requisite argument would proceed over a controversial call, she turned her attention back to Jonah. She smiled, rubbed her bare feet intimately against his hip. "Pretty good deal from my point of view. Good sex, good food and a ball game."

"To some…" He reached down to trace a finger up her instep. "Paradise."

"Since we're in paradise, can I ask you something really important?"

"All right."

"Are you going to eat all those fries?"

He grinned at her, shoved the plate in her direction, then leaned over to answer the phone. "Blackhawk. Yes." He held out the portable receiver. "For you, Detective."

"I left this number when I logged out," she told him, and took the phone. "Fletcher." She straightened on the sofa, and her eyes went flat. "Where? I'm on my way."

She was already on her feet when she tossed the receiver on the hook. "They found Jan."

"Where is she?"

"On her way to the morgue. I have to go."

"I'm going with you."

"There's no point in it."

"She worked for me," he said simply and walked into the bedroom.

Jonah had seen and done a great deal. In the first half of his life, he'd thought he'd seen and done everything. He'd seen death, but he'd never seen it stripped bare in cold, antiseptic surroundings.

He looked through the glass at the young woman and felt nothing but raw pity.

"I can verify ID," Ally said beside him. "But it's cleaner procedure if the visual comes from somebody else who knew her. Is that Janet Norton?"

"Yes."

She nodded to the technician behind the glass, and he lowered the blinds. "I don't know how long I'll be."

"I'll wait."

"There's coffee, down this corridor and to the left. It's crap, but it's usually hot and strong." She reached for the door, hesitated. "Listen, if you change your mind and want to go, just go."

"I'll wait," he said again.

It didn't take her long. When she came out he was sitting in one of the molded plastic chairs at the end of the hallway. Her footsteps clicked on the linoleum, and the clicks echoed.

"Nothing much to do until the autopsy report's in."

"How did she die?" When Ally shook her head he got to his feet. "How? It can't be that big a dent in the rules to tell me."

"She was stabbed. Multiple wounds, by what appears to be a long bladed knife with a serrated edge. Her body was dumped on the side of the road off southbound 85, just a few miles outside of Denver. He threw her purse out with her. He wanted us to find her and ID her quickly."

"And that's it for you? Just identify her and put another piece in the puzzle?"

She didn't snap back. She recognized the chill in his eyes as temper on a short leash, and her own was straining.

"Let's get out of here." Ally headed out. She wanted to fill her lungs with fresh air. "From the number of wounds, it appears she was killed with considerable rage."

"Where's yours?" He shoved the door open. "Or don't you feel any?"

She strode out ahead of him. "Don't slap at me."

He grabbed her arm, whirled her around. She led with her fist and pulled it an inch from his jaw. "You want rage." She shoved away from him. "I'll give you some rage. From the looks of things she was getting sliced to pieces while I was rolling around on the sheets with you. Now ask how I feel?"

He caught her before she got to the car and wrenched the door open. "I'm sorry."

She tried to shrug him off, then push him away, but when she spun around snarling he just wrapped his arms around her.

"I'm sorry." He said it quietly, pressing his lips to her hair. "I was out of line. We both know it wouldn't have made any difference where we were or what we were doing. This would have happened."

"No, it wouldn't have made any difference. And still, two people are dead." She drew away. "I can't afford rage. Can you understand that?"

"Yes." He took the clip out of her hair, rubbed the back of her neck. "I'd like to go home with you. I'd like to be with you tonight."

"Good, because that's what I'd like, too."

She slid into the car, waiting for him to climb into the passenger seat. They both needed to set aside the rage, she knew, and the guilt. "I have to get up really early."

He smiled at her. "I don't."

"Okay." She pulled out of the lot. "That means you get to make up the bed and do the dishes. That's the deal."

"Does it also mean that you make the coffee?"

"It does."

"I'll take the deal."

When she reached her building, she pulled into the underground garage. "Tomorrow might be a long one," she told him. "Does it matter what time I get to your place?"

"No." He got out of the car, came around to her side, then held out his hand for her keys.

"So what, did you take like a charm-school course or something?"

"Top of my class. I have a plaque." He pressed the button for the elevator. "Now some women are insecure and find the simple courtesy of a man opening doors for them or pulling out their chair, whatever, troubling. Naturally you're secure enough in your own power and femininity not to be troubled."

"Naturally," she agreed, and rolled her eyes as he gestured her into the elevator. Then he took her hand and made her smile.

"I like your style, Blackhawk. I haven't been able to pin it down, not exactly, but I like it." She angled her head to study him. "You used to play baseball, right?"

"That and your father kept me in high school."

"Basketball was my game. You ever shoot hoops?"

"Now and then."

"Want to shoot some with me, on Sunday?"

"I might." He walked out of the elevator with her. "What time?"

"Oh, let's say two. I'll pick you up. We can go—" She broke off, shifting in front of him fast and pulling her weapon. "Keep back. Don't touch anything."

He saw it now. The fresh scrape and pry marks on the door. She used two fingers on the knob, turned it, then booted the door open with her foot. She went in low, slapping the lights on, starting her sweep even as Jonah stepped in front of her.

"Get back. What are you crazy?"

"One of the things I learned in charm school was not to use a woman as a shield."

"This woman happens to be the one with the badge, and the gun."

"I noticed. Besides." He'd already scanned the debris of the room. "He's long gone."

She knew it, felt it, but there were rules and procedure.

"Well, pardon the hell out of me while I play cop and make sure. Don't touch anything," she said again, and stepping over a broken lamp, checked the rest of the apartment.

She was swearing in a low, steady voice as she headed for the phone.

"Your old friend Dennis?" Jonah asked.

"Maybe, but I don't think so. Lyle was heading south out of Denver." She jabbed her fingers into the keypad on the phone. "I think I just found out what he was doing here. This is Detective Fletcher. I've had a break-in."

Even before the crime scene unit arrived, Ally snapped on protective gloves and began to do inventory. Her stereo components, good ones, hadn't been stolen. But they had been smashed. Her laptop computer and the small TV that stood above the stereo had received the same treatment.

Every table lamp in the place—including the antique bookkeeper's light she'd bought for her desk—was broken. Her sofa had a long gash from end to end, and the guts of it spilled out in nasty puffs.

He'd poured the half gallon of paint she'd bought then had never gotten around to using, in the middle of her bed.

Over the bed, he'd slopped a message in the same paint.

Try To Sleep At Night

"He blames me for his sister's death. He knows I was the one. How does he know?"

"Jan," Jonah said from behind her. "She has to be the one who warned them something was wrong that night," he continued when Ally turned. "You got the Barneses back to their table, but they were still both gone for an unusual amount of time. They were nervous, upset. She picked up on it."

"Maybe." She nodded as she walked back out of the bedroom. "It was enough to make her start thinking. Worrying. She didn't notice when I left. She was busy, but Frannie did. She might have mentioned it to Jan in passing."

She picked her way through the living room, into the kitchen. "So she called it off, but just a little too late. Too late to save his sister. Doesn't look like he bothered much in here. Nothing worth smashing. I guess—" She broke off, walked slowly to the counter. "Oh, God."

When she turned her eyes were wide and horrified. "My bread knife." She laid her fingertips on the knife block, with one empty slot. "Long blade with serrated edge. God, Jonah. He killed her with my own knife."

Chapter 9

She wasn't going to let it shake her. She couldn't. For a cop, she reminded herself, nerves were as costly as rage and just as dangerous. The break-in at her apartment was a direct, and personal, attack. Her only choice was to stand up to it, maintain her objectivity, and do the job she'd sworn to do.

When the crime scene unit had left, adding their wreckage to what Lyle had left behind him, she hadn't argued with Jonah. He'd told her to pack what she thought she needed.

She was moving in with him until it was over.

Neither of them talked about the giant step they were taking; they told themselves it was simply a logical and convenient arrangement.

Then they had slept, tangled together, for what was left of the night.

"We've doubled the guards on Fricks," Kiniki told her at the morning briefing. "Lyle can't get to him."

"He's too smart to try." Ally stood in her lieutenant's office, hands in pockets. The horror had dulled, and the thin edge of fear was over. "He can wait, and he will. He's not in any hurry to pay Fricks back for what he might see as his part in his sister's death."

Behind the glass wall of Kiniki's office, the phones in the bull pen rang, and detectives went about the business of the day. Ally put herself into the mind of a dead woman she'd known for a matter of days.

"Jan Norton was easy. It was all an adventure to her, romantic, exciting. She was with him, and thought she was safe with him. The canvass of my building turned up two neighbors who saw a couple fitting Lyle's and Jan's description enter the building at around eight o'clock. Holding hands," she added. "She helped him trash my place, then once they were on the road again, he killed her. She stopped having a purpose."

She'd had plenty of time to think it through, lying awake through the darkest hours of the night in Jonah's bed. "He doesn't do anything without a purpose. There's a lot of anger in him for what he sees as the privileged class. There's a pattern in his background, in his previous arrests. All of them involve crimes against wealth—the hacking, the burglaries. Even the assaults were against wealthy superiors at his job when he held a computer programming position."

She pulled her hands out of her pockets, ticked off her fingers. "Wealth, authority, authority, wealth. They're synonymous to him, and both need to be taken down a peg. He's smarter than they are. Why should they have the easy life?"

In her mind she flipped through the steadily growing file

of data on Matthew Lyle. "He grew up on the bottom rung of lower middle class. Not quite poor, but never really comfortable. His father had a history of unemployment. Always moving from one job to another. His stepfather was arrogant and domineering. Lyle followed the same patterns. The supervisors and coworkers I've been able to contact all said the same basic thing. He's brilliant with tech stuff, but socially retarded. He's arrogant, belligerent and a loner. He came from a broken home, and both of his parents are dead. The only person he was ever close to was his sister."

Ally walked to the glass wall, looked out. "His sister played into his weaknesses, fed his monumental ego. One enabled the other. Now she's gone, and he's got no one but himself."

"Where would he go?"

"Not far," Ally calculated. "He's not finished yet. He has me to deal with, the Barneses, Blackhawk."

"I think your instincts are on target. We've put Mr. and Mrs. Barnes in a safe house. That leaves you, and Blackhawk."

She turned back. "I don't intend to take any unnecessary chances. But I have to keep visible, maintain a routine or he'll just go under and wait me out. He has my name, my address. He's probably got a reasonable description. He wants me to know it. To sweat it."

"We'll stake out your building."

"He may come back there. He doesn't want to just pick me off. It's not personal enough. And I don't think I'll be his first target."

"Blackhawk?"

"Yeah, in order of importance, Jonah's next. And as for Blackhawk, he's not cooperating."

And it still irked that he'd dismissed her idea of arranging protection.

"We can keep a couple of men on him, at a distance."

"You could keep them two miles away, and he'd spot them. Then he'd lose them on principle. Lieutenant, I'm…close to him. He trusts me. I can take care of it."

"You have an investigation to run, Detective, and your own butt to cover."

"I can do a considerable amount of all three at his club. And the fact is, I believe we might lure Lyle out, push him into making a move if he sees me with Blackhawk routinely."

"It's doubtful he knows you killed his sister. We've had a lid on that since the incident."

"But he knows I was part of the operation, the part inside the club. That Blackhawk and I worked together and started the steps that caused his sister's death."

"Agreed. I'm putting two men on Blackhawk, for the next seventy-two hours. Then we'll reevaluate."

"Yes, sir."

"On a different matter, you're aware that Dennis Overton's fingerprints were found on your hubcaps, your wheel wells. A search of his car turned up a recently purchased hunting knife. The lab work isn't back, but there were bits of tire rubber on the blade. He's been fired from the district attorney's office. They'd like to file formal charges."

"Sir—"

"Toughen your spine, Fletcher. If you don't file charges, he can walk. If you do, the D.A. will recommend psych evaluation. He needs it. Or do you want to wait until he shifts his obsession from you to somebody else?"

"No. No, I don't. I'll take care of it."

"Do it now. One lunatic out there after one of my detectives is enough."

The fact that he was right didn't make it any easier. Ally

walked out to the squad room, plopped down at her desk and decided she deserved at least thirty seconds to brood.

She'd made mistakes with Dennis, right from the beginning. Hadn't paid enough attention, hadn't picked up on the cues. None of that was any excuse for his behavior, but it did weigh into her part in triggering it.

"What's the problem, Fletcher? The boss ream you?"

She glanced up at Hickman who made himself at home with his butt on the edge of her desk. "No. I'm about to ream somebody."

He bit into his midmorning Danish. "That usually puts me in a pretty chipper mood."

"That's because you're a heartless jerk."

"I love it when you flatter me."

"If I tell you you're a brainless moron, would you do me a favor?"

He took another bite, sprinkled crumbs on her desk. "My life for you, baby."

"I have to file on Dennis Overton. When the warrant comes through, would you pick him up? He knows you. It might be a little easier on him."

"Sure. Ally, he's not worth the regrets."

"I know it." She got to her feet, pulled her jacket from the back of her chair. Then she smiled, broke off a corner of his Danish and popped it into her mouth. "You're ugly, too."

"Girl of my dreams. Marry me."

Grateful Hickman knew how to lighten her mood, Ally headed out.

Two hours later she was walking into her father's office.

He met her at the door this time, ran his hands up and down her arms while he studied her face. Then he simply pulled her into his embrace.

"Good to see you," he murmured.

She burrowed in, let herself absorb his strength, his stability. "You're always there, you and Mom. No matter what, you're right there. I just wanted to say that first."

"She's worried about you."

"I know. I'm sorry for it. Listen." She gave him an extra squeeze, then drew back. "I know you're up-to-date, but I wanted you to know I'm okay. And I'm handling it. Lyle can't wait long to make a move. He's got nobody now. Everything we've got on him indicates he needs somebody, a woman, to admire him, feed his ego, play his games with him. Alone, he'll break."

"I agree. And it's my assessment that it's a woman he'll want most to punish. You're elected."

"Agreed. He's already made his first big mistake by breaking into my place. He exposed himself. He left prints everywhere. His grief, his anger, pushed him to show me what he is and what he wants. Using my knife to kill Jan, that was his way of saying it could have been me."

"So far we have no argument. Why are you alone?"

"He won't move on me during the day. He works at night. I'm not going to take stupid chances, Dad. That's a promise. I wanted you to know I've filed charges against Dennis."

"Good. I don't want you hassled, and I don't want you distracted. I went by your apartment this morning."

"I've got some serious redecorating to do."

"You can't stay there. Come home for a few days. Until this is closed."

"I've, ah, already made arrangements." She tucked her hands into her pockets, rocked back on her heels. This part, she thought, would be tricky. "I'm staying at Blackhawk's."

"You can't bunk in a club," he began. Then it hit him, a sneaky jab to the solar plexus. "Oh." Boyd ran a hand through his hair, walked to his desk. Shook his head, walked to the coffeepot. "You, ah… Hell."

"I'm sleeping with Jonah."

His back still to her, Boyd lifted a hand, waved it from side to side. Acknowledging the signal, Ally closed her mouth and waited.

"You're a grown woman." He got that much out, then set the coffeepot back down. "Damn it."

"Is that a comment on my age, or my relationship with Blackhawk?"

"Both." He turned back. She was so lovely, he thought, this woman who'd come from him.

"Do you have anything against him?"

"You're my daughter. He's a man. There you go. Don't grin at me when I'm having a paternal crisis."

Obediently she folded her lips. "Sorry."

"If you don't mind, I think I'll imagine you and Jonah are spending your time together discussing great works of literature and playing gin rummy."

"Whatever gets you through, Dad. I'd like to bring him to the Sunday barbecue."

"He won't come."

"Oh, yes." Ally smiled thinly. "He will."

She spent the rest of her shift doing follow-ups on the case and dealing with the threads of two others assigned to her. She closed one on sexual assault, opened another on armed robbery.

She parked her car in a secured lot and backtracked the block and a half to Blackhawk's.

She spotted the stakeout car from the end of the block, and had no doubt Jonah had tagged it, as well.

The first person she saw when she walked into the club was Hickman sitting hunched at the bar. She figured she could have spotted his black eye from a block away, as well.

She went to him, tapped a finger under his chin and studied his face while he sulked. "Who popped you?"

"Your good friend and general jerk-face Dennis Overton."

"You're kidding. He resisted?"

"Ran like a jackrabbit." He glanced toward Frannie, tapped his glass for a refill. "Had to chase him down. Before I could cuff him, he caught me." He picked up his dwindling beer, sipped morosely. "Now I'm wearing this, and I've taken about all the razzing I'm going to."

"Sorry, Hickman." To prove it, she leaned over and touched her lips to the swollen bruise. When she leaned back, she noticed Jonah had turned the corner into the bar. He merely lifted a brow at seeing her with her arm around Hickman's shoulders, then signaled to Will.

"I never figured him for a rabbit." With a heavy sigh, Hickman scooped up a handful of bar nuts. "Then I take him down and got this." He shifted on the stool to show her the hole in the knee of his trousers. "And he's flopping around like a landed trout, and crying like a baby."

"Oh, God."

"One ounce, one ounce of sympathy in his direction, Fletcher, and I'll pop you myself." Instead Hickman began popping the nuts into his mouth. "He swings back and his elbow catches me, right here, right on the cheekbone. I saw whole planets erupt. Stupid son of a bitch can do his crying in a cage tonight. What the hell'd you ever see in him?"

"Beats me. Frannie, put my pal's drinks on my tab, will you?"

"I'm switching to the imported stuff then."

She laughed, then glanced over her shoulder when Will came up behind her.

"Never used to have cops in here." But he said it with an easy smile, and winked at Frannie. "You want some ice on that eye, Officer?"

Hickman shook his head. "Nah." He used his good one to give Will the once-over. "You got a problem with cops?"

"Not in about five years. Say, is Sergeant Maloney still down at the sixty-third? He busted me twice. Was always straight about it."

Amused, Hickman turned around on the stool. "Yeah, he's still there. Still working vice, too."

"You see him, you tell him, Will Sloan said hi. He was always square with me."

"I'll be sure to do that."

"Anyway, the man says I should have some dinner sent out to your friends in the Ford across the street. Figures they'll get hungry sitting out there all night twiddling their thumbs."

"I'm sure they'll appreciate that," Ally said dryly.

"Least we can do." Giving Hickman a friendly slap on the back, Will headed toward the kitchen.

"I've got a couple of things to do." Ally gave Hickman's black eye another look. "Put some ice on that," she advised, then made her way into the club area to track down Beth.

"Got a minute?"

Beth continued to key in codes on the register. "It's Friday night, we're booked solid. And we're a couple of waitresses short."

Ally acknowledged the sting of the cool tone, but didn't back down. "I can wait until your break."

"I don't know when I'll be able to take one. We're busy."

"I'll wait. I won't take up much of your time."

"Suit yourself." Without a glance at her, Beth strode away.

"She's feeling pretty raw," Will commented.

Ally turned around. "Are you everywhere?"

"Mostly." He lifted his shoulders. "That's my job. She trained Jan like, you know, she trained you. I guess we're all pretty shaken up about what happened."

"And blaming me?"

"I don't. You were doing your job. That's how it works. Beth, she'll come around. She thinks too much of the man not to. You want me to get you a table? Band's going to start in about an hour, and it's a hot one so there won't be a square inch of free space if you wait."

"No, I don't need a table."

"Give a yell if you change your mind."

"Will." She touched his arm before he could walk away. "Thanks."

He gave her a wide, easy smile. "No problem. I got nothing but respect for cops. In the last five years."

Beth made her wait an hour, and Ally was having her eardrums rattled by the band's second number, when the head waitress quickly strode up to her.

"I've got ten minutes. You can have five of them. That'll have to be enough."

"Fine." She had to lift her voice to a shout. "Can we go back in the employee lounge, or would you rather yell at each other right here?"

Saying nothing, Beth spun around and marched out of the club area. She unlocked the door to the lounge, walked to the sofa and, sitting, took off her shoes.

"More questions, Detective Fletcher?"

Ally closed the door and shut off the worst of the racket behind it. "I'll keep it brief and to the point. You're aware of what happened to Jan?"

"Yes. I'm very aware of it."

"Her next of kin have been notified," Ally said in the same flat tone. "Her parents will be in Denver tomorrow, and would like her things. I'd like to box up whatever she might have in her locker, and have it available for them. It would be easier on them that way."

Beth's lips trembled, and she looked away. "I don't have the combination to her lock."

"I do. She had it written down in her address book."

"Then do what you have to do. You don't need me."

"I need a witness. I'd appreciate it if you'd verify that I list any and all items in her work locker, that I put nothing in from the outside, or misappropriate any of her property."

"That's all it is to you? All what happened to her is to you? Another bit of business?"

"The sooner I cover every bit of business, the sooner we find the man who did this to her."

"She was nothing to you. None of us were. You lied to us."

"Yes, I lied. And since under the same circumstances I'd lie again, I can't apologize for it."

Ally walked to the locker, spun the combination lock. "To your knowledge did anyone have the combination to this except Janet Norton?"

"No."

Ally removed the lock, opened the door. As she scanned the contents, she took a large evidence bag from her purse.

"It smells like her." Beth's voice trembled, then broke. "You can smell her perfume. Whatever she did, she didn't deserve to be killed, to be thrown out on the side of the road like trash."

"No, she didn't. I want the man who did it to her to pay as much as you do. More."

"Why?"

"Because there has to be justice, or there's nothing. Because her parents loved her, and their hearts are broken. Because I can smell her perfume. Cosmetic bag," Ally snapped out, grabbing the hot-pink case, yanking the zipper. "Two lipsticks, powder compact, three eyeliner pencils—"

She broke off when Beth touched her arm. "Let me help you. I'll write it down."

She took a tissue out of her pocket, wiped her eyes, then stuffed it away again to take out her pad. "I liked you, you see. I liked who I thought you were. It was a kind of an insult to find out you were someone else."

"Now you know. Maybe we can start from here."

"Maybe." Beth pulled out her pencil and began to write.

Ally ordered a light meal at the bar and kept her eye on Jonah. His Friday night crowd was thick and they were rowdy. The longer she sat, watching, listening, the more she began to see the myriad problems of keeping him safe.

She saw just as many problems convincing him he needed to make adjustments in his lifestyle until Matthew Lyle was in custody.

Because she considered herself on duty, she stuck with coffee. And when the caffeine started to jiggle her system, switched to bottled water.

When the inactivity threatened to drive her mad, she

informed Frannie she was going to help out with the bar tables and grabbed a tray.

"I believe I fired you," Jonah said as she hauled a tray of empties to the bar.

"No, you didn't. I quit. House draft and a bump, Pete, campari and soda, Merlot with ice on the side and the complimentary ginger ale for the designated driver."

"You got it, Blondie."

"Go upstairs, get off your feet. You're tired."

Ally merely narrowed her eyes at Jonah's orders. "Pete, this guy's making insulting remarks about my looks. And he just put his hand on my butt."

"I'll break his face for you, honey, just as soon as I have a free hand."

"My new boyfriend here has biceps like oil tankers," Ally warned Jonah, and executed a stylish hair flip. "So you better watch your step, pretty boy."

He grabbed her chin, lifted her to her toes by it, then kissed her until her eyes threatened to roll back in her head. "I'm not paying you," he said mildly and strolled away.

"I'd work for that kind of tip," the woman on the stool beside her commented. "Anytime, anywhere."

"Yeah." Ally let out a long breath. "Who wouldn't?"

She worked through last call, then grabbed a table in the club and put her feet up while the band broke down and the staff prepared for closing.

And sitting, fell asleep.

Jonah sat across from her while the club went quiet.

"Anything I can do for you before I head out?"

He glanced up at Will. "No. Thanks."

"Guess she's worn-out."

"She'll bounce back."

"Well…" Will jiggled the change in his pockets. "I'm

just going to have my nightcap, then head home. I'll see Frannie off and lock up. See you tomorrow."

The man was sunk, was all Will could think as he walked back to the bar. Who could've figured it? The man was sunk, and over a cop.

"A cop." Will slid onto a stool. On cue, Frannie set down his nightly brandy. "The man's hooked on the cop."

"You just clued into that?"

"I guess." He tugged on his beard. "You think it'll work out?"

"I'm no judge of romantic relationships. They look good together, though, and they won't be able to run over each other since both of them have heads like bricks."

"She conked out in there." Will jerked his head toward the club, then sipped his brandy. "He's just sitting, watching her sleep. I think you can mostly tell what's going on in a man by the way he watches a woman."

And because he caught himself watching Frannie as she mopped up the bar, he flushed and stared down at his drink as if the brandy suddenly contained the solution to a very complex problem.

But she caught it, this time she caught it because she was looking for it. She continued to wipe the bar dry as she inventoried her reaction. A nice little tug, she realized, and just a little heat to go with it.

She hadn't felt—or hadn't let herself—feel either for a man in a very, very long time.

"I guess you're heading home," she said casually.

"I guess. You?"

"I was thinking about ordering a pizza and watching this horror movie marathon on cable."

He smiled over at her. "You always had a thing for monster movies."

"Yeah. Nothing like giant tarantulas or blood-sucking

vampires to chase away your troubles. Still… It's not a lot of fun by myself. You up for it?"

"Up for—" Brandy sloshed over the rim of his snifter and onto her clean bar. "Sorry. Damn. I'm clumsy."

"No, you're not." She slid the cloth over the spilled brandy, then looked him dead in the eye. "Do you want to split a pizza with me, Will, and watch old black-and-white monster movies, and neck on my sofa?"

"I— You—" He'd have gotten to his feet if he could have felt them. "Are you talking to me?"

She smiled, spread her cloth over the rim of the bar sink. "I'll get my jacket."

"I'll get it." He pushed to his feet, relieved when they held him upright. "Frannie?"

"Yes, Will?"

"I think you're beautiful. I just wanted to say that right out in case I'm too nervous later and forget."

"If you forget later, I'll remind you."

"Yeah. Okay. Good. I'll get your jacket," he said, and leaving her grinning, dashed off.

Jonah waited until the club was empty, until he heard Will and Frannie call out their good-nights. He rose, leaving Ally sleeping as he checked the locks and alarms himself. His heels clicked on the silver floor as he crossed it to go backstage. He chose the light pattern and music loop that suited his mood and set them.

Satisfied, he went back to Ally and bending down, kissed her awake.

She floated to the surface on the taste of him. Warm, a little rough, and very ready. When she opened her eyes, it was as though a thousand stars were twinkling against the night.

"Jonah."

"Dance with me." His mouth continued to nibble on hers as he lifted her to her feet.

She already was. Before the clouds cleared from her brain, she was moving with him, body molded to body as music rippled around them.

"The Platters." She stroked her cheek against his. "That's so weird."

"You don't like it? I can put on something else."

"No, I love it." She angled her head to give his lips freer access to her neck. "This number, it's my parents' song. 'Only You.' You know my mother was a night shift DJ at KHIP before she was station manager there. This is the song she played over the radio for my father the night she agreed to marry him. It's a nice story."

"I've heard pieces of it."

"You should see the way they look at each other when they dance to this. It's beautiful."

She dipped her fingers into his hair as they glided over the stars in the floor. "Very smooth," she whispered. "You're very smooth, Blackhawk. I should've figured it." She turned her head on his shoulder, watched the lights gleam. "Is everyone gone?"

"Yes." There's only you, he thought, brushing his lips over her hair. Only you.

Chapter 10

For the first time in weeks Ally woke without the need to jump out of bed and rush into the day.

Glorious Sunday.

Since Saturday night at Blackhawk's had been more crowded than the night before, she'd spent most of the time on her feet, and all of it mentally on duty.

Jonah might have shrugged off the guards outside the club, but she didn't think he'd take having her standing as his shield quite so casually.

Some things were best left undisclosed and undiscussed.

Besides, they were doing each other a favor. She couldn't stay in her apartment until it was cleaned out and refurnished. He was giving her a comfortable place to stay, and she was giving him a bodyguard. To her, it was a fair and rational deal.

And the deal had a distinctively superior side benefit.

Intent on indulging in it, she ran her hand over his chest and began to nibble on the body she was more than happy to shield and protect.

He shot awake, fully aroused, with her mouth hot and greedy on his.

"Let me. Let me." Exhilarated, she chanted it, already straddling him, already riding. She hadn't known her blood could leap so fast, that her own needs could bolt from lazy to desperate in one hammer beat of the heart.

She took him in, surrounded him, her own body shuddering and bowing back as the sharp claws of pleasure raked her.

He kept the bedroom dark. It was all shadows and movement as he reared up to wrap his arms around her. Possession. It drove them both. He found her mouth, her throat, her breast, fed the hunger she'd unleashed in him before he could think, before he could do anything but feel.

Her release came like a whiplash, snapping and slicing the system. And when she melted against him, he laid her back. Began to love her.

A kiss, soft as the shadows. A touch, tender as the night. When she reached for him, he took her hands, cupping them together and bringing them to his lips in a gesture that had something rich, something sumptuous sliding through her to tangle with needs still raw.

"Now let me."

This was different. This was patient and sweet and slow. A fire banked and left to simmer with light.

She yielded herself, a surrender as powerful as seduction. He was murmuring to her, quiet words that stirred the soul even as he stirred her blood. As her breathing thickened she floated on the thin and delicate layers of silky sensations.

The brush of his fingertips, of his hair, the warmth of his lips, the glide of his tongue urged her higher, gradually higher. As the rise of desire became a deep and liquid yearning that spread to an aching need, she moaned his name.

He slid her over the first satin edge.

He needed to touch her this way, to take her this way. He needed, at least in the shadows, to have the right to. Here, she could belong to him.

Her arms came around him as he sank into a kiss, took it deep, fathoms deeper, until he was lost in it. And lost, he slipped inside her, held there linked, and desperately, helplessly in love.

When at last they lay quiet, she turned her face into his throat, wanting the taste of him to linger just a little longer. "No, don't move," she whispered. "Not yet."

Her body was gold, pulsing gold. She would have sworn even the dark had gilt edges.

"It's still night." She stroked her hands down his back, up again. "As long as we're like this, it's still night."

"It can be night for as long as you want."

Her lips curved against him. "Just a little longer." She sighed again, content to hold and be held. "I was going to get up and use your equipment, but then…well, there you were, and it just seemed like a much better idea to use you."

"Good thinking." He closed his eyes and kept her close.

She let the morning slide away, enjoyed a fast, hard workout with him in his gym while they argued over sports' highlights that flashed by on the portable TV.

They shared a breakfast of bagels and coffee, along with the Sunday paper, while spread out lazily in bed. Natural, normal, almost domestic habits, Ally thought as they dressed for the day.

Not that a man like Blackhawk could or should be domesticated. But a slow, uncomplicated Sunday morning was a nice change of pace.

She sat on the side of the bed and laced up her ancient high-tops. Jonah tugged on a T-shirt, studied the endless line of her legs.

"Is your plan to wear those little shorts to distract me from whipping your excellent ass on the court?"

She lifted both eyebrows. "Please. With my innate skill I don't need such pitiful ploys."

"Good, because once I start a game, nothing distracts me until my opponent is crushed."

She stood, rolled strong shoulders shown to advantage in the sleeveless jersey. "We'll see who's crushed, Blackhawk, when the buzzer sounds. Now are you going to stand around here bragging, or are you ready to rock and roll?"

"More than ready, Detective Honey."

She waited until they were in his car. She thought the timing best. Besides, the longer she waited to bring it up, the shorter amount of time he'd have to argue with her.

Casually, she stretched out her legs and prepared to enjoy the ride. And smirked, just a little, when she saw his gaze shift, and slide down the length of her legs.

"So, are you ever going to let me drive this machine?"

Jonah switched on the engine. "No."

"I can handle it."

"Then buy your own Jag. Where's the court where you want to go down in inglorious defeat?"

"You mean where's the court where I plan to beat you into a whimpering pulp of humiliation? I'll give you directions. Of course, if I were driving, I could just take us there."

He merely flicked her a pitying glance, then slipped on his sunglasses. "Where's the court, Fletcher?"

"Out near Cherry Lake."

"Why the hell do you want to shoot hoops way out there? There are a half-dozen gyms around here."

"It's too nice a day to play indoors. Of course if you're afraid of a little fresh air…"

He reversed, and drove out of the parking lot.

"What do you do besides use that gorgeous equipment in your apartment over the club when you have a free day?" she asked him.

"Catch a game, check out a gallery." He sent her a slow smile. "Pick up women."

She tipped down her own sunglasses, peered at him over the tops. "What kind of game?"

"Depends on the season. If it's got a ball or a puck, I'll probably watch it."

"Me, too. I've got no resistance. What kind of gallery?"

"Whatever appeals at the time."

"You've got some great art. In the club and in your apartment."

"I like it."

"So… What kind of women?"

"The easy kind."

She laughed and tucked her glasses back in place. "You calling me easy, ace?"

"No, you're work. I like a change of pace now and again."

"Lucky me. You've got a lot of books," she commented. She studied his profile, the sexy, angular lines of it, the way the dark glasses concealed the fascinating contrast of those eyes of pure, light green. "It's hard to picture you curling up with a good book."

"Stretching out," he said, correcting her. "Women curl up with books, guys stretch out."

"Oh, I see. That's entirely different. This is your exit coming up. You'll take the two-two-five. And watch your speed. The traffic cops just love to nail pretty boys like you in their hot cars."

"I have pull in the police department."

"You think I'm going to fix a ticket for you when you won't even let me drive this thing?"

"It so happens I know the police commissioner."

As soon as he said it, it clicked.

"You said out in Cherry Lake?"

"That's right."

He got off the first exit and pulled into a convenience store parking lot.

"Problem?"

"Your family lives in Cherry Lake."

"That's right. And they have a basketball court—well half court. It was all we could push my parents into, even though my brothers and I campaigned pretty hard. They also have a barbecue pit, which my father puts to very good use. We try to get together a couple Sundays a month."

"Why didn't you tell me we were going to your parents'?"

She recognized the tone: anger, ruthlessly tethered. "What difference does it make?"

"I'm not intruding on your family." He shoved the car in Reverse again. "I'll drop you off. You can get a ride back when you're done."

"Hold on." She reached over, switched off the ignition. If he was angry, fine, they'd fight. But she'd be damned if he'd freeze her out. "What do you mean intruding? We're going to shoot some baskets, eat some steak. You don't need an engraved invitation."

"I'm not spending Sunday afternoon with your family."

"With a cop's family."

He pulled his sunglasses off, tossed them aside. "That has nothing to do with it."

"Then what does? I'm good enough to sleep with, but I'm not good enough for this?"

"That's ridiculous." He shoved out of the car, stalked to the end of the lot and stared out on a narrow grassy area.

"Then tell me something that isn't ridiculous." She marched up to him, jabbed his shoulder. "Why are you so angry that I want you to spend a few hours with my family?"

"You conned me into this, Allison. That's first."

"Why should I have to con you into it? Why is it, Jonah, that you've known my father for more than half your life but you've never accepted a single invitation to our home?"

"Because it's his home, and I have no place there. Because I owe him. I'm sleeping with his daughter, for God's sake."

"I'm aware of that. So is he. What? Do you think he's going to dig out his police issue and shoot you between the eyes when you walk in the door?"

"This isn't a joke. It's so easy for you, isn't it?"

Here's the heat, she thought, pumping.

"Everything was always just right in your world. Solid, balanced and steady. You have no idea what mine was before he came into it, and what it would be now if he hadn't. This is not the way I intend to pay him back."

"No, you pay him back by insulting him. By refusing to acknowledge your relationship with me, as if it was something to be ashamed of. You think I don't know what your life was like? You think my world was so rarefied, Blackhawk. I'm the daughter of a cop. There's nothing you've seen I haven't, through his eyes. And now my own."

She drilled a finger in his chest. "Don't you talk up to me, and don't you talk down. Wherever, however each of us started, we're on level ground now. And you'd better remember it."

He grabbed her hand. "Stop poking at me."

"I'd like to flatten you."

"Same goes."

He walked away, waiting until he was sure he had some level of control again. Her mention of shame had gotten through. He could be angry with himself for falling in love with her. But he wouldn't be ashamed of it.

"I'll make you a deal. You get rid of the tail." He gestured to the shadow car that had pulled in a minute behind them. "And we'll take a couple of hours at your parents'."

"Give me a second."

She walked to the dark sedan, leaned in and had a short conversation with the driver. She had her hands in her pockets as she strode back over to Jonah.

"I cut them loose for the rest of the afternoon. It's the best I can do." She circled her shoulders. Apologies always tensed her up. "Look, I'm sorry I played it this way. I should have done it straight and we could have argued about it back at your place."

"You didn't play it straight because you knew I wouldn't be here to argue with."

"Okay, you're right." She threw up her hands in defeat. "Sorry again. My family's important to me. I'm involved with you. It just follows that I want you to feel comfortable with them."

"Comfort might be asking a little too much. But I'm

not ashamed of my relationship with you. I don't want you to think I am."

"Fair enough. Jonah, it would mean a lot to me if you'd give it a try this afternoon."

"It's easier to argue with you when you're being obnoxious."

"Now see, that's what my brother Bryant always says. You'll get along fine." Hoping to soften things, she hooked her arm with his. "There's one thing, though," she began as they walked back to the car.

"What thing?"

"This deal at the house today? It's a little…more than I might have indicated. Sort of a kind of reunion. It's just that there'll be more people, that's all," she said quickly. "Aunts and uncles and cousins from back East, and my father's old partner and her family. It's really better for you this way," she insisted when he balled a fist and tapped it against her chin. "It's more a horde than a group, so nobody'll even notice you. Hey, why don't you let me drive the rest of the way?"

"Why don't I knock you unconscious and you can ride in the trunk the rest of the way?"

"Never mind. It was just a thought." She strolled around the car, reached for the door handle. But he beat her to it. It made her laugh and turn and take his face in her hands.

"You're a real case, Blackhawk." She gave him a noisy kiss, then climbed in. When he joined her, she leaned over, rubbed her knuckles over his cheek. "They're just people. Really nice people."

"I don't doubt it."

"Jonah. An hour. If you're uncomfortable being there after an hour, just tell me. I'll make an excuse and we'll go. No questions. Deal?"

"If I'm uncomfortable in an hour, I'll go. You stay with your family. That's the way it should be, so that's the deal."

"All right." She settled back, secured her belt. "Why don't I give you a quick rundown so you know the players? There's Aunt Natalie and her husband—Ryan Piasecki. She runs some of the interests of Fletcher Industries, but her real baby is Lady's Choice."

"Underwear?"

"Lingerie. Don't be a peasant."

"Terrific catalogues."

"Which you peruse for fashion's sake."

"Hell no. There are half-naked women in there."

She laughed, relieved they'd passed the crisis point. "Moving right along. Uncle Ry's an arson inspector in Urbana. They have three kids, fourteen, twelve and eight, if my math's right. Then there's my mother's sister, Aunt Deborah—Urbana's district attorney—her husband, Gage Guthrie."

"The Guthrie who has more money than the national treasury?"

"So rumor has it. Four kids for them. Sixteen, fourteen, twelve and ten. Like steps." She made upward motions with her hand. "Then there's Captain Althea Grayson, Dad's former partner, and her husband Colt Nightshade. Private Investigator. More of a troubleshooter really. Sort of a loose cannon. You'll like him. They have two kids, one of each, fifteen and twelve. No, thirteen now."

"So basically, I'm spending the afternoon with a teenage baseball team."

"They're fun," she promised him. "You don't like kids?"

"I have no idea. My exposure to their species has been limited."

"This exit," she told him. "Well, it won't be limited

after today. I think you might have met my brothers somewhere along the line. Bryant's in Fletcher Industries. I guess he's a kind of troubleshooter, too. Does a lot of traveling and nailing butts to the wall. He loves it. And Keenan's a firefighter. We visited my aunt Natalie right after she hooked up with Uncle Ry, and Keen, he fell for the big red truck. That was it for him. Left at the next light. That wraps it up."

"I have a headache."

"No, you don't. Right at the corner, left two blocks down."

He'd already gotten a solid impression of the neighborhood. Stable, rich and exclusive with its big, beautiful houses on big, beautiful grounds. It gave him an itch between the shoulder blades he'd never be able to explain.

He was comfortable in the city, where the streets reminded him he'd overcome something, and the faces that crowded him were anonymous. But here, with the majestic trees, the sloped lawns, green and lush with approaching summer, the explosion of flowers and rambling old homes, he wasn't just a stranger.

He was an intruder.

"That one there, on the left, the cedar and river rock, with the zigzagging decks. I guess everyone's here already. Looks like a parking lot."

The double driveway was packed. The house itself was a huge and unique study of rooflines, jutting decks, wide expanses of glass, all accented by trees and flowering bushes with a meandering slate path ribboning up the gentle hill.

"I've reassessed the deal," Jonah told her. "I'm adding exotic sexual favors. I think this deserves them."

"Fine. I'll take 'em."

She reached for the door, but his arm shot out, pinned

her back against the seat. She only laughed and rolled her eyes. "Okay, okay, we'll discuss exotic sexual favors later. Unless you're demanding a down payment on them here and now."

"Yeah, that'll put a cap on it." He jerked open his door, but before he could walk around the car, there was a war whoop, and a pretty young girl with a pixie cap of dark hair raced down the hill.

She grabbed Ally in a bear hug the minute she was out of the car. "There you are! Everyone's here. Sam already pushed Mick into the pool and Bing chased your neighbor's cat up a tree. Keenan got him down and my mom's inside putting something on the scratches. Hi."

She beamed a hundred-watt smile at Jonah. "I'm Addy Guthrie. You must be Jonah. Aunt Cilla said you were coming with Ally. You own a nightclub? What kind of music do you have?"

"She does shut up twice a year, for five minutes. We time it." Ally wrapped an arm around her cousin's neck and squeezed. "Sam is in the Piasecki branch, Mick is Addy's brother. And Bing is our family dog who has no manners whatsoever, so he fits in very well. Don't worry about remembering any of that, or you really will have a headache."

She reached out to take his hand, but Addy beat her to it. "Can I come to your club? We're not going home until Wednesday. Thursday if nagging works. I mean what's one more day? Gosh, you're really tall, aren't you? He looks great, too," she added peering around him to her cousin. "Nice job, Allison."

"Shut up, Addy."

"Somebody's always saying that to me."

Charmed despite himself, Jonah smiled at her. "Do you listen?"

"Absolutely not."

The noise level rose—screams, shouts. A couple of gangly teenagers of indeterminate sex raced by armed with enormous water guns. He saw a woman with a sunny sweep of hair in deep conversation with a striking redhead. A group of men—some stripped to the waist— battled it out brutally on a blacktopped basketball court. Another group of young people, dripping wet, raided a table loaded with food.

"Pool's around the other side of the house," Ally explained. "It's glassed in so we can use it all year."

One of the men on court pivoted, drove through the line of defense and dunked the ball. Then he caught sight of Ally, and deserted the field.

She met him halfway, shouting with laughter when he plucked her off her feet. "Put me down, moron. You're sweaty."

"So would you be if you were leading your team to a second consecutive victory." But he dropped her on her feet, wiped his hand on his jeans, then held it out to Jonah. "I'm Bryant, Ally's far superior brother. Glad you could make it. Want a beer?"

"Yes, actually."

Bryant eyed Jonah, measuring size and build. "You play any round ball?"

"Occasionally."

"Great, we're going to need fresh meat. Shirts and skins. Ally, get the man a beer while I finish trouncing these pansies."

"Come on inside." In a show of sympathy, Ally rubbed a hand up and down Jonah's arm. "Get your bearings. It's too confusing to try to meet everyone at once."

She drew him up onto a deck, where yet another table was spread with food and an enormous metal trough was filled with ice and cold drinks. She plucked out two beers and went in through the atrium doors.

The kitchen was spacious, broken up into family areas with counters and a banquette. In one corner a dark-haired man was trying to tug away from a dark-haired woman. "I'll live, Aunt Deb. Mom, get her off me."

"Don't be a baby." With her head stuck in the refrigerator, Cilla swore. "We're going to run out of ice. I knew it. Didn't I tell him we'd run out of ice?"

"Hold still, Keenan." Deborah covered the scratches with a gauze pad, taped it neatly. "There, now you can have a lollipop."

"I'm surrounded by smart alecks. Hey, speaking of which, here's Ally."

"Aunt Deb." Ally hurried over to hug her aunt, then reached over and grazed her knuckles over Keenan's cheek. "Hi, hero. This is Jonah Blackhawk. Jonah, my aunt, Deborah, my brother, Keenan. You've met my mother."

"Yes. Nice to see you again, Mrs. Fletcher."

A small army chose that moment to pour in through the door, full of shouted complaints and chased by an unbelievably large and ugly dog.

Ally was immediately absorbed into them. And before he could defend himself, so was Jonah.

Jonah intended to leave at the end of the hour. A deal was a deal. His plan was to make some polite conversation, keep as far out of the way as humanly possible, then fade back into his car and back into the city where he knew the rules.

And somehow, he was stripped out of his shirt and going elbow to gut in a vicious game of basketball with

Ally's uncles, cousins, brothers. In the heat of competition, he lost track of intentions.

But he damn well knew it was Ally herself who stomped on his instep and cost him game point.

She was fast and sneaky, he conceded that as he ripped the ball away from an opponent and gave her one deadly glare. But she hadn't grown up on the streets where a single basket could mean a buck for a burger against a painfully empty stomach.

That made him faster. And sneakier.

"I like him." Natalie ignored her son's bloodcurdling scream of revenge and tucked an arm through Althea's.

"He was a hard-ass, but Boyd always liked him. Ouch, he plays dirty."

"What other way is there? Whoa, Ryan's going to be limping tomorrow. Serves him right," Natalie said with a laugh. "Taking on a guy half his age. Nice butt."

"Ry's? I've always thought so."

"Keep your eye off my husband, Captain. I was referring to our Ally's young man."

"Does Ryan know you ogle young men?"

"Naturally. We have a system."

"Well, I am forced to agree. Ally's young man has a very nice butt. Oh, ouch, that had to hurt."

"I think I could take him," Natalie murmured, then laughed at Althea's arch look. "In basketball. Get your mind out of the gutter." She swung an arm over her old friend's shoulder. "Let's go get some wine and pump Cilla for info on this new and very interesting situation."

"You read my mind."

"I know nothing, I say nothing," Cilla claimed as she poured another bag of ice into the trough. "Go away."

"It's the first guy she's brought to one of the family deals," Natalie pointed out.

Cilla merely straightened and mimed zipping her own lips.

"Give it up," Deborah advised. "I've been interrogating her for a half hour, and I got zero."

"You lawyers are too soft." Althea moved forward, grabbing Cilla by the collar. "Now a good cop knows how to get to the truth. Spill it, O'Roarke."

"Do your worst, copper, I ain't no stool pigeon. Besides, I don't know anything yet. But I will," she murmured as she saw Ally dragging Jonah toward the deck. "Clear out, give me five minutes."

"It's nothing," Jonah insisted.

"It's blood. Rules of the house. If it bleeds, it gets mopped up."

"Ah, another victim." Cilla rubbed her hands together as her friends and relations conveniently scattered. "Bring him on."

"His face ran into something."

"Your fist," Jonah said with some bitterness. "Guarding the goal doesn't include left jabs."

"Around here it does."

"Let's see." Wisely Cilla kept her expression sober as she studied Jonah's bleeding lip. "Not so bad. Ally go help your father."

"But I—"

"Go help your father," Cilla repeated, and snagging Jonah's hand dragged him up to the deck and into the kitchen. "Now let's see, where did I put my instruments of torture?"

"Mrs. Fletcher."

"Cilla. Sit down, and button it up. Whining is severely

punished around here." She gathered up a damp cloth, ice and antiseptic. "Punched you, did she?"

"Yes, she did."

"Takes after her father. Sit," she ordered again and jabbed a finger into his bare stomach until he obeyed. "I appreciate your restraint in not hitting her back."

"I don't hit women." He winced when she dabbed at the cut.

"Good to know. She's a handful. Are you up to that?"

"I beg your pardon?"

"Is it just sex, or are you up for the whole package?"

He wasn't sure which shocked him more, the question or the sudden sting of antiseptic. He swore, ripely, then clenched his teeth. "Sorry."

"I've heard the word before. Was that your answer?"

"Mrs. Fletcher."

"Cilla." She leaned in close, then smiled into his eyes. Good eyes, she thought. Steady, clear. "I've embarrassed you. I didn't expect to. Almost done here. Hold this ice on it a minute."

She slid onto the bench across from him, crossed her arms on the table. By her calculations, she had two minutes tops before someone burst in the door and interrupted. "Boyd didn't think you would come today. I did. Allison is relentless when she's set her mind on something."

"Tell me about it."

"I don't know your mind, Jonah. But I know something about you, and I know what I see. So I want to tell you something."

"I didn't intend to stay this long—"

"Hush," she said mildly. "A lifetime ago. Nearly your lifetime ago, I met this cop. This irritating, fascinating, hardheaded cop. I didn't want to be interested. I certainly didn't want to be involved. My mother was a cop, and she died in the line of duty. I've never gotten over it. Not really."

She had to take a breath to steady herself, because it was perfectly true. "The last thing I wanted, the last thing I figured was good for me, was to find myself tangled up with a cop. I know how they think, what they are, what they risk. God, I didn't want that in my life. And here I am, a lifetime later. The wife of one, the mother of one."

She glanced out the window, caught sight of her husband, then her daughter. "Strange, isn't it, the way things turn out? It isn't easy, but I wouldn't give up a moment of it. Not one moment."

She patted the hand he'd laid on the table, then rose. "I'm glad you came today."

"Why?"

"Because it gave me a chance to see you and Ally together. It gave me a chance to look at you, close. An opportunity you haven't given me more than twice in, what is it, Jonah, seventeen years? And I like what I see."

Leaving him speechless, she turned to the fridge and pulled out a platter of burger patties. "Would you mind taking these to Boyd? If we don't feed the kids every couple of hours, it gets ugly."

"All right." He took the platter, struggled with himself while she just smiled at him out of the eyes Ally had inherited. "She's a lot like you, too."

"She inherited all of my and Boyd's most annoying qualities. Funny how that works." She rose on her toes, gently touched her lips to the wound at the corner of his mouth. "That comes with the treatment."

"Thanks." He shifted the tray, searched for something

Chapter 11

"It's all in the wrist," Boyd claimed, flipping a burger.

"I thought you said it was all in the timing." Ally stood, thumbs tucked into her pockets while her brother Bryant looked on, his elbow comfortably hooked on her shoulder.

"Timing is, of course, essential. There are many, many subtle aspects to the art of the barbecue."

"But when do we eat?" Bryant demanded.

"Two minutes if you're going for a burger. Another ten if you're holding out for steak." He peered through the billowing smoke as Jonah cut across the yard with a platter. "Looks like we have more supplies on the way."

"How about a burger, then steak?"

"You're tenth in line, I believe, for burger requests, son. Take a number." Boyd flipped another, sent it sizzling, then furrowed his brow as he caught sight of his wife on the side deck.

Dancing in place, she waved her arms, pointed at Jonah, pointed at Boyd, circled her fingers. He got the drift, and though he winced inwardly, gave a subtle shrug of acknowledgment.

Okay, okay, I'll talk to him. Damn it.

Cilla only smiled, then wagged her finger back and forth.

And I won't hurt him. Sheesh.

"Just set down the fresh rations, Jonah." Boyd jerked a thumb toward the high table beside the pit. "How's the lip?"

"I'll live." Jonah sent Ally a steely stare. "Especially since despite unsportsmanlike conduct by the opposing guard, I made the basket. And won."

"Lucky shot. We'll have a rematch after we eat."

"She loses," Bryant commented, "she demands a rematch. She wins, she rubs it in your face for days."

"And your point would be?" Ally fluttered her lashes at him.

"Mom would never let me hit her, because she was a girl." Bryant gave Ally's ear one hard tug. "I've always found that grossly unfair."

"Big deal. You just beat up on Keenan."

"Yeah." Instantly Bryant's face brightened. "Those were the days. I'm planning on punching on him later, for old times' sake."

"Can I watch? Like I used to."

"Naturally."

"Please. Your mother and I like to maintain the illusion we raised three well-balanced, competent adults. Don't shatter our dreams. Jonah, you haven't seen my workshop, have you?" At his daughter's answering snort, Boyd winged an eyebrow at her. "No comments. Bryant, this is a moment."

"Is it?"

"A monumental moment. I am passing the sacred tongs and spatula to you."

"Wait a minute, wait a minute." Ally elbowed her brother aside. "Why can't I do it?"

"Ah." Boyd held a hand to his heart. "How many times have I heard you say those very words in our long and exciting life together?"

Amused and fascinated by the family dynamics, Jonah watched mutiny settle over Ally's face. "Well, why can't I?"

"Allison, my treasure, there are some things a man must pass to his son. Son." Boyd laid a hand on Bryant's shoulder. "I'm trusting you with the Fletcher reputation. Don't let me down."

"Dad." Bryant wiped an imaginary tear from his eye. "I'm overwhelmed. Honored. I swear to uphold the family name, no matter what the cost."

"Take these." Boyd held out the barbecue tools. "Today, you are a man."

"That bites," Ally muttered as Boyd swung an arm around Jonah's shoulder.

"You're just a girl." Bryant leered and rubbed the tools together. "Live with it."

"She'll make him pay for that," Boyd murmured. "So, how are things?"

"Well enough." How the hell was Jonah supposed to make a quiet escape when someone or other was always dragging him somewhere? "I appreciate the hospitality today. I'm going to have to get back to the club."

"A business like that doesn't give you a lot of free time, especially in the early years." Still he steered Jonah toward a wooden structure in the far corner of the yard. "Know anything about power tools?"

"They make a great deal of noise."

Boyd gave a hoot of laughter and opened the door of the workshop. "What do you think?"

The garage-size room was full of tables, machines, shelves, tools, stacks of wood. There appeared to be a number of projects in progress, but Jonah couldn't tell what they were, or what they were intended to be.

"Impressive," he decided, diplomatically. "What do you do here?"

"I make a great deal of noise. Other than that, I haven't figured it out. I helped Keenan build a birdhouse about ten years ago. Came out pretty good. Cilla started buying me tools. Boy toys, she calls them."

He ran his hand over the guard of a skill saw. "Then I needed a place to keep them. Before I knew it, I had a fully equipped workshop. I think it was all a ploy to get me out of her hair."

"Pretty clever."

"That she is." They stood for a moment, hands in pockets, soberly studying the tools. "Okay, let's get this over with so we can both relax and get something to eat. What's going on with you and my daughter?"

Jonah couldn't say it was unexpected, but it still made his stomach clench. "We're seeing each other."

With a nod, Boyd walked over to a small square refrigerator and took out two beers. He twisted off the tops, held one out to Jonah. "And?"

Jonah tipped back the beer, then gave Boyd a level look. "What do you want me to say?"

"The truth. Though I realize what you'd like to say is that it's none of my business."

"Of course it's your business. She's your daughter."

"There we have no argument." Deciding to get comfortable, Boyd boosted himself up on a worktable. "There's a matter of intent, Jonah. I'm asking what you intend in regard to my daughter."

"I don't have any intentions. I should never have touched her. I know that."

"Really." Intrigued, Boyd cocked his head. "Mind explaining that?"

"What do you want from me? Damn it." Giving into frustration, Jonah dragged a hand through his hair.

"The first time you asked me that, in almost that same tone, you were thirteen. Your lip was bleeding then, too."

Jonah steadied himself. "I remember."

"I've never known you to forget anything, which means you'll remember what I said to you then, but I'll say it again. What do you want from *you,* Jonah?"

"I've got what I want. A decent life run in a way I can respect and enjoy. And I know why I have it. I know what I owe you, Fletch. Everything. Everything I've got, everything I am started with you. You opened doors for me, you took me on when you had no reason to."

"Whoa." Genuinely shocked, Boyd held up a hand. "Hold on."

"You changed my life. You gave me a life. I know where I'd be if it wasn't for you. I had no right to take advantage of that."

"You're sure putting a lot on me here," Boyd said quietly. "What I did, Jonah, was see a street kid with potential. And I hassled him."

Emotion swirled into Jonah's eyes. "You made me."

"Oh, Jonah, no, I didn't. You made yourself. Though God knows I'm proud to have played a part in it."

Boyd slid off the table, wandered the shop. Whatever he'd expected from this talk, it hadn't been to have his emotions stirred. To feel very much like a father being given a precious gift by a son.

"If you feel there's a debt, then pay it off now by being straight with me." He turned back. "Are you involved with Ally because she's mine?"

"In spite of it," Jonah corrected. "I stopped thinking about her being yours. If I hadn't, I wouldn't be involved with her."

It was the answer he wanted, so Boyd nodded. The boy's suffering, he thought, and couldn't find it in himself to be overly sorry about it. "Define involved."

"For God's sake, Fletch." Jonah took a long gulp of beer.

"I don't mean that area." Boyd spoke quickly, took a deep drink himself. "Let's just leave that particular area behind a firmly locked door so we don't have to punch each other."

"Fine. Good."

"I meant, what are your feelings for her?"

"I care about her."

Boyd waited a beat, nodded again. "Okay."

Jonah swore. Boyd had asked him to play straight, and he was circling. "I'm in love with her. Damn it." He closed his eyes, imagined flinging the bottle against the wall, shattering glass. It didn't help. "I'm sorry." Jonah opened his eyes again, got a slippery grip on control. "But that's as straight as it gets."

"Yeah, I'd say so."

"You know what I'm built on. You can't think I'm good enough for her."

"Of course you're not," Boyd said simply, and noticed those clear green eyes didn't so much as flicker. "She's my little girl, Jonah. No one's good enough for her. But knowing what you're built on, I'd say you're pretty close. I wonder why that surprises you. The one area I don't recall you ever being low in is esteem."

"I'm over my head here," Jonah murmured. "It's been a long time since I've been over my head in anything."

"Women do that to you. The right woman, you never really surface again. She's beautiful, isn't she?"

"Yes. She blinds me."

"She's also smart, and she's strong, and she knows how to deal with what's dished out."

Absently, Jonah rubbed his thumb over his sore lip. "No argument."

"Then my advice to you is to play it straight with her, too. She won't let you get away with less, not for long."

"She isn't looking for anything else from me."

"You keep thinking that, son." At ease again, Boyd crossed to Jonah, laid a hand on his shoulder. "There's just one thing," he said as they started toward the door. "If you hurt her, I'll take you out. They'll never find your body."

"Well, I feel better now."

"Good. So, how do you like your steak?"

Ally saw them come out of the workshop and relaxed for the first time since the moment she'd watched them go in. Her father had his arm swung companionably around Jonah's shoulder. It looked as if they'd done no more than share a friendly beer and grunt over the power tools.

If her father had done any poking or prying into her relationship with Jonah, at least he hadn't drilled any embarrassing holes.

She liked seeing them together, liked very much witnessing the very real bond of affection and mutual respect. Her family was paramount in her life, and though she would have given her heart where her heart yearned, it would never have settled with full happiness on a man her family couldn't love.

She bobbled the bowl of potato salad, would have dropped it if Cilla hadn't made the grab.

"Butter fingers," Cilla said and set the bowl on the deck table.

"Mom."

"Hmm? We're going to run out of ice again."

"I'm in love with Jonah."

"I know, baby. Who's not blocked in? I need somebody to get some ice."

"How can you know?" Ally grabbed her mother's wrist before Cilla could go to the deck rail and shout for an ice run. "I just figured it out this second."

"Because I know you, and I see the way you are with him." Gently, she smoothed a hand over Ally's hair. "Scared or happy?"

"Both."

"Good." Cilla turned, sighed once, then kissed Ally on each cheek. "That's perfect." She slipped an arm around Ally's waist, turned to the rail. "I like him."

"Me, too. I really like who he is."

Cilla tipped her head toward her daughter's. "It's nice, isn't it, having the family together like this."

"It's wonderful. Jonah and I had a fight about coming here today."

"Looks like you won."

"Yeah. We're going to have another fight when I tell him we're getting married."

"You're your father's daughter. My money's on you."

"Place your bets," Ally suggested, and walked down the steps, crossed the lawn. It was a calculated move. She didn't mind being calculating, not when she had a point to make.

She strolled up to her father and Jonah, cupped Jonah's face in her hands and pressed her lips hard to his. He hissed, reminding her about his sore mouth. But she just laughed, shook back her hair.

"Suck it in, tough guy," she suggested and kissed him again.

His hands came to her waist, fused there, drawing her up on her toes that intimate inch.

"Dad?" She eased back down. "Mom needs more ice."

"She's just saying that to make me look bad." Boyd scanned the yard, homed in on his target. "Keenan! Go get your mother more ice."

"So…" As her father chased down her brother, Ally linked her hands at the back of Jonah's neck. "What were you talking about with my father?"

"Man stuff. What are you doing?" he demanded as she brushed her lips over his again.

"If you have to ask, I must not be doing it right."

"I'm outnumbered here, Allison. Are you trying to coax your family into stomping me into dust?"

"Don't worry. We're very big on kissing in my family."

"I noticed. Still." He drew her back.

"You've got this quietly proper streak. It's really cute. Are you having a good time?"

"Except for a couple of minor incidents," he said, deliberately tapping his finger on the corner of his mouth. "You have a nice family."

"They're great. You forget sometimes how steadying, how comforting it is to have them. How much you depend on them for a hundred little things. My cousins will remember coming out here when they were kids, or all of us piling into that gorgeous gothic fortress of Uncle Gage's, or trooping up to the mountains to…"

"What?"

"Wait. Give me a minute." She had his hand and squeezed it as she shut her eyes and let the pieces of the puzzle tumble together. "You're drawn back," she murmured. "You're always drawn back to memories, and places where you were happy with the people who mean the most. That's why people are always going back to visit their hometown, or driving by the house where they grew up." She paused and opened her eyes as a new thought hit her. "Where did he grow up?"

She tapped a fist against Jonah's chest. "Where did he and his sister grow up? Where did they live together? Where was he happy? He has to go somewhere, has to find a place to hide, to plan. He's gone home."

She spun around and raced for the house.

She was already dialing the kitchen phone when Jonah caught up with her. "What are you doing?"

"My job. Stupid, stupid, not to think of it before! Carmichael? It's Fletcher. I need you to do a check for me. I need an address—Matthew Lyle's old address, addresses maybe. Going back to when he was a kid. There's, ah…"

She paused, forced it into focus. "He was born in Iowa, and they moved around some. I can't remember when he came to Denver. The parents are dead. Yeah, you can reach me at this number." She recited it. "Or my cell phone. Thanks."

"You think he's gone back home?"

"He needs to feel close to his sister to feel safe, to feel powerful." Allison paced the kitchen as she tried to remember details of the file. "The psych profile tags him as dependent on her, even as he sees himself as her protector. She's his only real consistency, the only constant in his life. Parents divorced, kids got bounced around.

Mother remarried, bounced around some more. Stepfather was...damn."

She pressed her fingers to her temple as if to push out the memory. "Ex-Marine. Very gung ho, and apparently very tough on the pudgy nerd and his devoted sister. Part of the whole authority complex comes from this instability of family life, ineffective father, the passive mother, the stern stepfather. Rocky foundations," she said as she paced.

"Lyle was bright, high IQ, but he was emotionally and socially inept. Except with his sister. His biggest trouble with the law was right after she got married. He got sloppy, careless. He was angry."

She checked her watch, urging Carmichael to hurry. "She stood by him, and it appears whatever rift there might have been between them was healed."

She leaped on the phone when it rang. "Fletcher. Yeah, what have you got?" She snatched up a pencil, began to scribble on the pad by the phone. "No, nothing out of state. He needs to stay close. Hold on." She covered the mouthpiece with her hand. "Do me a favor, Blackhawk. Would you tell my father I need to talk to him for a minute?"

It took more than a minute. She moved into her father's office, booted up his computer. With him beside her, and Carmichael on the phone, they worked through the files, picked through Matthew Lyle's history.

"See, ten years ago he was listing a P.O. Box as his address. He kept that listing for six years, even though he had a house on the lake. Bought that house nine years ago, the same year his sister married Fricks. But he held on to the P.O. Box."

"And his sister lists the same P.O. Box as her address through the same period."

"But where did they live? I'm going to go in and pin

Fricks down on this one." Then she pursed her lips, considered. "Carmichael, you up for another run? See what you can find me on property in the Denver metro area listed under the names Madeline Lyle or Madeline Matthews. Run Matthew and Lyle Madeline, too."

"Good move," Boyd approved. "Good thinking."

"He likes to own things," Ally noted. "Possessions are very important to him. If he stuck in the same spot for six years, more or less, he'd want his own place—or one for his sister."

She straightened in the chair. "Did you just say bingo? Carmichael, I think I love you. Yeah, yeah. All right. I've got it. I'll let you know. Really. Thanks."

She hung up, jumped out of the chair. "Lyle Madeline owns a condo in the center of downtown."

"Good work, Detective. Contact your lieutenant and assemble your team. And Ally," Boyd added, "I want in."

"Commissioner, I'm sure we can make room for you."

It ran like clockwork. Within two hours the building was surrounded, the stairways and exits blocked. Using hand signals a dozen cops wearing Kevlar vests ranged the hallway outside of Matthew Lyle's two-level condo.

Ally had the floor plan in her head, every inch of the blueprint she'd studied. She gave the nod, and the two officers beside her hit the door with the battering ram.

She went in first, went in low.

A stream of men rushed by her and up the stairs to her right. Others fanned out to the rooms at her left. It took less than ten minutes to determine the condo was empty.

"He's been staying here." Ally gestured to the dishes

in the sink. She dipped a finger into the dirt of an ornamental lemon tree potted by the kitchen window. "Damp. He's tending house. He'll be back."

In a bedroom upstairs they found three handguns, an assault rifle and a case of ammunition. "Be prepared," Ally murmured. "I see extra clips for a nine millimeter, but I don't see the nine millimeter, so he's armed."

"Detective Fletcher?" One of her team backed out of the closet, holding a long bladed knife with gloved fingers. "Looks like our murder weapon."

"Bag it." She picked up a black-and-silver matchbook from the dresser. "Blackhawk's." She shifted her eyes to her father. "That's his target. The only question is when."

Night had fallen when Ally confronted Jonah in his office. The man was mule stubborn, she thought. And more, he was just plain wrong.

"You close down for twenty-four hours. Forty-eight tops."

"No."

"I can close you down."

"No, you can't. And if you wrangle it, it'll take you longer than the forty-eight hours, which makes the entire process moot."

She dropped into a chair. It was important to stay calm, she reminded herself. Vital to stay in control. She hissed out a breath, then a stream of violent and inventive oaths.

"I don't believe your last suggestion is possible, regardless of my strength and flexibility."

She bolted forward. "Listen to me."

"No, you listen to me." His voice was quiet, cool, inflexible. "I could do what you're asking. What's to stop him from waiting me out? I close down, he goes under.

I open, he surfaces. We could play that game indefinitely. I prefer running my own game, on my own turf."

"I'm not going to say you don't have a point, because you do. But we'll nail him within two days. I promise you. All you have to do is shut the place down, take a little vacation. My parents have a great place in the mountains."

"Would you be coming with me?"

"Of course not. I have to stay here and close this thing."

"You stay. I stay."

"You're a civilian."

"Exactly, and until this is a police state, I have a right to run my business and come and go as I please."

She wanted to tear at her hair, but knew that would just amuse him. "It's my job to keep you alive to run your business."

He got to his feet. "Is that what you think? Are you my shield, Ally? Is that why you've been wearing your gun until we're up here behind locked doors? Is that why you keep it within reach even when we are here?"

He came around the desk, even as she cursed herself for the slip. "I don't like the implications of that."

She met him toe to toe. "You're a target."

"So are you."

"This is a waste of time."

He spun her around before she could stalk to the elevator. "You will not stand in front of me." He said it slowly, distinctly, with that rare glint of ready temper in his eyes. "Understand that."

"Don't tell me how to do my job."

"Don't tell me how to live my life."

She threw her head back, released a muffled scream. "All right. Okay. forget it. We do it the hard way. Here's the deal. Twenty-four-hour guards outside. Cops in soft clothes in the bar and club areas at all times. You take on undercover officers as kitchen and wait help."

"I don't like that deal."

"Tough. Take it or leave it. Leave it and I pull strings and have you slapped into protective custody so fast even a slick customer like you won't be able to slide through the knots. I can do it, Blackhawk, and I will. My father will help me do it, because he cares about you. Please." She grabbed him by the lapels. "Do it for me."

"Forty-eight hours," he agreed. "And in the meantime, I put out word on the street I'm looking for him."

"Don't—"

"That's the deal. It's fair."

"All right. That's the deal."

"Now, what would you like to bet that I can go downstairs right now and pick out every cop you've already planted?"

She puffed out her cheeks, then showed her teeth in a smile. "No bet. I don't suppose I can convince you to stay up here tonight?"

He traced a fingertip down the center of her body. "I will if you will."

"That's what I figured." Sometimes compromise, however annoying, was the only out. "Hold that thought until closing."

"That I have no problem with." He walked over to call for the elevator. "Tonight, or tomorrow night."

"Yeah. It's just as likely, more really, that they'll take him at the condo. But if he slips through the net, or senses anything, it'll be here. And it'll be soon."

"Will's got good eyes. He'll know what to look for."

"I don't want you, or any of your people, taking chances. If he's spotted, you tell me." She glanced over, caught him studying her. "What?"

"Nothing." But he traced his fingers over her cheek. "When you've closed this down, can you take any time?"

"What do you mean time?"

"A few days. Away. Somewhere away."

"I might be talked into that. Do you have anywhere in mind?"

"No. Pick it."

"Well, aren't you open-minded and daring? I'll start thinking." She took a step out of the elevator, already shifting her focus, but he took her arm.

"Ally?"

"Yeah."

There was too much to say. Entirely too much to feel. And it wasn't the time, not the time to play it straight or any other way. "Later. We'll get into it later."

Chapter 12

Traditionally business at Blackhawk's was light on Sunday nights. There was no live music as a lure, and the first day of the work week loomed heavily.

Ally decided a great many people in Denver were taking advantage of the gorgeous weather and mild evening, and most who strolled in out of the night lingered an hour or more over their drinks or bowls of guacamole and chips.

She watched the entrance, checked the exits, studied faces and counted heads. Throughout the evening she slipped into the lounge at regular intervals to check in with the stakeout at Lyle's condo.

An hour before closing, and still he hadn't been spotted.

Itchy, she roamed the floor, checking faces, watching doors. The crowd was thinning out, and she imagined there'd be no more than a scatter of customers left by last call.

Where was he? she asked herself. Where the hell was he? He'd run out of places to hide.

"Detective." Jonah danced his fingers over her shoulder. "I thought you'd be interested to know one of my sources reports a man fitting Lyle's description has been asking questions about me."

"When?" She gripped his arm and pulled him toward the alcove. "Where?"

"Tonight, actually. At my other place."

"Fast Break?" She swore, whipped out her phone. "We didn't put anyone there. They never hit there. It's not his style."

"I'd say that holds true." He laid a hand over hers before she could dial the phone. "The bartender there just got in touch. Apparently Lyle—I assume it was Lyle though he was wearing glasses and sporting a beard—dropped into Fast Break a few hours ago, loitered at the bar, started asking if I ever came in."

"Hold on." Ally tapped his hand away and put her call through. "Balou? Cut a pair of uniforms loose from the condo. Tell them to see the bartender at Fast Break. The address is…"

She looked at Jonah, repeated the address he gave her. "Lyle was in there tonight. He's reported to be wearing a beard and glasses. Make sure that gets out."

She disconnected, looked back at Jonah.

"As I was saying," he continued, "my man didn't think anything of it initially, then it started to bother him. He says Lyle was jumpy. Hung around about a half hour then said to tell me he'd see me around."

"His center's crumbling. He's psyching himself up to move." She wanted Jonah out of the way. "Look, why don't you go up, give your man another call. Let him know a couple of cops are on their way."

"Do I look like I'd fall for that lame a con?"

He strolled away from her to check on a table of customers who were preparing to leave.

The shouts came from the kitchen, followed by an explosive crash of dishes. Ally had her gun out, bolting for the door when it burst open.

He'd ditched the glasses, and the beard was a thin and scraggly dusting over his chin. But she saw she'd been right. He'd psyched himself up. His eyes were wide and wild.

And he had the barrel of the nine millimeter pressed to the soft underside of Beth's jaw.

"Don't move! Don't anybody move!" he shouted over the screams, the rush of running feet as customers scattered.

"Stay calm. Everybody stay calm." She sidestepped, kept her gun trained on him, her eyes trained on him. Forced herself to block out Beth's terrified face. "Lyle, take it easy. You want to let her go."

"I'll kill her. I'll blow her head off."

"You do that, I kill you. Think, you need to think. Where does that get you?"

"Put your gun down. Drop it, kick it over here, or she's dead."

"I'm not going to do that. And neither are any of the other cops in here. You know how many weapons you have aimed at you right now, Lyle? Look around. Do a count. It's over. Save yourself."

"I'll kill her." His gaze jittered around the room, bounced off guns. "Then I'll kill you. That'll be enough."

Someone was sobbing. Out of the corner of her eye she could see the bar area where civilians were being rushed outside to safety.

"You want to live, don't you? Madeline would want you to live."

"Don't you say her name! Don't you say my sister's name!" He shoved the gun harder against Beth's throat and made her cry out.

No place to run, Ally thought. His sister had had no place to run, and still she'd turned and fired.

"She loved you." Ally edged closer, keeping his focus on her. If she could get him to lower the gun, a few inches, get him to shift it toward her. Away from Beth. "She died for you."

"She was all I had! I got nothing to lose now. I want the cop who killed her, and I want Blackhawk. Now! Right now or she dies!"

Out of the corner of her eye, Ally saw Jonah move forward. "Look at me!" She shouted the words. "I'm the one who killed your sister."

He screamed, one long howl as he jerked the gun away from Beth, swung it toward Ally. There was a burst of gunfire, a blur of movement, wails of terror.

With fear locked in her throat, Ally rushed forward to where Jonah lay tangled with Lyle. Blood coated them both.

"Damn you! Damn, are you crazy?" With urgent hands she began to pat him down, looking for wounds. He'd thrown himself at the gun. In front of the gun.

He was breathing. She held on to that. He was breathing, and she would make sure he kept on breathing. "Jonah. Oh, God."

"I'm all right. Stop poking at me."

"All right? You jumped into cross fire. You nearly got yourself killed."

"You, too." He looked past her to where the starry floor was cracked an inch from where she'd stood.

"I'm wearing a vest."

"And that takes care of your hard head, too?" He sat back as a cop turned Lyle over.

"He's gone."

Jonah spared Lyle's face one glance, then looked into Ally's eyes. "I'd like to calm my customers down."

"You're not calming anyone down." Ally rose with him. "You've got blood all over you. Is all of it his?"

"Mostly."

"What do you mean mostly?"

"I'm going to deal with my customers and my people." He held her at arm's length before she could snatch at him again. "Do your job, and let me do mine."

He turned away to take Beth from the female officer who was holding her. "Come on, Beth, come on with me. Everything's all right now."

Ally pressed her fingers to her eyes then looked down at what was left of Matthew Lyle. "Yeah, everything's dandy."

"Slipped in the back," Hickman told her while they sat in the nearly empty club. The civilians were gone, the body had been removed and the crime scene unit was packing up.

She wondered idly what time it was, and how soon she could fall on her face and tune the world out. "He stopped being smart," she said. "He stopped thinking."

"You got that right," Hickman agreed. "Got himself one of those white kitchen uniforms, slapped on a wig and glasses. Before the cop who spotted him could call in or move, all hell broke loose."

"He didn't think we were smart enough to close him in. I saw his face when he spotted all the cops. Pure shock. My guess? He figured on breaking in here, taking

Jonah down, me if I was around, then he's got hostages. He'd demand we turn over the cop who killed his sister. He really figured we'd do it, and he'd get out."

"Arrogant. Speaking of which, it was pretty cocky, telling him you were the one he wanted."

"I don't know why he didn't spot me in the first place."

"You look different." Hickman scanned a look up, then down. "Very un-Fletcherlike."

"Give me a break, Hickman. I look how I look. I'll tell you how it was. He came in here for Jonah. When he looked at me, all he saw was cop—no face, no form, just another cop. He didn't put me together with the one who'd worked here."

"Maybe." He got to his feet. "I guess we'll never know."

He glanced over at the starburst crack in the floor. "Too bad about that—classy floor. Bet it'll cost an arm and two legs to fix it."

"Maybe he'll leave it like that. Conversation piece. Draw a crowd."

"Yeah." The idea tickled Hickman. "We'd've taken him out right away, you know, but he would've gotten that shot off anyway. At that range, the vest would've stopped the bullet. Probably. But one way or the other, if the shot hadn't been deflected, you'd have been seriously hurt."

Absently she rubbed a hand between her breasts, imagined the breathless pain. "You ever taken one in the vest?"

"Nope, but Deloy did. Had himself a softball-size bruise." Hickman held up his hands, made a circle. "Knocked him clean off his feet, too, and tossed him back like a rag doll. Ended up with a concussion where his head hit the pavement. That has to hurt."

"I'll take it over a bullet."

"Any day of the week. I'm going home." He got to his feet. "See you tomorrow."

"Yeah. Nice work."

"Back at you. Oh, your guy's in the kitchen, getting patched up."

"What do you mean patched up?"

"Caught a little friendly fire. Just a nick."

"He's shot? *Shot?* Why didn't anyone tell me?"

Hickman didn't bother to answer. She was already gone.

Ally slammed into the kitchen, her eyes dark and furious when she saw Jonah at one of the worktables, stripped to the waist, calmly drinking a brandy while Will rolled gauze over his upper arm.

"Hold it. Just hold it. Let me see that." She slapped Will away, unwound the gauze and poked at the long shallow cut until Jonah pushed her face up with the heel of his hand on her chin.

"Ouch," he said.

"Put that drink down, you're going to the hospital."

He kept his eyes on hers, lifted the brandy. Sipped. "No."

"No, my butt. What is this? Some idiot, male, macho deal? You've been shot."

"Not really. Grazed is more the accepted term. Now if you don't mind, Will's got a kinder touch with this than you. I'd like him to finish so he can go home."

"It could get infected."

"I could get hit by a truck, but I don't intend for either to happen."

"It's okay, Ally, really." Playing peacemaker, Will patted her shoulder before picking up the gauze again. "I cleaned it real good. We got some worse in the old days, didn't we, Jonah?"

"Sure did. Looks like I'm another scar up on you now."

"Well, isn't that nice?" Ally grabbed the brandy, glugged.

"I thought you hated brandy."

"I do."

"Why don't you get a glass of wine," Will suggested. "I'm nearly done here."

"I'm fine. I'm okay." Ally blew out a breath. Now, she thought, after everything, her hands wanted to shake. "Damn it, Blackhawk. I was probably the one who shot you."

"Probably. I've decided to weigh in the circumstances and not hold it against you."

"That's real big of you. Now listen to me—"

"Frannie went home with Beth," he added, wanting to distract her. "She's okay. Shaky yet, but okay. She wanted to thank you, but you were busy."

"There we go." Will stepped back. "Your arm's in a lot better shape than your shirt. I'd say that's a loss." He held up the bloodstained linen and made Ally's stomach turn over. "Want me to go up and get you a fresh one before I go?"

"No. Thanks." Jonah lifted his arm, flexed. "Nice job. Haven't lost your touch."

"All in a day's work." Will picked up his discarded jacket. "You sure stand up, Ally. Could've been an awful mess out there tonight. But you sure stand up."

"All in a day's work."

"I'll lock up. 'Night."

Ally sat at the table, waited until she heard silence. "Okay, smart guy, what the hell were you thinking? You interfered with a police operation."

"Oh, I don't know. Maybe I was thinking that lunatic

was going to kill you. It bothered me." He held out the brandy snifter. "How about a refill, since you drank mine."

"Fine. Sit here and swill brandy and look stoic." She shoved back, grabbed the glass, then gave in and wrapped her arms around his neck. "Don't *ever* scare me like that again."

"I won't if you won't. No, just stay right there a minute." He turned his face into her hair, breathed deep. "I'm going to see you stepping in front of that gun for a long time. That's hard."

"I know. I know it is."

"I'll deal with that, Ally, because that's the way it is." He drew her back, his eyes intense on hers. "There are some things you need to figure out if you can deal with. If you want to deal with."

"What are they?"

He rose to get the brandy himself, poured, set the bottle on the table. "Are there still cops in my place?"

"Other than me?"

"Yeah, other than you."

"No. We're clear."

"Then sit down."

"Sounds very serious." She pulled up her chair. "I'm sitting."

"My mother left when I was sixteen." He didn't know why he started there. It just seemed to be the spot. "I couldn't blame her, still don't. My father was a hard man, and she was tired of it."

"She left you with him?"

"I was self-sufficient."

"You were sixteen."

"Ally. I was never sixteen the way you were. And I had your father."

Everything inside her softened. "That's a lovely thing to say."

"It's just fact. He made me go to school. He came down on me when I needed it, which was most of the time. And he was the first person in my life to ever tell me I was worth anything. To ever see I might be. He's…I don't know anyone who comes up to him."

She reached across the table, took his hand. "I love him, too."

"Let me get through some of this." He squeezed her hand, then drew his away. "I didn't go to college, even Fletch couldn't browbeat me into that. I took some business courses because it suited me. When I was twenty, my father died. Three packs of cigarettes a day and a general meanness catches up with you. It was long and ugly, and when it was over, the only thing I felt was relief."

"Is that supposed to make me think less of you?"

"There's a contrast here, and you see it as well as I do."

"Yeah, you had a lousy childhood. I had a great one. As fate would have it, we both got lucky and ended up with Boyd Fletcher as a father. Don't look at me like that. That's exactly what he is to you."

"I'm going to make something clear to you before this goes any farther. I wasn't a victim, Allison. I was a survivor, and used whatever methods worked. I stole and cheated and conned, and I don't apologize for it. Things would've turned out differently if I hadn't had your father hounding me. But they didn't."

"I think that was my point."

"Don't interrupt. I'm a businessman. I don't steal or cheat because I don't have to. That doesn't mean I don't play the game my way."

"A real tough guy aren't you? Blackhawk, you're a

fraud. Cool customer, slick hands, icy stare. And this big, soft heart. Soft, hell, it's gooey."

Amused at the speechless shock on his face, she got up, sauntered to the fridge and hunted up an open bottle of white wine.

She wasn't tired anymore, she realized. She was revved.

"Do you think I didn't run you, pal? Run your friends, get the stories? You gather up your sick and wounded like a mama chick."

Enjoying herself now, Ally drew out the stopper, found a glass. "Frannie—got her off the streets, got her clean, gave her work. Will—straightened him up, paid off his debts before he got his knees capped, gave him a suit and some dignity."

"None of that's relevant."

"I'm not finished." She poured the wine. "The iceman got Beth into a woman's shelter, bought her kids presents from Santa Claus when she didn't have the money or the energy to deal with it. Jonah Blackhawk was buying Barbie dolls."

"I did not buy dolls." That was going just a little too far. "Frannie did. And it has nothing to do with this."

"Yeah, right. Then there's Maury, one of your line chefs." She sat down, wiggled into the chair and propped her feet up. "And the dough you lent him—and I use the word *lent* advisedly—to help his mother through a bad patch."

"Shut up."

She merely smiled, dipped a finger into her wine, licked it. "Sherry, the little busgirl, who's working her way through college. Who paid her tuition last semester when she couldn't scrape it together? Why, I believe it was you. And what about Pete the bartender's little problem last year when an uninsured driver totaled his car?"

"Investing in people is good business."

"That's your story, you stick to it."

Irritation and embarrassment warred for top gun inside him. He tossed his weight to the side of irritation. "You're ticking me off, Allison."

"*Ooooh,* really?" She leaned forward, leading with her chin. "Go ahead, hard case, slap me around and shut me up. Dare you."

"Be careful." He said it, meant it, then pushed to his feet. "This is irrelevant, and isn't getting us anywhere."

She crossed her ankles and made clucking noises.

"You're really asking for it."

"Yeah, yeah. I'm shaking. Sucker."

He cracked and lifted her right off the chair. "One more word. I swear, it's only going to take one more word."

She bit him, one quick nip on his already tender mouth. "Softy."

He pushed her aside and spun toward the door.

"Where you going?"

"To put on a damn shirt. I can't talk to you."

"Then I'll just have to rip it off you again. I've got a soft spot for wounded tough guys with gooey centers." And laughing, she launched herself at him, landed piggyback. "I'm crazy about you, Blackhawk."

"Go away. Go arrest somebody. I've had enough of cops for one day."

"You'll never get enough of me." She bit his earlobe, his shoulder. "Come on, shake me off."

He would have. He told himself he could have. It was just his bad luck he looked down and saw the scar in the floor. From a bullet meant for her.

He dragged her around, yanked her against him so

hard, so fast, she swore her ribs knocked together. His mouth was on hers, fused there with a heat borne of desperation.

"Better. Much better. Here, Jonah. Now. We both need to make it right again. I need you to love me. Like our lives depended on it."

He was on the floor with her, without any thought but to prove to himself that she was whole and safe and alive beneath him.

The cool, hard surface of the floor might have been a feather bed, or clouds, or the jagged, unforgiving peaks of a mountain. Nothing mattered but that she was wrapped around him, that her breath was fast and hot against his skin, that her heart beat like wild wings against his.

All the fear, the tension, the ugliness poured out of her when he touched her. Her hands tangled with his, fighting to strip away boundaries. Until they were free to drive together.

When he filled her—temper, passion, desperation—it was like coming home.

His breath was in rags, his system spent, and still he rocked against her.

"Just hold me a minute more." She pressed her face against his shoulder. "Just hold me." But she felt the warm wetness on her fingers, and pulled away. "Damn it. You're bleeding again. Let me fix it."

"It's fine. It's all right."

"It'll only take a minute."

"Ally, leave it be."

The snap of his voice had her eyes narrowing. "Don't think you can step back from me now. Don't think you'll get away with it this time."

"Just get dressed." He pushed back his hair and began to follow his own orders.

"Fine." She snatched at clothes, dragged them on. "You want to go another round, we'll go another round. You stupid son of a bitch."

He heard the tremor in her voice, cursed her. Cursed himself. "Don't cry. That's playing dirty."

"I'm not crying. You think I'd cry over you?"

He could feel his heart start to shatter as he brushed a tear off her cheek with his thumb. "Don't."

She sniffled, flicked her hands over her face to dry it and sneered. "Sucker."

Fury whipped into his eyes and scalded her. She couldn't have been more delighted. She got to her feet before he did, but it was close.

"You're in love with me." She punched her fist against his chest. "And you won't admit it. That doesn't make you tough, it makes you hardheaded."

"You weren't listening to me before."

"You weren't listening to me, either, so we're even."

"Listen now." He grabbed her face with both hands. "You have connections."

"Why, you insulting…" She wondered why the top of her head didn't fly off. "How dare you talk about my family's money at a time like this."

"I don't mean money." He jerked her up to her toes, then dropped her back on the flat of her feet again. "Now who's stupid? Money's nothing. I don't give a damn about your portfolio. I have my own. I'm talking about emotional connections. Foundations, roots, for God's sake."

"You have your own there, too. Frannie. Will. Beth. My father." She waved a hand, settling down again. "But I get you. You're saying, basically, that someone like me, who comes from the kind of place I come from, should hook herself up with a man who say, comes from a good, upstanding family. Probably upper-middle-class. He should have a good education, and hold a straight job. A profession. Like say a lawyer or a doctor. Is that the theme here?"

"More or less."

"Interesting. Yes, that's interesting," she said with a considering nod. "I can see the logic in that. Hey, you know who fits that bill to a tee? Dennis Overton. Remember him? Stalker, tire slasher, general pain in the ass?"

She'd turned it around and boxed him into his own corner. All he could do was steam.

"Don't cop to excuses, Blackhawk, if you haven't got the guts to tell me how you feel about me, and what you want for us."

She flipped her hair back, tucked in her shirt. "My work is done here. See you around, pal."

He got to the door before she did. He was good at that. But this time he slapped a hand on it, held it closed while she glared at him. "You don't walk until we're finished."

"I said I was finished." She jerked on the door.

"I'm not. Shut up and listen."

"You tell me to shut up one more time, and—"

He shut her up. One hard, exasperated kiss. "I've never loved another woman. Never even came close. So cut me a damn break here."

Her heart did a lovely bounding leap. But she nodded, stepped back. "Okay. Spill it."

"You hit me between the eyes the first minute you walked in the room. I still can't see straight."

"Well." She backed up, slid onto a stool. "I'm liking this so far. Keep going."

"You see that? That right there." He stabbed a finger at her. "Anyone else would want to deck you."

"But not you. You love that about me."

"Apparently." He crossed to her, laid his hands on the bar on either side of her. "I love you, so that's it."

"Oh, I don't think so. Make me a deal."

"You want a deal? Here it is. You ditch the apartment and move in, officially, upstairs."

"Full gym and sauna privileges?"

Half the knots in his stomach loosened when he laughed. "Yeah."

"So far, I can live with it. What else are you offering me?"

"Nobody's ever going to love you like I do. I guarantee it. And nobody's ever going to put up with you. But I will."

"Same goes. But that's not enough."

Those wonderful eyes narrowed on her face. "What do you want?"

She rested her back against the bar. "Marriage."

Now those narrowed eyes darkened. "Do you mean that?"

"I say what I mean. Now I could ask you, but I have to figure that a guy who makes a habit of opening doors for women, and buying Christmas presents for little children—"

"Leave that part alone."

"Okay." But she sat up, brushed her knuckles over his cheek. "We'll just say I figure you've got enough of a traditional-guy streak to want to propose on your own. So, I'll let you." She linked her hands at the back of his neck. "I'm waiting."

"I'm just thinking. It's the middle of the night. We're in a bar and my arm's bleeding."

"So's your mouth."

"Yeah." He swiped at it with the back of his hand. "I guess that makes it close to perfect for you and me."

"Works for me. Jonah. You work for me."

He pulled the clip out of her hair, tossed it aside. "First tell me you love me. Use my name."

"I love you, Jonah."

"Then marry me, and let's see where it takes us."

"That's a deal."

Epilogue

With a howl of outrage, Ally bolted up from the sofa. "Off side! Off side! What, are those refs blind? Did you see that?" Instead of kicking in the TV, which occurred to her, she settled for leaning down and pounding on Jonah's shoulder.

"You're just mad because your team's losing, and you're going to owe me."

"I don't know what you're talking about." She sniffed, pushing back her hair. "My team is *not* going to lose, despite corrupt and myopic officials." But it looked very dim for her side. She planted her hands on her hips. "Besides, must I remind you there is no bet because you don't have a license for gambling."

He skimmed his eyes down her long black robe. "You're not wearing your badge."

"Metaphorically, Blackhawk." She leaned over to kiss him. "I'm always wearing my badge." Then she narrowed her eyes. "You swear you didn't hear who won this game? You have no information?"

"Absolutely not."

But she didn't like the way he smiled at her. They'd missed the regular Monday night broadcast and were watching the hotly contested football game on videotape. "I don't know about you. You're slippery."

"We made a deal." He skimmed his hand up the sleeve of her robe, trailing his fingers over flesh. "I never go back on a deal." He reached for the remote, paused the screen. "Since you're up…" He held up his empty glass. "How about a refill?"

"I got it last time."

"You were up last time, too. If you'd sit down and stay down, you wouldn't get tagged."

Conceding his point, she took the glass. "Don't start the game until I get back."

"Wouldn't think of it."

She headed back to the kitchen. There were times she missed the apartment on top of the club. But even a couple of die-hard urbanites needed a little elbow room, she thought. And the house suited them. So did marriage, she thought with a contented sigh as she poured Jonah's habitual bottled water over ice.

There'd been a lot of changes in the eighteen months since they, well, closed the deal, she supposed. Good changes. The kind lives were built on. They were building strong, and they were building solid.

Sipping his water, she walked back to the great room and frowned when she found it empty. Then with a shake of her head, she set the glass down. She knew just where to find him.

She wound her way quietly through the house, and stopped at the door to the bedroom.

The winter moonlight streamed through the windows, glowing over him, and the infant he held in his arms. Love burst through her, a nova of feeling, then settled again to a steady warmth.

"You woke her up."

"She was awake."

"You woke her up," Ally repeated, crossing to him. "Because you can't keep your hands off her."

"Why should I?" He pressed his lips to his daughter's head. "She's mine."

"No question of that." Ally traced a finger over the baby's soft black hair. "She's going to have your eyes."

The idea of it was a staggering thrill. He looked down at that perfect little face, with those dark and mysterious eyes of the newborn. He could see his whole life in those eyes. Sarah's eyes.

"You can't tell at two weeks. The books say it takes longer."

"She's going to have your eyes," Ally repeated. She draped an arm around his waist and together they studied their miracle. "Is she hungry?"

"No. She's just a night person." And his, like the woman beside him was his. Two years before they hadn't existed for him. Now they were the world.

He turned his head, leaning down as Ally lifted her mouth. As the kiss sweetened, the baby stirred in his arms. He shifted, tucking Sarah's head on his shoulder with a natural grace that never failed to make Ally smile.

He'd taken to fatherhood as if he'd only been waiting for the moment. Then again, she thought, thinking of her own father, he'd had a wonderful teacher.

She angled her head, studied the two of them. "I guess she wants to watch the game now."

Jonah rubbed his cheek over his daughter's hair. "She mentioned it."

"She'll just fall asleep."

"So will you."

With a laugh, Ally took the blanket from the bassinet. "Give her up," she said, holding out her arms.

"No."

Ally rolled her eyes. "Okay, you get her till halftime, then it's my turn."

"Deal."

With the baby on his shoulder and his hand linked with the woman's he loved, he went out to enjoy the night.

* * * * *

NIGHT MOVES

To the mountains I live in,
and the people who love them.

Chapter 1

"What the hell are you doing in a place like this?"

Maggie, on her hands and knees, didn't look up. "C.J., you're playing the same old song."

C.J. pulled down the hem of his cashmere sweater. He was a man who made worry an art, and he worried about Maggie. Someone had to. Frustrated, he looked down at the sable-brown hair twisted untidily into a knot on top of her head. Her neck was slender, pale, her shoulders curved slightly forward as she rested her weight on her forearms. She had a delicate build, with the kind of fragility C.J. had always associated with nineteenth-century English aristocratic ladies. Though perhaps they, too, had possessed endless stores of strength and endurance under frail bones and porcelain skin.

She wore a T-shirt and jeans that were both faded and slightly damp from perspiration. When he looked at her hands, fine-boned, elegant hands, and saw they were grimy, he shuddered. He knew the magic they were capable of.

A phase, he thought. She was just going through a phase. After two marriages and a few affairs, C.J. understood that women went through odd moods from time to time. He brushed at his trim, sandy mustache with one finger. It was up to him to guide her back, gently, to the real world.

As he glanced around at nothing but trees and rocks and isolation, he wondered, fleetingly, if there were bears in the woods. In the real world, such things were kept in zoos. Keeping a nervous lookout for suspicious movements, he tried again.

"Maggie, just how long are you going to go on this way?"

"What way is that, C.J.?" Her voice was low, husky, as if she'd just been awakened. It was a voice that made most men wish they'd awakened her.

The woman was infuriating. C.J. tugged a hand through his carefully styled, blow-dried hair. What was she doing three thousand miles from L.A., wasting herself on this dirty work? He had a responsibility to her and, damn it, to himself. C.J. blew out a long breath, an old habit he had whenever he met with opposition. Negotiations were, after all, his business. It was up to him to talk some sense into her. He shifted his feet, careful to keep his polished loafers out of the dirt. "Babe, I love you. You know I do. Come home."

This time Maggie turned her head, looking up with a flash of a smile that involved every inch of her face—the mouth that stopped just short of being too wide, the chin a bit pointed, the sweep of cheekbones that gave her face a diamond shape. Her eyes, big, round and shades darker than her hair, added that final spark of animation. It wasn't a stunning face. You'd tell yourself that while you tried to focus in on the reason you were stunned. Even now, without makeup, with a long streak of topsoil across one cheek, the face involved you. Maggie Fitzgerald involved you because she was exactly what she seemed. Interesting. Interested.

Now she sat back on her haunches, blowing a wisp of hair out of her eyes as she looked up at the man who was frowning at her. She felt a tug of affection, a tug of amusement. Both had always come easily to her. "C.J., I love you, too. Now stop acting like an old woman."

"You don't belong here," he began, more exasperated than insulted. "You shouldn't be grubbing around on your hands and knees—"

"I like it," she said simply.

It was the very simplicity of the tone that told him he had a real problem. If she'd shouted, argued, his chances of turning her around would've been all but secured. But when she was like this, calmly stubborn, changing her mind would be like climbing Mount Everest. Treacherous and exhausting. Because he was a clever man, C.J. changed tactics.

"Maggie, I can certainly understand why you might like to get away for a while, rest a bit. No one deserves it more." That was a nice touch, he thought, because it was true. "Why don't you take a couple weeks in Cancún, or go on a shopping spree in Paris?"

"Mmm." Maggie shifted on her knees and fluffed up the petals of the pansies she was planting. They looked, she decided, a bit sick. "Hand me that watering can, will you?"

"You're not listening."

"Yes, I am." Stretching over, she retrieved the can herself. "I've been to Cancún, and I have so many clothes now I left half of them in storage in L.A."

Without breaking stride, C.J. tried a different turn. "It's not just me," he began again, watching as she drenched the pansies. "Everyone who knows you, who knows about this, thinks you've—"

"Slipped a gear?" Maggie supplied. Overdid the water, she decided as the saturated blossoms drooped. She had a lot to learn about the basics of country life. "C.J., instead of nagging me and trying to talk me into doing something I've no intention of doing, why don't you come down here and give me a hand?"

"A hand?" His voice held the slightly appalled note it might have if she'd suggested he dilute prime scotch with tap water. Maggie chuckled.

"Pass me that flat of petunias." She stuck the small spade in the ground again, fighting the rocky soil. "Gardening's good for you. It gets you back in touch with nature."

"I've no desire to touch nature."

This time she laughed and lifted her face to the sky. No, the closest C.J. would come to nature would be a chlorinated pool—solar-heated. Up to a few months ago she'd barely gotten much closer herself. She'd certainly never attempted to. But now she'd found something—something she hadn't even been looking for. If she hadn't come to the East Coast to collaborate on the score for a new musical, if she hadn't taken an impulsive drive south after the long, grueling sessions had ended, she never would've happened on the sleepy little town tucked into the Blue Ridge.

Do we ever know where we belong, Maggie wondered, unless we're lucky enough to stumble onto our own personal space? She only knew that she'd been heading nowhere in particular and she'd come home.

Maybe it had been fate that had led her into Morganville, a cluster of houses cupped in the foothills that boasted a population of 142. From the town proper, it spread out into farms and isolated mountain homes. If fate had taken her to Morganville, it had again taken her past the sign that listed the sale of a house and twelve acres. There'd been no moment of indecision, no quibbling over the price, no last-minute doubts. Maggie had met the terms and had had the deed in her hand within thirty days.

Looking up at the three-story frame house, with shutters still hanging crooked, Maggie could well imagine her friends and colleagues wondering about her mental state. She'd left her Italian-marble entrance hall and mosaic-tiled pool for rusty hinges and rocks. She'd done it without a backward glance.

Maggie patted the dirt around the petunias, then sat back. They looked a bit more spritely than her pansies. Maybe she was beginning to get the hang of it. "What do you think?"

"I think you should come back to L.A. and finish the score."

"I meant the flowers." She brushed off her jeans as she rose. "In any case, I am finishing the score—right here."

"Maggie, how can you work here?" C.J. exploded. He tossed out both arms in a gesture she'd always admired for its unapologetic theatrics. "How can you live here? This place isn't even civilized."

"Why? Because there's no health club and boutique on every other corner?" Wanting to temper the words, she tucked a hand through C.J.'s arm. "Go ahead, take a deep breath. The clean air won't hurt you."

"Smog's underrated," he mumbled as he shifted his feet again. Professionally he was her agent, but personally C.J. considered himself her friend, perhaps her best friend since Jerry had died. Thinking of that, he changed his tone again. This time it was gentle. "Look, Maggie, I know you've been through some rough times. Maybe L.A. has too many memories for you to deal with right now. But you can't bury yourself."

"I'm not burying myself." She put her hands on his forearms, squeezing for both emphasis and support. "And I buried Jerry nearly two years ago. That was another part of my life, C.J., and has nothing to do with this. This is home. I don't know how else to explain it." She slid her hands down to his, forgetting hers were smeared with earth. "This is my mountain now, and I'm happier here, more settled, than I ever was in Los Angeles."

He knew he was beating his head against a wall, but opted to give it one more shot. "Maggie." He slipped an arm around her shoulder, as if, she thought ruefully, she was a small child needing guidance. "Look at that place." He let the silence hang a moment while they both studied the house on the rise above. He noticed that the porch was missing several boards and that the paint on the trim was peeling badly. Maggie saw the sun reflecting off the window glass in rainbows. "You can't possibly be serious about living there."

"A little paint, a few nails." She shrugged it away. Long ago she'd learned that surface problems were best ignored. It was the problem simmering under the surface, not quite visible, that had to be dealt with. "It has such possibilities, C.J."

"The biggest one is that it'll fall down on your head."

"I had the roof fixed last week—a local man."

"Maggie, I'm not at all convinced there are any local men, or women, within ten miles. This place doesn't look fit for anything but elves and gnomes."

"Well, he might've been a gnome." Her sense of fun

spurred her on as she stretched her back muscles. "He was about five foot five, stocky as a bull and somewhere around a hundred and two. His name was Bog."

"Maggie—"

"He was very helpful," she went on. "He and his boy are coming back to deal with the porch and some of the other major repairs."

"All right, so you've got a gnome to do some hammering and sawing. What about this?" He swept his hand around to take in the surrounding land. It was rocky, uneven and overgrown with weeds and thickets. Not even a dedicated optimist could've considered any part of it a lawn. A burly tree slanted dangerously toward the house itself, while thorny vines and wildflowers scrambled for space. There was a pervading smell of earth and green.

"Like Sleeping Beauty's castle," Maggie murmured. "I'll be sorry in a way to hack it down, but Mr. Bog has that under control, too."

"He does excavation work, too?"

Maggie tilted her head and arched her brows. It was a look that made anyone over forty remember her mother. "He recommended a landscaper. Mr. Bog assures me that Cliff Delaney is the best man in the county. He's coming by this afternoon to take a look at the place."

"If he's a smart man, he'll take one look at that gully you call a road leading up here and keep on going."

"But you brought your rented Mercedes all the way up." Turning, she threw her arms around his neck and kissed him. "Don't think I don't appreciate that or the fact that you flew in from the Coast or that you care enough to be concerned. I appreciate all of it. I appreciate you." She ruffled his hair, something no one else would've gotten away with. "Trust my judgment on this, C.J. I really do know what I'm doing. Professionally, my work can't do anything but improve here."

"That's yet to be seen," he muttered, but lifted a hand to touch her cheek. She was still young enough to have foolish dreams, he thought. Still sweet enough to believe in them. "You know it's not your work I'm worried about."

"I know." Her voice softened, and with it her eyes, her mouth. She was not a woman who guided her emotions, but one who was guided by them. "I need the peace here. Do you know, this is the first time in my life I've gotten off the merry-go-round? I'm enjoying the solid ground, C.J."

He knew her well and understood that there was no moving her, for the moment, from the position she'd taken. He understood, too, that from birth her life had been ribboned with the stuff of fantasies—and of nightmares. Perhaps she did need to compensate, for a time.

"I've got a plane to catch," he grumbled. "As long as you insist on staying here, I want you to call me every day."

Maggie kissed him again. "Once a week," she countered. "You'll have the completed score for *Heat Dance* in ten days." With her arm around his waist, she led him to the end of the uneven, overgrown path where his Mercedes sat in incongruous splendor. "I love the film, C.J. It's even better than I thought it would be when I first read the script. The music's all but writing itself."

He only grunted and cast one look behind him at the house. "If you get lonely—"

"I won't." With a quick laugh, Maggie nudged him into the car. "It's been enlightening discovering how self-sufficient I can be. Now, have a nice trip back and stop worrying about me."

Fat chance, he thought, automatically reaching in his

briefcase to make certain his Dramamine was there. "Send me the score, and if it's sensational, I might stop worrying…a little."

"It is sensational." She backed off from the car to give him room to turn around. "*I'm* sensational!" she shouted as the Mercedes began to inch around. "Tell everyone back on the Coast that I've decided to buy some goats and chickens."

The Mercedes stopped dead. "Maggie…"

Laughing, she waved at him and backed down the path. "Not yet…but maybe in the fall." She decided it was best to reassure him, or else he might get out and start again. "Oh, and send me some Godiva chocolates."

That was more like it, C.J. thought, and put the car in gear again. She'd be back in L.A. in six weeks. He glanced in his rearview mirror as he started to drive away. He could see her, small and slender, still laughing, against the backdrop of the overgrown land, greening trees and dilapidated house. Once again he shuddered, but this time it wasn't from an offense of his sensibilities. This time it was from something like fear. He had a sudden flash of certainty that she wasn't safe there.

Shaking his head, C.J. reached in his pocket for his antacids as the car bumped noisily over a rock. Everyone told him he worried too much.

Lonely, Maggie thought as she watched the Mercedes bump and wind its way down her excuse for a lane. No, she wasn't lonely. She was as certain as she'd ever been about anything that she'd never be lonely here. She felt an unexpected sense of foreboding that she shrugged off as ridiculous.

Wrapping her arms around herself, she turned in two slow circles. Trees rose up out of the rocky hillside. The leaves were hardly more than buds now, but in a few weeks they would grow and spread, turning the woods into a lush cover of green. She liked to imagine it that way and to try to picture it in the dead of winter—white, all white and black with ice clinging to the branches and shimmering on the rocks. In the fall there'd be a tapestry outside every window. She was far from lonely.

For the first time in her life, she had a chance to put her own stamp on a place. It wouldn't be a copy of anything she'd had before or anything that'd been given to her. It was hers, absolutely, and so were any mistakes she made here, any triumphs. There'd be no press to compare this isolated spot in western Maryland with her mother's mansion in Beverly Hills or her father's villa in the south of France. If she was lucky, very, very lucky, Maggie thought with a satisfied sigh, there'd be no press at all. She could make her music and live her life in peace and solitude.

If she stood very still, if she closed her eyes and didn't move, she could hear the music all around her. Not birdsong but the ruffle of air through branches and tiny leaves. If she concentrated, she could hear the faint trickle of the narrow creek that ran along the other side of the lane. The quality of silence was rich, flowing over her like a symphony.

There was a place for glitz, she mused, and for glamour. She simply didn't want that place any longer. The truth was she hadn't wanted that place for a very long time but hadn't known the way out. When your birth had been celebrated by the international press, your first step, your first words, cataloged for the public, it was natural to forget there was another way of life.

Her mother had been one of the greatest blues and ballad singers in America, her father a child actor turned successful film director. Their courtship and marriage had been followed religiously by fans around the world. The birth of their daughter had been an event treated like the birth of royalty. And Maggie had lived the life of a pampered princess. Gold carousels and white fur coats. She'd been lucky because her parents had adored her, and each other. That had compensated for the make-believe, often hard-edged world of show business, with all its demands and inconstancy. Her world had been cushioned by wealth and love, rippled continually with publicity.

The paparazzi haunted her on dates through her teenage years—to her amusement but often to the boys' frustration. Maggie had accepted the fact that her life was public domain. It had never been otherwise.

And when her parents' private plane had crashed into the Swiss Alps, the press had frozen her grief in glossies and newsprint. She hadn't tried to stop it; she'd realized that the world had mourned with her. She'd been eighteen when the fabric of her world had torn.

Then there had been Jerry. First friend, then lover, then husband. With him, her life had drifted into more fantasy, and more tragedy.

She wouldn't think of any of that now, Maggie told herself as she picked up her spade and began to fight the tough soil again. All that was really left of that portion of her life was her music. That she would never give up. She couldn't have if she'd tried. It was part of her the way her eyes and ears were part of her. She composed words and music and twined them together, not effortlessly, as it sometimes seemed from the fluid finished result, but obsessively, wonderingly, constantly. Unlike her mother, she didn't perform but fed other performers with her gift.

At twenty-eight, she had two Oscars, five Grammies

and a Tony. She could sit at the piano and play any song she'd ever written from memory. The awards were still in the packing boxes that had been shipped from L.A.

The little flower plot she was planting in a spot perhaps no one would see but herself was a labor of love with no guarantee of success. It was enough that it gave her pleasure to add her own peculiar spot of color to the land she'd claimed as hers. Maggie began to sing as she worked. She'd completely forgotten her former feeling of apprehension.

Normally he didn't do the estimating and initial planning on a job himself. Not anymore. For the past six years Cliff Delaney had been in the position of being able to send one or two of his best men out on the first stage of a project; then he would fine-tune. If the job was interesting enough, he would visit the site while work was in progress, perhaps handle some of the grading and planting himself. He was making an exception.

He knew the old Morgan place. It had been built by a Morgan, even as the tiny community a few miles away had been named after one. For ten years, since William Morgan's car had crashed into the Potomac, the house had stood empty. The house had always been stern, the land formidable. But with the right touch, the right insight, Cliff knew, it could be magnificent. He had his doubts that the lady from L.A. had the right insight.

He knew of her. Naturally he knew of her. Anyone who hadn't spent the last twenty-eight years in a cave knew Maggie Fitzgerald. At the moment, she was the biggest news in Morganville—all but eclipsing the hot gossip of Lloyd Messner's wife running off with the bank manager.

It was a simple town, the kind that moved slowly. The

kind of town where everyone took pride in the acquisition of a new fire engine and the yearly Founder's Day parade. That's why Cliff chose to live there after he'd reached a point where he could live anywhere he chose. He'd grown up there and understood the people, their unity and their possessiveness. He understood their failings. More, perhaps much more, than that, he understood the land. He had serious doubts that the glamorous songwriter from California would understand either.

C.J. had estimated six weeks before she flew back. Cliff, without ever setting eyes on her, cut that in half. But perhaps before Maggie Fitzgerald grew bored with her shot at rural living, he could put his own mark on the land.

He turned off the paved road onto the quarter-mile lane that cut through the Morgan property. It had been years since he'd been on it, and it was worse than he remembered. Rain and neglect had worn ruts in the dirt. From both sides of the lane, branches reached out to whip at the truck. The first order of business would be the lane itself, Cliff thought as his small pickup bounced over ruts. It would be graded, leveled, filled. Drainage ditches would have to be dug, gravel spread.

He went slowly, not for the truck's sake but because the land on either side of the lane appealed to him. It was wild and primitive, timeless. He'd want to work with that, incorporate his own talents with the genius of nature. If Maggie Fitzgerald wanted blacktop and hothouse plants, she'd come to the wrong place. He'd be the first one to let her know.

If he had a distrust of outsiders, Cliff considered he'd come by it honestly. They came, often from the rich suburbs of D.C., and wanted their lawns flat and free of the poplar and oak that had first claim. They wanted neat little flowers in orderly rows. Lawns should be even, so that their mowers could handle the weekly cutting effortlessly. What they wanted, Cliff thought derisively, was to say they lived *in the country* while they brought city attitudes and city tastes with them. By the time he rounded the last bend, he was already out of patience with Maggie Fitzgerald.

Maggie heard the truck coming before it was in sight. That was something else she liked about her new home. It was quiet—so quiet that the sound of a truck, which would have been ignored in the city, brought her to attention. Halfheartedly brushing her hands on the seat of her pants, she rose from her planting, then shielded her eyes against the sun.

While she watched, the truck rounded the curve and parked where the Mercedes had been only an hour before. A bit dusty from the road, with its chrome dull rather than gleaming, the truck looked much more comfortable than the luxury car had. Though she couldn't yet see the driver through the glare of sun on windshield, Maggie smiled and lifted a hand in greeting.

The first thing Cliff thought was that she was smaller than he'd expected, more delicate in build. The Fitzgeralds had always been larger than life. He wondered, with a quick grunt, if she'd want to raise orchids to match her style. He got out of the truck, convinced she was going to annoy him.

Perhaps it was because she'd been expecting another Mr. Bog that Maggie felt a flutter of surprise when Cliff stepped out of the truck. Or perhaps, she thought with her usual penchant for honesty, it was because he was quite simply a magnificent example of manhood. Six-two, Maggie decided, with an impressive breadth of shoulders. Black hair that had been ruffled by the wind through the open truck windows fell over his forehead and ears in loose waves. He didn't smile, but his mouth was sculpted, sensual. She had a fleeting regret that he wore dark glasses so that his eyes were hidden. She judged people from their eyes.

Instead, Maggie summed him up from the way he moved—loosely, confidently. Athletic, she concluded, as he strode over the uneven ground. Definitely self-assured. He was still a yard away when she got the unmistakable impression that he wasn't particularly friendly.

"Miss Fitzgerald?"

"Yes." Giving him a neutral smile, Maggie held out a hand. "You're from Delaney's?"

"That's right." Their hands met, briefly, hers soft, his hard, both of them capable. Without bothering to identify himself, Cliff scanned the grounds. "You wanted an estimate on some landscaping."

Maggie followed his gaze, and this time her smile held amusement. "Obviously I need something. Does your company perform miracles?"

"We do the job." He glanced down at the splash of color behind her, wilted pansies and soggy petunias. Her effort touched something in him that he ignored, telling himself she'd be bored long before it was time to pull the first weeds. "Why don't you tell me what you have in mind?"

"A glass of iced tea at the moment. Look around while I get some—then we'll talk about it." She'd been giving orders without a second thought all her life. After giving this one, Maggie turned and climbed the rickety steps to the porch. Behind the tinted glasses, Cliff's eyes narrowed.

Designer jeans, he thought with a smirk as he watched

the graceful sway of hips before the screen door banged shut at her back. And the solitaire on the thin chain around her neck had been no less than a carat. Just what game was little Miss Hollywood playing? She'd left a trace of her scent behind, something soft and subtle that would nag at a man's senses. Shrugging, he turned his back on the house and looked at the land.

It could be shaped and structured without being tamed. It should never lose its basic unruly sense by being manicured, though he admitted the years of neglect had given the rougher side of nature too much of an advantage. Still, he wouldn't level it for her. Cliff had turned down more than one job because the client had insisted on altering the land's personality. Even with that, he wouldn't have called himself an artist. He was a businessman. His business was the land.

He walked farther away from the house, toward a grove of trees overrun with tangling vines, greedy saplings and thistles. Without effort he could see it cleared of undergrowth, richly mulched, naturalized perhaps with jonquils. That one section would personify peace, as he saw it. Hitching his thumbs in his back pockets, Cliff reflected that from the reams that had been written about Maggie Fitzgerald over the years, she didn't go in much for peace.

Jet-setting, the fast lane, glitter and glitz. What the hell had she moved out here for?

Before he heard her, Cliff caught a fresh whiff of her perfume. When he turned, she was a few paces behind him, two glasses in her hand. She watched him steadily with a curiosity she didn't bother to hide. He learned something more about her then as she stood with her eyes on his face and the sun at her back. She was the most alluring woman he'd ever met, though he'd be damned if he knew why.

Maggie approached him and offered a glass of frosty tea. "Want to hear my ideas?"

The voice had something to do with it, Cliff decided. An innocent question, phrased in that sultry voice, conjured up a dozen dark pleasures. He took a slow sip. "That's what I'm here for," he told her with a curtness he'd never shown any potential client.

Her brow lifted at the tone, the only sign that she'd noticed his rudeness. With that attitude, she thought, he wouldn't have the job for long. Then again, he didn't strike her as a man who'd work for someone else. "Indeed you are, Mr….?"

"Delaney."

"Ah, the man himself." That made more sense, she decided, if his attitude didn't. "Well, Mr. Delaney, I'm told you're the best. I believe in having the best, so…" Thoughtfully, she ran a fingertip down the length of her glass, streaking the film of moisture. "I'll tell you what I want, and you tell me if you can deliver."

"Fair enough." He didn't know why her simple statement should annoy him any more than he could understand why he was just noticing how smooth her skin was and how compelling were those large velvet eyes. Like a doe's, Cliff realized. He wasn't a man who hunted but a man who watched. "I'll tell you up front that my company has a policy against destroying the natural terrain in order to make the land into something it's not. This is rough country, Miss Fitzgerald. It's supposed to be. If you want an acre or two of manicured lawn, you've bought the wrong land and called the wrong landscaper."

It took a great deal to fire up her temper. Maggie had worked long and hard to control a natural tendency toward quick fury in order to block the label of temperamental daughter of temperamental artists. "Decent of you to point it out," she managed after three long, quiet breaths.

"I don't know why you bought the place," he began.

"I don't believe I've offered that information."

"And it's none of my business," Cliff finished with an acknowledging nod. "But this—" he indicated the property with a gesture of his hand "—is my business."

"You're a bit premature in condemning me, aren't you, Mr. Delaney?" To keep herself in check, Maggie took a sip of tea. It was cold, with a faint bite of lemon. "I've yet to ask you to bring on the bulldozers and chain saws." She ought to tell him to haul his buns into his truck and take off. Almost before she could wonder why she didn't, the answer came. Instinct. Instinct had brought her to Morganville and to the property she now stood on. It was instinct that told her he was indeed the best. Nothing else would do for her land. To give herself a moment to be sure she didn't do anything rash, Maggie took another sip from her glass.

"That grove there," she began briskly. "I want it cleared of undergrowth. It can't be enjoyed if you have to fight your way through thorns and thickets to walk in it." She shot him a look. "Don't you want to take notes?"

He watched her, consideringly. "No. Go on."

"All right. This stretch right here, in front of the porch—I imagine that was a lawn of sorts at one time." She turned, looking at the knee-high weeds. "It should be again, but I want enough room to plant, I don't know, some pines, maybe, to keep the line between lawn and woods from being too marked. Then there's the way the whole thing just sort of falls away until it reaches the lane below."

Forgetting her annoyance for the moment, Maggie made her way across the relatively flat land to where it sloped steeply down. Weeds, some of them as tall as she, grew in abundance wherever the rocks would permit. "It's certainly too steep for grass to be practical," she said half to herself. "But I can't just let all these weeds have their way. I'd like some color, but I don't want uniformity."

"You'll want some evergreens," he said from behind her. "Some spreading junipers along the bottom edge of the whole slope, a few coming farther up over there, with some forsythia mixed in. Here, where the grade's not so dramatic, you'd want some low ground cover." He could see phlox spilling and bumping over the rocks. "That tree's got to come down," he went on, frowning at the one that leaned precariously toward her roof. "And there's two, maybe three, on the rise behind the house that've got to be taken down before they fall down."

She was frowning now, but she'd always believed in letting an expert set the plan. "Okay, but I don't want you to cut down anything that doesn't have to be cleared."

Maggie could only see her own reflection in his glasses when he faced her. "I never do." He turned and began to walk around the side of the house. "That's another problem," Cliff continued without checking to see if she was following. "The way that dirt wall's eroding down from the cliff here. You're going to end up with a tree or a boulder in your kitchen when you least expect it."

"So?" Maggie tilted her head so she could scan the ridge behind her house. "You're the expert."

"It'll need to be recut, tapered back some. Then I'd put up a retaining wall, three, maybe four, foot high. Crown vetch'd hold the dirt above that. Plant it along the entire slope. It's hardy and fast."

"All right." It sounded reasonable. He sounded more reasonable, Maggie decided, when he was talking about his business. A man of the land, she mused, and wished again she could see beyond the tinted glass to his eyes. "This part behind the house has to be cleared." She began to fight her way through the weeds and briars as she talked. "I think if I had a walkway of some kind from here to the lane, I could have a rockery…here." A vague gesture of her hands indicated the spot she had in mind. "There're plenty of rocks," she muttered, nearly stumbling over one. "Then down here—"

Cliff took her arm before she could start down the slope on the far side of the house. The contact jolted both of them. More surprised than alarmed, Maggie turned her head.

"I wouldn't," Cliff said softly, and she felt a tiny trickle, an odd excitement, sprint up her spine.

"Wouldn't what?" Her chin automatically tilted, her eyes challenged.

"Walk down there." Her skin was soft, Cliff discovered. With his hand wrapped around her arm, he could touch his fingertips to his thumb. Small and soft, he mused, enjoying the feel of his flesh against hers. Too small and soft for land that would fight back at you.

Maggie glanced down to where he held her. She noticed the tan on the back of his hand; she noticed the size and the strength of it. When she noticed her pulse wasn't quite steady, she lifted her gaze again. "Mr. Delaney—"

"Snakes," he said simply, and had the satisfaction of seeing her take two quick steps back. "You're almost sure to have some down in a spot like that. In fact, with the way this place is overgrown, you're likely to have them everywhere."

"Well, then—" Maggie swallowed and made a Herculean effort not to shudder "—maybe you can start the job right away."

For the first time, he smiled, a very slight, very cautious, curving of lips. They'd both forgotten he still held her, but they were standing much closer now, within a hand span of touching. She certainly hadn't reacted the way he'd expected. He wouldn't have been surprised if she'd screeched at the mention of snakes, then had dashed into the house, slamming and locking the door. Her skin was soft, Cliff mused, unconsciously moving his thumb over it. But apparently she wasn't.

"I might be able to send a crew out next week, but the first thing that has to be dealt with is your road."

Maggie dismissed this with a shrug. "Do whatever you think best there, excluding asphalt. It's only a means of getting in and out to me. I want to concentrate on the house and grounds."

"The road's going to run you twelve, maybe fifteen, hundred," he began, but she cut him off again.

"Do what you have to," she told him with the unconscious arrogance of someone who'd never worried about money. "This section here—" She pointed to the steep drop in front of them, making no move this time to go down it. At the base it spread twenty feet wide, perhaps thirty in length, in a wicked maze of thorny vines and weeds as thick at the stem as her thumb. "I want a pond."

Cliff brought his attention back to her. "A pond?"

She gave him a level look and stood her ground. "Allow me one eccentricity, Mr. Delaney. A small one," she continued before he could comment. "There's certainly enough room, and it seems to me that this section here's the worst. It's hardly more than a hole in the ground in a very awkward place. Do you have an objection to water?"

Instead of answering, he studied the ground below them, running through the possibilities. The truth was, she couldn't have picked a better spot as far as the lay of the land and the angle to the house. It could be done, he mused. It wouldn't be an easy job, but it could be done. And it would be very effective.

"It's going to cost you," he said at length. "You're going to be sinking a lot of cash into this place. If you're weighing that against resale value, I can tell you, this property won't be easy to sell."

It snapped her patience. She was tired, very tired, of having people suggest she didn't know what she was doing. "Mr. Delaney, I'm hiring you to do a job, not to advise me on real estate or my finances. If you can't handle it, just say so and I'll get someone else."

His eyes narrowed. The fingers on her arm tightened fractionally. "I can handle it, Miss Fitzgerald. I'll draw up an estimate and a contract. They'll be in the mail tomorrow. If you still want the job done after you've looked them over, call my office." Slowly, he released her arm, then handed her back the glass of tea. He left her there, near the edge where the slope gave way to gully as he headed back toward his truck. "By the way," he said without turning around, "you overwatered your pansies."

Maggie let out one long, simmering breath and dumped the tepid tea on the ground at her feet.

Chapter 2

When she was alone, Maggie went back inside, through the back door, which creaked ominously on its hinges. She wasn't going to think about Cliff Delaney. In fact, she doubted if she'd see him again. He'd send crews out to deal with the actual work, and whatever they had to discuss would be done via phone or letter. Better that way, Maggie decided. He'd been unfriendly, abrupt and annoying, though his mouth had been attractive, she reflected, even kind.

She was halfway through the kitchen when she remembered the glasses in her hand. Turning back, she crossed the scarred linoleum to set them both in the sink, then leaned on the windowsill to look out at the rise behind her house. Even as she watched, a few loose stones and dirt slid down the wall. A couple of hard rains, she mused, and half that bank would be at her back door. A retaining wall. Maggie nodded. Cliff Delaney obviously knew his business.

There was just enough breeze to carry a hint of spring to her. Far back in the woods a bird she couldn't see sang out as though it would never stop. Listening, she forgot the eroding wall and the exposed roots of trees that were much too close to its edge. She forgot the rudeness, and the attraction, of a stranger. If she looked up, far up, she could see where the tops of the trees met the sky.

She wondered how this view would change with the seasons and found herself impatient to experience them all. Perhaps she'd never realized how badly she'd needed a place to herself, time to herself, until she'd found it.

With a sigh, Maggie moved away from the window. It was time to get down to work if she was to deliver the finished score as promised. She walked down the hall, where the wallpaper was peeling and curled, and turned into what had once been the back parlor. It was now her music room.

Boxes she hadn't even thought of unpacking stood in a pile against one wall. A few odd pieces of furniture that had come with the house sat hidden under dustcovers. The windows were uncurtained, the floor was uncarpeted. There were pale squares intermittently on the walls where pictures had once hung. In the center of the room, glossy and elegant, stood her baby grand. A single box lay open beside it, and from this Maggie took a sheet of staff paper. Tucking a pencil behind her ear, she sat.

For a moment she did nothing else, just sat in the silence while she let the music come and play in her head. She knew what she wanted for this segment— something dramatic, something strong and full of power. Behind her closed eyelids she could see the scene from the film sweep by. It was up to her to underscore, to accentuate, to take the mood and make it music.

Reaching out, she switched on the cassette tape and began.

She let the notes build in strength as she continued to visualize the scene her music would amplify. She only worked on films she had a feeling for. Though the Oscars told her she excelled in this area of work, Maggie's true affection was for the single song—words and music.

Maggie had always compared the composing of a score to the building of a bridge. First came the blueprint, the overall plan. Then the construction had to be done, slowly, meticulously, until each end fit snugly on solid ground, a flawless arch in between. It was a labor of precision.

The single song was a painting, to be created as the mood dictated. The single song could be written from nothing more than a phrasing of words or notes. It could encapsulate mood, emotion or a story in a matter of minutes. It was a labor of love.

When she worked, she forgot the time, forgot everything but the careful structuring of notes to mood. Her fingers moved over the piano keys as she repeated the same segment again and again, changing perhaps no more than one note until her instincts told her it was right. An hour passed, then two. She didn't grow weary or bored or impatient with the constant repetition. Music was her business, but it was also her lover.

She might not have heard the knock if she hadn't paused to rewind the tape. Disoriented, she ignored it, waiting for the maid to answer before she recalled where she was.

No maids, Maggie, she reminded herself. *No gardener, no cook. It's all up to you now.* The thought pleased her. If there was no one to answer to her, she had no one to answer to.

Rising, she went back into the hall and down to the

big front door. She didn't have to develop the country habit of leaving the doors unlocked. In L.A., there'd been servants to deal with bolts and chains and security systems. Maggie never gave them a thought. Taking the knob in both hands, she twisted and tugged. She reminded herself to tell Mr. Bog about the sticking problem as the door swung open.

On the porch stood a tall, prim-looking woman in her early fifties. Her hair was a soft, uniform gray worn with more tidiness than style. Faded blue eyes studied Maggie from behind rose-framed glasses. If this was the welcome wagon lady, Maggie thought after a glance at the unhappy line of the woman's mouth, she didn't seem thrilled with the job. Much too used to strangers' approaches to be reserved, Maggie tilted her head and smiled.

"Hello, can I help you?"

"You are Miss Fitzgerald?" The voice was low and even, as subdued and inoffensive as her plain, pale coatdress.

"Yes, I am."

"I'm Louella Morgan."

It took Maggie a moment; then the name clicked. Louella Morgan, widow of William Morgan, former owner of the house that was now hers. For an instant Maggie felt like an intruder; then she shook the feeling away and extended her hand. "Hello, Mrs. Morgan. Won't you come in?"

"I don't want to disturb you."

"No, please." As she spoke, she opened the door a bit wider. "I met your daughter when we settled on the house."

"Yes, Joyce told me." Louella's gaze darted around and behind Maggie as she stepped over the threshold.

"She never expected to sell so quickly. The property had only been on the market a week."

"I like to think it was fate." Maggie put her weight against the door and pushed until she managed to close it. Definitely a job for Bog, she decided.

"Fate?" Louella turned back from her study of the long, empty hall.

"It just seemed to be waiting for me." Though she found the woman's direct, unsmiling stare odd, Maggie gestured toward the living room. "Come in and sit down," she invited. "Would you like some coffee? Something cold?"

"No, thank you. I'll stay only a minute." Louella did wander into the living room, and though there was a single sofa piled with soft, inviting pillows, she didn't accept Maggie's invitation to sit. She looked at the crumbling wallpaper, the cracked paint and the windows that glistened from Maggie's diligence with ammonia. "I suppose I wanted to see the house again with someone living in it."

Maggie took a look at the almost-empty room. Maybe she'd start stripping off the wallpaper next week. "I guess it'll be a few weeks more before it looks as though someone is."

Louella didn't seem to hear. "I came here as a newlywed." She smiled then, but Maggie didn't see anything happy in it. The eyes, she thought, looked lost, as if the woman had been lost for years. "But then, my husband wanted something more modern, more convenient to town and his business. So we moved, and he rented it out."

Louella focused on Maggie again. "Such a lovely, quiet spot," she murmured. "A pity it's been so neglected over the years."

"It is a lovely spot," Maggie agreed, struggling not to sound as uncomfortable as she felt. "I'm having some work done on both the house and the land…" Her voice trailed off when Louella wandered to the front window and stared out. *Heavens,* Maggie thought, searching for something more to say, *what have I got here?* "Ah, of course I plan to do a lot of the painting and papering and such myself."

"The weeds have taken over," Louella said with her back to the room.

Maggie's brows lifted and fell as she wondered what to do next. "Yes, well, Cliff Delaney was out this afternoon to take a look around."

"Cliff." Louella's attention seemed to focus again as she turned back. The light coming through the uncurtained windows made her seem more pale, more insubstantial. "An interesting young man, rather rough-and-ready, but very clever. He'll do well for you here, for the land. He's a cousin of the Morgans, you know." She paused and seemed to laugh, but very softly. "Then, you'll find many Morgans and their kin scattered throughout the county."

A cousin, Maggie mused. Perhaps he'd been unfriendly because he didn't think the property should've been sold to an outsider. Resolutely, she tried to push Cliff Delaney aside. He didn't have to approve. The land was hers.

"The front lawn was lovely once," Louella murmured.

Maggie felt a stirring of pity. "It will be again. The front's going to be cleared and planted. The back, too." Wanting to reassure her, Maggie stepped closer. Both women stood by the window now. "I'm going to have a rock garden, and there'll be a pond where the gully is on the side."

"A pond?" Louella turned and fixed her with another long stare. "You're going to clear out the gully?"

"Yes." Uncomfortable again, Maggie shifted. "It's the perfect place."

Louella ran a hand over the front of her purse as if she were wiping something away. "I used to have a rock garden. Sweet william and azure Adams. There was wisteria beneath my bedroom window, and roses, red roses, climbing on a trellis."

"I'd like to have seen it," Maggie said gently. "It must've been beautiful."

"I have pictures."

"Do you?" Struck with an idea, Maggie forgot her discomfort. "Perhaps I could see them. They'd help me decide just what to plant."

"I'll see that you get them. You're very kind to let me come in this way." Louella took one last scan of the room. "The house holds memories." When she walked out into the hall, Maggie went with her to tug open the front door again. "Goodbye, Miss Fitzgerald."

"Goodbye, Mrs. Morgan." Her pity stirred again, and Maggie reached out to touch the woman's shoulder. "Please, come again."

Louella looked back, her smile very slight, her eyes very tired. "Thank you."

While Maggie watched, she walked to an old, well-preserved Lincoln, then drove slowly down the hill. Vaguely disturbed, Maggie went back into the music room. She hadn't met many residents of Morganville yet, she mused, but they were certainly an interesting bunch.

The noise brought Maggie out of a sound sleep into a drowsy, cranky state. For a moment, as she tried to bury her head under the pillow, she thought she was in New

York. The groan and roar sounded like a big, nasty garbage truck. But she wasn't in New York, she thought as she surfaced, rubbing her hands over her eyes. She was in Morganville, and there weren't any garbage trucks. Here you piled your trash into the back of your car or pickup and hauled it to the county dump. Maggie had considered this the height of self-sufficiency.

Still, something was out there.

She lay on her back for a full minute, staring up at the ceiling. The sunlight slanted, low and thin, across her newly purchased quilt. She'd never been a morning person, nor did she intend to have country life change that intimate part of her nature. Warily, she turned her head to look at the clock: 7:05 a.m. Good heavens.

It was a struggle, but she pushed herself into a sitting position and stared blankly around the room. Here, too, boxes were piled, unopened. There was a precariously stacked pile of books and magazines on decorating and landscaping beside the bed. On the wall were three fresh strips of wallpaper, an ivory background with tiny violets, that she'd hung herself. More rolls and paste were pushed into a corner. The noise outside was a constant, irritating roar.

Resigned, Maggie got out of bed. She stumbled over a pair of shoes, swore, then went to the window. She'd chosen that room as her own because she could see out over the rolling pitch of what would be her front yard, over the tops of the trees on her own property to the valley beyond.

There was a farmhouse in the distance with a red roof and a smoking chimney. Beside it was a long, wide field that had just been plowed and planted. If she looked farther still, she could see the peaks of mountains faintly blue and indistinct in the morning mist. The window on the connecting wall would give her a view of the intended pond and the line of pines that would eventually be planted.

Maggie pushed the window up the rest of the way, struggling as it stuck a bit. The early-spring air had a pleasant chill. She could still hear the constant low sound of a running engine. Curious, she pressed her face against the screen, only to have it topple out of the window frame and fall to the porch below. One more thing for Mr. Bog to see to, Maggie thought with a sigh as she leaned through the opening. Just then the yellow bulk of a bull-dozer rounded the bend in her lane and broke into view.

So, she thought, watching it inch its way along, leveling and pushing at rock and dirt, Cliff Delaney was a man of his word. She'd received the promised estimate and contract two days after his visit. When she'd called his office, Maggie had spoken to an efficient-sounding woman who'd told her the work would begin the first of the week.

And it's Monday, she reflected, leaning her elbows on the sill. Very prompt. Narrowing her eyes, she looked more closely at the man on top of the bulldozer. His build was too slight, she decided, his hair not quite dark enough. She didn't have to see his face to know it wasn't Cliff. Shrug-ging, she turned away from the window. Why should she have thought Cliff Delaney would work his own machines? And why should she have wanted it to be him? Hadn't she already decided she wouldn't see him again? She'd hired his company to do a job; the job would be done, and she'd write out a check. That was all there was to it.

Maggie attributed her crankiness to the early awaken-ing as she snatched up her robe and headed for the shower.

Two hours later, fortified with the coffee she'd made

for herself and the bulldozer operator, Maggie was on her knees on the kitchen floor. Since she was up at a barbaric hour, she thought it best to do something physical. On the counter above her sat her cassette tape player. The sound of her score, nearly completed, all but drowned out the whine of machinery. She let herself flow with it while words to the title song she'd yet to compose flitted in and out of her mind.

While she let her thoughts flow with the music she'd created, Maggie chipped away at the worn tile on the kitchen floor. True, her bedroom had only one wall partially papered, and only the ceiling in the upstairs bath was painted, *and* there were two more steps to be stripped and lacquered before the main stairway was finished, but she worked in her own way, at her own speed. She found herself jumping from project to project, leaving one partially done and leaping headlong into the next. This way, she reasoned, she could watch the house come together piece by piece rather than have one completed, out-of-place room.

Besides, she'd gotten a peek at the flooring beneath the tile when she'd inadvertently knocked an edge off a corner. Curiosity had done the rest.

When Cliff walked to the back door, he was already annoyed. It was ridiculous for him to be wasting time here, with all the other jobs his firm had in progress. Yet he was here. He'd knocked at the front door for almost five minutes. He knew Maggie was inside, her car was in the driveway, and the bulldozer operator had told him she'd brought out coffee an hour or so before. Didn't it occur to her that someone usually knocked when they wanted something?

The music coming through the open windows caught his attention, and his imagination. He'd never heard the melody before. It was compelling, sexy, moody. A lone piano, no backdrop of strings or brass, but it had the power of making the listener want to stop and hear every note. For a moment he did stop, both disturbed and moved.

Shifting the screen he'd found into his other hand, Cliff started to knock. Then he saw her.

She was on her hands and knees, prying up pieces of linoleum with what looked like a putty knife. Her hair was loose, falling over one shoulder so that her face was hidden behind it. The deep, rich sable brown picked up hints of gold from the sunlight that streamed through the open door and window.

Gray corduroys fit snugly over her hips, tapering down to bare ankles and feet. A vivid red suede shirt was tucked into the waist. He recognized the shirt as one sold in exclusive shops for very exclusive prices. Her wrists and hands looked impossibly delicate against it. Cliff was scowling at them when Maggie got too enthusiastic with the putty knife and scraped her knuckle against a corner of the tile.

"What the hell are you doing?" he demanded, swinging the door open and striding in before Maggie had a chance to react. She'd barely put the knuckle to her mouth in an instinctive move when he was crouched beside her and grabbing her hand.

"It's nothing," she said automatically. "Just a scratch."

"You're lucky you didn't slice it, the way you're hacking at that tile." Though his voice was rough and impatient, his hand was gentle. She left hers in it.

Yes, his hand was gentle, though rough-edged, like his voice, but this time she could see his eyes. They were gray; smoky, secret. Evening mists came to her mind. Mists that were sometimes dangerous but always compelling. That was the sort of mist she'd always believed had cloaked Brigadoon for a hundred years at a time. Maggie decided she could like him, in a cautious sort of way.

"Who'd be stupid enough to put linoleum over this?" With the fingers of her free hand, she skimmed over the hardwood she'd exposed. "Lovely, isn't it? Or it will be when it's sanded and sealed."

"Get Bog to deal with it," Cliff ordered. "You don't know what you're doing."

So everyone said. Maggie withdrew a bit, annoyed by the phrase. "Why should he have all the fun? Besides, I'm being careful."

"I can see that." He turned her hand over so that she saw the scrape over her thumb. It infuriated him to see the delicacy marred. "Doesn't someone in your profession have to be careful with their hands?"

"They're insured," she tossed back. "I think I can probably hit a few chords, even with a wound as serious as this." She pulled her hand out of his. "Did you come here to criticize me, Mr. Delaney, or did you have something else in mind?"

"I came to check on the job." Which wasn't necessary, he admitted. In any case, why should it matter to him if she was careless enough to hurt her hand? She was just a woman who had touched down in his territory and would be gone again before the leaves were full-blown with summer. He was going to have to remember that, and the fact that she didn't interest him personally. Shifting, he picked up the screen he'd dropped when he'd taken her hand. "I found this outside."

It wasn't often her voice took on that regal tone. He seemed to nudge it out of her. "Thank you." She took the screen and leaned it against the stove.

"Your road'll be blocked most of the day. I hope you weren't planning on going anywhere."

Maggie gave him a level look that held a hint of challenge. "I'm not going anywhere, Mr. Delaney."

He inclined his head. "Fine." The music on the tape player changed tempo. It was more hard-driving, more primitive. It seemed something to be played on hot, moonless nights. It drew him, pulled at him. "What is that?" Cliff demanded. "I've never heard it before."

Maggie glanced up at the recorder. "It's a movie score I'm composing. That's the melody for the title song." Because it had given her a great deal of trouble, she frowned at the revolving tape. "Do you like it?"

"Yes."

It was the most simple and most direct answer he'd given her thus far. It wasn't enough for Maggie.

"Why?"

He paused a moment, still listening, hardly aware that they were both still on the floor, close enough to touch. "It goes straight to the blood, straight to the imagination. Isn't that what a song's supposed to do?"

He could have said nothing more perfect. Her smile flashed, a quick, stunning smile that left him staring at her as though he'd been struck by lightning. "Yes. Yes, that's exactly what it's supposed to do." In her enthusiasm she shifted. Their knees brushed. "I'm trying for something very basic with this. It has to set the mood for a film about a passionate relationship—an intensely passionate relationship between two people who seem to have nothing in common but an uncontrollable desire for each other. One of them will kill because of it."

She trailed off, lost in the music and the mood. She could see it in vivid colors—scarlets, purples. She could feel it, like the close, sultry air on a hot summer night. Then she frowned, and as if on cue, the music stopped. From the tape came a sharp, pungent curse, then silence.

"I lost something in those last two bars," she muttered. "It was like—" she gestured with both hands, bringing them up, turning them over, then dropping them again "—something came unmeshed. It has to build to desperation, but it has to be more subtle than that. Passion at the very edge of control."

"Do you always write like that?" Cliff was studying her when she focused on him again, studying her as he had her land—thoroughly, with an eye both for detail and an overview.

She sat back on her haunches, comfortable now with a conversation on her own turf. He could hardly frustrate her in a discussion of music. She'd lived with it, in it, all her life. "Like what?" she countered.

"With the emphasis on mood and emotions rather than notes and timing."

Her brows lifted. With one hand, she pushed back the hair that swept across her cheek. She wore an amethyst on her finger, wine-colored, square. It caught the light, holding it until she dropped her hand again. As she thought it over, it occurred to her that no one, not even her closest associates, had ever defined her style so cleanly. It pleased her, though she didn't know why, that he had done so. "Yes," she said simply.

He didn't like what those big, soft eyes could do to him. Cliff rose. "That's why your music is good."

Maggie gave a quick laugh, not at the compliment, but at the grudging tone with which he delivered it. "So, you can say something nice, after all."

"When it's appropriate." He watched her stand, noting that she moved with the sort of fluidity he'd always associated with tall, willowy women. "I admire your music."

Again, it was the tone, rather than the words, that

spoke to her. This time it touched off annoyance, rather than humor. "And little else that has to do with me."

"I don't know you," Cliff countered.

"You didn't like me when you drove up that hill the other day." With her temper rising, Maggie put her hands on her hips and faced him squarely. "I get the impression you didn't like me years before we met."

That was direct, Cliff decided. Maggie Fitzgerald, glamour girl from the Coast, didn't believe in evasions. Neither did he. "I have a problem with people who live their lives on silver platters. I've too much respect for reality."

"Silver platters," Maggie repeated in a voice that was much, much too quiet. "In other words, I was born into affluence, therefore, I can't understand the real world."

He didn't know why he wanted to smile. Perhaps it was the way color flooded her face. Perhaps it was because she stood nearly a foot beneath him but gave every appearance of being ready to Indian-wrestle and win. Yet he didn't smile. Cliff had the impression that if you gave an inch to this lady, you'd soon be begging to give a mile. "That about sums it up. The gravel for the lane'll be delivered and spread by five."

"Sums it up?" Accustomed to ending a conversation when she chose, Maggie grabbed his arm as he started to turn for the door. "You're a narrow-minded snob, and you know nothing about my life."

Cliff looked down at the delicate hand against his tanned muscled arm. The amethyst glowed up at him. "Miss Fitzgerald, everyone in the country knows about your life."

"That is one of the most unintelligent statements I've ever heard." She made one final attempt to control her temper, then forgot it. "Let me tell you something, Mr. Delaney—" The phone interrupted what would have been a stream of impassioned abuse. Maggie ended up swearing. "You stay there," she ordered as she turned to the wall phone.

Cliff's brows lifted at the command. Slowly, he leaned against the kitchen counter. He'd stay, he decided. Not because she'd told him to, but because he'd discovered he wanted to hear what she had to say.

Maggie yanked the receiver from the wall and barked into it. "Hello."

"Well, it's nice to hear that country life's agreeing with you."

"C.J." She struggled to hold down her temper. She wanted neither questions nor I-told-you-sos. "Sorry, you caught me in the middle of a philosophical discussion." Though she heard Cliff's quick snort of laughter, she ignored it. "Something up, C.J.?"

"Well, I hadn't heard from you in a couple of days—"

"I told you I'd call once a week. Will you stop worrying?"

"You know I can't."

She had to laugh. "No, I know you can't. If it relieves your mind, I'm having the lane fixed even as we speak. The next time you visit, you won't have to worry about your muffler falling off."

"It doesn't relieve my mind," C.J. grumbled. "I have nightmares about that roof caving in on your head. The damn place is falling apart."

"The place is not falling apart." She turned, inadvertently kicking the screen and sending it clattering across the floor. At that moment, her eyes met Cliff's. He was still leaning against the counter, still close enough to the back door to be gone in two strides. But now he was grinning. Maggie looked at the screen, then back at Cliff, and covered her mouth to smother a giggle.

"What was that noise?" C.J. demanded.

"Noise?" Maggie swallowed. "I didn't hear any noise." She covered the mouth of the receiver with her hand when Cliff laughed again. "Shh," she whispered, smiling. "C.J.," she said back into the phone, knowing she needed to distract him, "the score's nearly finished."

"When?" The response was immediate and predictable. She sent Cliff a knowing nod.

"For the most part, it's polished. I'm a little hung up on the title song. If you let me get back to work, the tape'll be in your office next week."

"Why don't you deliver it yourself? We'll have lunch."

"Forget it."

He sighed. "Just thought I'd try. To show you my heart's in the right place, I sent you a present."

"A present? The Godiva?"

"You'll have to wait and see," he said evasively. "It'll be there by tomorrow morning. I expect you to be so touched you'll catch the next plane to L.A. to thank me in person."

"C.J.—"

"Get back to work. And call me," he added, clever enough to know when to retreat and when to advance. "I keep having visions of you falling off that mountain."

He hung up, leaving her, as he often did, torn between amusement and annoyance. "My agent," Maggie said as she replaced the receiver. "He likes to worry."

"I see."

Cliff remained where he was; so did she. That one silly shared moment seemed to have broken down a barrier between them. Now, in its place, was an awkwardness neither of them fully understood. He was suddenly aware of the allure of her scent, of the slender line of her throat. She was suddenly disturbed by his basic masculinity, by the memory of the firm, rough feel of his palm. Maggie cleared her throat.

"Mr. Delaney—"

"Cliff," he corrected.

She smiled, telling herself to relax. "Cliff. We seem to've gotten off on the wrong foot for some reason. Maybe if we concentrate on something that interests us both—my land—we won't keep rubbing each other the wrong way."

He found it an interesting phrase, particularly since he was imagining what it would feel like to run his hands over her skin. "All right," he agreed as he straightened from the counter. He crossed to her, wondering who he was testing, himself or her. When he stopped, she was trapped between him and the stove.

He didn't touch her, but both of them could sense what it would be like. Hard hands, soft skin. Warmth turning quickly to heat. Mouth meeting mouth with confidence, with knowledge, with passion.

"I consider your land a challenge." He said it quietly, his eyes on hers. She didn't think of mists now but of smoke—of smoke and fire. "Which is why I've decided to give this project quite a bit of my personal attention."

Her nerves were suddenly strung tight. Maggie didn't back away, because she was almost certain that was what he wanted. Instead, she met his gaze. If her eyes weren't calm, if they'd darkened with the first traces of desire, she couldn't prevent it. "I can't argue with that."

"No." He smiled a little. If he stayed, even moments longer, he knew he'd find out how her lips tasted. That might be the biggest mistake he'd ever make. Turning, he went to the back door. "Call Bog." He tossed this over his shoulder as he pushed the screen door open. "Your fingers belong on piano keys, not on putty knives."

Maggie let out a long, tense breath when the screen door slammed. Did he do that on purpose, she wondered as she pressed a hand to her speeding heart. Or was it a natural talent of his to turn women into limp rags? Shaking her head, she told herself to forget it. If there was one thing she had experience in, it was in avoiding and evading the professional lothario. She was definitely uninterested in going a few rounds with Morganville's leading contender.

With a scowl, she dropped back to her knees and picked up the putty knife. She began to hack at the tile with a vengeance. Maggie Fitzgerald could take care of herself.

Chapter 3

For the third morning in a row, Maggie was awakened by the sound of men and machinery outside her windows. It occurred to her that she'd hardly had the chance to become used to the quiet when the chaos had started.

The bulldozer had been replaced by chain saws, industrial weed eaters and trucks. While she was far from getting used to the early risings, she was resigned. By seven-fifteen she had dragged herself out of the shower and was staring at her face in the bathroom mirror.

Not so good, she decided, studying her own sleepy eyes. But then she'd been up until two working on the score. Displeased, she ran a hand over her face. She'd never considered pampering her skin a luxury or a waste of time. It was simply something she did routinely, the same way she'd swim twenty laps every morning in California.

She'd been neglecting the basics lately, Maggie decided, squinting at her reflection. Had it been over two months since she'd been in a salon? Ruefully, she tugged at the bangs that swept over her forehead. It was showing, and it was time to do something about it.

After wrapping her still-damp hair in a towel, she pulled open the mirrored medicine-cabinet door. The nearest Elizabeth Arden's was seventy miles away. There were times, Maggie told herself as she smeared on a clay mask, that you had to fend for yourself.

She was just rinsing her hands when the sound of quick, high-pitched barking reached her. C.J.'s present, Maggie thought wryly, wanted his breakfast. In her short terry-cloth robe, which was raveled at the hem, her hair wrapped in a checked towel and the clay mask hardening on her face, she started downstairs to tend to the demanding gift her agent had flown out to her. She had just reached the bottom landing when a knock on the door sent the homely bulldog puppy into a frenzy.

"Calm down," she ordered, scooping him up under one arm. "All this excitement and I haven't had my coffee yet. Give me a break." The pup lowered his head and growled when she pulled on the front door. Definitely city-oriented, she thought, trying to calm the pup. She wondered if C.J. had planned it that way. The door resisted, sticking. Swearing, Maggie set down the dog and yanked with both hands.

The door swung open, carrying her a few steps back with the momentum. The pup dashed through the closest doorway, poking his head around the frame and snarling as if he meant business. Cliff stared at Maggie as she stood, panting, in the hall. She blew out a breath, wondering what could happen next. "I thought country life was supposed to be peaceful."

Cliff grinned, tucking his thumbs in the front pockets of his jeans. "Not necessarily. Get you up?"

"I've been up for quite some time," she said loftily.

"Mmm-hmm." His gaze skimmed over her legs, nicely exposed by the brief robe, before it lingered on the puppy crouched in the doorway. Her legs were longer, he mused, than one would think, considering the overall size of her. "Friend of yours?"

Maggie looked at the bulldog, which was making fierce sounds in his throat while keeping a careful distance. "A present from my agent."

"What's his name?"

Maggie sent the cowering puppy a wry look. "Killer."

Cliff watched the pup disappear behind the wall again. "Very apt. You figure to train him as a guard dog?"

"I'm going to teach him to attack music critics." She lifted a hand to push it through her hair—an old habit—and discovered the towel. Just as abruptly, she remembered the rest of her appearance. One hand flew to her face and found the thin layer of hardened clay. "Oh, my God," Maggie murmured as Cliff's grin widened. "Oh, damn." Turning, she raced for the stairs. "Just a minute." He was treated to an intriguing glimpse of bare thighs as she dashed upstairs.

Ten minutes later, she walked back down, perfectly composed. Her hair was swept back at the side with mother-of-pearl combs; her face was lightly touched with makeup. She'd pulled on the first thing she'd come to in her still-unpacked trunk. The tight black jeans proved an interesting contrast to the bulky white sweatshirt. Cliff sat on the bottom landing, sending the cowardly puppy into ecstasy by rubbing his belly. Maggie frowned down at the crown of Cliff's head.

"You weren't going to say a word, were you?"

He continued to rub the puppy, not bothering to look up. "About what?"

Maggie narrowed her eyes and folded her arms under her breasts. "Nothing. Was there something you wanted to discuss this morning?"

He wasn't precisely sure why that frosty, regal tone appealed to him. Perhaps he just liked knowing he had the ability to make her use it. "Still want that pond?"

"Yes, I still want the pond," she snapped, then gritted her teeth to prevent herself from doing so again. "I don't make a habit of changing my mind."

"Fine. We'll be clearing out the gully this afternoon." Rising, he faced her while the puppy sat expectantly at his feet. "You didn't call Bog about the kitchen floor."

Confusion came and went in her eyes. "How do you—"

"It's easy to find things out in Morganville."

"Well, it's none of your—"

"Hard to keep your business to yourself in small towns," Cliff interrupted again. It amused him to hear her breath huff out in frustration. "Fact is, you're about the top news item in town these days. Everybody wonders what the lady from California's doing up on this mountain. The more you keep to yourself," he added, "the more they wonder."

"Is that so?" Maggie tilted her head and stepped closer. "And you?" she countered. "Do you wonder?"

Cliff knew a challenge when he heard one, and knew he'd answer it in his own time. Impulsively, he cupped her chin in his hand and ran his thumb over her jawline. She didn't flinch or draw back, but became very still. "Nice skin," he murmured, sweeping his gaze along the path his thumb took. "Very nice. You take good care of it, Maggie. I'll take care of your land."

With this, he left her precisely as she was—arms folded, head tilted back, eyes astonished.

* * *

By ten, Maggie decided it wasn't going to be the quiet, solitary sort of day she'd moved to the country for. The men outside shouted above the machinery to make themselves heard. Trucks came and went down her newly graveled lane. She could comfort herself that in a few weeks that part of the disruption would be over.

She took three calls from the Coast from friends who wondered how and what she was doing. By the third call, she was a bit testy from explaining she was scraping linoleum, papering walls, painting woodwork and enjoying it. She left the phone off the hook and went back to her putty knife and kitchen floor.

More than half of the wood was exposed now. The progress excited her enough that she decided to stick with this one job until it was completed. The floor would be beautiful, and, she added, thinking of Cliff's comments, she'd have done it herself.

Maggie had barely scraped off two more inches when there was a knock behind her. She turned her head, ready to flare if it was Cliff Delaney returned to taunt her. Instead, she saw a tall, slender woman of her own age with soft brown hair and pale blue eyes. As Maggie studied Joyce Morgan Agee, she wondered why she hadn't seen the resemblance to Louella before.

"Mrs. Agee." Maggie rose, brushing at the knees of her jeans. "Please, come in. I'm sorry." Her sneakers squeaked as she stepped on a thin layer of old glue. "The floor's a bit sticky."

"I don't mean to disturb your work." Joyce stood uncertainly in the doorway, eyeing the floor. "I would've called, but I was on my way home from Mother's."

Joyce's pumps were trim and stylish. Maggie felt the glue pull at the bottom of her old sneakers. "We can talk outside, if you don't mind." Taking the initiative, Maggie walked out into the sunshine. "Things are a little confused around here right now."

"Yes." They heard one of the workers call to a companion, punctuating his suggestion with good-natured swearing. Joyce glanced over in their direction before she turned back to Maggie. "You're not wasting any time, I see."

"No." Maggie laughed and eyed the crumbling dirt wall beside them. "I've never been very patient. For some reason, I'm more anxious to have the outside the way I want it than the inside."

"You couldn't have picked a better company," Joyce murmured, glancing over at one of the trucks with *Delaney's* on the side.

Maggie followed her gaze but kept her tone neutral. "So I'm told."

"I want you to know I'm really glad you're doing so much to the place." Joyce began to fiddle with the strap of her shoulder bag. "I can hardly remember living here. I was a child when we moved, but I hate waste." With a little smile, she looked around again and shook her head. "I don't think I could live out here. I like being in town, with neighbors close by and other children for my children to play with. Of course, Stan, my husband, likes being available all the time."

It took Maggie a moment; then she remembered. "Oh, your husband's the sheriff, isn't he?"

"That's right. Morganville's a quiet town, nothing like Los Angeles, but it keeps him busy." She smiled, but Maggie wondered why she sensed strain. "We're just not city people."

"No." Maggie smiled, too. "I guess I've discovered I'm not, either."

"I don't understand how you could give up—" Joyce seemed to catch herself. "I guess what I meant was, this must be such a change for you after living in a place like Beverly Hills."

"A change," Maggie agreed. Was she sensing undercurrents here, too, as she had with Louella's dreaminess? "It was one I wanted."

"Yes, well, you know I'm glad you bought the place, and so quickly. Stan was a little upset with my putting it on the market when he was out of town, but I couldn't see it just sitting here. Who knows, if you hadn't come along so fast, he might've talked me out of selling it."

"Then we can both be grateful I saw the sign when I did." Mentally, Maggie was trying to figure out the logistics of the situation. It seemed the house had belonged exclusively to Joyce, without her husband or her mother having any claim. Fleetingly, she wondered why Joyce hadn't rented or sold the property before.

"The real reason I came by, Miss Fitzgerald, is my mother. She told me she was here a few days ago."

"Yes, she's a lovely woman."

"Yes." Joyce looked back toward the men working, then took a deep breath. Maggie no longer had to wonder if she was sensing undercurrents. She was sure of it. "It's more than possible she'll drop in on you again. I'd like to ask you a favor, that is, if she begins to bother you, if you'd tell me instead of her."

"Why should she bother me?"

Joyce let out a sound that was somewhere between fatigue and frustration. "Mother often dwells on the past. She's never completely gotten over my father's death. She makes some people uncomfortable."

Maggie remembered the discomfort she'd felt on and off during Louella's brief visit. Still, she shook her head.

"Your mother's welcome to visit me from time to time, Mrs. Agee."

"Thank you, but you will promise to tell me if—well, if you'd like her to stay away. You see, she'd often come here, even when the place was deserted. I don't want her to get in your way. She doesn't know who you are. That is—" Obviously embarrassed, Joyce broke off. "I mean, Mother doesn't understand that someone like you would be busy."

Maggie remembered the lost eyes, the unhappy mouth. Pity stirred again. "All right, if she bothers me, I'll tell you."

The relief in Joyce's face was quick and very plain. "I appreciate it, Miss Fitzgerald."

"Maggie."

"Yes, well..." As if only more uncertain of her ground, Joyce managed a smile. "I understand that some-one like you wouldn't want to have people dropping by and getting in the way."

Maggie laughed, thinking how many times the phone calls from California had interrupted her that morning. "I'm not a recluse," she told Joyce, though she was no longer completely sure. "And I'm not really very temperamental. Some people even consider me normal."

"Oh, I didn't mean—"

"I know you didn't. Come back when I've done some-thing with that floor, and we'll have some coffee."

"I'd like to, really. Oh, I nearly forgot." She reached into the big canvas bag on her shoulder and pulled out a manila envelope. "Mother said you wanted to see these. Some pictures of the property."

"Yes." Pleased, Maggie took the envelope. She hadn't thought Louella would remember or bother to put them together for her. "I hoped they might give me some ideas."

"Mother said you could keep them as long as you liked." Joyce hesitated, fiddling again with the strap of her bag. "I have to get back. My youngest gets home from kindergarten at noon, and Stan sometimes comes home for lunch. I haven't done a thing to the house. I hope I see you sometime in town."

"I'm sure you will." Maggie tucked the envelope under her arm. "Give my best to your mother."

Maggie started back into the house, but as she put her hand on the doorknob, she noticed Cliff crossing to Joyce. Curiosity had her stopping to watch as Cliff took both the brunette's hands in his own. Though she couldn't hear the conversation over the din of motors, it was obvious that they knew each other well. There was a gentleness on Cliff's face Maggie hadn't seen before, and something she interpreted as concern. He bent down close, as if Joyce were speaking very softly, then touched her hair. The touch of a brother? Maggie wondered. Or a lover?

As she watched, Joyce shook her head, apparently fumbling with the door handle before she got into the car. Cliff leaned into the window for a moment. Were they arguing? Maggie wondered. Was the tension she sensed real or imaginary? Fascinated with the silent scene being played out in her driveway, Maggie watched as Cliff withdrew from the window and Joyce backed out to drive away. Before she could retreat inside, Cliff turned, and their gazes locked.

There were a hundred feet separating them, and the air was full of the sounds of men and machines. The sun was strong enough to make her almost too warm in the sweatshirt, yet she felt one quick, unexpected chill race up her spine. Perhaps it was hostility she felt. Maggie tried to tell herself it was hostility and not the first dangerous flutters of passion.

There was a temptation to cross those hundred feet and test both of them. Even the thought of it stirred her blood. He didn't move. He didn't take his eyes from her. With fingers gone suddenly numb, Maggie twisted the handle and went inside.

Two hours later, Maggie went out again. She'd never been one to retreat from a challenge, from her emotions or from trouble. Cliff Delaney seemed connected with all three. While she'd scraped linoleum, Maggie had lectured herself on letting Cliff intimidate her for no reason other than his being powerfully male and sexy.

And different, she'd admitted. Different from most of the men she'd encountered in her profession. He didn't fawn—far from it. He didn't pour on the charm. He wasn't impressed with his own physique, looks or sophistication. It must have been that difference that had made her not quite certain how to handle him.

A very direct, very frank business approach, she decided as she circled around the back of the house. Maggie paused to look at the bank fronting her house.

The vines, briars and thick sumac were gone. Piles of rich, dark topsoil were being spread over what had been a tangled jungle of neglect. The tree that had leaned toward her house was gone, stump and all. Two men, backs glistening with sweat, were setting stone in a low-spreading wall where the edge of the slope met the edge of the lawn.

Cliff Delaney ran a tight ship, Maggie concluded, and made her way through the new dirt toward the side yard. Here, too, the worst had been cleared out. An enormous bearded man in bib overalls sat atop a big yellow backhoe as easily as another might sit in an armchair. At the push of a lever, the digger went down into the gully, bit into earth and rock and came up full.

Maggie shaded her eyes and watched the procedure while the puppy circled her legs and snarled at everything in sight. Each time the digger would open its claws to drop its load, the dog would send up a ruckus of barks. Laughing, Maggie crouched down to scratch his ears and soothe him.

"Don't be a coward, Killer. I won't let it get you."

"I wouldn't get any closer," Cliff said from behind her.

She turned her head, squinting against the sun. "This is close enough." Disliking the disadvantage of looking up and into the sun, Maggie stood. "You seem to be making progress."

"We need to get the plants in and the wall of this thing solid—" he gestured toward the gully "—before the rain hits. Otherwise, you'll have a real mess on your hands."

"I see." Because he wore the frustratingly tinted glasses again, she turned from him to watch the backhoe work. "You certainly have a large staff."

Cliff's thumbs went into his pockets. "Large enough." He'd told himself he'd imagined that powerful sexual pull hours before. Now, feeling it again, he couldn't deny it.

She wasn't what he wanted, yet he wanted her. She wasn't what he would have chosen, yet he was choosing her. He could turn away logic until he'd learned what it was like to touch her.

Maggie was very aware of how close they stood. The stirring she'd felt hours before began to build again, slowly, seductively, until she felt her whole body tense with it. She understood that you could want someone you didn't know, someone you passed on the street. It all had to do with chemistry, but her chemistry had never reacted this way before. She had a wild urge to turn into his arms, to demand or offer the fulfillment, or whatever it was, that simmered between them. It was something that offered excitement and pleasure she had only glimpsed before. So she did turn, completely uncertain as to what she would say.

"I don't think I like what's happening here."

Cliff didn't pretend to misunderstand her. Neither of their minds was on the pond or the machine. "Do you have a choice?"

Maggie frowned, wishing she was more certain of her moves. He wasn't like the men she'd known before; therefore, the standard rules didn't apply. "I think so. I moved here because it was where I wanted to live, where I wanted to work. But I also moved here because I wanted to be on my own. I intend to do all those things."

Cliff studied her a moment, then gave the backhoe driver an absent wave as he shut off the machine to take his lunch break. "I took this job because I wanted to work this land. I intend to do it."

Though she didn't feel the slightest lessening of tension, Maggie nodded. "Then we understand each other."

As she started to turn away, Cliff put a hand on her shoulder, holding her still. "I think we both understand quite a bit."

The muscles in her stomach tightened and loosened like a nervous fist. With his fingers so light on the bulky sweatshirt, she shouldn't have felt anything. But hundreds of pulses sprang to life in her body. The air seemed to grow closer, hotter, the sounds of men more distant. "I don't know what you mean."

"Yes, you do."

Yes, she did. "I don't know anything about you," Maggie managed.

Cliff caught the tips of her hair in his fingers. "I can't say the same."

Maggie's temper flared, though she knew when she

was being baited. "So, you believe everything you read in the tabloids and glossies." She tossed her head to free her hair from his fingers. "I'm surprised that a man who's obviously so successful and talented could be so ignorant."

Cliff acknowledged the hit with a nod. "I'm surprised a woman who's obviously so successful and talented could be so foolish."

"Foolish? What the hell's that supposed to mean?"

"It seems foolish to me to encourage the press to report every area of your life."

She clenched her teeth and tried deep breathing. Neither worked. "I don't encourage the press to do anything."

"You don't discourage them," Cliff countered.

"Discouragement *is* encouragement," she tossed back. Folding her arms under her breasts as she'd done earlier, she stared out over the open gully. "Why am I defending myself?" she muttered. "You don't know anything about it. I don't need you to know anything about it."

"I know you gave an interview about yourself and your husband weeks after his death." He heard her quick intake of breath even as he cursed himself for saying something so personal, and so uncalled-for.

"Do you have any idea how the press hammered at me during those weeks?" Her voice was low and strained, and she no longer looked at him. "Do you know all the garbage they were printing?" Her fingers tightened on her own arms. "I chose a reporter I could trust, and I gave the most honest, most straightforward interview I could manage, knowing it was my only chance to keep things from sinking lower. That interview was for Jerry. It was the only thing I had left to give him."

He'd wanted to prod, perhaps even to prick, but he

hadn't wanted to hurt. "I'm sorry." Cliff put his hand on her shoulder again, but she jerked away.

"Forget it."

This time he took both of her shoulders, turning her firmly to face him. "I don't forget blows below the belt, especially when I'm the one doing the punching."

She waited to speak until she was certain she had some control again. "I've survived hits before. My advice to you is not to criticize something you have no capacity for understanding."

"I apologized." He didn't release her shoulders when she tried to draw away. "But I'm not very good at following advice."

Maggie became still again. Somehow they had gotten closer, so that now their thighs brushed. The combination of anger and desire was becoming too strong to ignore. "Then you and I don't have any more to say to each other."

"You're wrong." His voice was very quiet, very compelling. "We haven't begun to say all there is to say."

"You work for me—"

"I work for myself," Cliff corrected.

She understood that kind of pride, admired it. But admiration wouldn't remove his hands from her shoulders. "I'm paying you to do a job."

"You're paying my company. That's business."

"It's going to be our only business."

"Wrong again," he murmured, but released her.

Maggie opened her mouth to hurl something back at him, but the dog began to bark in quick, excited yelps. She decided turning her back on him to investigate her pet was a much grander insult than the verbal one she'd planned. Without a word, she began to make her way around the slope of the gully to the pile of earth and rock and debris the backhoe had dumped.

"All right, Killer." The going was so rough that she swore under her breath as she stumbled over stones. "You'll never find anything worthwhile in that pile, anyway."

Ignoring her, the puppy continued to dig, his barking muffled as his nose went farther in, his backside wriggling with either effort or delight in the new game.

"Cut it out." She bent to pull him out of the heap and ended up sitting down hard. "Damn it, Killer." Staying as she was, she grabbed the dog with one hand, dragging him back and unearthing a small avalanche of rock.

"Will you be careful?" Cliff shouted from above her, knowing she'd been lucky not to have one of the rocks bounce off her shin.

"It's the stupid dog!" Maggie shouted back as she lost her grip on him again. "God knows what he thinks is so fascinating about this mess. Nothing but dirt and rocks," she muttered, pushing at the pile that had landed near her hip.

"Well, grab him and get back up here before you're both hurt."

"Yeah," she muttered under her breath. "You're a big help." Disgusted, she started to struggle up when her fingers slid into the worn, rounded rock her hand had rested on. Hollow, she thought curiously. Her attention torn between the gully and the dog's unrelenting barks, Maggie glanced down.

Then she began to scream, loud and long enough to send the puppy racing for cover.

Cliff's first thought as he raced down the slope to her was snakes. When he reached her, he dragged her up and into his arms in an instinctive move of protection. She'd stopped screaming, and though her breathing was shallow, Maggie grabbed his shirt before he could carry her back up the slope. "Bones," she whispered. Closing her eyes, she dropped her head on his shoulder. "Oh, my God."

Cliff looked down and saw what the machine and dog had unearthed. Mixed with the rock and debris was a pile of what might have been mistaken for long white sticks layered with dirt.

But lying on the bones, inches from where Maggie had sat, was a human skull.

Chapter 4

"I'm all right." Maggie sat at the kitchen table and gripped the glass of water Cliff had handed her. When the pain in her fingers finally registered, she relaxed them a bit. "I feel like an idiot, screaming that way."

She was still pale, he noted. Though the hands on the glass were steady now, they were still white at the knuckles. Her eyes were wide and shocked, suddenly too big for the rest of her face. He started to stroke her hair, then stuck his own hands in his pockets. "A natural enough reaction."

"I guess." She looked up and managed a shaky smile. She was cold, but prayed she wouldn't begin to shiver in front of him. "I've never found myself in that sort of…situation before."

Cliff lifted a brow. "Neither have I."

"No?" Somehow she'd wanted to think it had happened before. If it had, it might make it less horrible—and less personal. She looked down at the floor, not realizing until that moment that the dog lay across her feet, whimpering. "But don't you dig up a lot of—" She hesitated, not sure just how she wanted to phrase it. "Things—" Maggie decided weakly "—in your line of work?"

She was reaching, Cliff thought, and whether she knew it or not, those big brown eyes were pleading with him for some sort of easy explanation. He didn't have one to give her. "Not that kind of thing."

Their gazes held for one long, silent moment before Maggie nodded. If there was one thing she'd learned in the hard, competitive business she'd chosen, it was to handle things as they came. "So, neither of us has a tidy explanation." The little expulsion of breath was the last sign of weakness she intended to show him. "I guess the next step is the police."

"Yeah." The more determined she became to be calm, the more difficult it became for him. She was weakening something in him that he was determined to keep objective. His hands were balled into fists inside his pockets in his struggle not to touch her. Distance was the quickest defense. "You'd better call," Cliff said briskly. "I'll go out and make sure the crew keeps clear of the gully."

Again, her answer was a nod. Maggie watched as he crossed to the screen door and pushed it open. There he hesitated. He'd have cursed if he'd understood what it was he wanted to swear at. When he looked back, she saw the concern on his face she'd seen when he'd spoken to Joyce. "Maggie, are you all right?"

The question, and the tone, helped her to settle. Perhaps it had something to do with her knowing just what it was like to be pressured by another's weakness. "I will be. Thanks." She waited until the screen door banged shut behind him before she dropped her head on the table.

Good heavens, what had she walked into here? People didn't find bodies in their front yard. C.J. would've said it was totally uncivilized. Maggie choked back a hysterical giggle and straightened. The one unarguable fact she had to face was that she had found one. Now she had to deal with it. Taking deep breaths, she went to the phone and dialed the operator.

"Get me the police," she said quickly.

A few minutes later, Maggie went outside. Though she'd hoped the practical routine of reporting what she'd found would calm her, it hadn't worked. She didn't go near the gully, but she found she couldn't sit inside, waiting alone. Circling around the front of the house, she found a convenient rock and sat. The puppy stretched out in the patch of sunlight at her feet and went to sleep.

She could almost believe she'd imagined what she'd seen in that pile of dirt and rock. It was too peaceful here for anything so stark. The air was too soft, the sun too warm. Her land might be unruly, but it held a serenity that blocked out the harsher aspects of life.

Was that why she'd chosen it, Maggie wondered. Because she wanted to pretend there wasn't any real madness in the world? Here she could cocoon herself from so many of the pressures and demands that had threaded through her life for so long. Was this spot the home she'd always wanted, or was it in reality just an escape for her? She squeezed her eyes shut. If that were true, it made her weak and dishonest, two things she couldn't tolerate. Why had it taken this incident to make her question what she hadn't questioned before? As she tried to find her tranquillity again, a shadow fell over her. Opening her eyes, Maggie looked up at Cliff.

For some reason it toughened her. She wouldn't admit

to him that she'd begun to doubt herself or her motives. No, not to him.

"Someone should be here soon." She linked her folded hands over one knee and looked back into the woods.

"Good." Several minutes passed while they both remained silent, looking into the trees.

Eventually, Cliff crouched down beside her. Funny, but he thought that she looked more apt to fall apart now than she had when he'd carried her into her kitchen. Reaction, he decided, had different speeds for different people. He wanted to hold her again, hard and close, as he'd done all too briefly before. The contact had made something strong and sultry move through him. Like her music—something like her music.

He wished like hell he'd turned down the job and had walked away the first time he'd seen her. Cliff looked past her to the slope that led to the gully.

"You talked to Stan?"

"Stan?" Blankly, Maggie stared at Cliff's set profile. At that moment, he was close enough to reach but seemed miles away. "Oh, the sheriff." She wished he'd touch her, just for a moment. Just a hand on her. "No, I didn't call him. I called the operator and asked for the police. She connected me with the state police in Hagerstown." She lapsed into silence, waiting for him to make some comment on her typical city response.

"Probably for the best," Cliff murmured. "I let the crew go. It'll be less confusing."

"Oh." She must've been in a daze not to notice that the trucks and men were gone. When she forced herself to look, she saw that the backhoe remained, sitting on the rise above the gully, big and yellow and silent. The sun was warm on her back. Her skin was like ice. Time to snap out of it, Maggie told herself, and straightened her shoulders. "Yes, I'm sure you're right. Should I call your office when the police say it's all right to start work again?" Her voice was businesslike. Her throat was dry with the thought of being left alone, completely alone, with what was down by the gully.

Cliff turned his head. Without speaking, he took off his sunglasses so that their eyes met. "Thought I'd hang around."

Relief washed over her. Maggie knew it must've shown in her face, but she didn't have the will to put pride first. "I'd like you to. It's stupid, but—" She glanced over in the direction of the gully.

"Not stupid."

"Maybe weak's a better word," she mumbled, trying to smile.

"Human." Despite his determination not to, Cliff reached out and took her hand. The touch, one designed to comfort, to reassure her, set off a chain reaction of emotion too swift to stop.

It ran through her head that she should rise swiftly and go inside. He might stop her, or he might let her go. Maggie didn't ask herself which she wanted, nor did she move. Instead, she sat where she was, meeting his gaze and letting the sensation of torrid, liquid heat flow through her. Nothing else existed. Nothing else mattered.

She felt each of his fingers tense individually on her hand. There was a sense of power there; whether it was his or hers, she wasn't sure. Perhaps it was the melding of both. She saw his eyes darken until the irises were only shades lighter than the pupils. It was as if he were looking through her, into her chaotic thoughts. In the quiet of midafternoon, she heard each breath he drew in and expelled. The sound stirred the excitement that vibrated in the air between them.

Together they moved toward each other until mouth molded itself to mouth.

Intensity. She hadn't known anything between two people could be so concentrated, such pure sensation. She understood that if years passed, if she was blind and deaf, she would know this man just by the touch of his lips. In one instant she became intimate with the shape of his mouth, the taste and texture of his tongue. Her mouth was on his, his hand on hers, and they touched nowhere else. In that moment there was no need to.

There was an aggressiveness, even a harshness, to the kiss that Maggie hadn't expected. It held none of the sweetness, the hesitation, that first kisses often do, yet she didn't back away from it. Perhaps it was all part of the attraction that had begun the moment he'd stepped from the truck. Different, yes, he was different from the other men who'd touched her life—different still from the man she'd shared her body with. She'd known that from the first encounter. Now, with his mouth stirring her senses, she found herself grateful for it. She wanted nothing to be the same as it had been, no reminders of what she'd had once and lost. This man wouldn't pamper or worship. He was strong enough to want strength in return. She felt his tongue tangle with hers, probing deeper. Maggie reveled in the demands.

It was easy, almost too easy, to forget her delicate build, her fragile looks, when her mouth was so ardent on his. He should've known there'd be deep, restless passion in a woman who created music with such sexuality. But how could he have known that passion would call to him as though he'd been waiting for years?

It was much too easy to forget she wasn't the kind of woman he wanted in his life when her taste was filling him. Again, he should have known she'd have the power to make a man toss aside all logic, all intellect. Her lips were warm, moist, the taste as pungent as the scent of newly turned earth around them. The urge rose to take her in his arms and fulfill, there under the clear afternoon sun, all the needs that welled inside him. Cliff drew back, resisting that final painful twist of desire.

Breathless, throbbing, Maggie stared at him. Could that one searing meeting of lips have moved him as it had moved her? Were his thoughts swimming as hers were? Was his body pulsing with wild, urgent needs? She could tell nothing from his face. Though his eyes were fixed on hers, their expression was unreadable. If she asked, would he tell her that he, too, had never known a wave of passion so overwhelming or so mesmerizing? She would ask, and would know, as soon as she had the voice to question. As she sat, struggling to catch her breath, the events of the day came flashing back into her mind. Abruptly, Maggie sprang to her feet.

"God, what are we doing?" she demanded. With a hand that shook, she pushed the hair away from her face. "How can we sit here like this when that—that thing's only a few yards away?"

Cliff took her arm, turning her back to face him. "What does one have to do with the other?"

"Nothing. I don't know." With her insides churning, she looked up at him. Her emotions had always been too dominant. Though she knew it, Maggie had never been able to change it. It had been years since she'd really tried. Confusion, distress, passion, radiated from her as tangible things. "What we found, it's dreadful, unbelievably dreadful, and a few moments ago I was sitting there wondering what it would be like to make love with you."

Something flashed in his eyes, quickly controlled.

Unlike Maggie, Cliff had learned long ago to channel his emotions and keep them to himself. "You obviously don't believe in evading the issue."

"Evasions take too much time and effort." After letting out a long breath, Maggie managed to match his even, casual tone. "Listen, I didn't expect that sort of— eruption," she decided. "I suppose I'm wound up over all of this, and a bit too susceptible."

"Susceptible." Her choice of words made him smile. Somehow, when she became cool and calm, he became tempted to prod. Deliberately, he lifted a hand and ran his fingertips down her cheek. Her skin was still warm with desire. "I wouldn't have described you that way. You seem to be a woman who knows what she wants and how to get it."

If he'd wanted to fire her up, he'd found the perfect key. "Stop it." In one sharp move, she pushed his hand from her face. "I've said it before—you don't know me. Every time we're together, I become more certain that I don't want you to. You're a very attractive man, Cliff. And very unlikable. I stay away from people I don't like."

It occurred to him that he'd never gone out of his way to argue with anyone before. A lot of things were changing. "In a small community like this, it's hard to stay away from anyone."

"I'll put more effort into it."

"Nearly impossible."

She narrowed her eyes and fought to keep her lips from curving. "I'm very good when I put my mind to something."

"Yeah." He put his sunglasses back on. When he grinned, the deliberate cockiness was almost too appealing to resist. "I bet you are."

"Are you trying to be smart, or are you trying to be charming?"

"I never had to try to be either one."

"Think again." Because she was having trouble controlling the grin, Maggie turned away. As luck would have it, she found herself staring out over the gully. A chill raced up her spine. Swearing, she folded her arms under her breasts. "I can't believe it," she muttered. "I can't believe I'm standing here having a ridiculous conversation when there's a—" She found she couldn't say it and detested herself. "I think the whole world must be going mad."

He wasn't going to let her get shaky on him again. When she was vulnerable, she was much more dangerous. "What's down there's been there for a long time." His voice was brisk, almost hard. "It doesn't have anything to do with you."

"It's my land," Maggie tossed back. She whirled around, eyes glowing, chin angled. "So it has everything to do with me."

"Then you better stop shaking every time you think about it."

"I'm not shaking."

Without a word, he drew her hand away from her elbow so they could both see the tremor. Furious, Maggie snatched it away again. "When I want you to touch me, I'll let you know," she said between her teeth.

"You already have."

Before she could think of an appropriate response, the dog scrambled up and began to bark furiously. Seconds later, they both heard the sound of an approaching car.

"He might make you a decent watchdog, after all," Cliff said mildly. The pup bounded around in circles like a mad thing, then hid behind the rock. "Then again…"

As the official car came into sight, he bent down to pat

the dog on the head before he walked toward the end of the drive. Maggie hurried to keep pace. Her land, her problem, her responsibility, she told herself. *She'd* do the talking.

A trooper climbed out of the car, adjusted his hat, then broke into a grin. "Cliff, didn't expect to see you out here."

"Bob." Because the greeting didn't include a handshake, Maggie assumed the men knew each other well and saw each other often. "My company's handling the landscaping."

"The old Morgan place." The trooper looked around with interest. "Been a while since I was back here. You dig up something we should know about?"

"So it seems."

"It's the Fitzgerald place now," Maggie cut in briskly.

The trooper touched the brim of his hat and started to make a polite comment. His eyes widened when he took his first good look at her. "Fitzgerald," he repeated. "Hey, aren't you Maggie Fitzgerald?"

She smiled, though the recognition, with Cliff beside her, made her uncomfortable. "Yes, I am."

"I'll be damned. You look just like your pictures in all the magazines. I guess there isn't a song you've written I can't hum. You bought the Morgan place."

"That's right."

He pushed the hat back on his head in a gesture that made her think of cowboys. "Wait till I tell my wife. We had 'Forever' played at our wedding. You remember, Cliff. Cliff was best man."

Maggie tilted her head to look at the man beside her. "Really?"

"If you've finished being impressed," Cliff said mildly, "you might want to take a look at what's down by the gully."

Bob grinned again, all amiability. "That's why I'm here." They began to walk toward the gully together. "You know, it isn't easy to tell what's from a human and what's from an animal just by looking. Could be, ma'am, that you uncovered a deer."

Maggie glanced over at Cliff. She could still feel the way her hand had slid into the hollow opening of what she'd taken for a rock. "I wish I could think so."

"Down here," Cliff said without acknowledging the look. "The going's rough." In a smooth, calculated move, he blocked Maggie's way before she could start down. It forced her to pull up short and grab his arm for support. "Why don't you wait here?"

It would've been easy to do so. Much too easy. "It's my land," Maggie said, and, brushing by him, led the way down herself. "The dog started digging in this pile." She heard the nerves in her own voice and fought against them. "I came down to pull him away, and that's when I saw…" Trailing off, she pointed.

The trooper crouched down, letting out a low whistle. "Holy hell," he murmured. He turned his head, but it was Cliff he looked at, not Maggie. "It doesn't look like you dug up any deer."

"No." In a casual move, Cliff shifted so that he blocked Maggie's view. "What now?"

Bob rose. He wasn't smiling now, but Maggie thought she detected a gleam of excitement. "I'll have to call the investigation section. Those boys are going to want to take a look at this."

Maggie didn't speak when they climbed up the slope again. She waited in silence while the trooper went to his car to radio in his report. When she did speak, she deliberately avoided the reason they were all standing outside in the middle of the afternoon.

"So you two know each other," she commented as though it were any normal remark made on any normal day.

"Bob and I went to school together." Cliff watched a big black crow swoop over the trees. He was remembering the look on Maggie's face the moment before she'd begun to scream. "He ended up marrying one of my cousins a couple of years ago."

Bending over, she plucked a wildflower and began to shred it. "You have a lot of cousins."

He shrugged. The crow landed and was still. "Enough."

"A few Morgans."

That caught his attention. "A few," he said slowly. "Why?"

"I wondered if it was your connection with them that made you resent my having this land."

Cliff wondered why, when he normally respected candor, it annoyed him from her. "No."

"But you did resent it," Maggie insisted. "You resented me before you even saw me."

He had, and perhaps the resentment had grown since he'd had a taste of her. "Joyce had the right to sell this property whenever, and to whomever, she wanted."

Maggie nodded, looking down to where the puppy scrambled in the new dirt. "Is Joyce a cousin, too?"

"What are you getting at?"

Lifting her head, Maggie met his impatient look. "I'm just trying to understand small towns. After all, I'm going to be living here."

"Then the first thing you should learn is that people don't like questions. They might volunteer more information than you want to hear, but they don't like to be asked."

Maggie acknowledged this with a lift of a brow. "I'll

keep that in mind." Rather pleased that she'd annoyed him, Maggie turned to the trooper as he approached.

"They're sending out a team." He glanced from her to Cliff, then over his friend's shoulder toward the gully. "Probably be here for a while, then take what they find with them."

"What then?"

Bob brought his attention back to Maggie. "Good question." He shifted his feet as he considered it. "To tell you the truth, I've never been in on anything like this before, but my guess would be they'd ship everything off to the medical examiner in Baltimore. He'd have to check the, ah, everything out before they could start an investigation."

"Investigation?" she repeated, and felt something tighten in her throat. "What kind of investigation?"

The trooper ran his thumb and forefinger down his nose. "Well, ma'am, as far as I can see, there's no reason for anything like that to be buried down in that gully unless—"

"Unless someone buried it there," Cliff finished.

Maggie stared out into the peaceful spread of greening wood across the lane. "I think we could all use some coffee," she murmured. Without waiting for an acknowledgment, she went back toward the house.

Bob took off his hat and wiped at the sweat on his forehead. "This is one for the books."

Cliff followed his friend's long look at the woman climbing the rickety front steps. "Which? Her or that?" With one hand he gestured toward the gully.

"Both." Bob took out a pack of gum and carefully unwrapped a piece. "First place, what's a woman like her, a celebrity, doing holed up here in the woods?"

"Maybe she decided she likes trees."

Bob slipped the gum into his mouth. "Must be ten, twelve acres of them here."

"Twelve."

"Looks to me like she bought more than she bargained for. Holy hell, Cliff, we haven't had anything like this down in this end of the county since crazy Mel Stickler set those barn fires. Now, in the city—"

"Taken to the fast pace, have you?"

Bob knew Cliff well enough to catch both the dig and the humor. "I like some action," he said easily. "Speaking of which, the lady songwriter smells like heaven."

"How's Carol Ann?"

Bob grinned at the mention of his wife. "Just fine. Look, Cliff, if a man doesn't look, and appreciate, he'd better see a doctor. You're not going to tell me you haven't noticed just how nice that lady's put together."

"I've noticed." He glanced down at the rock beside him. She'd sat there when he'd kissed her. It wouldn't take any effort to remember each separate sensation that had run through him in that one moment. "I'm more interested in her land."

Bob let out a quick laugh. "If you are, you've done a lot of changing since high school. Remember when we used to come up here—those blond twins, the cheer-leaders whose parents rented the place for a while? That old Chevy of yours lost its muffler right there on that turn."

"I remember."

"We had some interesting walks up there in the woods," Bob reminisced. "They were the prettiest girls in school till their daddy got transferred and they moved away."

"Who moved in after that?" Cliff wondered, half to himself. "That old couple from Harrisburg—the Fara-days. They were here a long time, until the old man died and she went to live with her kids." Cliff narrowed his eyes as he tried to remember. "That was a couple months before Morgan ran off the bridge. Nobody's lived here since."

Bob shrugged; then both of them looked toward the gully. "Guess it's been ten years since anybody lived here."

"Ten years," Cliff repeated. "A long time."

They both looked over at the sound of a car. "The investigators," Bob said, adjusting his hat again. "They'll take over now."

From the corner of the porch, Maggie watched the proceedings. She'd decided that if the police crew needed her, they'd let her know. It appeared to her that they knew their business. She would just be in the way down there, Maggie reasoned as she drank another cup of black coffee.

She watched them shovel, sift and systematically bag what they'd come for. Maggie told herself that once it was off her property, she'd forget it. It would no longer concern her. She wished she could believe it. What was now being transferred into plastic bags had once been a living being. A man or a woman who'd had thoughts and feelings had lain, alone, only yards from what was now her home. No, she didn't believe she'd be able to forget that.

Before it was over, she'd have to know who that person had been, why they had died and why their grave had been on her land. She'd have to have the answers if she were to live in the home she'd chosen. She finished the last swallow of coffee as one of the police crew broke away from the group and came toward the porch. Maggie went to the steps to meet him.

"Ma'am." He nodded to her but, to her relief, didn't offer his hand. Instead, he took out a badge, flashing the cover up briefly. "I'm Lieutenant Reiker."

She thought he looked like a middle-aged accountant and wondered if he carried a gun under his jacket. "Yes, Lieutenant."

"We're just about finished up. Sorry for the inconvenience."

"That's all right." She gripped her hands together over the cup and wished she could go inside, to her music.

"I've got the trooper's report, but I wonder if you could tell me how you happened to find the remains."

Remains, Maggie thought with a shudder. It seemed a very cold word. For the second time, she related her story of the puppy's digging. She did so calmly now, without a tremor.

"You just bought the place?"

"Yes, I only moved in a few weeks ago."

"And you hired Delaney to do some landscaping."

"Yes." She looked down to where Cliff stood talking to another of the team. "The handyman I hired recommended him."

"Mmm-hmm." In a very casual way, the investigator took notes. "Delaney tells me you wanted the gully there dug out for a pond."

Maggie moistened her lips. "That's right."

"Nice place for one," he said conversationally. "I'd like to ask you to hold off on that for a while, though. We might need to come back and take another look around."

Maggie's hands twisted on the empty cup. "All right."

"What we'd like to do is block off that area." He hitched at his belt, then settled one foot on the step above the other. "Some chicken wire," he said easily, "to keep your dog and any other stray animal from digging around in there."

And people, Maggie thought, deciding it didn't take a genius to read between the lines. Before the day was over, this would be the biggest news flash in the county. She was learning fast. "Do whatever you need to do."

"We appreciate the cooperation, Miss Fitzgerald." He twirled the pen in his fingers, hesitating.

"Is there something else?"

"I know it's a bad time," he said with a sheepish smile, "but I can't pass it up. Would you mind signing my pad? I was a big fan of your mother's, and I guess I know most all of your songs, too."

Maggie laughed. It was far better to laugh. The day had been a series of one ludicrous event after another. "Of course." She took the offered pad and pen. "Would you like me to say anything special?"

"Maybe you could just write—to my good friend Harvey."

Before she could oblige, she glanced up and caught Cliff's eyes on her. She saw his lips twist into something between a sneer and a smile. With a silent oath, she signed the pad and handed it back.

"I don't know much about this kind of thing," she began briskly, "but I'd appreciate it if you kept me informed on whatever's being done."

"We'll have the medical examiner's report in a few days." Pocketing his pad, the investigator became solidly professional again. "We'll all know more then. Thanks for your time, Miss Fitzgerald. We'll be out of your way as soon as we can."

Though she felt Cliff's gaze still on her, Maggie didn't look over. Instead, she turned and walked back into the house. Moments later, music could be heard through the open windows.

Cliff remained where he was, though he'd answered all the questions that he could answer. His thoughts were focused on the sounds coming from the music room. It wasn't one of her songs, he concluded, but something from the classics, something that required speed, concentration and passion. Therapy, he wondered, frowning up at the window. With a shrug, he started toward his car. It wasn't his concern if the lady was upset. Hadn't she told him she'd moved back here to be on her own?

Turning his head, he saw the investigators preparing to leave. Within moments, he reflected, she'd be alone. The music pouring out of the windows was tense, almost desperate. Swearing, Cliff stuffed his keys back in his pocket and strode toward the steps.

She didn't answer his knock. The music played on. Without giving it a second thought, he pushed open the front door. The house vibrated with the storm coming from the piano. Following it into the music room, he watched her from the doorway.

Her eyes were dark, her head was bent, though he didn't think she even saw the keys. Talent? There was no denying it, any more than there could be any denying her tension or her vulnerability. Later, he might ask himself why all three made him uncomfortable.

Perhaps he did want to comfort her, he told himself. He'd do the same for anyone, under the circumstances. She didn't have to mean anything to him for him to want to offer a diversion. Strays and wounded birds had always been weaknesses of his. Dissatisfied with his own logic, Cliff waited until she'd finished.

Maggie looked up, startled to see him in the doorway. Damn her nerves, she thought, carefully folding her hands in her lap. "I thought you'd gone."

"No. They have."

She tossed the hair out of her eyes and hoped she looked composed. "Was there something else?"

"Yeah." He walked over to run a finger over the piano

keys. No dust, he noted, in a house nearly choked with it. Her work was obviously of first importance.

When he didn't elaborate, Maggie frowned. Cliff preferred the impatience he saw in her eyes now. "What?"

"I had a steak in mind."

"I beg your pardon?"

The cool response made his lips curve. Yes, he definitely preferred her this way. "I haven't eaten."

"Sorry." Maggie began to straighten her sheet music. "I don't happen to have one handy."

"There's a place about ten miles out of town." He took her arm to draw her to her feet. "I have a feeling they'd treat a steak better than you would, anyway."

She pulled away, stood her ground and studied him. "We're going out to dinner?"

"That's right."

"Why?"

He took her arm again, so that he wouldn't ask himself the same question. "Because I'm hungry," Cliff said simply.

Maggie started to resist, though he didn't appear to notice. Then it struck her how much she wanted to get out, to get away, just for a little while. Sooner or later, she'd have to be alone in the house, but right then— No, right then, she didn't want to be alone anywhere.

He knew, understood, and whatever his approach, Cliff was offering her exactly what she needed.

Though their thoughts weren't particularly calm, neither of them spoke as they walked through the door together.

Chapter 5

Maggie set aside the next day to complete the title song for the movie score. She made a conscious effort to forget everything that had happened the day before. Everything. She wouldn't think of what had been buried and unearthed so close to her house, nor would she think of police or investigators or medical examiners.

In exactly the same way, she refused to think of Cliff, of the one wildly exciting kiss or of the oddly civilized dinner they'd shared. It was difficult to believe that she'd experienced both with the same man.

Today, she was Maggie Fitzgerald, writer of songs, creator of music. If she thought of only that, *was* only that, perhaps she could convince herself that everything that had happened yesterday had happened to someone else.

She knew there were men outside spreading seed, planting. There were shrubs going in, mulch being laid, more brush being cleared. If the landscape timbers she'd seen brought in that morning meant what she thought, construction was about to begin on her retaining wall.

None of that concerned her. The score demanded to be completed, and she'd complete it. The one form of discipline she understood perfectly was that a job had to be done no matter what went on around you. She'd seen her father direct a movie when his equipment had broken down and his actors had thrown tantrums. She'd known her mother to perform while running a fever. Much of her life might have been lived in a plush, make-believe world, but she'd learned responsibility.

The score came first today, and the title song would be written. Perhaps she'd even add some clever little aside to C.J. at the end of the tape before she mailed it off.

It certainly wouldn't do to mention what was going on in her side yard, Maggie thought as she meticulously copied notes onto staff paper. C.J. wouldn't be able to find enough antacids in L.A. to handle it for him. Poor man, she mused, he'd been worried about the roof caving in on her. In a totally unexpected way, it certainly had. If he knew there'd been policemen swarming over her land with plastic bags, he'd catch the next plane and drag her back to L.A.

She wondered if Cliff would've dragged her from the house the night before if she hadn't gone voluntarily. Fortunately, it hadn't been an issue, because Maggie thought him perfectly capable of it. Yet he'd been the ideal dinner companion. While she hadn't expected consideration from him, he'd been considerate. She hadn't expected subtle kindness, but it had been there. Finding both had made it difficult to remember she considered him an unlikable man.

They hadn't spoken of what had been found on her property that day, nor had there been any speculation on the whys and hows. They hadn't discussed his work or hers, but had simply talked.

Looking back, Maggie couldn't say precisely what they'd talked about, only that the mood had been easy. So easy, she had almost forgotten the passion they'd pulled from each other in the quiet afternoon sunlight. Almost forgotten. The memory had been there, quietly nagging at her throughout the evening. It had made her blood move a little faster. It had made her wonder if he'd felt it, too.

Maggie swore and erased the last five notes she'd copied down. C.J. wouldn't appreciate the fact that she was mixing her bass and tenor. She was doing exactly what she'd promised herself she wouldn't do, and as she'd known it would, the upheaval of yesterday was affecting her work. Calmly, she took deep breaths until her mind was clear again. The wisest course was to switch the recorder back on to play and start from the beginning. Then the knock on the front door disrupted her thoughts. Quiet country life. She asked herself where she'd ever heard that expression as she went to answer.

The gun on the man's hip made her stomach twist. The little badge pinned to the khaki shirt told her he was the sheriff. When she took her gaze up to his face, she was surprised by his looks. Blond, tanned, with blue eyes fanned by lines that spoke of humor or sun. For a moment, she had the insane notion that C.J. had sent him out from central casting.

"Miss Fitzgerald?"

She moistened her lips as she tried to be rational. C.J. worried too much for practical jokes. Besides, the gun looked very, very real. "Yes."

"I'm Sheriff Agee. Hope you don't mind me dropping by."

"No." She tried a polite smile, but found it strained. Guns and badges and official vehicles. Too many police in too short a time, Maggie told herself.

"If it wouldn't put you out too much, I'd like to come in and talk to you for a few minutes."

It did put her out. She wanted to say it did, then close the door on him and everything he wanted to talk about. *Coward,* she told herself, and stepped back to let him in. "I suppose you're here about what we found yesterday." Maggie put her shoulder to the door to shut it. "I don't know what I can tell you."

"I'm sure it was a nasty experience, Miss Fitzgerald, and one you'd just as soon forget." His voice held just the right trace of sympathy mixed with professionalism. She decided he knew his business. "I wouldn't feel I was doing my duty as sheriff or as a neighbor if I didn't give you whatever help I can."

Maggie looked at him again. This time her smile came a bit more easily. "I appreciate that. I can offer you coffee, if you don't mind the mess in the kitchen."

He smiled and looked so solid, so pleasant, Maggie almost forgot the gun at his hip. "I never turn down coffee."

"The kitchen's down here," she began, then laughed. "I don't have to tell you, do I? You'd know this house as well as I do."

He fell into step beside her. "Tell you the truth, I've been around the outside, hacking at the weeds now and again or hunting, but I've only been inside a handful of times. The Morgans moved out when Joyce was still a kid."

"Yes, she told me."

"Nobody's lived here for more'n ten years. Louella just let it go after the old man died." He glanced up at the cracked ceiling paint. "She held it in trust till Joyce inherited it at twenty-five. You probably heard I held Joyce off from selling."

"Well…" Uncertain how to respond, Maggie busied herself at the stove.

"Guess I thought we'd fix it up eventually, rent it out again." To her, he sounded like a man who knew about dreams but never found the time for them. "But a big old place like this needs a lot of time and money to put right. Joyce probably did the right thing, selling out."

"I'm glad she did." After switching on the coffee-maker, Maggie indicated a chair.

"With Bog handling repairs and Delaney working on the grounds, you picked the right men." When Maggie just looked at him, the sheriff grinned again. "Nothing travels fast in small towns but news."

"No, I suppose not."

"Look, what happened yesterday…" He paused, clearing his throat. "I know it must be rough on you. I gotta tell you, Joyce was worked up about it. A lot of people who'd find something like that a stone's throw from their house would just pull up stakes and take off."

Maggie reached in the cabinets for cups. "I'm not going anywhere."

"Glad to hear it." He was silent a moment, watching her pour the coffee. Her hands looked steady enough. "I understand Cliff was here yesterday, too."

"That's right. He was overseeing some of the work."

"And your dog dug up—"

"Yes." Maggie set both cups on the table before she sat down. "He's just a puppy. Right now he's asleep upstairs. Too much excitement."

The sheriff waved away her offer of cream, sipping the coffee black. "I didn't come to press you for details. The state police filled me in. I just wanted to let you know I was as close as the phone if you needed anything."

"I appreciate that. I'm not really familiar with the procedure, but I suppose I should've called you yesterday."

"I like to take care of my own territory," he said slowly, "but with something like this—" He shrugged. "Hell, I'd've had to call in the state, anyway." She watched his wedding ring gleam dully in the sunlight. Joyce had had a matching one, Maggie recalled. Plain and gold and solid. "Looks like you're redoing this floor."

Maggie looked down blankly. "Oh, yes, I took up the old linoleum. I've got to get to the sanding."

"You call George Cooper," the sheriff told her. "He's in the book. He'll get you an electric sander that'll take care of this in no time. Just tell him Stan Agee gave you his name."

"All right." She knew the conversation should've eased her mind, but her nerves were jumping again. "Thank you."

"Anything else you need, you just give us a call. Joyce'll want to have you over for dinner. She bakes the best ham in the county."

"That'd be nice."

"She can't get over someone like you moving here to Morganville." He sipped at his coffee while Maggie's grew cold. While he leaned back in the chair, relaxed, she sat very straight with tension. "I don't keep up with music much, but Joyce knows all of your songs. She reads all those magazines, too, and now somebody's who's in them's living in her old house." He glanced idly at the back door. "You ought to speak to Bog about putting some dead bolts on."

She looked over at the screen, remembering the hinges needed oiling. "Dead bolts?"

With a laugh, he finished off his coffee. "That's what happens when you're sheriff. You're always thinking of security. We've got a nice, quiet community, Miss Fitzgerald. Wouldn't want you to think otherwise. But I'd feel better knowing you had some good solid locks on the doors, since you're back here alone." Rising, he tugged absently at his holster. "Thanks for the coffee. You just remember to call if you need anything."

"Yes, I'll remember."

"I'll go on out this way and let you get back to work. You call George Cooper, now."

"All right." Maggie walked to the back door with him. "Thank you, Sheriff."

For a moment she just stood there by the door, her head resting against the jamb. She hated knowing she could be so easily worked up. The sheriff had come to reassure her, to show her that the community she'd chosen to live in had a concerned, capable law enforcer. Now her nerves were raw from talking to so many police. So many police, Maggie mused, just as it had been when Jerry died. All the police, all the questions. She thought she'd been over it, but now everything was coming back again, much too clearly.

"Your husband drove off the road, Mrs. Browning. We haven't located his body yet, but we're doing everything we can. I'm sorry."

Yes, there'd been sympathy at first, Maggie remembered. She'd had sympathy from the police, from her friends, Jerry's friends. Then questions: "Had your husband been drinking when he left the house?" "Was he upset, angry?" "Were you fighting?"

God, hadn't it been enough that he'd been dead? Why

had they picked and pulled at all the reasons? How many reasons could there be for a twenty-eight-year-old man to turn his car toward a cliff and drive over it?

Yes, he'd been drinking. He'd done a lot of drinking since his career had started to skid and hers had kept climbing. Yes, they'd been fighting, because neither of them had understood what had happened to the dreams they'd once had. She'd answered their questions; she'd suffered the press until she had thought she'd go mad.

Maggie squeezed her eyes tight. That was over, she told herself. She couldn't bring Jerry back and solve his problems now. He'd found his own solution. Turning from the door, she went back to the music room.

In her work she found the serenity and the discipline she needed. It had always been that way for her. She could escape into the music so that her emotions found their outlet. She could train her mind on timing and structure. Her drive had always been to release the emotions, hers by the creation of a song and the listener's by hearing it. If she was successful in that, she needed no other ambition.

Talent wasn't enough in itself, she knew. It hadn't been enough for Jerry. Talent had to be harnessed by discipline; discipline, guided by creativity. Maggie used all three now.

As time passed, she became absorbed in the music and in the goal she'd set. The title song had to be passionate, full of movement and sexuality, as the title itself suggested. When it was played, she wanted it to stir the senses, touch off needs, build longings.

No one had been signed to perform it yet, so she was free to use whatever style she chose. She wanted something bluesy, and in her mind she could hear the moan of a sax. Sexy, sultry. She wanted the quiet wail of brass and the smoky throb of bass. Late the night before, when she'd been restless, she'd written down a few phrases. Now she experimented with them, twining words to music.

Almost at once she knew she'd found the key. The key was unexplained passion, barely controlled. It was desire that promised to rip aside anything civilized. It was the fury and heat that a man and woman could bring to each other until both were senseless from it. She had the key now, Maggie thought as her pulse began to pound with the music, because she'd experienced it herself. Yesterday, on the rise, in the sun, with Cliff.

Madness. That was the word that streamed through her mind. Desire was madness. She closed her eyes as words and melody flowed through her. Hadn't she felt that madness, the sweetness and the ache of it, when his mouth had moved on hers? Hadn't she wanted to feel him against her, flesh to flesh? He'd made her think of dark nights, steamy, moonless nights when the air was so thick you'd feel it pulse on your skin. Then she hadn't thought at all, because desire was madness.

She let the words come, passionate, wanton promises that simmered over the heat of the music. Seductive, suggestive, they poured out of her own needs. Lovers' words, desperate words, were whispered out in her low, husky voice until the room was charged with them. No one who heard would be unmoved. That was her ambition.

When she was finished, Maggie was breathless and moved and exhilarated. She reached up to rewind the recorder for playback when, for the second time, she saw Cliff standing in the doorway.

Her hand froze, and her pulse, already fast, went racing. Had she called him with the song? she wondered frantically. Was the magic that strong? When he said nothing, she switched off the recorder and spoke with studied calm. "Is it an accepted habit in the country for people to walk into homes uninvited?"

"You don't seem to hear the door when you're working."

She acknowledged this with an inclination of her head. "That might mean I don't like to be disturbed when I'm working."

"It might." Disturbed. The word almost made him laugh. Perhaps he had disturbed her work, but that was nothing compared to what the song had done to him—to what watching her sing had done to him. It had taken every ounce of his control not to yank her from the piano stool and take her on the littered, dusty floor. He came closer, knowing before it reached him that her scent would be there to add to her allure.

"I lost quite a bit of time yesterday." Maggie swallowed whatever was trying to block her voice. Her body was still throbbing, still much too vulnerable from the passion she'd released. "I have a deadline on this score."

He glanced down at her hands. He wanted to feel them stroke over him with the same skill she'd used on the piano keys. Slowly, he took his gaze up her arms, over the curve of her shoulder to her face. For both of them, it was as if he'd touched her.

Her breath wasn't steady; her eyes weren't calm. That was as he wanted it now. No matter how often or how firmly he told himself to back off from her, Cliff knew he was reaching a point when it would be impossible. She wasn't for him—he could convince himself of that. But they had something that had to be freed and had to be tasted.

"From what I heard," he murmured, "you seem to be finished."

"That's for me to decide."

"Play it back." It was a challenge. He saw from her

eyes that she knew it. A challenge could backfire on either of them. "The last song—I want to hear it again."

Dangerous. Maggie understood the danger. As she hesitated, his lips curved. It was enough. Without a word, she punched the rewind button. The song was a fantasy, she told herself as the tape hurried backward. It was a fantasy, just as the film was a fantasy. The song was for the characters in a story and had nothing, absolutely nothing, to do with her. Or with him. She flicked the recorder to play.

She'd listen objectively, Maggie decided as the music began to spill into the room. She'd listen as a musician, as a technician. That was what her job demanded. But she found, as her own voice began to tempt her, that she was listening as a woman. Rising, she walked to the window and faced out. When a hunger was this strong, she thought, distance could mean everything.

> Wait for night when the air's
> hot and there's madness
> I'll make your blood swim
> Wait for night when passion rises like
> a flood in the heat dance
> Desire pours over the rim

He listened, as he had before, and felt his system respond to the music and the promises that low voice made. He wanted all that the song hinted at. All that, and more.

When Cliff crossed the room, he saw her tense. He thought he could feel the air snap, hissing with the heat the song had fanned. Before he reached her, Maggie turned. The sun at her back shot a nimbus around her. In contrast, her eyes were dark. Like night, he thought. Like her night music. The words she'd written filled the room around them. It seemed those words were enough.

He didn't speak, but circled the back of her neck with his hand. She didn't speak, but resisted, forcing her body to stiffen. There was anger in her eyes now, as much for herself as for him. She'd taken herself to this point by allowing her own needs and fantasies to clear the path. It wasn't madness she wanted, Maggie told herself as she drew back. It was stability. It wasn't the wild she sought, but serenity. He wouldn't offer those things.

His fingers only tightened as she pulled back. That surprised them both. He'd forgotten the rules of a civilized seduction, just as he'd forgotten he'd only come there to see how she was. The music, the words, made the vulnerability that had concerned him a thing of the past. Now he felt strength as his fingers pressed into her skin. He saw challenge in her stance, and a dare, mixed with the fury in her eyes. Cliff wanted nothing less from her.

He stepped closer. When she lifted a hand in protest, he took her wrist. The pulse throbbed under his hand as intensely as the music throbbed on the air. Their eyes met, clashed, passion against passion. In one move, he pulled her against him and took her mouth.

She saw the vivid colors and lights she'd once imagined. She tasted the flavor of urgent desire. As her arms pulled him yet closer to her, Maggie heard her own moan of shuddering pleasure. The world was suddenly honed down to an instant, and the instant went on and on.

Had she been waiting for this? This mindless, melting pleasure? Were these sensations, these emotions, what she'd poured out into music for so long? She could find no answers, only more needs.

He'd stopped thinking. In some small portion of his brain, Cliff knew he'd lost the capacity to reason. She made him feel, outrageously, so that there was no room for intellect. His hands sought her, skimming under her shirt to find the soft, heated skin he knew he'd dreamed about. She strained against him, offering more. Against his mouth, he felt her lips form his name. Something wild burst inside him.

He wasn't gentle, though as a lover he'd never been rough before. He was too desperate to touch to realize that he might bruise something more fragile than he. The kiss grew savage. He knew he'd never be able to draw enough from her to satisfy him. More, and still more, he wanted, though her mouth was as crazed and demanding as his.

He was driving her mad. No one had ever shown her a need so great. Hunger fueled hunger until she ached with it. She knew it could consume her, perhaps both of them. With a fire so hot, they could burn each other out and be left with nothing. The thought made her moan again, and cling. She wanted more. Yet she feared to take more and find herself empty.

"No." His lips at her throat were turning her knees to water. "No, this is crazy," she managed.

He lifted his head. His eyes were nearly black now, and his breathing was unsteady. For the first time, Maggie felt a twinge of fear. What did she know of this man? "You called it madness," he murmured. "You were right."

Yes, she'd been right, and it had been him she'd thought of when she'd written the words. Yet she told herself it was sanity she needed. "It's not what either of us should want."

"No." His control was threatening to snap completely.

Deliberately, he ran a hand down her hair. "But it's already too far along to stop. I want you, Maggie, whether I should or not."

If he hadn't used her name— Until then she hadn't realized that he could say her name and make her weak. As needs welled up again, she dropped her head on his chest. It was that artless, unplanned gesture that cleared his frenzied thoughts and tugged at something other than desire.

This was the kind of woman who could get inside a man. Once she did, he'd never be free of her. Knowing that, he fought back the overwhelming need to hold her close again. He wanted her, and he intended to have her. That didn't mean he'd get involved. They both knew that what had ignited between them would have to be consummated sooner or later. It was basic; it was simple. And they'd both walk away undamaged.

Whereas the arousal he'd felt hadn't worried him, the tenderness he was feeling now did. They'd better get things back on the right road. He took her by the shoulders and drew her back.

"We want each other." It sounded simple when he said it. Cliff was determined to believe it could be.

"Yes." She nodded, almost composed again. "I'm sure you've learned, as I have, that you can't have everything you want."

"True enough. But there's no reason for either of us not to have what we want this time."

"I can think of a few. The first is that I barely know you."

He frowned as he studied her face. "Does that matter to you?"

Maggie jerked away so quickly his hands fell to his sides. "So, you do believe everything you read." Her voice was brittle now, and her eyes were cold. "Los Angeles, land of sinning and sinners. I'm sorry to disappoint you, Cliff, but I haven't filled my life with nameless, faceless lovers. This fills my life." She slapped her hand down on the piano so that papers slid off onto the floor. "And since you read so much, since you know so much about me, you'll know that up to two years ago I was married. I had a husband, and as ridiculous as it sounds, was faithful for six years."

"My question didn't have anything to do with that." His voice was so mild in contrast to hers that she stiffened. Maggie had learned to trust him the least when he used that tone. "It was more personal, as in you and me."

"Then let's just say I have a rule of thumb not to hop into bed with men I don't know. You included."

He crossed the room, then laid his hand over hers on the piano. "Just how well do you have to know me?"

"Better, I think, than I ever will." She had to fight the urge to snatch her hand away. She'd made a fool of herself enough for one day. "I have another rule about steering clear of people who don't like who and what I am."

He looked down at the hand beneath his. It was pale, slender and strong. "Maybe I don't know who and what you are." His gaze lifted to lock on hers. "Maybe I intend to find out for myself."

"You'll have to have my cooperation for that, won't you?"

He lifted a brow, as if amused. "We'll see."

Her voice became only more icy. "I'd like you to leave. I've a lot of work to do."

"Tell me what you were thinking about when you wrote that song."

Something fluttered over her face so quickly he

couldn't be certain if it was panic or passion. Either would have suited him.

"I said I want you to leave."

"I will—after you tell me what you were thinking of."

She kept her chin angled and her eyes level. "I was thinking of you."

He smiled. Taking her hand, he brought her palm to his lips. The unexpected gesture had thunderbolts echoing in her head. "Good," he murmured. "Think some more. I'll be back."

She closed her fingers over her palm as he walked away. He'd given her no choice but to do as he'd asked.

It was late, late into the night, when she woke. Groggy, Maggie thought it had been the dream that had disturbed her. She cursed Cliff and rolled onto her back. She didn't want to dream of him. She certainly didn't want to lie awake in the middle of the night, thinking of him.

Staring up at the ceiling, she listened to the quiet. At times like this, it struck her how alone she was. There were no servants sleeping downstairs, as there had been all her life. Her closest neighbor was perhaps a quarter of a mile away through the woods. No all-night clubs or drugstores, she mused. So far, she'd yet to even deal with getting an outside antenna for television. She was on her own, as she'd chosen.

Then why, Maggie wondered, did her bed suddenly seem so empty and the night so long? Rolling to her side, she struggled to shake off the mood and her thoughts of Cliff.

Overhead, a board creaked, but she paid no attention. Old houses made noises at night. Maggie had learned that quickly. Restless, she shifted in bed and lay watching the light of the waning moon.

She didn't want Cliff there, with her. Even allowing herself to think that she did was coming too close to dangerous ground. It was true her body had reacted to him, strongly. A woman couldn't always control the needs of her body, but she could control the direction of her thoughts. Firmly, she set her mind on the list of chores for the next day.

When the sound came again, she frowned, glancing automatically at the ceiling. The creaks and groans rarely disturbed her, but then, she'd always slept soundly in this house. Until Cliff Delaney, she thought, and determinedly shut her eyes. The sound of a door shutting quietly had them flying open again.

Before panic could register or reason overtake it, her heart was lodged in her throat, pounding. She was alone, and someone was in the house. All the nightmares that had ever plagued a woman alone in the dark loomed in her mind. Her fingers curled into the sheets as she lay stiffly, straining to hear.

Was that a footstep on the stairs, or was it all in her imagination? As terror flowed into her, she thought of the gully outside. She bit down on her lip to keep herself from making a sound. Very slowly, Maggie turned her head and made out the puppy sleeping at the foot of the bed. He didn't hear anything. She closed her eyes again and tried to even her breathing.

If the dog heard nothing that disturbed him, she reasoned, there was nothing to worry about. Just boards settling. Even as she tried to convince herself, Maggie heard a movement downstairs. A soft squeak, a gentle scrape. The kitchen door? she asked herself as the panic buzzed in her head. Fighting to move slowly and quietly, she reached for the phone beside the bed. As she held it to her ear, she heard the buzz that reminded her she'd left the kitchen extension off the hook earlier so as not to be disturbed. Her phone was as good as dead. Hysteria bubbled and was swallowed.

Think, she ordered herself. *Stay calm and think.* If she was alone, with no way to reach help, she had to rely on herself. How many times in the past few weeks had she stated that she could do just that?

She pressed a hand against her mouth so that the sound of her own breathing wouldn't disturb her concentrated listening. There was nothing now, no creaks, no soft steps on wood.

Careful to make no sound, she climbed out of bed and found the fireplace poker. Muscles tense, Maggie propped herself in the chair, facing the door. Gripping the poker in both hands, she prayed for morning.

Chapter 6

After a few days, Maggie had all but forgotten about the noises in her house. As early as the morning after the incident, she'd felt like a fool. She'd been awakened by the puppy licking her bare feet while she sat, stiff and sore from the night in the chair. The fireplace poker had lain across her lap like a medieval sword. The bright sunlight and birdsong had convinced her she'd imagined everything, then had magnified every small noise the way a child magnifies shadows in the dark. Perhaps she wasn't quite as acclimated to living alone as she'd thought. At least she could be grateful she'd left the downstairs extension off the hook. If she hadn't, everyone in town would know she was a nervous idiot.

If she had nerves, Maggie told herself, it was certainly understandable under the circumstances. People digging up skeletons beside her house, the local sheriff suggesting she lock her doors, and Cliff Delaney, Maggie added, keeping her up at night. The only good thing to come out of the entire week was the completed score. She imagined that C.J. would be pleased enough with the finished product not to nag her about coming back to L.A., at least for a little while.

Maggie decided the next constructive thing to do was to take the tape and sheet music she'd packaged to the post office and mail it off. Perhaps later she'd celebrate her first songs written in her new home.

She enjoyed the trip to town and took it leisurely. The narrow little roads were flanked by trees that would offer a blanket of shade in a few short weeks. Now the sun streamed through the tiny leaves to pour white onto the road. Here and there the woods were interrupted by fields, brown earth turned up. She could see farmers working with their tractors and wondered what was being planted. Corn, hay, wheat? She knew virtually nothing of that aspect of the home she'd chosen. Maggie thought it would be interesting to watch things grow until the summer or autumn harvest.

She saw cows with small calves nursing frantically. There was a woman carrying a steel bucket to what must have been a chicken coop. A dog raced along a fenced yard, barking furiously at Maggie's car.

Her panic of a few nights before seemed so ridiculous she refused to think of it.

She passed a few houses, some of them hardly more than cabins, others so obviously new and modern they offended the eyes. She found herself resenting the pristine homes on lots where trees had been cleared. Why hadn't they worked with what was there, instead of spoiling it? Then she laughed at herself. She was sounding too much like Cliff Delaney. People had a right to live where and how they chose, didn't they? But she couldn't deny that she preferred the old weathered brick or wood homes surrounded by trees.

As she drove into Morganville, she noted the homes were closer together. That was town life, she decided. There were sidewalks here, and a few cars parked along the curb. People kept their lawns trimmed. Maggie decided that from the look of it, there was quite a bit of pride and competition among the flower gardens. It reminded her to check her own petunias.

The post office was on the corner, a small redbrick building with a two-car parking lot. Beside it, separated by no more than a two-foot strip of grass, was the Morganville bank. Two men stood beside the outside mailbox, smoking and talking. They watched as Maggie pulled into the lot, as she stepped out of the car and as she walked toward the post office. Deciding to try her luck, she turned her head and flashed them a smile.

"Good morning."

"Morning," they said in unison. One of them pushed back his fishing cap. "Nice car."

"Thank you."

She walked inside, pleased that she had had what could pass for a conversation.

There was one woman behind the counter already engaged in what appeared to be casual gossip with a younger woman who toted a baby on her hip. "No telling how long they've been there," the postmistress stated, counting out stamps. "Nobody's lived out there since the Faradays, and that's been ten years last month. Old lady Faraday used to come in for a dollar's worth of stamps once a week, like clockwork. 'Course, they were cheaper then." She pushed the stamps across the counter. "That's five dollars' worth, Amy."

"Well, I think it's spooky." The young mother jiggled

the baby on her hip while he busied himself gurgling at Maggie. Gathering up the stamps, she stuffed them into a bag on her other shoulder. "If I found a bunch of old bones in my yard, I'd have a For Sale sign up the next day." Hearing the words, Maggie felt some of her pleasure in the day fade. "Billy said some drifter probably fell in that gully and nobody ever knew about it."

"Could be. Guess the state police'll figure it out before long." The postmistress closed the conversation by turning to Maggie. "Help you?"

"Yes." Maggie stepped up to the counter. The young woman gave her one long, curious look before she took her baby outside. "I'd like to send this registered mail."

"Well, let's see what it weighs." The postmistress took the package and put it on the scale. "You want a return receipt?"

"Yes, please."

"Okay." She took the pencil from behind her ear to run the tip along a chart taped to the scale. "Cost you a bit more, but you'll know it got there. Let's see, it's going to zone—" She broke off as she caught the return address on the corner of the package. Her gaze lifted, focusing sharply on Maggie, before she began to fill out the form. "You're the songwriter from California. Bought the Morgan place."

"That's right." Because she wasn't sure what to say after the conversation she'd overheard, Maggie left it at that.

"Nice music." The postmistress wrote in meticulously rounded letters. "Lot of that stuff they play I can't even understand. I got some of your mama's records. She was the best. Nobody else comes close."

Maggie's heart warmed, as it always did when someone spoke of her mother. "Yes, I think so, too."

"You sign this here." As she obeyed, Maggie felt the postmistress's eyes on her. It occurred to her that this woman saw every piece of correspondence that came to or from her. Though it was an odd feeling, she found it wasn't unpleasant. "Big old house, the Morgan place." The woman figured the total on a little white pad. "You settling in all right out there?"

"Bit by bit. There's a lot to be done."

"That's the way it is when you move into a place, 'specially one's been empty so long. Must be a lot different for you."

Maggie lifted her head. "Yes. I like it."

Perhaps it was the direct eyes or perhaps it was the simple phrasing, but the postmistress seemed to nod to herself. Maggie felt as though she'd found her first full acceptance. "Bog'll do well by you. So will young Delaney."

Maggie smiled to herself as she reached for her wallet. Small towns, she thought. No secrets.

"You had a shock the other day."

Because she'd been expecting some kind of comment, Maggie took it easily. "I wouldn't care to have another like it."

"Nope, guess nobody would. You just relax and enjoy that old house," the postmistress advised. "It was a showcase in its day. Louella always kept it fine. Let the police worry about the rest of it."

"That's what I'm trying to do." Maggie pocketed her change. "Thank you."

"We'll get this off for you right away. You have a nice day."

Maggie was definitely feeling pleased with herself when she walked back outside. She took a deep breath of soft spring air, smiled again at the two men still talking beside the mailbox, then turned toward her car. The smile faded when she saw Cliff leaning against the hood.

"Out early," he said easily.

He'd told her it was difficult to avoid anyone in a town that size. Maggie decided it was his accuracy that annoyed her. "Shouldn't you be working somewhere?"

He grinned and offered her the bottle of soda he held. "Actually, I just came off a job site and was on my way to another." When she made no move to take the soda, he lifted the bottle to his lips again and drank deeply. "You don't see too many of these in Morganville." He tapped a finger against the side of her Aston Martin.

She started to move around him to the driver's door. "If you'll excuse me," she said coolly, "I'm busy."

He stopped her effortlessly with a hand on her arm. Ignoring her glare, as well as the interested speculation of the two men a few yards away, Cliff studied her face. "You've shadows under your eyes. Haven't you been sleeping?"

"I've been sleeping just fine."

"No." He stopped her again, but this time he lifted a hand to her face, as well. Though she didn't seem to know it, every time her fragile side showed, he lost ground. "I thought you didn't believe in evasions."

"Look, I'm busy."

"You've let that business in the gully get to you."

"Well, what if I have?" Maggie exploded. "I'm human. It's a normal reaction."

"I didn't say it wasn't." The hand on her face tilted her chin back a bit farther. "You fire up easily these days. Is it just that business that has you tense, or is there something else?"

Maggie stopped trying to pull away and stood very still. Maybe he hadn't noticed the men watching them, or the postmistress in the window, but she had. "It's none of your business whether I'm tense or not. Now, if you'll stop making a scene, I have to go home and work."

"Do scenes bother you?" Amused now, he drew her closer. "I wouldn't have thought so, from the number of times you've had your picture snapped."

"Cliff, cut it out." She put both hands on his chest. "For heaven's sake, we're standing on Main Street."

"Yeah. And we've just become the ten-o'clock bulletin."

A laugh escaped before she even knew it was going to happen. "You get a real kick out of that, don't you?"

"Well…" He took advantage of her slight relaxing and wrapped his arms around her. "Maybe. I've been meaning to talk to you."

A woman walked by with a letter in her hand. Maggie noticed that she took her time putting it into the box. "I think we could find a better place." At his snort of laughter, she narrowed her eyes. "I didn't mean that. Now, will you let go?"

"In a minute. Remember when we went out to dinner the other night?"

"Yes, I remember. Cliff—" She turned her head and saw that the two men were still there, still watching. Now the woman had joined them. "This really isn't funny."

"Thing is," he continued easily, "we have this custom around here. I take you out to dinner, then you reciprocate."

Out of patience, she wriggled against him and found that only made her blood pressure rise. "I haven't the time to go out to dinner right now. I'll get back to you in a few weeks."

"I'll take potluck."

"Potluck?" she repeated. "At *my* house?"

"Good idea."

"Wait a minute. I didn't say—"

"Unless you can't cook."

"Of course I can cook," she tossed back.

"Fine. Seven o'clock?"

She aimed her most deadly, most regal stare. "I'm hanging wallpaper tonight."

"You have to eat sometime." Before she could comment, he kissed her, briefly but firmly enough to make a point. "See you at seven," he said, then strolled over to his truck. "And Maggie," he added through the open window, "nothing fancy. I'm not fussy."

"You—" she began, but the roar of the truck's engine drowned her out. She was left standing alone, fuming, in the center of the parking lot. Knowing there were at least a dozen pair of eyes on her, Maggie kept her head high as she climbed into her own car.

She cursed Cliff repeatedly, and expertly, on the three-mile drive back to her house.

Maggie expected the men from Cliff's crew to be there when she returned. The discreet black car at the end of her driveway, however, was unexpected. She discovered as she pulled alongside it that she wasn't in the mood for visitors, not for neighbors calling to pay their respects or for curiosity-seekers. She wanted to be alone with the sander she'd rented from George Cooper.

As she stepped from the car, she spotted the rangy man with the salt-and-pepper hair crossing her front yard from the direction of the gully. And she recognized him.

"Miss Fitzgerald."

"Good morning. Lieutenant Reiker, isn't it?"

"Yes, ma'am."

What was the accepted etiquette, Maggie wondered, when you came home and found a homicide detective on your doorstep? Maggie decided on the practical, marginally friendly approach. "Is there something I can do for you?"

"I'm going to have to ask for your cooperation, Miss Fitzgerald." The lieutenant kept his weight on one foot, as if his hips were troubling him. "I'm sure you'd like to get on with all your landscaping plans, but we want you to hold off on the pond a while longer."

"I see." She was afraid she did. "Can you tell me why?"

"We've received the medical examiner's preliminary report. We'll be investigating."

It might've been easier not to ask, not to know. Maggie wasn't certain she could live with herself if she took the coward's way out that she was obviously being offered. "Lieutenant, I'm not sure how much you're at liberty to tell me, but I do think I have a right to know certain things. This is my property."

"You won't be involved to any real extent, Miss Fitzgerald. This business goes back a long way."

"As long as my land's part of it, I'm involved." She caught herself worrying the strap of her bag, much as Joyce had done on her visit. She forced her hands to be still. "It'd be easier for me, Lieutenant, if I knew what was going on."

Reiker rubbed his hand over his face. The investigation was barely under way, and he already had a bad taste in his mouth. Maybe things that'd been dead and buried for ten years should just stay buried. Some things, he decided grimly. Yes, some things.

"The medical examiner determined that the remains belonged to a Caucasian male in his early fifties."

Maggie swallowed. That made it too real. Much too real. "How long—" she began, but had to swallow again. "How long had he been there?"

"The examiner puts it at about ten years."

"As long as the house has been empty," she murmured.

She brought herself back, telling herself that it wasn't personal. Logically, practically, it had nothing to do with her. "I don't suppose they could determine how he died?"

"Shot," Reiker said flatly, and watched the horror fill her eyes. "Appears to've been a thirty-gauge shotgun, probably at close range."

"Good God." Murder. Yet hadn't she known it, sensed it almost from the first instant? Maggie stared out into the woods and watched two squirrels race up the trunk of a tree. How could it have happened here? "After so many years—" she began, but had to swallow yet again. "After so many years, wouldn't it be virtually impossible to identify the—him?"

"He was identified this morning." Reiker watched as she turned to him, pale, her eyes almost opaque. It gave him a bad feeling. He told himself it was because, like every other man in the country, he'd had a fantasy love affair with her mother twenty years before. He told himself it was because she was young enough to be his daughter. At times like this, he wished he'd chosen any other line of work.

"We found a ring, too, an old ring with a lot of fancy carving and three small diamond chips. An hour ago, Joyce Agee identified it as her father's. William Morgan was murdered and buried in that gully."

But that was wrong. Maggie dragged a hand through her hair and tried to think. No matter how bluntly, how practically, Reiker put it, it was wrong. "That can't be. I was told that William Morgan had an accident—something about a car accident."

"Ten years ago, his car went through the guardrail of the bridge crossing into West Virginia. His car was dragged out of the Potomac, but not his body. His body was never found...until a few days ago."

Through the rail, into the water, Maggie thought numbly. Like Jerry. They hadn't found Jerry's body, either, not for nearly a week. She'd lived through every kind of hell during that week. As she stood, staring straight ahead, she felt as though she were two people in two separate times. "What will you do now?"

"There'll be an official investigation. It has nothing to do with you, Miss Fitzgerald, other than we need for you to keep that section of your property clear. There'll be a team here this afternoon to start going over it again, just in case we missed something."

"All right. If you don't need anything else—"

"No, ma'am."

"I'll be inside."

As she walked across the lawn toward the house, she told herself that something that had happened ten years before had nothing to do with her. Ten years before, she'd been dealing with her own tragedy, the loss of her parents. Unable to resist, she looked back over her shoulder at the gully as she climbed the steps to the porch.

Joyce Agee's father, Maggie thought with a shudder. Joyce had sold her the house without knowing what would be discovered. She thought of the pretty, tense young woman who had been grateful for a simple kindness to her mother. Compelled, Maggie went to the pad scrawled with names and numbers beside the phone. Without hesitating, she called the number for Joyce Agee. The voice that answered was soft, hardly more than a whisper. Maggie felt a stab of sympathy.

"Mrs. Agee—Joyce, this is Maggie Fitzgerald."

"Oh… Yes, hello."

"I don't want to intrude." Now what? Maggie asked herself. She had no part of this, no link other than a plot of land that had lain neglected for a decade. "I just wanted you to know that I'm terribly sorry, and if there's anything I can do…I'd like to help."

"Thank you, there's nothing." Her voice hitched, then faltered. "It's been such a shock. We always thought—"

"Yes, I know. Please, don't think you have to talk to me or be polite. I only called because somehow—" She broke off, passing a hand over her hair. "I don't know. I feel as though I've set it all off."

"It's better to know the truth." Joyce's voice became suddenly calm. "It's always better to know. I worry about Mother."

"Is she all right?"

"I'm not— I'm not sure." Maggie sensed fatigue now, rather than tears. She understood that form of grief, as well. "She's here now. The doctor's with her."

"I won't keep you, then. Joyce, I understand we hardly know each other, but I would like to help. Please let me know if I can."

"I will. Thank you for calling."

Maggie replaced the receiver. That accomplished nothing, she reflected. It accomplished nothing, because she didn't know Joyce Agee. When you grieved, you needed someone you knew, the way she'd needed Jerry when her parents had been killed. Though she knew Joyce had a husband, Maggie thought of Cliff and the way he'd taken the woman's hands, the look of concern on his face, when he'd spoken to her. He'd be there for her, Maggie mused, and wished she knew what they meant to each other.

To give her excess energy an outlet, she switched on the rented sander.

The sun was low, the sky rosy with it, when Cliff drove toward the old Morgan property. His mind was full of questions. William Morgan murdered. He'd been shot, buried on his own property; then someone had covered the trail by sending his car into the river.

Cliff was close enough to the Morgans and to the people of Morganville to know that every other person in town might've wished William Morgan dead. He'd been a hard man, a cold man, with a genius for making money and enemies. But could someone who Cliff knew, someone he'd talk to on the street any day of the week, have actually murdered him?

In truth, he didn't give a damn about the old man, but he worried about Louella and Joyce—especially Joyce. He didn't like to see her the way she'd been that afternoon, so calm, so detached, with nerves snagged at the edge. She meant more to him than any other woman he'd known, yet there seemed to be no way to help her now. That was for Stan, Cliff thought, downshifting as he came to a corner.

God knew if the police would ever come up with anything viable. He didn't have much faith in that after ten years. That meant Joyce would have to live with knowing that her father had been murdered and that his murderer still walked free. Would she, Cliff mused, look at her neighbors and wonder?

Swearing, Cliff turned onto the lane that led to the Morgan place. There was someone else he worried about, he thought grimly, though he didn't have the excuse of a long, close friendship with this woman.

Damned if he wanted to worry about Maggie Fitzgerald. She was a woman from another place, who liked glittery parties and opening nights. Where he'd choose solitude, she'd choose crowds. She'd want champagne; he, cold beer. She'd prefer trips to Europe; he, a quiet ride down the river. She was the last person he needed to worry about.

She'd been married to a performer who'd flamed like a comet and who'd burned out just as quickly. Her escorts had been among the princes of the celebrity world. Tuxedos, silk scarves and diamond cuff links, he thought derisively. What the hell was she doing in the middle of a mess like this? And what the hell, he asked himself, was she doing in his life?

He pulled up behind her car and stared broodingly at her house. Maybe with all that was going on she'd decide to go back West. He'd prefer it that way. Damned if he didn't want to believe he would. She had no business crashing into his thoughts the way she had lately. That music. He let out a long stream of curses as he remembered it. That night music. Cliff knew he wanted her the way he'd wanted no woman before. It was something he couldn't overcome. Something he could barely control.

So why was he here? Why had he pushed his way into a meeting she hadn't wanted? Because, he admitted, when he thought of the way it had been between them, he didn't want to overcome it. Tonight he didn't want control.

As he walked toward the front door, he reminded himself that he was dealing with a woman who was different from any he'd known. Approach with caution, he told himself, then knocked at the front door.

From the other side, Maggie gripped the knob with both hands and tugged. It took two tries before she opened the door, and by that time Killer was barking nonstop.

"You should have Bog take care of that," Cliff suggested. He bent down to ruffle the dog's fur. Killer flopped on his back, offering his belly.

"Yeah." She was glad to see him. Maggie told herself she would've been glad to see anyone, but when she looked at him, she knew it was a lie. All through the afternoon she'd waited. "I keep meaning to."

He saw tension in the way she stood, in the way one hand still gripped the doorknob. Deliberately, he gave her a cocky smile. "So, what's for dinner?"

She let out a quick laugh as some of the nerves escaped. "Hamburgers."

"Hamburgers?"

"You did invite yourself," she reminded him. "And you did say not to fuss."

"So I did." He gave Killer a last scratch behind the ears, then rose.

"Well, since it's my first dinner party, I thought I'd stick with my speciality. It was either that or canned soup and cold sandwiches."

"If that's been your staple since you moved in, it's no wonder you're thin."

Frowning, Maggie glanced down at herself. "Do you realize you make a habit of criticizing?"

"I didn't say I didn't like thin women."

"That's not the point. You can come back and complain while I cook the hamburgers."

As they walked down the hall, Cliff noticed a few bare spots where she'd removed strips of wallpaper. Apparently she was serious about taking on the overwhelming job of redoing the house. When they passed the music room, he glanced in at her piano and wondered why. She was in the position of being able to hire a fleet of decorators and craftsmen. The job could be done in weeks, rather than the months, even years, it promised to take this way. The freshly sanded floor in the kitchen caught his eye.

"Nice job." Automatically, he crouched down to run his fingers over the floor's surface. The dog took this as an invitation to lick his face.

Maggie lifted a brow. "Well, thank you."

Catching the tone, he looked up at her. He couldn't deny that he'd been giving her a hard time from the outset. He had his reasons. The primary one as Cliff saw it now was her effect on him. "The question is," he said, rising again, "why you're doing it."

"The floor needed it." She turned to the counter to begin making patties.

"I meant why *you're* doing it."

"It's my house."

He wandered over to stand beside her. Again, he found himself watching her hands. "Did you sand your own floors in California?"

"No." Annoyed, she set the patties under the broiler. "How many can you eat?"

"One'll do. Why are you sanding floors and hanging wallpaper?"

"Because it's my house." Maggie grabbed a head of lettuce from the refrigerator and began to shred it for salad.

"It was your house in California, too."

"Not the way this is." She dropped the lettuce and faced him. Impatience, annoyance, frustration—the emotions were plainly on the surface for him to see. "Look, I don't expect you to understand. I don't *care* if you understand. This house is special. Even after everything that's happened, it's special."

No, he didn't understand, but he discovered he wanted to. "The police have contacted you, then."

"Yes." She began to shred lettuce with a vengeance. "That investigator, Lieutenant Reiker, was here this morning." Her fingers dug into the cold, wet leaves. "Damn it, Cliff, I feel gruesome. I called Joyce and felt like an idiot, an intruder. There was nothing I could say."

"Did you?" he murmured. Strange that Joyce hadn't said anything about it, he thought. Then again, Joyce had said very little to him. "There isn't anything for you to say." He put his hands on her shoulders and felt the tension ripple. "This is something Joyce and her mother and the police have to deal with. It's nothing to do with you."

"I tell myself that," she said quietly. "Intellectually, I know it's true, but—" She turned, because she needed someone. Because, she admitted, she needed him. "It happened right outside. I'm involved, connected, whether I want to be or not. A man was murdered a few yards from my house. He was killed in a spot where I'd planned to put a nice quiet pond, and now—"

"And now," Cliff said, interrupting, "it's ten years later."

"Why should that matter?" she demanded. "My parents were killed ten years ago— Time doesn't make any difference."

"That," he countered, less gently than he'd intended, "had everything to do with you."

With a sigh, she allowed herself the weakness of resting her head against him. "I know how Joyce is feeling now. Everywhere I look, something draws me into this."

The more Maggie talked of Joyce, the less Cliff thought of the quiet brunette, and the more he thought of Maggie. His fingers tangled in her hair. It wasn't desire he felt now, but an almost fierce, protective urge he'd never expected. Perhaps there was something he could do, he decided, drawing her away.

"You didn't know William Morgan."

"No, but—"

"I did. He was a cold, ruthless man who didn't believe

in words like *compassion* or *generosity*." Deliberately, he set Maggie aside and tended to the meat under the broiler himself. "Half the town would've cheered ten years ago if it hadn't been for Louella. She loved the old man. Joyce loved him, too, but both of them feared him every bit as much. The police won't have an easy time proving who killed him, and the town won't care. I detested him myself, for a lot of reasons."

She didn't like knowing that he could speak of a man's murder so calmly, so coldly. But then, as she'd told him herself before, they really didn't understand each other. To keep her hands busy, Maggie went back to the salad. "Joyce?" she asked casually.

He glanced at her sharply, then leaned on the counter again. "Yeah, for one. Morgan believed in discipline. Old-fashioned discipline. Joyce was like my kid sister. When I caught Morgan going at her with a belt when she was sixteen, I threatened to kill him myself."

He said it so casually Maggie's blood froze. He saw the doubts and the questions in her eyes when she looked at him.

"And so," Cliff added, "as the stories go, did half the population of Morganville. No one grieved when they fished William Morgan's car out of the river."

"No one has the right to take a life," Maggie said in a shaky voice. "Not their own or anyone else's."

He remembered that they had fished her husband's car out of the water, too. He remembered that the final verdict had been suicide. "You'd be better off not making comparisons," he said roughly.

"They seem to make themselves."

"What happened to Jerry Browning was a tragic waste of a life and of a talent. Do you plan on taking the blame for that, too?"

"I never took the blame," Maggie said wearily.

"Did you love him?"

Her eyes were eloquent, but her voice was steady. "Not enough."

"Enough to be faithful to him for six years," Cliff countered.

She smiled as her own words came back to her. "Yes, enough for that. Still, there's more to love than loyalty, isn't there?"

His hand was gentle again when he touched her face. "You said you hadn't taken the blame."

"Responsibility and blame are different things."

"No." He shook his head. "There's no responsibility or blame this time, either. Don't you think it's the height of egotism to feel responsible for someone else's actions?"

She started to snap at him, but the words hit home. "Maybe. Maybe it is." It wasn't easy, but she shook off the mood and smiled. "I think the hamburgers are done. Let's eat."

Chapter 7

Maggie found the kitchen cozy with the smell of hot food and the patter of raindrops that had just begun to strike the windows. When she thought of it, she decided she'd never really experienced coziness before. Her parents had lived on a grand scale: huge, elegant rooms and huge, elegant parties; boisterous, eccentric friends. With her own home in Beverly Hills, Maggie had followed the same pattern. Extravagance might've been what she needed during that phase of her life, or it might've been a habit. She wasn't sure when it had begun to wear on her, any more than she was certain if she'd ever been as relaxed as she was at that moment, eating in her half-finished kitchen with a man she wasn't quite sure of.

He was strong, she mused. Perhaps she'd never allowed a strong man into her life. Her father had been strong, Maggie remembered. He'd been the type of man who could do and get precisely what he wanted simply because he wanted it. The strength hadn't been a physical one, but one of personality and will. But then, her mother had matched him with her own combination of grit and exuberance. Maggie had never seen a more perfect relationship than theirs.

Theirs had been an all-consuming, enduring love, with qualities of practicality, compassion and fire. They'd never competed, never envied each other's success. Support, she thought. Perhaps that had been the real key to the quality and lasting power of their relationship. Unquestioning mutual support. She hadn't found that in her own marriage, and she'd come to think her parents had been unique.

Something had happened to the balance in her relationship with Jerry. As he'd grown weaker, she'd grown stronger. Eventually, they'd come to a point where all the support had been on her side and all the need on his. Yet she'd stayed, because it had been impossible to forget that they'd been friends. Friends don't break promises.

She wondered, as she studied Cliff, what sort of friend he would be. And she wondered, though she tried not to, what he would be like as a lover.

"What're you thinking of?"

The question came so abruptly that Maggie almost overturned her glass. Quickly, she sorted out her thoughts and chose the least personal. She could hardly tell him what had been the last thing on her mind. "I was thinking," she began, picking up her wine again, "how cozy it is eating here in the kitchen. I'll probably demote the dining room to the last thing on my list."

"That's what you were thinking?" By the way he held her gaze, she knew he sensed there'd been other things.

"More or less." A woman who'd been interviewed and

questioned all her life knew how to evade and dodge. Lifting the bottle, she filled Cliff's glass again. "The Bordeaux's another present from my agent. Or another bribe," she added.

"Bribe?"

"He wants me to give up this mad scheme of camping out in the wilderness and come back to civilization."

"He thinks he can persuade you with puppies and French wine?"

With a bubbling laugh, Maggie sipped. "If I weren't so attached to this place, either one might've worked."

"Is that what you are?" Cliff asked thoughtfully. "Attached?"

At the question, her eyes stopped laughing, and her soft, wide mouth sobered. "In your business you should know that some things root quickly."

"Some do," he agreed. "And some that do can't acclimate to the new territory."

She tapped the side of her glass with a fingertip, wishing she understood why his doubts dug at her so deeply. "You don't have much faith in me, do you?"

"Maybe not." He shrugged as if to lighten a subject he wasn't so certain of any longer. "In any case, I'm finding it interesting to watch you make the adjustments."

She decided to go with his mood. "How'm I doing?"

"Better than I'd thought." He lifted his glass in a half toast. "But it's early yet."

She laughed, because arguing seemed like a waste of time. "Were you born cynical, Cliff, or did you take lessons?"

"Were you born an optimist?"

Both brows lifted to disappear under the fringe of sable bangs. *"Touché,"* Maggie said. No longer interested in the meal, she studied him, finding that while his face was very much to her liking, she still couldn't judge him by his eyes. Too much control, she thought. A person would only get inside his head if he or she was invited. "You know," she began slowly, "after I'd stopped being annoyed, I decided I was glad you were coming by this evening." Now she grinned. "I don't know when I might've opened the wine otherwise."

This time he grinned. "I annoy you?"

"I think you're well aware of that," Maggie returned dryly. "And that for your own personal reasons it pleases you to do so."

Cliff tasted the wine again. It was warm and rich, reminding him of her mouth. "Actually, I do."

He said it so easily that Maggie laughed again. "Is it just me, or is annoying people a hobby of yours?"

"Just you." Over the rim of his glass, he studied her. She'd pinned her hair up in a loose Gibson style that accentuated her delicate, old-fashioned features. She wore some dark contouring shadow that made her eyes seem even larger, but her mouth was naked. This was a woman, Cliff thought, who knew how to accentuate her own looks to the best advantage, subtly, so that a man would be caught before he analysed what was Maggie and what was illusion. "I like your reactions," Cliff continued after a moment. "You don't like to lose your temper."

"So you like to provoke me until I do."

"Yeah." He smiled again. "That about sizes it up."

"Why?" she demanded in a voice filled with exasperated amusement.

"I'm not immune to you," Cliff said, so quietly her fingers tightened on the stem of her glass. "I wouldn't like to think you were immune to me."

She sat for a moment, stirred and baffled. Before her emotions could rise any closer to the surface, she stood and began to clear the table. "No, I'm not. Would you like more wine or some coffee?"

His hands closed over hers on the dishes. Slowly, he rose, his gaze fixed on her face. Maggie felt as though the kitchen had shrunk in size. Like Alice in the rabbit hole, she thought confusedly, unsure whether to sample that tempting little bottle or not. The patter of rain outside seemed to grow to a roar.

"I want to make love with you."

She wasn't a child, Maggie told herself. She was an adult, and men had wanted her before. She'd resisted temptations before. But had any ever been quite so alluring? "We've already been through this."

His hands tightened on hers when she tried to turn away. "But we never resolved it."

No, she couldn't turn away, or run away, from a man like this, Maggie realized. She'd have to stand her ground. "I was sure we had. Perhaps coffee would be best, since you have to drive this evening and I have to work."

Cliff took the dishes and set them back on the table. With her hands empty, Maggie found herself at a loss. She folded her arms under her breasts, a habit Cliff had discovered she used whenever she was upset or disturbed. At the moment, he didn't care which she was, as long as she wasn't unmoved.

"We haven't resolved it," he repeated, and plucked a pin from her hair. "We haven't begun to resolve it."

Though her eyes remained steady, she backed up when he stepped closer. It made him feel as though he were stalking her, an odd and thrilling sensation. "I really thought I'd made myself clear," Maggie managed, in what sounded to her like a firm, dismissive tone.

"It's clear when I touch you." Cliff backed her up

against the counter, then pulled another pin from her hair. "It's clear when you look at me like you're looking at me now."

Maggie's heart began to pound at the base of her throat. She was weakening; she felt it in the heaviness of her limbs, the lightness in her head. Desire was temptation, and temptation a seduction in itself. "I didn't say I didn't want you—"

"No, you didn't," Cliff interrupted. When he drew out the next pin, her hair fell heavily to her shoulders and lay there, dark and tousled. "I don't think lying comes easily to you."

How could she have been so relaxed a few moments before and so tense now? Every muscle in her body was taut in the effort to combat what seemed to be inevitable. "No, I don't lie." Her voice was lower, huskier. "I said I didn't know you. I said you didn't understand me."

Something flashed into him. Perhaps it was rage; perhaps it was need. "I don't give a damn how little we know each other or how little we understand each other. I know I want you." He gathered her hair in one hand. "I only have to touch you to know you want me."

Her eyes grew darker. Why did it always seem her desire was mixed with anger and, though she detested it, a certain weakness she couldn't control? "Can you really believe it's that simple?"

He had to. For the sake of his own survival, Cliff knew, he had to keep whatever was between them purely physical. They'd make love through the night until they were exhausted. In the morning, the need and the bond would be gone. He had to believe it. Otherwise... He didn't want to dwell on otherwise. "Why should it be complicated?" he countered.

The anger and the longing flowed through her. "Why indeed?" Maggie murmured.

The room had lost its cozy ambience. Now she felt she'd suffocate if she didn't escape it. Her eyes were stormy, his almost brutally calm, but she kept her gaze level on his while her thoughts raged. Why should she feel the need to rationalize, to romanticize? she asked herself. She wasn't an innocent young girl with misty dreams, but an adult, a widow, a professional woman who'd learned to live with reality. In reality, people took what they wanted, then dealt with the consequences. Now so would she.

"The bedroom's upstairs," she told him, and, brushing by him, walked out of the kitchen.

Disturbed, Cliff frowned after her. This was what he wanted, he thought. The lack of complications. Yet her abrupt acceptance had been so unexpected, so cool. No, he realized as he started after her, that wasn't what he wanted.

Maggie was at the base of the steps before he caught up with her. When she looked over her shoulder, he saw the fury in her eyes. The moment he took her arm, he felt the tension. This, he discovered, was what he wanted. He didn't want her cool, emotionless agreement or a careless acquiescence. He wanted to build that fury and tension until the passion that spawned them broke through. Before the night was over, he'd draw it all from her and purge himself, as well.

In silence, they climbed the stairs to the second floor.

The rain fell, strong and steady, against the windows and the newly seeded earth below. The sound made Maggie think of the subtle rhythmic percussion she'd imagined in the arrangement of the song she'd just completed. There was no moon to guide the way, so she moved from memory. Darkness was deep and without shadows. She didn't look when she entered the bedroom, but she knew Cliff was still beside her.

What now? she thought with sudden panic. What was she doing, bringing him here, to the single spot she considered purely private? He might learn more than she wanted before he left again, yet she might learn nothing more than she already knew. They wanted each other; it was unexplainable. It was undeniable.

As her nerves stretched tighter, Maggie was grateful for the dark. She didn't want him to see the doubts that would be clear on her face. As the need grew stronger, she knew she wouldn't have been able to conceal that, either. Darkness was better, she told herself, because it was anonymous. When he touched her, her body went rigid with a dozen conflicting emotions.

Feeling it, Cliff ran his hands over the slope of her shoulders, down to her lower back. He found he didn't want her to be too relaxed, to be too yielding. Not yet. He wanted to know she struggled against something deeper, something unnamed, even as he did.

"You don't want to give in to this," Cliff said quietly. "Or to me."

"No." Yet she felt the tremor, not fear but pleasure, course through her body when he slipped his hands under her thin wool sweater. "No, I don't."

"What choice is there?"

She could see his face through the gloom of darkness, close, very close, to hers. "Damn you," she whispered. "There's none at all."

He slid his hands up her naked back, through the neck opening of her sweater, until his fingers found her hair. "No, not for either of us."

His body was firm against hers. His voice, soft and

low, was faintly edged with anger. She caught the scent of soap, sharp, unrepentantly male, that lingered on his skin. His face was mysterious, indistinct in the darkness. He might've been anyone. As Maggie felt the next fierce pull of desire, she almost wished he was.

"Make love with me," she demanded. A decision made quickly, freely, would leave no room for regrets. "Take me now. It's all either of us wants."

Was it? The question had barely formed in his mind when his mouth was on hers. Then there were no questions, just flame and flash and power. Understanding, if there had been any before, dimmed. Reason vanished. Sensation, and only sensation, ruled. While perhaps both of them had expected it, they were caught in a maelstrom in which neither of them had any control. Racked by it, they fell together onto the bed and let the fire rage.

He could find no gentleness to give her, but it seemed she neither demanded nor expected any. He wanted her naked but not vulnerable, soft but not yielding. If he had spoken the needs aloud, she could have been no more than what he'd asked for. As she arched against him, her lips clung in a wild, urgent kiss that was only a prelude to passion. He pulled at her clothes, forgetting finesse, then caught his breath when, in an equal frenzy, she began to strip him.

Clothes were tossed aside as if they were meaningless. Her scent rose up from her skin, from her hair, clouding whatever logic he might have tried to regain. The mattress swayed and dipped as they rolled over it, mindless now of the rain, of the dark, of time and place.

Then they were naked, heated flesh to heated flesh. The desperation grew in each to have all there could be of the other. Whispered demands, labored breathing, moans and sighs of pleasure, drowned out the sound of falling rain. Her body was small and supple and surprisingly strong. All three aspects combined to drive him mad.

This was what it meant to be consumed. Maggie knew it as his hands skimmed over her, inciting thrill after thrill. She hungered, no, starved, for each new demand. Greedy for what pleasure he would give and what pleasure she would take, she allowed him whatever he wanted. She felt no shame, no hesitation, in tasting, in touching, in asking for more or in taking it.

If his body had been designed to her wish, it could have been no more perfect. She reveled in the leanness, the cords of muscle, the long, narrow bones that ran along his hips. Wherever, whenever, she touched, she could almost feel the blood throb under his skin.

She wanted to know he had no more control than she. She wanted to know they were both victims of their own combined power. The fuse that had been lit between them with a look was burning quickly. Desire was madness, and if the words she'd written were true, she'd cast aside her reason for it.

With a savageness they both craved, they came together, fighting to prolong an outrageous passion, greedy to capture that final flash of pleasure. She thought of whirlpools and high winds and the bellow of thunder. She felt the spin, the speed and heard the roar. Then both her mind and body shuddered from the last violent surge.

Love? Maggie thought some dim time later, when her thoughts began to clear again. If this was making love, she'd been innocent all her life. Could something with so gentle a name have such a violent effect on the body? Hers was pulsing and throbbing as if she'd raced up one side of a mountain and fallen off the other. She'd written songs about love, songs about passion, yet she'd never fully understood her own words until now.

Until now, she thought, when the man who lay beside her had dared her to live her own fantasies. With him she'd found the answer to the dark, driving needs that gave the grit, or the wistfulness, to most of her music. She understood, but understanding opened the door to dozens of questions.

Maggie ran a hand up her own body, astonished at the lingering sense of power and of wonder. How long had she been waiting for this night to come? Perhaps it was possible for passion to lie dormant, unexplored, until it was triggered by a certain person at a certain time.

Maggie thought of the film her music would score. It had been that way for the female character. She'd been content with life, almost smug, until one day a man had entered it, a man she'd shared little common ground with, a man who'd ignited a spark that had changed everything. It hadn't mattered that the woman was intelligent, successful, independent. The man, merely by existing, had altered the scope and pattern of her life.

If the same thing was happening to her, there was still time to stop it before she, too, became so consumed by needs, so ruled by desire, that nothing would ever be the same again.

In the film, the relationship had spawned violence. Instinct told her that there was something between her and Cliff that could do the same. There was little moderation in either of them. It was extremes, she knew, that played havoc with human nature.

Maybe fate had brought her to this serene little plot of land with its undertones of violence. The same fate might have brought her to this taciturn, physical man who seemed connected with both the tranquillity and the danger. The question now was whether she was strong enough to deal with the consequences of each.

What, Maggie asked herself while she stared into the darkness, would happen next?

Because nothing was as he'd expected it, Cliff was silent. He'd wanted passion, but he'd never imagined the scope of it. He'd wanted what her song had whispered of, but the reality had been much more dramatic than any words or any melody. He'd been certain that once the tension between them had been released, once the lure had been accepted, the needs would lessen.

It was true his body was sated with a pleasure more intense than anything he'd known, but his mind— Cliff closed his eyes, wishing his mind would rest as easy. But it was too full of her. So full that he knew even a touch would set his body raging again. That kind of need was a shade too close to dependence for comfort. They had nothing to offer each other, he reminded himself, nothing but outrageous mutual desire.

And suddenly he remembered a line from her song. "Desire is madness."

If he could have stopped himself, he wouldn't have touched her again. He was already reaching for her.

"You're cold," he murmured, automatically drawing her against him to warm her.

"A bit." There was an awkwardness she didn't know how to alleviate and a need she didn't know how to explain.

"Here." He tugged the tangled spread over her, then pulled her close again. "Better?"

"Yes." Her body relaxed against his, even as her thoughts continued to race.

They lapsed into silence again, neither knowing quite how to deal with what had flared between them. Cliff listened to the rain beat against the window glass, adding to the sense of isolation. Even on a clear night, he knew, you would see no light from a neighboring house. "Are you having trouble staying out here alone?"

"Trouble?" Maggie hedged. She wanted to stay exactly as she was, wrapped close around him, warm and safe and untroubled. She didn't want to think now of staying in the big house alone, of sleeping alone.

"This place is more isolated than most around here." How soft she was, he thought. It brought him an odd sort of contentment to feel her hair lie against his shoulder. "A lot of people, even if they were raised here, would have trouble being this far back and alone, especially after everything that's happened."

No, she didn't want to talk about it. Maggie closed her eyes, reminding herself that she'd come here determined to take care of herself, to deal with whatever came. She drew a deep breath, but when she started to shift away, Cliff held her still.

"You are having trouble."

"No. No, not really." Her biggest problem at the moment was to keep her mind and body from wanting more of him. Opening her eyes again, she stared at the rain-drenched window. "I'll admit I've had a couple of restless nights since—well, since we started to dig the pond. It isn't easy knowing what happened in that gully ten years ago, and I have a very active imagination."

"Part of the job?" He turned toward her a bit more, so that her leg slid casually between his. Her skin was smooth as polished glass.

"I suppose." She laughed, but he thought he detected nerves in it. "One night I was certain I heard someone in the house."

He stopped stroking her hair, drawing her back far enough to see her eyes. "In the house?"

"Just my imagination," she said with a shrug. "Boards creaking in the attic, stealthy footsteps on the stairs, doors opening and closing. I worked myself up into quite a state."

He didn't like the sound of it, even in her dismissive tone of voice. "Don't you have a phone in this room?" Cliff demanded.

"Well, yes, but—"

"Why didn't you call the police?"

Maggie sighed and wished she'd never mentioned anything about it. He sounded like a cranky older brother scolding his scatterbrained sister. "Because I'd left the kitchen extension off the hook. I'd been trying to work that afternoon, and—" The word scatterbrained flowed back into her head. Embarrassed, she trailed off. "Anyway, it's better that I didn't call. I felt like an idiot in the morning in any case."

Imagination or not, Cliff reflected, she was still a woman alone, isolated, and everyone in a ten-mile radius knew it. "Are you locking your doors?"

"Cliff—"

"Maggie." He rolled until she was on her back and he was looking down at her. "Are you locking your doors?"

"I wasn't," she said, annoyed. "But after the sheriff came by, I—"

"Stan was here?"

A breath hissed out between her teeth. "Damn it, do you know how often you cut me off in the middle of a sentence?"

"Yes. When did Stan come by?"

"The day after the state police were here. He wanted to reassure me." She wasn't cold now, not with the way his body was pressed against hers. Desire began to stir again, not too quiet, not too slow. "He seems to know his job."

"He's been a good sheriff."

"But?" Maggie prompted, sensing more.

"Just a personal thing," Cliff murmured, shifting away again. Maggie felt the chill return immediately.

"Joyce," she said flatly, and started to rise. Cliff's arm came out to pin her down.

"You have a habit of saying little and implying a lot." His voice was cool now, his hold firm. "It's quite a talent."

"It seems we have little to say to each other."

"I don't have to explain myself to you."

She lay stiff and still. "I'm not asking you to."

"The hell you aren't." Angry, he sat up, drawing her with him so that the cover dropped away. Her skin was pale, her hair like a flood of night over her shoulders. Despite a strong will and a keen sense of privacy, he felt compelled to clarify. "Joyce's been like my sister. When she married Stan, I gave her away. I'm godfather to her oldest girl. It might be difficult for you to understand that kind of friendship."

It wasn't. It had been like that between herself and Jerry. The friendship had gradually deteriorated during marriage, because the marriage had been a mistake. "No, I understand it," Maggie said quietly. "I don't understand why you seem so concerned about her."

"That's my business."

"It certainly is."

He swore again. "Look, Joyce has been going through a difficult time. She never wanted to stay in Morganville. When she was a kid, she'd had ideas about going to the city and studying to be an actress."

"She wanted to act?"

"Pipe dreams, maybe." Cliff moved his shoulders. "Maybe not. She let them go when she married Stan, but she's never been happy staying in Morganville. One of the reasons she sold the house was so they'd have enough money to move. Stan won't budge."

"They could compromise."

"Stan doesn't understand how important it is to her to get away from here. She was eighteen when she married. Then she had three children over the next five years. She spent the first part of her life following her father's rules, the second caring for her children and her mother. A woman like you wouldn't understand that."

"I'm sick of that!" Maggie exploded, jerking away from him. "I'm sick to death of you putting me in some category. Pampered celebrity with no conception of how real people feel or live." Anger rocketed through her, so quick and powerful she never thought to repress it. "What kind of man are you, going to bed with a woman you haven't an ounce of respect for?"

Stunned by the sudden, passionate outburst, he watched her spring from the bed. "Wait a minute."

"No, I've made enough mistakes for one evening." She began to search for her clothes among those scattered on the floor. "You had your dinner and your sex," she said in a brittle tone. "Now get out."

Fury rose so that he had to fight it back. She was right, Cliff told himself. He'd come to take her to bed; that was all. Intimacy didn't always equal closeness. He wasn't interested in being close to her or in becoming involved with anything more than her body. Even as he thought it, the emptiness of it washed over him. The contentment he'd felt so briefly vanished. He could hear her unsteady breathing as she pulled on her sweater. Reaching for his clothes, he tried to concentrate on the sound of the rain instead.

"We're not finished, you and I," he murmured.

"Aren't we?" Enraged, aching, Maggie turned. She could feel the tears well in her eyes, but felt secure in the darkness. The sweater skimmed her thighs, leaving the length of her legs naked. She knew what he thought of her, and this time would give him the satisfaction of believing he was right. "We went to bed, and it was good for both of us," she said easily. "Not all one-night stands are as successful. You get a high rating as a lover, Cliff, if that helps your ego."

This time there was no controlling the temper that roared into him. Grabbing both her arms, he pulled her toward him. "Damn you, Maggie."

"Why?" she tossed back. "Because I said it first? Go home and curl up with your double standard, Cliff. I don't need it."

Everything she said hit home, and hit hard. If he stayed, he wasn't certain what he might do. Throttle her? It was tempting. Drag her back to bed and purge himself of the angry desire that pounded in him? More temptation. As he held her, he wasn't sure if it was he who was shaking or her, but he knew if he stayed, something volatile, perhaps irrevocable, would burst.

Dropping his hands, he walked from the room. "Lock your doors," he called out, and cursed her as he strode down the stairs.

Maggie wrapped her arms around herself and let the tears overflow. It was much too late for locks, she thought.

Chapter 8

For the next few days, Maggie worked like a Trojan. Her kitchen floor was sealed, making it her first fully and successfully completed project. She added three fresh strips of wallpaper to her bedroom, found a rug for the music room and cleaned the trim in the downstairs hall.

In the evenings, she worked at her piano until she was too tired to see the keys or hear her own music. She kept her phone off the hook. All in all, she decided, the life of a recluse had its advantages. She was productive, and no one interfered with the flow of her days. It became almost possible to believe that was what she wanted and no more.

Perhaps she was pushing herself. She might admit that, but she wouldn't admit she did so to prevent herself from thinking about her night with Cliff. That had been a mistake. It wasn't wise to dwell on mistakes.

She saw no one, spoke to no one, and told herself she was content to go on that way indefinitely.

But of course complete solitude lasts only so long. Maggie was painting the window trim in the music room when she heard the sound of an approaching car. She debated whether she might just ignore the caller until he or she went away again. As a beginning recluse, it was certainly her right. Then she recognized the old Lincoln. Setting the paint bucket on the drop cloth at her feet, Maggie went to the front door to meet Louella Morgan.

She looked even more frail this time, Maggie mused. Her skin seemed almost translucent against the tidy white hair. It was an odd, somewhat eerie combination of youth and age. As Maggie watched, Louella looked over toward the gully. For a moment she seemed like a statue, unmoving, unblinking, unbreathing. When Maggie saw her take a step toward the fenced-off section, she walked outside.

"Good morning, Mrs. Morgan."

Louella glanced up, her eyes focusing slowly. The hand she lifted to pat at her hair shook lightly. "I wanted to come."

"Of course." Maggie smiled and hoped she was doing the right thing. "Please come in. I was about to fix some coffee."

Louella walked up the sagging steps Maggie had yet to contact Bog about. "You've made some changes."

Unsure which route to take, she decided on light, cheerful chatter. "Yes, inside and out. The landscapers work faster than I do." Killer stood in the doorway, snarling and backing up. Maggie hushed him as they went inside.

"This wallpaper was here when we moved in," Louella murmured, looking around the hall. "I always meant to change it."

"Did you?" Maggie led her gently toward the living room as she spoke. "Perhaps you could give me some suggestions. I haven't quite made up my mind yet."

"Something warm," Louella said softly. "Something warm, with subtle color, so people would feel welcome. That's what I wanted."

"Yes, I'm sure that's just what it needs." She wanted to put her arm around the woman and tell her she understood. Perhaps it was kinder not to.

"A house like this should smell of lemon oil and flowers."

"It will," Maggie told her, wishing she could change the scent of dust and paint.

"I always felt it should be filled with children." She gazed around the room with the kind of misty concentration that made Maggie think she was seeing it as it had been more than twenty years before. "Children give a house its personality, you know, more than its decorating. They leave their mark on it."

"You have grandchildren, don't you?" Maggie steered her toward the sofa.

"Yes, Joyce's children. The baby's in school now. Time goes so quickly for the young. You've looked at the pictures?" Louella asked suddenly.

"The pictures?" Maggie's brow creased, then cleared. "Oh, yes, I've really only had a chance to glance at them. I've been a bit tied up." Remembering, she walked to the mantel and retrieved the envelope. "Your roses looked beautiful. I'm not sure I'd have that kind of talent."

Louella took the envelope and stared down at it. "Roses need love and discipline. Like children."

Maggie decided against another offer of coffee. Instead, she sat down beside Louella. "Perhaps if we looked at them together it would help."

"Old pictures." Louella opened the flap and drew them out. "There's so much to see in old pictures if you know where to look. Early spring," she murmured, looking down at the first snapshot. "You see, the hyacinths are blooming, and the daffodils."

Maggie studied the square, pristine black and white, but it was the man and small girl who caught her attention rather than the flowers. He was tall, broad in the chest, with a sharp-boned, lantern-jawed face. The suit he wore was severe and proper. Beside him, the little girl wore a frilly dress, ribboned at the waist with black strap shoes and a flowered bonnet.

It must've been Easter, Maggie concluded. The little girl smiled determinedly at the camera. Joyce would've been around four then, Maggie calculated, and perhaps a bit uncomfortable in the organdy and flounces. William Morgan didn't look cruel, she thought as she studied his set, unreadable face. He simply looked untouchable. She fought back a shudder and spoke lightly.

"I want to plant some bulbs myself. Things should be a little more settled by fall."

Louella said nothing as she turned over the next picture. This time Maggie was looking at a young Louella. The style of hair and dress told her the picture was more than twenty years old. The lopsided angle of the shot made her suspect that Joyce had taken it as a child.

"The roses," Louella murmured, running a finger over the picture where they grew in profusion. "Gone now, with no one to care for them."

"Do you have a garden now?"

"Joyce does." Louella set the picture aside and took up another. "I tend it now and then, but it isn't the same as having your own."

"No, it's not, but Joyce must be grateful for your help."

"She's never been easy in town," Louella said, half to

herself. "Never easy. A pity she took after me rather than her father."

"She's lovely," Maggie told her, searching for something to say. "I hope to see more of her. Her husband suggested that we have dinner."

"Stan's a good man. Solid. He's always loved her." The sad, elusive smile touched her lips. "He's been kind to me."

When she turned over the next picture, Maggie felt her stiffen. She saw the smile freeze rather than fade. Looking down, she saw William Morgan and a young, perhaps teenaged Stan Agee. This more recent photo was in color, and the trees in the background were vibrant with fall. The two men were dressed in flannel shirts and caps, and each wore a drab-colored vest with what looked to Maggie like small weights around the hem. Each carried a shotgun.

Shells, not weights, Maggie realized as she looked at the vests again. They must've been hunting. And they stood, she noted, near the slope of the gully. Disturbed, she looked at the trees again, at the tapestry she wanted to see for herself.

"Joyce would've taken this," Louella murmured. "She hunted with her father. He taught her how to handle guns before she was twelve. It didn't matter that she hated them—she learned to please him. William looks pleased," Louella continued, though Maggie couldn't see it. "He liked to hunt this land. Now we know he died here. Here," she repeated, placing a palm over the picture. "Not three miles away, in the river. He never left his land. Somehow I think I always knew."

"Mrs. Morgan." Maggie set the pictures aside and laid a hand on her arm. "I know this must be difficult for you; it must be like going through it all over again. I wish there was something I could do."

Turning her head, Louella fixed Maggie with a long, unsmiling stare. "Put in your pond," she said flatly. "Plant your flowers. That's as it should be. The rest is over."

When she started to rise, Maggie found herself more disturbed by the emotionless reply than she would've been with a bout of tears. "Your pictures," she began helplessly.

"Keep them." Louella walked to the doorway before she turned. "I've no need for them anymore."

Should she have been depressed? Maggie wondered as she listened to the car drive away. Was her reaction normal empathy for another's tragedy, or was she allowing herself to become personally involved again? Over the last few days, she'd nearly convinced herself that the Morgan business had nothing to do with her. Now, after one brief contact, it was beginning again.

Yet it was more than a sense of involvement, Maggie admitted as she rubbed her arms to bring back warmth. There'd been something eerie in the way Louella had looked at the pictures. As if, Maggie reflected, she'd been putting the people in them to rest, though only one was dead.

Imagination again, she scolded herself. An overactive one. Yet hadn't there been something odd in the way Louella had studied that last snapshot? It had been as if she'd been searching for details, looking for something. With a frown, Maggie walked over and sifted through the pictures herself, stopping when she came to the color print.

There was William Morgan again, his hair a bit thinner, his eyes a bit sterner than they'd been in the Easter photo. Sheriff Agee stood beside him, hardly more than a boy, his build not quite filled out, his hair a little shaggy. He'd looked even more like a beachcomber in his youth, Maggie decided, though he held the gun as if he were very familiar with firearms. Looking at him, Maggie could easily see why Joyce had fallen for him hard enough to give up dreams of fame and fortune. He was young, handsome, with a trace of cocky sexuality around his mouth.

She could understand, too, why Joyce had feared and obeyed and struggled to please the man beside him. William Morgan looked straight at the camera, legs spread, the gun held in both hands. Cliff had described him as a hard, cold man. Maggie had no trouble believing him, but it didn't explain why Louella had been so disturbed by this one picture. Or why, Maggie added, she herself became uneasy when she looked at it.

Annoyed by her own susceptibility, she started to study the picture more closely when the rumble outside warned of another approaching vehicle.

When it rains it pours, she thought bad-temperedly. Tossing the picture carelessly on top of the others, she walked to the window. When Cliff's pickup came into view, the flare of excitement left her shaken. *Oh, no,* Maggie warned herself. *Not again. A woman who makes the same mistake twice deserves what she gets.* Determined, she picked up her brush and began to paint in long, hard strokes. Let him knock all he wanted, she thought with an angry toss of her head. She had work to do.

Minutes passed, but he didn't come to her door. Maggie continued to paint, telling herself it didn't matter to her what he was doing outside. When she tried to lean closer to the window to look through, paint smeared from the sill to her jeans. Swearing, she wiped at it and made it worse.

She didn't give a damn about Cliff Delaney, Maggie told herself. But she did care about having people wander around on her land. It was her right to go out and see what he was up to and order him away, she told herself as she set down her brush. If he were only checking on how her grass was growing, she fumed as she headed for the door, he should still have the courtesy to announce himself. By not announcing himself, he was denying her the satisfaction of ignoring him.

She yanked open the door but didn't, as she'd expected, see him bending over the little green sprouts that had begun to shoot up through the topsoil. Neither was he looking out over the plugs of phlox or the juniper shrubs on her front bank. Perhaps, Maggie thought with a frown, he'd gone around to check on the last project to be completed, the crown vetch on her eroding rear bank.

Annoyed that she hadn't thought of that in the first place, she started to turn back into the house when a movement near the gully caught her eye. For an instant, basic, primitive fear that slept in her awoke. She thought of ghouls and phantoms and legends of shades that never rest. In the next instant she recognized Cliff. As infuriated as she was embarrassed by her own reaction, she went to confront him.

As she drew closer, Maggie saw the willow, slender, small and tenderly green. Cliff was setting the ball of roots into a hole he'd dug out of the rocky soil with a pick and shovel. He stood perhaps six feet from the slope of the gully, his shirt tossed carelessly on the ground. She could see the muscles in his back ripple as he began to shovel dirt back into the hole. The twinge of her stomach told her that her reaction to him was no less powerful now than it had been before they'd made love.

Maggie straightened her shoulders and angled her chin. "What're you doing?"

Because he continued to shovel without breaking

rhythm, she decided he'd known she was coming. "Planting a tree," Cliff said easily.

Her eyes narrowed dangerously. "I can see that. As far as I remember, I didn't order a willow from you."

"No." He knelt down to mound and smooth the dirt at the base of the tree. She watched his hands, knowing now what they could do on her body. It seemed he had the same talent with soil. "No charge."

Impatient with his nonanswers and with her own growing arousal, she folded her arms. "Why are you planting a tree I didn't buy?"

Satisfied that the willow was secure, he rose. Leaning casually on the shovel, he studied her. No, he hadn't gotten her out of his system, Cliff decided. Seeing her again didn't relieve the knots of tension he'd been living with for days. Somehow he'd known it wouldn't, but he'd had to try. "Some people might call it a peace offering," he told her at length, then watched her mouth open and close again.

Maggie looked at the tree. It was so young, so fragile, but one day she would see it in full sweep, spreading over her pond, and— She stopped, realizing that it was the first time she'd thought of going through with the pond since the discovery. He must have known that, just as he'd known the willow might be enough to make her see the beauty and serenity again. Most of her anger had drained before she remembered to hold on to any of it.

"A peace offering," she repeated, running a finger down one delicate leaf. "Is that what you call it?"

Her voice had been cool, but he saw that her eyes had already started to warm. He wondered how many strong men she'd slain with that one look. "Maybe." He sliced the shovel into the ground where it stood, tilting slightly to the left. "Got anything cold in there to drink?"

It was an apology, Maggie decided, perhaps the only kind a man like him could give. It only took her five seconds to decide to accept it. "Maybe," she said in an equal tone, then turned to walk back toward the house. A smile curved her lips when he fell into step beside her. "Your men did an excellent job," she continued while they circled around toward the rear of the house. "I'm anxious to see how the stuff over the retaining wall's going to look."

"Crown vetch," Cliff supplied before he stopped to check the job, as she'd suspected he would. "You should see something come through in four or five more days. It'll spread fast enough to cover this bank before summer's over." He kept his hands in his back pockets as he studied the work his men had done and thought of the woman beside him. "You've been busy?"

Maggie lifted a brow. "I suppose so. The house needs a lot of attention."

"Seen the paper?"

"No," she said, puzzled. "Why?"

Cliff shrugged, then walked ahead to the screen door to open it. "There was a big story on finding William Morgan buried on his old land. Land," he continued when Maggie moved by him into the kitchen, "recently purchased by a celebrated songwriter."

She turned sharply. "They had my name?"

"Yeah, it was mentioned—several times."

"Damn," she whispered, and, forgetting he'd asked for a drink, she dropped into a chair. "I'd wanted to avoid that." Half hopefully, she glanced up. "The local paper?"

Helping himself, Cliff went to the refrigerator and searched out a soda. "Morganville doesn't have a paper. There were stories in the *Frederick Post* and the *Herald Mail*." As he twisted off the top, he nodded toward the phone sitting off the hook. "If you hadn't done that, you'd have already answered a flood of calls from reporters." And from himself, Cliff thought silently. In the past twenty-four hours, he'd called her a dozen times. He'd vacillated between being frantic and furious every time he'd gotten a busy signal. What kind of woman left her phone off the hook for hours at a time? One who was independent of the outside world, he mused, or one who was hiding from it. Lifting the bottle, he drank. "That your escape route these days?"

In defense, Maggie rose and slammed the receiver back in place. "I don't need to escape from anything. You said yourself that this whole business doesn't have anything to do with me."

"So I did." He examined the liquid left in the bottle. "Maybe you were escaping from something else." He shifted his gaze until it locked on hers. "Were you hiding from me, Maggie?"

"Certainly not." She swept over to the sink and began to scrub the paint splatters from her hands. "I told you, I've been busy."

"Too busy to answer the phone?"

"The phone's a distraction. If you want to start an argument, Cliff, you can just take your peace offering and—" The phone shrilled behind her so that she ended her suggestion with an oath. Before she could answer it herself, Cliff had picked up the phone.

"Yes?" He watched the fury spring into her eyes as he leaned on the counter. He'd missed that, he discovered, just as he'd missed the subtle sexiness of the scent she wore. "No, I'm sorry, Miss Fitzgerald isn't available for comment." He replaced the receiver while Maggie wiped her damp hands on her jeans.

"I can screen my own calls, thank you. When I want a liaison, I'll let you know."

He drank from the bottle again. "Just saving you some aggravation."

"I don't want you or anyone to save me aggravation," she fumed. "It's my aggravation, and I'll do whatever I want with it." He grinned, but before she could think of any retaliation, the phone rang again. "Don't you dare," she warned. Shoving him aside, she answered herself.

"Hello."

"Damn it, Maggie, you've been leaving the phone off the hook again."

She let out a huff of breath. A reporter might've been easier to deal with. "Hello, C.J. How are you?"

"I'll tell you how I am!"

Maggie drew the phone back from her ear and scowled at Cliff. "There's no need for you to hang around."

He took another long sip from the bottle before he settled back comfortably. "I don't mind."

"Maggie!" C.J.'s voice vibrated in her ear. "Who the hell are you talking to?"

"Nobody," she mumbled, deliberately turning her back on Cliff. "You were going to tell me how you were."

"For the past twenty-four hours I've been frantic trying to get through to you. Maggie, it's irresponsible to leave your phone off the hook when people're trying to reach you."

There was a bag of cookies on the counter. Maggie dug into it, then bit into one with a vengeance. "Obviously I left it off the hook so I couldn't be reached."

"If I hadn't gotten you this time, I was going to send a telegram, and I'm not even sure they deliver telegrams in that place. What the hell have you been doing?"

"I've been working," she said between her teeth. "I can't work when the phone's ringing off the wall and people are forever coming by. I moved out here to be alone. I'm still waiting for that to happen."

"That's a nice attitude," he tossed back. In Los Angeles, C.J. searched through his desk drawer for a roll of antacids. "You've got people all over the country worried about you."

"Damn it, people all over the country don't have to worry about me. I'm fine!"

"You sound fine."

With an effort, Maggie controlled her precarious temper. When she lost it with C.J., she invariably lost the bout, as well. "I'm sorry I snapped at you, C.J., but I'm tired of being criticized for doing what I want to do."

"I'm not criticizing you," he grumbled over the peppermint-flavored pill. "It's just natural concern. For God's sake, Maggie, who wouldn't be concerned after that business in the paper?"

She tensed and, without thinking, turned back to face Cliff. He was watching her intently, the neck of the bottle held loosely in his fingers. "What business in the paper?"

"About that man's—ah, what was left of that man being dug up on your property. Good God, Maggie, I nearly had a heart attack when I read it. Then, not being able to reach you—"

"I'm sorry." She dragged a hand through her hair. "I'm really sorry, C.J. I didn't think it would hit the papers, at least not out there."

"So what I didn't know wouldn't hurt me?"

She smiled at the offended tone of voice. "Yes, something like that. I'd've called you with the details if I'd realized the news would get that far."

"Get this far?" he retorted, unappeased. "Maggie, you know that anything with your name in it's going to hit the press on both sides of the Atlantic."

She began to rub one finger slowly up and down her right temple. "And you know that was one of the reasons I wanted to get out."

"Where you live isn't going to change that."

She sighed. "Apparently not."

"Besides, that doesn't have anything to do with what's happened now," C.J. argued. He pressed a hand to his nervous stomach and wondered if a glass of Perrier would calm him. Maybe scotch would be a better idea.

"I haven't seen the paper," Maggie began in an even tone, "but I'm sure the whole thing was blown out of proportion."

"Blown out of proportion?" Again, she had to move the receiver back from her ear. A few steps away, Cliff heard C.J.'s voice clearly. "Did you or did you not stumble over a pile of—of bones?"

She grimaced at the image. "Not exactly." She had to concentrate harder on keeping her voice calm. "Actually, it was the dog that found them. The police came right out and took over. I really haven't been involved." She saw Cliff lift a brow at her final statement but made no comment.

"Maggie, it said that man had been murdered and buried right there, only yards from your house."

"Ten years ago." She pressed her fingers more firmly against her temple.

"Maggie, come home."

She closed her eyes, because his voice held the kind of plea that was hard to resist. "C.J., I am home."

"Damn it, how am I supposed to sleep at night thinking of you alone out in the middle of nowhere? For God's sake, you're one of the most successful, wealthiest, most celebrated women in the world, and you're living in Dogpatch."

"If I'm successful, wealthy and celebrated, I can live

wherever I want." She struggled against temper again. However he phrased it, whatever his tone, the concern was real. It was better to concentrate on that. "Besides, C.J., I have the vicious guard dog you sent me." She looked down to where Killer was sleeping peacefully at Cliff's feet. When she lifted her gaze, she found herself smiling into Cliff's face. "I couldn't be safer."

"If you hired a bodyguard—"

Now she laughed. "You're being an old woman again. The last thing I need's a bodyguard. I'm fine," she went on quickly before he could comment. "I've finished the score, I've a dozen ideas for new songs running around in my head, and I'm even considering another musical. Why don't you tell me how brilliant the score was?"

"You know it's brilliant," he mumbled. "It's probably the best thing you've done."

"More," she insisted. "Tell me more. My ego's starving."

He sighed, recognizing defeat. "When I played it for the producers, they were ecstatic. It was suggested that you come out and supervise the recording."

"Forget it." She began to pace to the sink and back again.

"Damn it, we'd come to you, but there's no studio in Hicksville."

"Morganville," she corrected mildly. "You don't need me for the recording."

"They want you to do the title song."

"What?" Surprised, she stopped her restless pacing.

"Now listen to me before you say no." C.J. straightened in his chair and put on his best negotiator's voice. "I realize you've always refused to perform or record, and I've never pressed you. But this is something I really think you should consider. Maggie, that song's dynamite, absolute dynamite, and nobody's going to be able to put into it what you did. After I played the tape, everyone in the room needed a cold shower."

Though she laughed, Maggie couldn't quite put the idea aside. "I can think of a half-dozen artists who could deliver that number, C.J. You don't need me."

"I can think of a dozen who could deliver it," he countered. "But not like you. The song needs you, Maggie. At least you could think about it."

She told herself she'd already refused him enough for one day. "Okay, I'll think about it."

"You let me know in a week."

"C.J.—"

"Okay, okay, two weeks."

"All right. And I'm sorry about the phone."

"You could at least get one of those hateful answering machines."

"Maybe. Take care of yourself, C.J."

"I always do. Just take your own advice."

"I always do. Bye." She hung up, heaving a long sigh. "I feel like I've just been taken to task by the school principal."

Cliff watched her pick up a folded dish towel, crumple it, then set it down again. "You know how to handle him."

"I've had plenty of practice."

"What's C.J. stand for?"

"Constant Jitters," she murmured, then shook her head. "No, to tell you the truth, I haven't any idea."

"Does he always give you a hard time?"

"I suppose." She picked up the dish towel again. "It seems the news hit the papers on the Coast. Then, when he couldn't reach me…" She trailed off, frowning out the window.

"You're tense."

She dropped the cloth over the edge of the sink. "No."

"Yes," Cliff corrected. "I can see it." Reaching out, he ran his hand down the side of her neck to the curve of her shoulder. "I can feel it."

The brush of his fingers made her skin hum. Slowly, she turned her head. "I don't want you to do that."

Deliberately, he took his other hand on a like journey, so that he could knead at the tension in both of her shoulders. Was it her nerves he sought to soothe or his own? "To touch you?" he said quietly. "It's difficult not to."

Knowing she was already weakening, Maggie lifted her hands to his wrists. "Put some effort into it," she advised as she tried to push him aside.

"I have for the past few days." His fingers pressed into her skin and released, pressed and released, in a rhythm that caused her bones to liquefy. "I decided it was a misdirection of energy when I could put the same effort into making love to you."

Her mind was starting to haze, her breath beginning to tremble. "We've nothing to give each other."

"We both know better than that." He lowered his head so that his lips could brush along the temple he'd seen her stroke while on the phone.

A sigh escaped before she stopped it. This wasn't what she wanted—it was everything she wanted. "Sex is—"

"A necessary and enjoyable part of life," Cliff finished before he moved his lips down to tease hers.

So this was seduction, Maggie thought as her mind began to float. This was arousal without will. She knew she wasn't resisting, but yielding, melting, submitting, just as she knew that when surrender was complete, her bridges would be in flames behind her.

"We'll only be two people sharing a bed," she murmured. "There's nothing else."

Whether it was a question or a statement, Cliff tried to believe it was true. If there was more, it wouldn't end, and he'd find himself tangled around a woman he barely understood for the rest of his life. If there were only needs, he could relinquish his control and race with them. If there was only desire, he could take whatever he wanted with no consequences. When she was softening and heating in his arms, what did he care for consequences?

"Let me feel you," he murmured against her lips. "I want your skin under my hands, smooth and hot, your heart pounding."

Anything, she thought dizzily. She'd give him anything, as long as he stayed close like this, as long as his mouth continued that dark, desperate, delirious seduction of her senses. He tugged her T-shirt over her head, then ran his hands down her sides, up again, so that the friction had her nearly mad for more. His shirt scraped against her taut nipples until his hands came between them to possess.

He could feel her heart beat now, and she could hear it pounding in her own head. Her thighs pressed against his with only two layers of thin, soft denim between. She could remember every slope and plane of his body, how it had felt warm and urgent and naked on hers.

He smelled of work and the outdoors, traces of sweat and turned earth. As the scent raced through her senses, she took her lips over his face and throat to draw in the taste.

Uncivilized, like the land that held them both. Alluring and not quite tamed, like the thick woods that surrounded them. If she thought at all, this is how she thought of the need that burned between them. There was danger in both, and pleasure and wonder. Throwing aside all reason, Maggie gave herself to it.

"Now," she demanded huskily. "I want you now."

With no sense of time or place, no hesitation, they lowered onto the floor. The struggle with clothes only added to the aura of desperation and unrelenting desire that sprang back whenever they touched. Warmth against warmth, they found each other.

When the phone shrilled on the wall beside them, neither heard. Whether it was by choice or the will of fate, there was nothing for either of them but each other.

A tremble, a moan, a rough caress, the scent and fury of passion; that was their world. Urgently and more urgently, they sought the taste and touch of each other, as if the hunger would never abate, as if neither would allow it to. The floor was hard and smooth beneath them. They rolled over it as if it were layered with feathers. Sunlight streamed in, falling over them. They explored all the secrets of the night.

Man for woman, woman for man—time had no place and place no meaning. Hot and open, his mouth found hers, and finding it, he burned with the need to possess her completely. His fingers dug into her hips as he shifted her on top of him so that her skin slid tantalizingly over his. He felt her throb, just as he felt the flood of passion beat against the weakened dam of his control. At the moment of joining, her body arched back in stunned pleasure. The pace was frenetic, leaving them both helpless and raging. On and on they drove each other, mercilessly, ruthlessly.

Through half-closed eyes, Cliff saw her shudder with the speed of the crest. Then he was swept up with her in the power of the ultimate heat dance.

Chapter 9

Had hours passed, or was his sense of time still distorted? Cliff tried to gauge the hour by the slant of the sun through the window, but couldn't be sure. He felt more than rested; he felt vitalized. Turning his head, he watched Maggie as she slept beside him. Though his own actions were vague in his mind, like a half dream that blurs on awakening, he could remember carrying her upstairs where they'd tumbled into bed. Wrapped around each other, they'd fallen into an exhausted sleep. Yes, that part was vague, he mused, but the rest—

On the kitchen floor. He ran a hand over his face, uncertain if he was pleased or astonished. Cliff discovered he was both.

He'd made love to her on the kitchen floor like a frantic teenager in the first spin of desire. By the time a man of experience had reached his thirties, he should be able to show a bit more control, use a bit more finesse. Yet he'd had neither both times he'd made love with her. Cliff wasn't certain that would change if he'd loved her a hundred times. She had some power over him that went deep and triggered frenzy rather than style. And yet... Because she was asleep and unaware, he brushed the hair from her cheek so that he could see more of her face. Looking at her was becoming a habit he wasn't sure could be easily broken. Yet when they lay quiet like this, he was overwhelmed by a sense of protective tenderness. As far as he could remember, no other woman had elicited either response from him before. The knowledge wasn't comfortable.

Perhaps it was because when she slept as she did now, she looked frail, defenseless, small. He'd never been able to resist fragility. When she was in his arms, she was all fire and flare, with a power so potent she seemed indestructible. Challenges were something else he'd never been able to resist.

Just who was Maggie Fitzgerald? Cliff wondered while he traced the shape of her mouth with a fingertip. He wouldn't have said she was beautiful, yet her face had the power to both stun and haunt a man. He hadn't expected her to be kind or compassionate, yet he'd seen the qualities in her. He hadn't expected her to be self-sufficient, yet she was proving to be just that under an uneasy set of circumstances.

He frowned and unconsciously drew her closer. Maggie murmured but slept on. Though he'd told her that she had no connection with what had happened there ten years before, Cliff didn't like knowing she was alone in the big, remote house. Knowing Morganville was a quiet, settled town didn't change that. Even the quiet, the settled, had undercurrents. That had been made plain in the past two weeks.

Whoever had killed William Morgan had gone unpunished for a decade. Whoever had murdered him had probably walked the streets of town, chatted outside the bank, cheered at Little League games. It wasn't a pleasant thought. Nor was it pleasant to conclude that whoever had killed once might do anything necessary to go on living a quiet, settled life in a town where everyone knew your name and your history. It might be a cliché about the murderer returning to the scene of the crime, but—

She woke up alone, her mind still disoriented. Was it morning? she wondered groggily. When she shifted, lifting both hands to push back her hair, she felt the sweet heaviness in her limbs that came from lovemaking. Abruptly awake, she looked over to see the bed beside her empty.

Perhaps she'd been dreaming. But when she felt the sheets beside her, they were still warm, and when she turned her face into the pillow, his scent lingered on the case.

They'd made love on the kitchen floor, she remembered with a reaction that directly paralleled Cliff's. But she also remembered quite clearly the sensation of being carried up the stairs, gently, as if she'd been something precious. It was a warm memory, different from the erotic scene that had preceded it. A memory like that was something she could hold on to during some long, restless night in the future.

But he'd left, saying nothing.

Grow up, Maggie, she ordered herself. *Be sensible.* From the beginning she'd known this wasn't romance but desire. The only thing she'd gain from dwelling on the first was pain. Romance was for the impractical, the vulnerable, the naive. Hadn't she spent a great deal of her time training herself to be none of those things?

He didn't love her; she didn't love him. There was a twinge in her stomach at the second denial that had her biting her lip. No, she insisted, she didn't love him. She couldn't afford to.

He was a hard man, though she'd seen some softer aspects of him. He was intolerant, impatient and more often rude than not. A woman didn't need to fix her heart on a man like that. In any case, he'd made it clear that he wanted her body, and her body only. Twice she'd made the decision to give it to him, so she had no right to regrets, even though he'd left without a word.

Maggie flung her arms over her eyes and refused to acknowledge the growing fear that she'd already given him more than her body, without either of them being aware of it.

Then she heard it, the soft creak directly overhead. Slowly, she lowered her arms, then lay still. When it came the second time, the panic fluttered in her throat. She was awake, it was midafternoon, and the sounds came from the attic, not her imagination.

Though she was shaking, she climbed quietly out of bed. This time she wouldn't cower in her room while someone invaded her home. This time, she thought, moistening her lips as she slipped into her T-shirt, she'd find out who it was and what they wanted. Cold and clearheaded, she took the poker from the fireplace and slipped into the hallway.

The attic stairs were to her right. When she saw that the door at the top was open, fear sliced through her again. It hadn't been opened since she'd moved in. Shaking, determined, she took a firmer grip on the poker and started up the stairs.

At the doorway, she paused, hearing the faint whisper

of movement inside. She pressed her lips together, swallowed, then stepped inside.

"Damn it, Maggie, you could hurt someone with that thing."

She jumped back, banging smartly into the doorjamb. "What are you doing up here?" she demanded as Cliff scowled back at her.

"Just checking. When's the last time you were up here?"

She expelled a breath, releasing pent-up tension. "Never. It's far down on my lists of priorities, so I haven't been up since I moved in."

He nodded, taking another glance around. "Someone has."

For the first time, she looked into the room. As she'd suspected, it contained little more than dust and cobwebs. It was high enough that Cliff could stand upright with an inch or so to spare, though at the sides it sloped down with the pitch of the roof. There was an old rocker that might prove interesting after refinishing, a sofa that was hopeless, two lamps without shades and a large upright traveling chest.

"It doesn't look as though anyone's been up here for years."

"More like a week," Cliff corrected. "Take a look at this."

He walked toward the chest, and making a face at the layer of dust on the floor, Maggie padded after him in her bare feet. "So?" she demanded. "Joyce mentioned that there were some things up here she didn't have any use for. I told her not to bother with them, that I'd take care of hauling them out when I was ready."

"I'd say someone already took something out." Cliff crouched in front of the dust-covered chest, then pointed.

Annoyed, stifling the urge to sneeze, Maggie bent toward the dust-covered chest. Then she saw it. Just near the lock, and very faint, was the imprint of a hand. "But—"

Cliff grabbed her wrist before she could touch the imprint herself. "I wouldn't."

"Someone was here," she murmured. "I didn't imagine it." Struggling for calm, she looked back at Cliff. "But what could anyone have wanted up here, in this thing?"

"Good question." He straightened, but kept her hand in his.

She wanted to play it light. "How about a good answer?"

"I think we might see what the sheriff thinks."

"You think it has something to do with—the other thing."

Her voice was steady enough, but with his fingers on her wrist, he knew her pulse wasn't. "I think it's odd that everything's happening at once. Coincidences are curious things. You wouldn't be smart to let this one go."

"No." This wasn't ten years ago, she thought. This was now. "I'll call the sheriff."

"I'll do it."

She stopped in the doorway, bristling. "It's my house," she began.

"It certainly is," Cliff agreed mildly, then stunned her by running both hands up her naked thighs to her hips. "I don't mind looking at you half dressed, but it's bound to distract Stan."

"Very funny."

"No, very beautiful." While she stared, wide-eyed, he lowered his head and kissed her with the first true gentleness he'd shown. She didn't move or speak when he lifted his head again. Her eyes were still open. "I'll call the sheriff," Cliff said roughly. "You get some pants on."

Without waiting for her reply, he was heading down

the steps, leaving her staring after him. Dazed, Maggie lifted a finger to trace over her own lips. That, she decided, had been as unexpected and as difficult to explain as anything else that had happened between them.

Utterly confused, Maggie left the poker tilted against the door and went back to her room. She couldn't have known he could kiss like that—tenderly, exquisitely. If she couldn't have known that, she couldn't have known that her heart could stop beating and her lungs could choke up. The totally different kiss had brought on a totally different reaction. This reaction, she knew, had left her without any form of defense.

A passionate, aggressive demand she could meet with passion and aggression of her own. There they were equal, and if she had no control, neither did he. Urgency would be met with urgency, fire with fire, but tenderness... What would she do if he kissed her like that again? And how long would she have to wait until he did? A woman could fall in love with a man who kissed like that.

Maggie caught herself. Some women, she corrected, hastily dragging on her jeans. Not her. She wasn't going to fall in love with Cliff Delaney. He wasn't for her. He wanted no more than—

Then she remembered that he hadn't left without a word. He hadn't left at all.

"Maggie!"

The voice from the bottom of the stairs had her jolting. "Yes." She answered him while she stared at her own astonished face in the mirror.

"Stan's on his way."

"All right, I'm coming down." In a minute, she added silently, in just a minute. Moving like someone who wasn't sure her legs could be trusted, she sat on the bed.

If she was falling in love with him, she'd better admit it now, while there was still time to do something about it. Was there still time? It washed over her that her time had been up days before, perhaps longer. Perhaps it had been up the moment he'd stepped out of his truck onto her land.

Now what? she asked herself. She'd let herself fall for a man she hardly knew, barely understood and wasn't altogether sure she liked a great deal of the time. He certainly didn't understand her and didn't appear to want to.

Yet he'd planted a willow in her yard. Perhaps he understood more than either of them realized. Of course, there couldn't be anything between them, really, she reminded herself hastily. They were poles apart in attitude. Still, for the moment, she had no choice but to follow her heart and hope that her mind would keep her somewhat level. As she rose, Maggie remembered fatalistically that it never had before.

It was quiet downstairs, but as soon as she came to the landing, she smelled coffee. She stood there a moment, wondering if she should be annoyed or pleased that Cliff was making himself at home. Unable to decide, she walked back to the kitchen.

"Want a cup?" Cliff asked as she entered. He was already leaning against the counter in his habitual position, drinking one of his own.

Maggie lifted a brow. "As a matter of fact, I would. Have any trouble finding what you needed?"

He ignored the sarcasm and reached in a cupboard for another cup. "Nope. You haven't eaten lunch."

"I generally don't." She came up behind him to pour the cup herself.

"I do," he said simply. With a naturalness Maggie

thought bordered on arrogance, he opened the refrigerator and began to search through it.

"Just help yourself," she muttered before she scalded her tongue on the coffee.

"You'd better learn to stock up," Cliff told her when he found her supplies discouragingly slim. "It isn't unusual to get snowed in on a back road like this for a week at a time in the winter."

"I'll keep that in mind."

"You eat this stuff?" he asked, pushing aside a carton of yogurt.

"I happen to like it." She strode over, intending to slam the refrigerator door whether his hand was inside or not. Cliff outmaneuvered her by plucking out a single chicken leg, then stepping aside. "I'd just like to mention you're eating my dinner."

"Want a bite?" Apparently all amiability, he held out the drumstick. Maggie concentrated on keeping her lips from curving.

"No."

"Funny." Cliff took a bite and chewed thoughtfully. "Just coming into this kitchen seems to work up my appetite."

She shot him a look, well aware that she was now standing on the spot where they'd made wild love only a short time before. If he was trying to get a rise out of her, he was succeeding. If he was trying to distract her from what they'd discovered in the attic, he was succeeding, as well. Either way, Maggie found she couldn't resist him.

Deliberately, she took a step closer, running her hands slowly up his chest. It was time, she decided, to give him back a bit of his own. "Maybe I'm hungry, after all," she murmured, and, rising on her toes, brushed her lips teasingly over his.

Because he hadn't expected the move from her, Cliff did nothing. From the start he'd stalked and seduced. She was the lady, the crown princess with the wanton passion men often fantasize about on long, dark nights. Now, looking into those deep, velvet eyes, he thought her more of a witch. And who, he wondered as his blood began to swim, had been stalked and seduced?

She took his breath away—just the scent of her. She made his reason cloud—just the touch of her. When she looked at him like this, her eyes knowing, her lips parted and close, she was the only woman he wanted, the only woman he knew. At times like this, he wanted her with a fire that promised never to be banked. Quite suddenly and quite clearly, she terrified him.

"Maggie." He put a hand up to ward her off, to draw her closer; he'd never know, for the dog began to bark, and the rumble of a car laboring up the lane sounded from outside. Cliff dropped the hand to his side again. "That'll be Stan."

"Yes." She studied him with an open curiosity he wasn't ready to deal with.

"You'd better get the door."

"All right." She kept her gaze direct on his for another moment, rather pleased with the uncertainty she saw there. "You coming?"

"Yeah. In a minute." He waited until she had gone, then let out a long, uneasy breath. That had been too close for comfort. Too close to what, he wasn't certain, but he was certain he didn't like it. With his appetite strangely vanished, Cliff abandoned the drumstick and picked up his coffee. When he noticed his hands weren't quite steady, he downed the contents in one swallow.

Well, she certainly had enough to think about, Maggie mused as she walked down the hall. The sheriff was at her door again, Cliff was standing in her kitchen looking as though he'd been struck with a blunt instrument, and her own head was so light from a sense of—was it power?—that she didn't know what might happen next. Her move to the country certainly hadn't been quiet. She'd never been more stimulated in her life.

"Miss Fitzgerald."

"Sheriff." Maggie scooped Killer up in one arm to quiet his barking.

"Quite a beast you've got there," he commented. Then, holding out a hand, he allowed the puppy to sniff it cautiously. "Cliff gave me a call," he continued. "Said it looked like somebody's broken into the house."

"That seems to be the only explanation." Maggie stepped back to struggle with both the puppy and the door. "Although it doesn't make any sense to me. Apparently someone was in the attic last week."

"Last week?" Stan took care of the door himself, then rested his hand lightly, it seemed negligently, on the butt of his gun. "Why didn't you call before?"

Feeling foolish, Maggie set the dog down, giving him an impatient nudge on the rear that sent him scampering into the music room. "I woke up sometime in the middle of the night and heard noises. I admit it panicked me at the time, but in the morning..." She trailed off and shrugged. "In the morning, I thought it'd been my imagination, so I more or less forgot the whole thing."

Stan listened, and his nod was both understanding and prompting. "And now?"

"I happened to mention it to Cliff this...ah...this morning," she finished. "He was curious enough to go up into the attic."

"I see." Maggie had the feeling he saw everything, very well.

"Stan." Cliff strode down the hall from the kitchen, looking perfectly at ease. "Thanks for coming by."

I should've said that, Maggie thought, but before she could open her mouth again, the men were talking around her.

"Just part of the job," Stan stated. "You're doing quite a job yourself on the grounds outside."

"They're coming along."

Stan gave him a crooked, appealing smile. "You've always liked a challenge."

They knew each other well enough that Cliff understood he referred to the woman, as well as her land. "Things would be dull without them," he said mildly.

"Heard you found something in the attic."

"Enough to make me think someone's been poking around."

"I'd better have a look."

"I'll show you," Maggie said flatly, then, sending Cliff a telling look, led the way upstairs.

When they came to the attic door, Stan glanced down at the poker still leaning against it. "Somebody could trip over that," he said mildly.

"I must have left it there before." Ignoring Cliff's grin, she picked it up and held it behind her back.

"Doesn't look like anyone's been up here in a long time," Stan commented as he brushed a cobweb away from his face.

"I haven't been up at all until today." Maggie shivered as a large black spider crawled sedately up the wall to her left. She hadn't admitted to anyone yet that the prospect of insects and mice was primarily what had kept her out. "There's been so much else to do in the house." Deliberately, she stepped farther away from the wall.

"Not much up here." Stan rubbed a hand over his chin. "Joyce and I cleared out everything we were interested in when she first inherited. Louella already had everything she wanted. If you haven't been up," he continued, peering slowly around, "how do you know anything's missing?"

"I don't. It's this." For the second time, Maggie crossed the dusty floor to the trunk. This time it was she who crouched down and pointed.

Stan bent down over her, close enough that she could smell the simple department-store aftershave he wore. She recognized it and, on a wave of nostalgia, remembered her mother's driver had worn it, too. For no other reason, her sense of trust in him was confirmed.

"That's curious," Stan murmured, careful not to smear the faint outline. "Did you open this?"

"Neither of us touched it," Cliff said from behind.

With another nod, Stan pushed the button on the latch. His other hand came up automatically, stopping just short of gripping the trunk in the same spot the handprint was. "Looks like somebody did." Cautiously, he put his hand on the closure and tugged. "Locked." Sitting back on his haunches, he frowned at the trunk. "Damn if I can remember what's in this thing or if there's a key. Joyce might know—more'n likely Louella, though. Still..." With a shake of his head, he straightened. "It doesn't make much sense for somebody to break in and take something out of this old trunk, especially now that the house is occupied for the first time in ten years." He looked back at Maggie. "Are you sure nothing's missing from downstairs?"

"No—that is, I don't think so. Almost everything I shipped out's still in crates."

"Wouldn't hurt to take a good look."

"All right." She started back toward the second floor, realizing she hoped something would be missing. That would make sense; that would be tangible. The faint handprint on the trunk and no explanation gave her a queasy feeling in the stomach. A cut-and-dried burglary would only make her angry.

With the two men following, she went into her bedroom, checking her jewelry first. Everything was exactly as it should've been. In the next bedroom were crates that at a glance she could see were untouched and unopened.

"That's all up here. There's more crates downstairs and some paintings I haven't had reframed yet."

"Let's take a look."

Going with the sheriff's suggestion, Maggie headed for the stairs again.

"I don't like it," Cliff said to Stan in an undertone. "And you don't think she's going to find anything missing downstairs."

"Only thing that makes sense is a burglary, Cliff."

"A lot of things haven't made sense since we started digging in that gully."

Stan let out a quiet breath, watching Maggie's back as she descended the steps. "I know, and a lot of times there just aren't any answers."

"Are you going to tell Joyce about this?"

"I might have to." Stan stopped at the base of the stairs, running a hand over the back of his neck as though there were tension or weariness there. "She's a strong woman, Cliff. I guess I didn't know just how strong until this business started. I know when we first got married, a lot of people thought I did it for her inheritance."

"Not anyone who knew you."

Stan shrugged. "Anyway, that died down after a while,

died completely after I became sheriff. I guess there were times I wondered whether Joyce ever thought it."

"She'd have told me if she had," Cliff said bluntly.

With a half laugh, Stan turned to him. "Yes, she would've at that."

Maggie came back into the hall from the music room. "There's nothing missing in there, either. I've a few things in the living room, but—"

"Might as well be thorough," Stan told her, then strode across the hall and over the threshold. "Doing some painting?" he asked when he noticed the can and brush by the window.

"I'd planned to have all the trim done in here today," she said absently as she examined a few more packing boxes, "but then Mrs. Morgan stopped by, and—"

"Louella," Stan interrupted.

Because he was frowning, Maggie began to smooth it over. "Yes, though she didn't stay very long. We just looked over the pictures she'd lent me." Distracted, she picked up the stack. "Actually, I'd wanted to show these to you, Cliff. I wondered if you could tell me how to deal with getting some climbing roses like these started."

With the men flanking her, Maggie flipped through the snapshots.

"Louella certainly had a feel for making flowers look like they'd grown up on their own," she murmured. "I don't know if I have the talent for it."

"She always loved this place," Stan said. "She—" Then he stopped when she flipped to the color shot of himself and Morgan. "I'd forgotten about that one," he said after a moment. "Joyce took that the first day of deer season."

"Louella mentioned that she hunted."

"She did," Cliff put in, "because he wanted her to. Morgan had an—affection for guns."

And died by one, Maggie thought with a shudder. She turned the pictures facedown. "There's nothing missing anywhere that I can see, Sheriff."

He stared down at the pile of photos. "Well, then, I'll do a check of the doors and windows, see if anything's been forced."

"You can look," Maggie said with a sigh, "but I don't know if the doors were locked, and half the windows at least were open."

He gave her the look parents give children when they do something foolish and expected. "I'll just poke around, anyway. Never can tell."

When he'd gone out, Maggie flopped down on the sofa and lapsed into silence. As if he had nothing better to do, Cliff wandered to the clock on the mantel and began to wind it. Killer came out from under the sofa and began to dance around his legs. The tension in the room was palpable. Maggie had almost given up wondering if it would ever be resolved.

Why would anyone break into an old trunk that had been neglected for years? Why had Cliff been in on the discovery, just as he'd been in on the discovery in the gully? What had caused her to fall in love with him, and would this need between them fade, as flash fires had a habit of doing? If she could understand any of it, perhaps the rest would fall into place and she'd know what move to make.

"There doesn't seem to be any forced entry," Stan said as he came back into the room. "I'll go into town, file a formal report and get to work on this, but—" He shook his head at Maggie. "I can't promise anything. I'd suggest you keep your doors locked and give some more thought to those dead bolts."

"I'll be staying here for the next few days," Cliff announced, throwing Stan and Maggie into surprised silence. He continued as if he hadn't noticed the reaction his statement caused. "Maggie won't be alone, though it would seem that whatever was wanted in the house was taken."

"Yeah." Stan scratched his nose, almost concealing a grin. "I'd better get back. I'll just let myself out."

Maggie didn't rouse herself to say goodbye but stared at Cliff until the front door shut. "Just what do you mean, you'll be staying here?"

"We'll have to do some grocery shopping first. I can't live off what you keep in that kitchen."

"Nobody asked you to live off it," she said, springing to her feet. "And nobody asked you to stay here. I don't understand why I have to keep reminding you whose house and land this is."

"Neither do I."

"You told *him*," she continued. "You just as good as announced to the town in general that you and I—"

"Are exactly what we are," Cliff finished easily. "You'd better get some shoes on, if we're going to town."

"I'm not going to town, and you're not staying here."

He moved so quickly she was caught completely off guard. His hands closed over both her arms. "I'm not letting you stay here alone until we know exactly what's going on."

"I've told you before I can take care of myself."

"Maybe you can, but we're not putting it to the test right now. I'm staying."

She gave him a long stare. The truth was she didn't want to be alone. The truth was, she wanted him, perhaps too much for her own good. Yet he was the one insisting, she thought as her temper began to cool. Since he was insisting, perhaps he cared more than he was willing to admit. Maybe it was time she took a gamble on that.

"If I let you stay…" she began.

"I am staying."

"If I let you stay," she repeated coolly, "you have to cook dinner tonight."

He lifted a brow, and the grip on her arms relaxed slightly. "After sampling your cooking, you won't get any argument."

Refusing to be insulted, she nodded. "Fine. I'll get my shoes."

"Later." Before she knew what he was up to, they were tumbling back onto the sofa. "We've got all day."

Chapter 10

Maggie considered it ironic that she'd just begun to become accustomed to living alone and she was no longer living alone. Cliff made the transition unobtrusively. No fuss, no bother. A brisk, rather subtle sense of organization seemed to be a part of his makeup. She'd always respected organized people—from a safe distance.

He left early each morning, long before she considered it decent for a person to be out of his bed. He was quiet and efficient and never woke her. Occasionally, when she groped her way downstairs later in the morning, she'd find a scrawled note next to the coffeepot.

"Phone was off the hook again," it might say. Or "Milk's low. I'll pick some up."

Not exactly love letters, Maggie thought wryly. A man like Cliff wouldn't put his feelings down on paper the way she was compelled to. It was just one more area of opposition between them.

In any case, Maggie wasn't certain Cliff had any feelings about her other than impatience and an occasional bout of intolerance. Though there were times she suspected she touched some of his softer edges, he didn't act much like a lover. He brought her no flowers, but she remembered he'd planted a willow tree. He gave her no smooth, clever phrases, but she remembered the look she'd sometimes catch in his eyes. He wasn't a poet, he wasn't a romantic, but that look, that one long, intense look, said more than most women ever heard.

Perhaps, despite both of them, she was beginning to understand him. The more she understood, the more difficult it became to control a steadily growing love. He wasn't a man whose emotions could be pushed or channeled. She was a woman who, once her feelings were touched, ran with them in whatever direction they went.

Though she'd lived in the house outside of Morganville for only a month, Maggie understood a few basics of small-town life. Whatever she did became common knowledge almost before she'd done it. Whatever it was she did would draw a variety of opinions that would lead to a general consensus. There were a few key people whose opinion could sway that consensus. Cliff, she knew, was one of them, if he chose to bother. Stan Agee and the postmistress were others. It didn't take her long to discover that Bog was another whose opinion was sought and carefully weighed.

The politics in Morganville might've been on a smaller scale than those in Southern California's music industry, but Maggie saw that they ran in the same vein. In L.A., however, she'd been second-generation royalty, while here she was an outsider. An outsider, she knew, whose notoriety could be either scorned or accepted. To date, she'd been fortunate, because most of the key people had decided to accept. Thinking of small, close-knit towns, she realized she'd taken a chance on that acceptance by living with Cliff.

Not living with, Maggie corrected as she spread adhesive on her newly stripped bathroom floor. He wasn't living with her; he was staying with her. There was a world of difference between the two. He hadn't moved in, bag and baggage, nor had there been any discussion about the length of his stay. It was, she decided, a bit like having a guest whom you didn't feel obligated to entertain or impress.

Unnecessarily, and through his own choice, he'd opted to be her bodyguard. And at night, when the sun went down and the woods were quiet, her body was his. He accepted her passion, her hungers and desires. Perhaps, just perhaps, one day he might accept her emotions, which raged just as hot, and just as high. First he had to come to understand her as she was beginning to understand him. Without that, and the respect that went with it, emotions and desires would wither and die.

Maggie set the next square of tile into position, then sat back to judge the outcome. The stone-patterned ceramic was rustic and would leave her free to use an infinite range of color combinations. She wanted nothing in her home to be too restricted or regimented, just as she wanted to do most of the changes and improvements herself.

Looking at the six pieces of tile she'd installed, Maggie nodded. She was becoming quite handy these days. Though her pansies had never recovered, they were her only major failure.

Pleased and ready for more, Maggie debated whether

to mix up another batch of adhesive or to start the next wall of paper in her bedroom. There was only a wall and a half left to cover, she remembered; then it would be time to make a decision on curtains. Priscillas, cafés, Cape Cods… Nothing monumental, most people would say, she mused, but then she'd always left such things up to decorators before. Now, if something didn't work, she had no one to blame but herself.

With a laugh, she reached into the box of tiles again, swearing halfheartedly as she scraped her finger against a sharp edge. The price of being your own handyman, Maggie decided, going to the sink to run water over the cut. Maybe it was time to turn in the tiles for wallpaper and paste.

When the dog began to bark, she knew that either project would have to wait. Resigned, she turned off the tap just as the sound of a car reached her. Going to the tiny latticed window, she watched Lieutenant Reiker pull around the last curve.

Why was he back? she wondered, frowning. There couldn't possibly be any more information she could give him. When he didn't approach the house immediately, Maggie stayed where she was. He walked along the path of flagstone Cliff's crew had set just that week. When he reached the end, he didn't turn toward the porch, but looked out over the gully. Slowly, he drew out a cigarette, then lit it with a short wooden match. For several moments he just stood there, smoking and watching the dirt and rocks as if they had the answers he wanted. Then, before she could react, he turned and looked directly up at the window where she stood. Feeling like an idiot, she started down to meet him.

"Lieutenant." Maggie went cautiously down the porch steps and onto the sturdy new flagstone.

"Miss Fitzgerald." He flipped the cigarette stub into the tangle of brush near the gully. "Your place is coming along. Hard to believe what it looked like a few weeks ago."

"Thank you." He looked so harmless, so pleasant. She wondered if he carried a gun in a shoulder holster under his jacket.

"Noticed you planted a willow over there." But he looked at her, not at the gully. "It shouldn't be much longer before you can have your pond put in."

Like Reiker, Maggie didn't look toward the gully. "Does that mean the investigation's almost over?"

Reiker scratched along the side of his jaw. "I don't know if I'd say that. We're working on it."

She bit back a sigh. "Are you going to search the gully again?"

"I don't think it's going to come to that. We've been through it twice now. Thing is—" He stopped, shifting his weight to ease his hip. "I don't like loose ends. The more we look into this thing, the more we find. It's hard to tie up ends that've been dangling for ten years."

Was this a social call or an official one? she wondered, trying not to be annoyed. Maggie could remember how embarrassed he'd been when he'd asked for her autograph. At the moment, she didn't need a fan. "Lieutenant, is there something I can do?"

"I wondered if you'd had anyone coming around, someone you know, maybe someone you don't know."

"Coming around?"

"The murder happened here, Miss Fitzgerald, and the more we dig, the more people we find who had reason to kill Morgan. A lot of them still live in town."

She folded her arms under her breasts. "If you're trying to make me uneasy, Lieutenant, you're doing a good job."

"I don't want to do that, but I don't want to keep you in the dark, either." He hesitated, then decided to go with his instincts. "We discovered that Morgan withdrew twenty-five thousand cash from his bank account on the day he disappeared. His car was found, now his body's been found, but the money's never showed up."

"Twenty-five thousand," Maggie murmured. A tidy sum, even tidier ten years ago. "You're telling me you think the money was the motive for murder?"

"Money's always a motive for murder, and it's a loose end. We're checking a lot of people out, but it takes time. So far, nobody around here's ever flashed that kind of money." He started to reach for another cigarette, then apparently changed his mind. "I've got a couple of theories…"

She might've smiled if her head wasn't beginning to ache. "And you'd like to tell me?"

"Whoever killed Morgan was smart enough to cover his tracks. He might've been smart enough to know that coming up with twenty-five thousand dollars wouldn't go unnoticed in a town like this. Maybe, just maybe, he panicked and got rid of the money. Or maybe he hid it so he could wait a good long time, until any rumors about Morgan had died down—then it'd just be waiting for him."

"Ten years is a very long time, Lieutenant."

"Some people're more patient than others." He shrugged. "It's just a theory."

But it made her think. The attic, and the trunk and the handprint. "The other night—" she began, then stopped.

"Something happen the other night?" he prompted.

It was foolish not to tell him, to feel as though, if she did, she would be forging another link in the chain that bound her to everything that had happened. He was, after all, in charge of the investigation. "Well, it seems someone broke in and took something out of a trunk in the attic. I didn't realize it until days later—then I reported it to Sheriff Agee."

"That was the thing to do." His gaze lifted to the dormer window. "He come up with anything?"

"Not really. He did find a key. That is, his wife found one somewhere. He came back and opened the trunk, but it was empty."

"Would you mind if I had a look myself?"

She wanted it over, yet it seemed every step she took brought her in deeper. "No, I don't mind." Resigned, Maggie turned to lead him into the house. "It seems odd that anyone would hide money in the attic, then wait until someone was living here to claim it."

"You bought the place almost as soon as the sign was posted," Reiker reminded her.

"But it was nearly a month before I'd moved in."

"I heard Mrs. Agee kept quiet about the sale. Her husband didn't like the idea."

"You hear a lot of things, Lieutenant."

He gave her the slow, half-embarrassed smile he'd given her when he'd asked for her autograph. "I'm supposed to."

Maggie lapsed into silence until they reached the second floor. "The attic's up here. For what it's worth, I haven't found anything missing in the house."

"How'd they get in?" he asked as he began to climb the steeper, more narrow staircase.

"I don't know," she mumbled. "I wasn't locking my doors."

"But you are now?" He looked back over his shoulder.

"Yes, I'm locking them."

"Good." He went directly to the trunk, and, crouching down, studied the lock. The handprint had faded back to dust. "You say Mrs. Agee had the key?"

"Yes, or one of them. It seems this trunk belonged to the last people who rented the house, an old couple. The woman left it here after her husband died. Apparently there were at least two keys, but Joyce could only find one of them."

"Hmm." Reiker opened the now-unlocked trunk and peered inside, much as he'd peered into the gully. And it, Maggie thought, was just as empty now.

"Lieutenant, you don't really think there's a connection between this and—what you're investigating?"

"I don't like coincidences," he muttered, echoing Cliff's earlier statement. "You say the sheriff's looking into it?"

"Yes."

"I'll talk to him before I head back. Twenty-five thousand doesn't take up much room," he said. "It's a big trunk."

"I don't understand why anyone would let it sit in one for ten years."

"People're funny." He straightened, grunting a little with the effort. "Of course, it's just a theory. Another is that Morgan's mistress took the money and ran."

"His mistress?" Maggie repeated blankly.

"Alice Delaney," Reiker said easily. "She'd been having an affair with Morgan for five or six years. Funny how people'll talk once you get them started."

"Delaney?" Maggie said it quietly, hoping she'd heard incorrectly.

"That's right. As a matter of fact, it's her son who's been doing your landscaping. Coincidences," he repeated. "This business is full of them."

Somehow she managed to remain composed as they walked back downstairs. She spoke politely when he told her again how much he admired her music. Maybe she even smiled when she closed the door on him. When she was alone, Maggie felt her blood turn to ice, then drain.

Cliff's mother had been Morgan's mistress for years; then she'd disappeared, right after his death? Cliff would've known. Everyone would've known, she thought, and covered her face with both hands. What had she fallen into, and how would she ever get out again?

Maybe he was going crazy, but Cliff was beginning to think of the long, winding drive up the hill as going home. He'd never have believed he could consider the old Morgan place as home. Not with the way he'd always felt about William Morgan. Nor would he have believed the woman who lived there could make him think that way. It seemed a great deal was happening that he could neither stop nor harness. Yet staying with Maggie had been his own choice, just as leaving again would be— when he was ready. From time to time he found he needed to remind himself that he could and would leave again.

Yet when she laughed, the house was so warm. When she was angry, it was so full of energy. When she sang— when she worked in the music room in the evening, Cliff thought. When the woods were quiet, before the moon had risen, she'd play. She'd sing snatches of words, sentences, phrases, as she composed. Long before she'd finished, he'd find himself in a frenzy of need. He wondered how she worked hour after hour, day after day, with such passion and feeling driving her.

It was the discipline, Cliff decided. He'd never expected her to be so disciplined about her music. The talent he'd admired all along, but in the few days he'd lived with her, he'd learned that she drove herself hard in the hours she worked.

A contrast, Cliff decided. It was an implausible contrast to the woman who jumped sporadically from one project to another in that big, dusty house. She left walls half papered, ceilings half painted. There were crates and boxes everywhere, most of which hadn't been touched. Rolls of supplies were tucked into every corner. He'd say her work on the house was precise, even creative, to the point where she'd leave off for something new.

She wasn't like anyone he'd ever known, and he realized that somewhere along the way he'd begun to understand her. It had been easier when he could dismiss her as a spoiled Hollywood princess who'd bought a dilapidated country house on a whim or for a publicity stunt. He knew now that she'd bought the house for no other reason than she'd loved it.

Perhaps she was a bit spoiled. She tended to give orders a little too casually. When she didn't get her own way, she tended to bristle or to freeze up. Cliff grinned. The same could be said of himself, he admitted.

To give Maggie her due, she hadn't run from the trouble or unpleasantness that had begun so shortly after she'd moved in. If he'd seen another woman stick as Maggie was sticking, he'd have said she'd indeed taken root. Cliff still had his doubts. Perhaps he fostered them purposely, because if he believed Maggie Fitzgerald would stay in Morganville, he might have to admit he wanted her to. He might have to admit that coming home every night to a woman who made him laugh and fume and throb wasn't something he'd give up without a fight.

He drove the last few yards, then stopped at the edge of the drive. The phlox was blooming on the bank. The new grass was like a green shadow over the soil. Maggie's petunias were a splash of color.

They'd both put part of themselves into the land

already, he realized. Perhaps that in itself was a bond that would be difficult to break. Even as he stepped out of the truck, he wanted her, just the scent, just the softness of her. There was nothing he could do to change it.

There was no music. Cliff frowned as he slowly climbed the front steps. Maggie was always at her piano at this time of day. There were times he'd come back earlier and work on the yard himself. He'd know it was five o'clock, because that's when the music would begin, and it would continue for no less than an hour, often longer. Cliff looked at his watch: 5:35 p.m. Uneasy, he turned the knob on the front door.

Of course it was unlocked, he thought, annoyed. He'd left her a note that morning, telling her none of his crew would be there that day and to keep the doors locked. Senseless woman, he thought as he shoved the door open. Why couldn't she get it through her head that she was completely isolated here? Too many things had happened, and simply by living in this house, she was in the center of them.

Quiet. Too damn quiet, Cliff realized as annoyance began to fade into anxiety. The dog wasn't barking. The house had that echoing, empty feeling almost everyone can sense but can't explain. Though instinct told him no one was there, he began to go from room to room, calling her. Her name bounced back off the walls in his own voice and taunted him.

Where the hell was she, Cliff demanded as he took the stairs two at a time to check the second floor. He didn't like to admit that he could feel panic at nothing more than coming home to an empty house, but panic was exactly what he felt. Every day that week he'd been sure he'd had a crew, or part of one, working outside until he'd been there. He hadn't wanted her left alone, but because he couldn't explain it, Cliff had broken the ritual that day. And now he couldn't find her.

"Maggie!" Desperately, he searched the second floor, not even certain what he expected, or wanted, to find. He'd never experienced this kind of raw, basic fear. He only knew the house was empty and his woman was gone. A pair of her shoes sat carelessly in the center of the bedroom rug. A blouse was tossed negligently over a chair. The earrings he'd watched her take off the night before still lay on the dresser, beside a silver-backed brush engraved with her mother's initials. The room held her scent; it always did.

When he saw the new tiles in the bathroom, he tried to calm himself. In her helter-skelter way, she'd started a new project. But where in the hell—

Then, in the bowl of the sink, he saw something that stopped his heart. Against the pristine white porcelain were three drops of blood. He stared while panic swirled through him, making his head swim and his skin ice.

From somewhere outside, the dog began to bark frantically. Cliff was racing down the steps, not even aware that he called her name again and again.

He saw her as soon as he burst through the back door. She was coming slowly through the woods to the east, the dog dancing around her legs, leaping and nipping. She had her hands in her pockets, her head down. His mind took in every detail while the combination of fear and relief made his legs weak.

He ran toward her, seeing her head lift as he called her again. Then he had her in his arms, holding tight, closing his eyes and just feeling her, warm and whole and safe. He was too overcome with emotions that had no precedent to notice that she stood stiff and unyielding against him.

He buried his face in the soft luxury of her hair. "Maggie, where've you been?"

This was the man she'd thought she was beginning to understand. This was the man she was beginning to love. Maggie stared straight ahead over his shoulder to the house beyond. "I went for a walk."

"Alone?" he demanded irrationally, drawing her back. "You went out alone?"

Everything turned cold; her skin, her manner, her eyes. "It's my land, Cliff. Why shouldn't I go out alone?"

He caught himself before he could rage that she should've left him a note. What was happening to him? "There was blood in the sink upstairs."

"I cut my finger on a tile."

He found he wanted to rage at her for that. She had no business hurting herself. "You're usually playing this time of day," he managed.

"I'm not locked into a routine any more than I'm locked into the house. If you want a placid little female who's waiting to fall at your feet every night when you come home, you'd better look somewhere else." Leaving him staring, she broke away and went into the house.

Calmer but more confused, Cliff went into the kitchen to see her pouring a drink. Scotch, he noted, another first. With his mind a bit clearer, he could see that the normal color was absent from her cheeks and that her shoulders were stiff with tension. This time he didn't go to her or touch her.

"What's happened?"

Maggie swirled the scotch once before she swallowed. She found it too warm, too strong, but she sipped again. "I don't know what you mean." The kitchen was too small. Maggie took the glass and went out. The air was warm and soft. Outside there were no walls or ceilings to make her feel closed in. Circling around, she sat down on the spread of new grass. She'd sit here in the summer, Maggie thought, and read—Byron, if that was her mood. She'd let the sun fall over her, the silence cloak her, and read until she slept. Maggie continued to look out over the woods when Cliff's shadow slanted over her.

"Maggie, what's wrong with you?"

"I'm having a mood," she said flatly. "You'd expect spoiled celebrities to have moods, wouldn't you?"

Keeping his temper in check, Cliff sat down beside her, then took her chin in his hand. He waited until their eyes had met and held. "What?"

She'd known she'd have to tell him. It was the not knowing what there would be afterward that left her insides cold and knotted. "Lieutenant Reiker was here today," she began, but carefully removed Cliff's hand from her face.

Cliff swore, cursing himself for leaving her alone. "What'd he want?"

Maggie shrugged and sipped at the scotch again. "He's a man who doesn't like loose ends. Apparently he's been finding quite a number. It seems William Morgan withdrew twenty-five thousand dollars from his bank account on the day he was murdered."

"Twenty-five thousand?"

He sounded surprised, Maggie noted. Genuinely surprised. She recognized his expression, that thoughtful, narrow-eyed look that meant he was considering all the details and angles. How could she be certain of anything any longer? "The money was never recovered. One of Reiker's theories is that the murderer hid it away, patiently waiting until people forgot about Morgan."

Cliff's eyes sharpened. Automatically, he turned his head and looked back to the house. "Here?"

"Possibly."

"Ten years is a damn long time to sit on twenty-five thousand," Cliff muttered. Still, he didn't care for loose ends, either. "Did you tell him about the trunk in the attic?"

"Yes, he had a look at it himself."

He touched her shoulder, just his fingertips, so lightly that the touch offered whatever support she might want to take. "It's upset you." Maggie said nothing, nor did she look at him. Tension began to work at his own muscles. "There's more."

"There's always more," Maggie said quietly. Now she looked at him; she had to. "He mentioned that Morgan's mistress had disappeared right after his death." She felt Cliff's fingers tighten convulsively on her shoulder just as she felt the waves of anger.

"She wasn't his mistress," Cliff said tightly. "My mother might've been foolish enough to fall in love with a man like Morgan, she might've been unwise enough to sleep with him, but she wasn't his mistress."

"Why didn't you tell me before?" Maggie demanded. "Why did you wait until I found out this way?"

"It doesn't have anything to do with you or with anything that's happened here." As restless anger swarmed in him, he rose.

"Coincidences," Maggie said quietly, but Cliff turned and stared down at her. "Weren't you the one who said not to trust coincidences?"

He was trapped, by an old anger and by a pair of depthless brown eyes. Again he found himself compelled to explain what he'd never explained before. "My mother was lonely and very vulnerable after my father died. Morgan knew how to exploit that. I was living outside of D.C. at the time. If I'd been here, I might've stopped it." Resentment welled up and was controlled. "He knew how to play on weaknesses, and he played on my mother's. When I found out they were lovers, I wanted to kill him."

He said it as he had once before, coldly, calmly. Maggie swallowed on a dry throat. "She was already too involved for anything to be done, deluded into believing she loved him, or maybe she did love him. Other intelligent women had. She'd been friends with Louella for years, but that didn't matter. When they found his car in the river, she snapped."

It was painful to look back on it, but Maggie's solemn brown eyes insisted he go on. "She didn't disappear—she came to me. She was frantic, and for the first time since she'd become involved with Morgan, she was seeing clearly again. Shame affects different people in different ways. My mother broke all ties with Morganville and everyone in it. She knew her relationship with Morgan wasn't a secret, and now that it was over, she simply couldn't face the gossip. She's still in D.C. She has a new life, and I don't want any of this to touch her."

Was he always so unflaggingly protective of the women in his life? Maggie wondered. Joyce, his mother… Where, she wondered, did she fit in? "Cliff, I understand how you feel. My mother was one of the most precious people in my life, too. But there might not be anything you can do about it. They're reconstructing what happened ten years ago, and your mother has a part in it."

But that wasn't all she was thinking, Cliff realized. Deliberately, he sat down beside her, struggling to keep the tension from his fingers when he took her shoulders. "You're wondering how much a part I might've had in it."

"Don't." She tried to stand, but he held her still.

"It's possible that I could've shot Morgan to end a destructive relationship with my mother."

"You hated him."

"Yes."

Her eyes never left his. They looked deep, searching. Logic might implicate him; his own temperament might make him suspect. Maggie stared into the smoky gray of his eyes and believed what she saw. "No," she murmured, drawing him against her. "No, I understand you too well."

Her faith—the warm flood of it—almost destroyed him. "Do you?"

"Maybe too well," she murmured. "I was so frightened before." Closing her eyes, she drew in the familiar scent of him. He was real, he was solid, and for as long as she could hold on, he was hers. "Not now, not now that you're here."

He could feel the pull, that slow, gentle pull. If he wasn't careful, he'd soon forget there was anything or anyone but her in his life. "Maggie." His fingers were already tangling in her hair. "You shouldn't trust without questions."

"It isn't trust with questions," she countered. She wanted it to be only the two of them, with the rest of the world locked out, forgotten. Framing his face with her hands, she drew his mouth down to hers.

She'd expected fire, aggression, but his lips were soft and sweet. Confused, moved, Maggie drew back to stare at him. The eyes that had fascinated her from the beginning held hers as seconds edged closer to a minute. She was lost in the mists and the smoke. Without a word, he brought her close again.

With his eyes on hers, he lightly traced the shape of her face with a fingertip. This, he discovered, was the only face he ever needed to see again. Lightly, he outlined the shape of her lips. These, he knew, were the only lips he'd ever need to taste. With a gentleness he'd shown to no other lover, he laid her back. This was the only body he ever wanted to possess.

Tenderness left her stunned, weak. His mouth lingered on hers, but with such poignancy, the kiss alone made her bones liquefy. The grass was cool beneath her, the sun warm. Swimming in emotion, Maggie closed her eyes while his lips traveled over her face.

Had she ever been touched like this before? As if she were spun glass, his hands stroked over her. As if she were the rarest of delicacies, his lips tasted. And she was helplessly caught in the silken web that was more love than passion.

"Cliff—"

She might've told him, if his lips hadn't captured hers with a sweetness that left her speechless.

He'd never felt a stronger need to savor. It was as if each moment could be stretched to an hour as long as they lay together in the fragrant spring grass. The color in her cheeks was delicate; the sunlight combed through her hair. The look in her eyes was one no man could resist. It told him as clearly as words that she was his. He had only to claim. Knowing it, he moved only more slowly and touched only more reverently.

He undressed her while his kisses continued to hold her in the honey-steeped prison of pleasure. When she was naked, he watched how the sun streamed over her skin. Her large, expressive eyes were half closed. He could feel the pliancy in her body when, with a sigh, she lifted her hands to help him undress.

The raw, primitive need she so often incited in him didn't rise up. Instead, she drew out the softer emotions he normally held back. He wanted only to please her.

Gently, he lowered his mouth to her breast. He could hear her heartbeat increase in pace as he lingered there with his tongue tracing, his teeth nibbling. The tip grew taut, so that when he drew it into his mouth, he heard her breath shudder out, then catch again. Her hand moved through his hair as she lay back, saturated with sensation.

Her body was like a treasure to be discovered and admired before possession. Slowly, almost leisurely, he took those moist kisses and gentle hands over it, stopping, lingering, when he felt her shuddering response. He knew she was steeped in that dim, heavy world where passions hover around the edges and desires lick temptingly, like tiny tongues of fire. He wanted to keep her there for hours or days or years.

Her thighs were slender and long and pearl-white. He loitered there, nudging them both closer, still closer to the edge. But not yet.

She'd forgotten where she was. Though her eyes were half opened, she saw nothing but mists and dreams. She could feel, oh, yes, she could feel each stroke of his hand, each warm brush of lips. She could hear gentle murmurs, quiet sighs that might've been his or hers. There was no reason to ever feel or hear anything else. She was slowly, inevitably, being drawn through the sweetness and into the heat. She began to crave it.

He felt the change in her body, heard the change in the breaths that whispered through her lips. He swept his mouth farther up her thigh, but still he didn't hurry. She would have all he had to give before they were finished.

She arched, catapulted with the sudden intensity of pleasure. She crested, quickly, shatteringly, with an abandonment of self and will. He wanted, demanded, just that. Before she could settle, he drove her up again until the madness once more began to creep into both of them.

Cliff held it off, almost delirious with the knowledge that he could give her what a woman might only dream of. Her body was alive with sensations only he could bring to her. Her mind was swirling with thoughts of only him.

Knowing it, reveling in it, he slipped into her, taking her with a tenderness that lasted and lasted and lasted.

Chapter 11

Saturday morning, Maggie decided she could lie there, half dozing, until it was Saturday afternoon. She could feel the weight of Cliff's arm across her waist, his warm breath fluttering over her cheek. Without opening her eyes, she snuggled closer, wallowing in lazy contentment.

If she'd been certain he could be so gentle, she'd have fallen in love with him willingly. But how satisfying it was to have discovered it after her heart had already been lost. He had such emotion in him. Perhaps he was cautious with it, but she could love him much more comfortably knowing it was there and that now and again, unexpectedly, it would reach out to her.

No, it wasn't flowery phrases she wanted, but his stability. She didn't need smooth charm. When a woman found a man who was capable of such passion and such tenderness, she'd be a fool to want to change him in any way. Maggie Fitzgerald, she thought with a little satisfied smile, was no fool.

"What're you smiling at?"

Opening her eyes, Maggie looked directly into Cliff's. Because his were alert and direct, she knew he'd been awake for some time. She tried to blink away the mists and smiled again. "It feels good," she murmured, snuggling even closer. "You feel good."

He ran a hand down her back, over her hip and thigh. Yes, it felt very good. "Soft," Cliff said quietly. "So soft and smooth." He wondered how he'd gone so many years without being able to touch her like this, when she was lazy and warm and naked. He felt no tension in her, none of the subtle little signs he'd grown so adept at spotting. The need was very strong in him to keep that tension away for as long as he could. She'd walked unwittingly into a whirlpool, and somehow he was connected with it. If it was only for a day, he'd keep the problems at bay.

He rolled, pressed her down into the mattress so that she laughingly murmured a complaint. "Are you going to cook breakfast?" he demanded.

Maggie pillowed her head on her hands, giving him arrogant look for arrogant look. "You don't like my cooking."

"I've decided to be tolerant this morning."

"Have you?" She arched a brow. "How lucky for me."

"Floppy bacon and sloppy eggs," he told her before he nuzzled at her neck.

She shifted, enjoying the rough feel of the night's growth of beard against her skin. "What?"

"I don't like my bacon too crisp—" he nipped at the pulse in her throat "—or my eggs too set."

With a sigh, she closed her eyes again. She wanted to bottle this moment, so that she could take it out again whenever she needed to feel content. "I like my bacon so crisp it crumbles, and I don't like eggs at all."

"They're good for you." Cliff took his lips up her throat to nibble at her ear. "Might put some meat on you." As he spoke, he took his hand down her side again.

"Complaining?"

"Uh-uh." He ran his hand back up again so that his fingers brushed the side of her breast. "Though you do tend toward the lean side. We could build you up with three square meals a day and some exercise."

"No one needs three meals a day," she began, a bit huffily. "And as for exercise—"

"Do you like to dance?"

"Yes, but I—"

"Not much muscle," he noted, pinching her arm. "How's your endurance?"

She gave him a saucy look. "You should know."

With a laugh, he pressed his lips to hers. "You've a very quick, very wicked mind."

"Thanks."

"Now, about dancing. Ever been in a contre line?"

"A what?"

"I thought so." He shook his head, then shifted so that he could look down at her with pity. "Country dancing, Maggie."

Her brows drew together. "Square dancing?"

"No." It was time to educate the lady, Cliff decided, and drew her up to a sitting position. Her hair flowed wildly over her shoulders, the way he liked it best. "Square dancing's more formal, more regimented, than country dancing, but there'd be traditional music and a caller."

Maggie ran a finger up his chest. "Swing your partner and do-si-do?"

He felt the little thrill inch along his skin behind the trail of her finger. Did she know it? he wondered. From the smile that hovered on her lips, he thought she knew it very well. "Among other things."

Maggie linked her hands around his neck and let her head fall back so that she could look at him from beneath lowered lashes. "I'm sure it's all very fascinating, but I don't know why we're doing all this talking when you could be kissing me."

For an answer he gave her a long, searing kiss that left her breathless and pleased. "Because," he said, and nipped at her ear, "I want to go dancing with you."

Sighing, content, Maggie enjoyed the sensation of feeling her own blood begin to sizzle. "Where and when?"

"Tonight, in the park outside of town."

"Tonight?" She opened one eye. "Dancing in the park?"

"It's a tradition." He laid her back again but kept himself propped up so that his hand was free to skim her body. "A sort of Founder's Day celebration combined with rites of spring. Most of the town'll show. There'll be dancing till midnight, then a potluck supper. Then…" He cupped her breast, enjoying the way her eyes clouded when he brushed a fingertip over the point. "There's dancing till dawn for anybody who can handle it."

"Until dawn?" Intrigued and already hopelessly aroused, Maggie arched under him.

"You've danced until dawn before, I imagine."

He'd said the wrong thing or used the wrong tone, because her body stiffened. No, he didn't want to bring up their differences now. At the moment, he could hardly recognize them. He lay down beside her and cradled her in his arms. "We could watch the sun come up," he murmured. "And the stars go out."

She lay against him, but her mind was clear now. The doubts had returned. "You never mentioned this to me before."

"I didn't think you'd be much interested in country dances and potluck suppers. I guess I realized I was wrong."

It was another kind of apology. Maggie accepted this one as easily as she had the first. Smiling again, she tilted her head back from him. "Are you asking me for a date?"

He liked it when her eyes held that half teasing, half challenging light. "Looks like it."

"I'd love to."

"Okay." Her hair fell onto his shoulder. Absently, he twisted the end around his finger. "Now, about breakfast."

She grinned, lowering her mouth to his. "We'll have it for lunch."

She didn't know what she expected, but Maggie looked forward to an evening out, away from the house, an evening to spend with other people. After her brief stab at being a hermit, she'd discovered that she could indeed take total command of her own needs. Being able to live with herself for long periods of time simply showed her that she didn't always have to in order to prove her independence. Perhaps she hadn't been attempting to learn anything with the dramatic change in her lifestyle, but she'd learned something, anyway. She could take charge of the tiny details of day-to-day living that she'd always left to others, but she didn't have to cut herself off from everyone to do it.

No, she didn't know what to expect, perhaps a quaint little festival with tinny music and warm lemonade in paper cups. She didn't expect to be particularly impressed. She certainly didn't expect to be enchanted.

The line of cars that sloped down the winding drive to the park surprised her. She'd thought most of the people in town would simply walk. When she mentioned it to Cliff, he shrugged and negotiated his pickup into a spot behind a yellow van.

"They come from all over the county, and from as far away as D.C. and Pennsylvania."

"Really?" Pursing her lips, she climbed out of the truck into the warm, clear night. There'd be a full moon, though the sun was just beginning to set. She wondered if the town had planned it that way or if it had been the luck of the draw. Either way, it was one more thing to be enjoyed. Putting her hand in Cliff's, she began to walk with him to the crest of the hill.

As she watched, the sun dropped lower behind the mountains in the west. She'd seen the sun sink gloriously into the sea and been awed by the colors and brilliance of sunsets in the snow-covered Alps. She'd seen the desert vibrate with color at dusk and cities glow with twilight. Somehow, watching the gold and mauve and pink layer over what were hardly more than foothills of a great range, she was more deeply affected. Perhaps it was foolish, perhaps it was fanciful, but she felt more a part of this place, more involved with the coming of this night, than she'd been of any other. On impulse, she threw her arms around Cliff's neck and held on.

Laughing, he put his hands on her hips. "What's this for?"

"It feels good," she said, echoing her morning words.

Then with a bang that shattered the silence, the music burst out. As a musician, she recognized each individual instrument—violin, banjo, guitar, piano. As a music lover, she felt her excitement leap.

"It's fabulous!" she exclaimed, drawing quickly away.

"Absolutely fabulous. Hurry, I have to see." Maggie grabbed his hand and raced the rest of the way up the hill.

Her first impression was of a maze of people, two hundred, perhaps two hundred fifty, crowded together in a covered pavilion. Then she saw they were in lines, six, no, eight, she realized after a quick count. There would be a line of men facing a line of women, and so on, until they simply ran out of room. And they were moving to the music in a system that looked both confusing and fluid.

Some of the women wore skirts that flared out as they dipped, swayed or spun. Others wore jeans. Men's attire was no more consistent and no more formal than the women's. Some of the dancers wore sneakers, while a great many more wore what seemed to be old-fashioned black leather shoes that tied and had thick, sturdy heels. Still others wore what looked like oriental slippers with a single strap across the instep. It didn't seem to matter what was worn; everyone moved. Petticoats flashed, heels stomped, laughter rang out.

A woman stood at the edge of a small wooden stage in front of the band and belted out instructions in a singsong voice. Maggie might not have understood most of the words, but she understood rhythm. Already she was itching to try it herself.

"But how do they know what do to?" she shouted over the music. "How do they understand her?"

"It's a sequence of moves repeated over and over," Cliff told her. "Once you've got the sequence down, you don't even need a caller; she just adds to it."

A sequence, Maggie mused and tried to find it. At first, she only saw bodies moving in what seemed a helter-skelter pattern, but gradually she began to see the repetition. Counting off the beats, she concentrated on one couple while trying to anticipate their next move. It pleased her to be able to find the sequence, just as the music pleased her ear and the swirling colors pleased her eye. She could smell a mixture of colognes, men's and women's, and the bursting fragrance of the spring flowers that skirted the pavilion.

As the sun dropped lower, the lights, strung overhead, spilled over the dancers. The floor vibrated under her feet so that she felt she was already dancing herself. With Cliff's arm around her, she watched with the undiluted fascination of discovering something new and exciting. She recognized the postmistress. The rather severe-looking middle-aged woman spun by like a dervish and flirted like a young girl.

Flirtation was part of it, Maggie realized as she began to watch faces instead of feet and bodies. Eye contact was essential, as were the saucy smiles she noted and the quick head tosses. It was, as perhaps dances had always been, a kind of mating ritual.

He hadn't thought she'd be fascinated or excited, but he recognized both in the look in her eyes. It gave Cliff overwhelming pleasure to know he'd brought that to her. Her face was flushed, her body already moving to the beat, and her eyes were everywhere at once. She didn't make him think of Maggie Fitzgerald, star baby and glamorous celebrity, but of Maggie, a woman he could hold on to and dance with until the sun came up again.

When the music ended, Maggie burst into raucous applause with everyone else. Laughing, her face tilted back, she grabbed his hand. "I have to try the next one, even if I make a fool of myself."

"Just listen to the calls and follow the music," he said simply as the lines began to form again. "They always run through the dance once before the music starts."

She listened as the next dance sequence was explained

by the caller. Though she didn't understand half of the terms, Maggie tried to link them in her mind with the moves that followed. As Cliff guided her slowly through the paces, she enjoyed the sense of camaraderie and the lack of inhibitions around her.

Though she could sense that she was being watched with speculation and interest, Maggie refused to be perturbed by it. They had a right to look, she decided. It was, after all, the first time she'd participated in a town function, and she was being partnered by a man everyone seemed to know.

"This one's called, 'Whiskey before Breakfast,'" the caller sang out. "If you've tried it, you know it ain't as good for you as dancing." She stomped her foot on the platform, one, two, three, and the music began.

The dance was fast and exuberant. Maggie was caught up in the moves before she'd fully registered them. Right, then left; join left hands with your corner and turn around twice. Pass through. Balance and swing.

The first time Cliff whirled her around, she felt the rush of air on her face and laughed.

"Watch my eyes," he warned. "Or you'll be too dizzy to stand up."

"I like it!" she tossed back, then "Whoops!" as she botched the next step and hurried to keep up with the rest of the line.

She didn't mind the sense of confusion or the crowd. Shoulders bumped, feet tangled, her waist was gripped, and she was whirled around by people she'd never met. Teenagers danced with grandmothers. Ladies in frilly dresses swirled with men in jeans with bandannas in their back pockets. Obviously anyone was welcome to line up and dance, and Maggie had already noticed that women picked men for partners just as often as men picked women. It was a free-for-all, and the rules were loose.

As the steps became more repetitive and more instinctive, she began to enjoy it even more. Her steps became more animated, her concentration less focused on the moves and more on the music. She could see why it drove people to dance. Feet couldn't be still with that rhythm jangling out. She knew, as Cliff grabbed her and swung her in fast circles, that she could've danced for hours.

"That's it," he said, laughing as she clung to him.

"Already?" She was breathless but not nearly finished. "It was wonderful, but too short. When do we do another?"

"Anytime you like."

"Now," she told him, sliding in as new lines formed.

She was fitting in as if she'd been to country dances in rural parks all her life. Perhaps he shouldn't have been surprised; she'd proved him wrong time and time again in his preconception of her. Yet in other ways, Cliff mused, he'd been right. She had an elegance that was too ingrained to be missed, whether she was scraping linoleum or lying in his arms. There was a polish that came from affluence and classy schools that set her apart from the other women around her. For days he'd been telling himself that it was that difference that attracted him as much as it put his back up. He couldn't explain the reason for either. He couldn't explain now, as he watched her begin the next dance as if she'd been moving to the call all her life, why she made him uneasy.

Circumstances, he told himself, and turned her back and around in a butterfly swing. The circumstances almost from the moment they'd met had been uneasy. That was bound to affect the way he felt when he looked at her—when he thought of her. And he thought of her, Cliff admitted, more often than he should; he looked at her less often than he wanted to.

Living with her for the past few days had given him the odd sensation of having something he hadn't known he'd wanted. There was something just a little too appealing about waking each morning with her warm beside him, about coming home to Maggie and her music. It would be wiser, much wiser, if he remembered those differences between them. No real common ground, he told himself again. But when she whirled into his arms, laughing, it was as though he'd been waiting for her.

The first few dances were a blur of color and sound and music. Maggie let herself go, realizing it had been weeks since she'd felt this free of tension and trouble. She'd danced in trendy clubs with celebrities, twirled in ballrooms with royalty, but she knew she'd never had as much simple fun as she was having now, following the caller and the fiddle.

As she turned to her next partner, she found her hand gripped by Stan Agee. Without his badge and gun, he might've been an attractive athlete in his prime. For a reason Maggie couldn't analyze, she tensed immediately on contact.

"Glad to see you're out, Miss Fitzgerald."

"Thank you." Determined not to give in to the mood, she smiled, lifting a hand to his shoulder as he began the spin. She caught his scent, the familiar department-store cologne, but it didn't soothe her.

"You catch on fast."

"It's wonderful. I can't believe I've missed it all my life." Out of the corner of her eye, she saw Cliff spinning with Joyce. The tension wouldn't dissolve.

"Save out a dance for me," he ordered before they whirled back to their original partners for the next step.

The moment he touched her, Cliff felt the rigidity of her muscles. "What's wrong?"

"Nothing." It was nothing, Maggie told herself, because she couldn't explain it. But now, as she swirled and turned from one pair of arms to another, it came to her that each time she danced with someone, she might be dancing with a murderer. How was she to know? It could be anyone—the real estate agent who'd sold her the house, the butcher who'd recommended the pork chops only the day before, the postmistress, the bank teller. How was she to know?

Maggie's mind began to whirl. For an instant, her eyes locked on Lieutenant Reiker's as he stood on the sidelines, watching. Why here? she asked herself as she was snatched up and spun again. Why would he come here? Perhaps he was watching her—but why? Protecting her—from what?

Then she was in Cliff's arms again, grateful that her feet could follow the mindless repetition of the dance while her thoughts raced in dozens of directions. Hadn't Cliff said people came from all over to this all-night festival? Maybe Reiker was a country-dance enthusiast. More likely, she thought grimly, he'd wanted to see all the townspeople together, observe, dissect. She shuddered. It was his job, she reminded herself. He was only doing his job. But how she wished he'd go away.

There was Louella, seeming to float through the dance. Rather than verve, she had a restrained dignity in her movements that was both lovely and uncomfortable to watch. Lovely, Maggie realized, because Louella had the grace of a natural dancer. Uncomfortable—though she wasn't able to put her finger on it, Maggie sensed there was something beneath the restraint that struggled for release.

Fanciful, she berated herself. She was being foolish and fanciful, imagining things that weren't there. But the feeling of discomfort was persistent. She was being watched, she knew. By Reiker? Stan Agee, Joyce, Louella? By everyone, Maggie thought. They all knew one another; they'd all known William Morgan. She was the outsider who'd uncovered what had been dead and buried for a decade. Logic indicated that at least one of them would resent her for that—perhaps all of them.

Suddenly, the music was too loud, the steps were too fast and the air was too full of scent.

Then she was caught up in Bog's short, wiry arms and spun at a breathless pace. "You're a good spinner, Miss Maggie," he told her, grinning and showing several gaps instead of teeth. "One helluva spinner."

Looking down into his homely, wrinkled face, she broke into a grin of her own. She was being ridiculous. No one resented her. Why should they? She wasn't involved in a tragedy that was ten years old. It was time she stopped looking beneath the surface and accepted things as she saw them. "I love to spin!" she shouted to Bog, leaning back into it. "I could spin for hours."

He gave a cackling laugh and released her for the next sequence. The music built, but it no longer seemed too loud. The tempo increased, but she could've danced faster and faster. When it was over, she had her hands linked around Cliff's neck and was laughing.

There was no tension in her now, but there had been. He thought he understood the reason. Deliberately, he steered her away from the Agees and Louella. "I could use a beer."

"Sounds perfect. I'd like to watch another one, anyway. It's the best show in town."

"You want a beer?"

Maggie glanced up, brow lifted. "Aren't I allowed?"

He shrugged and passed a man in overalls a dollar. "You just don't look like the beer type."

"You type too easily," Maggie countered, watching as beer was tapped from a wooden keg into paper cups.

"Maybe," he murmured as she sipped at the froth. "You're having a good time?"

"Yes." She laughed over the rim. The beer was luke-warm, but it was wet. Her foot was already tapping. They'd added a mandolin, she noticed. The sound was sweet and old-fashioned. "Didn't you think I would?"

"I thought you'd enjoy the music." He leaned against the wall so that he could see her with the dancers at her back. "I thought you needed to get out. But I didn't expect you to take to all this as if you'd been born doing it."

She lowered her half-empty cup and gave him a solemn smile. "When are you going to stop putting me in that shiny glass cage, Cliff? I'm not a delicate hothouse flower or a spoiled Hollywood bitch. I'm Maggie Fitz-gerald, and I write music."

The look held for a long time while the music pulsed around them. "I think I know who you are." Lifting a hand, he ran the back of it down her cheek. "I think I know Maggie Fitzgerald. It might've been safer for both of us with you in that glass cage."

She felt the heat rise. It only took a touch. "We'll have to see, won't we?" With one brow still lifted in question, she touched her cup to his. "To new understanding?"

"All right." He cradled her chin in his hand before he kissed her. "We'll give it a shot."

"Miss Fitzgerald?"

Maggie turned to see a short man in his early twenties

running a felt hat around and around in his hands. Until that moment, she'd been so intent on Cliff that she hadn't noticed the music had stopped. "You're the piano player." Her eyes lit, and the smile that could stun so unexpectedly curved on her lips. "You're wonderful."

He'd been nervous before; now he was overwhelmed. "I just— Thank you," he managed, staring at her with his soul in his eyes.

She doesn't even know it, Cliff realized. She wasn't aware that she could make a man want to grovel. Sipping his beer, he watched the piano player try to find his voice again.

"I couldn't believe it when I heard you were here."

"I live here," she told him simply.

The way she said it, so matter-of-factly, had Cliff looking at her again. She'd said it before, countless times in countless ways, but he realized now he hadn't listened. Yes, she lived here. She'd chosen to live here just as he had. It hardly mattered where she'd lived or how she'd lived before. She was here now because she'd chosen to be. And she was staying. For the first time, he fully believed it.

"Miss Fitzgerald…" The piano player crushed the brim of his hat in his fingers, torn between pleasure and anxiety. "I just wanted you to know it's great having you here. We don't want to push you into anything, but if you'd like to play anything, anything at all—"

"Are you asking?" she interrupted.

The boy stumbled over uncertain ground. "We just wanted you to know that if you'd like—"

"I don't know any of the songs," she told him, taking a last sip of beer. "Do you trust me to improvise?"

His mouth dropped open. "Are you kidding?"

She laughed and handed her cup to Cliff. "Hang on to this."

He shook his head, leaning back against the wall as she walked to the stage with the piano player. She had a habit of giving orders, he mused. Then he thought of the look of stunned admiration in the boy's eyes. Maybe it was worth it.

She played for an hour. It was, she discovered, as much fun making the music as it was dancing to it. She enjoyed the challenge of the unfamiliar music and the freewheeling style. Before she'd gone through the second number, Maggie had decided to write one of her own.

From the vantage point of the stage, she could see the dancers. She saw Louella again, partnered by Stan. Automatically, she searched the crowd for Joyce and found her facing Cliff. As if she'd known he'd be there, her gaze was drawn to the left. Reiker leaned against a post, smoking, watching the dancers.

Who? Maggie wondered. Who is he watching? As the lines merged and shifted, she couldn't be sure, only that the direction of his gaze rested on where Stan danced with Louella and Cliff with Joyce.

If he saw one of them as a murderer, it didn't show in his eyes. They were calm and steady and made Maggie's stomach queasy. Deliberately, she turned her head and concentrated on the music.

"I didn't expect to lose my partner to a piano," Cliff said when the music paused again.

Maggie sent him an arch look. "You didn't appear to lack for any."

"A lone man's easy prey around here." Grabbing her hand, he drew her to her feet. "Hungry?"

"Is it midnight already?" Maggie pressed a hand to her stomach. "I'm starving."

They piled their plates high, though the light was so

dim it was impossible to tell what they were eating until it was tasted. They sat on the grass under a tree and chatted easily to the people who passed by. It was easy, Maggie thought. They were just people drawn to one place by music. Again she felt a sense of camaraderie and connection. Leaning back, Maggie scanned the crowd.

"I don't see Louella."

"Stan would've taken her home," Cliff said between bites. "She never stays past midnight. He'll come back."

"Mmm." Maggie sampled what turned out to be Waldorf salad.

"Miss Fitzgerald."

Maggie set down her fork as Reiker crouched down beside her. "Lieutenant."

"I enjoyed your playing." He gave her the quiet smile that had her cursing her reaction to him. "I've listened to your music for years, but I never expected to be able to hear you play."

"I'm glad you liked it." She knew she should leave it at that, but felt compelled to go on. "I haven't noticed you dancing."

"Me?" The smile turned sheepish. "No, I don't dance. My wife, now, she likes to come."

Maggie felt herself relax. So the explanation had been a simple one, an innocent one. "Most people who appreciate music like to dance."

"I'd like to. My feet don't." His gaze shifted to Cliff. "I want to thank you for your cooperation. It might help us tie up a few loose ends."

"Whatever I can do," Cliff said briskly. "We'd all like this business tied up."

Reiker nodded, then, with some effort, rose. "I hope you'll play some more before the night's over, Miss Fitzgerald. It's a real pleasure listening to you."

When he was gone, Maggie let out a long breath. "It isn't fair that he makes me uncomfortable. He's only doing his job." She began to pick at her food again when Cliff remained silent. "What did he mean by cooperation?"

"I contaeted my mother. She's coming up Monday to give a statement."

"I see. That must be difficult for her."

"No." Cliff shrugged it off. "It was ten years ago. It's behind her. It's behind all of us," he added quietly, "but one."

Maggie closed her eyes on a shudder. She wouldn't think of it now, not tonight. "Dance with me again," she insisted when the musicians began to tune. "There are hours yet before dawn."

She never tired, even after the moon began to set. The music and the movement gave her the release she needed for nervous energy. Some dancers faded; others became only more exuberant as the night grew later. The music never stopped.

As the sky began to lighten, there were no more than a hundred dancers left on their feet. There was something mystical, something powerful, in watching the sun rise from behind the mountains while the music poured onto the air. As the light grew rosy with the new day, the last waltz was called.

Cliff folded Maggie in his arms and circled the floor. He could feel the life vibrate from her—exciting, strong. Once she'd stopped, he thought as he gathered her closer, she'd sleep for hours.

She moved with him, snug against him. Her heartbeat was steady, her hair soft. He watched the colors spread over the mountains to the east. Then she tilted back her head and smiled at him.

And when he realized he was in love with her, Cliff was stunned and speechless.

Chapter 12

Maggie might've noticed Cliff's abrupt withdrawal if she hadn't been so full of the night and the music. "I can't believe it's over. I've hours more dancing in me."

"You'll be asleep before you're home," Cliff told her, but made certain he wasn't touching her. He must be crazy, falling in love with a woman like her. She couldn't decide whether to hang wallpaper or lay tile. She gave orders. She wore silk under her jeans. He must be crazy.

But she could dance with him through the night. There was a ridge of strength and courage under the delicate features. She made music that was part heaven and part sin. Hadn't he known, and hadn't he fought so hard, because he'd known almost from the first that she was a woman he'd never get out of his mind?

Now she was climbing into the cab of his pickup and resting her head against his shoulder as if it belonged there. It did belong there. Though the acceptance didn't come easily to him, Cliff put his arm around her, drawing her closer. She belonged there.

"I don't know when I've had such a good time." The energy was draining out of her swiftly. Through sheer will, Maggie kept her eyes open.

"The music's still running around in your head."

She tilted her head so that she could see his profile. "I think you are beginning to understand me."

"Some."

"Some's enough." She yawned hugely. "It was fun playing tonight. You know, I've always avoided performing, mainly because I knew it would only open the door for more comparisons. But tonight…"

Cliff frowned, not certain if he liked the drift. "You're thinking of performing?"

"No, not on a regular basis. If I'd had a drive to do it, I'd have done it long before this." She shifted into a more comfortable position. "But I've decided to take C.J.'s advice and do the title song for *Heat Dance*. It's a compromise, a recording rather than a performance. And I do feel rather personally toward that song."

"You decided this tonight?"

"I've been leaning toward it for quite a while. It seems foolish to live by rules so strict you can't do something you really want to do. I really want to do that song." As her head began to droop, she noticed they were turning into her lane. "It'll mean flying back to L.A. for a few days for the taping, which'll thrill C.J." She gave a sleepy laugh. "He'll pull out every trick in the book to keep me from coming back."

Cliff felt the panic in his chest. He pulled the truck up at the end of the drive and set the brake. "I want you to marry me."

"What?" Half-asleep, Maggie shook her head, certain she'd misunderstood.

"I want you to marry me," Cliff repeated, but this time he took her shoulders so that she wasn't slumped down in the seat any longer. "I don't care if you record a dozen songs. You're going to marry me before you go back to California."

To say she was stunned would've been an immeasurable understatement. Maggie stared at him as if one of them had lost his mind. "I must be a little foggy at the moment," she said slowly. "Are you saying you want to marry me?"

"You know damn well what I'm saying." It was too much to know the fear of losing her just when he'd realized he couldn't live without her. He couldn't be calm; he couldn't be rational; he couldn't let her go without a pledge that she'd come back. "You're not going to California until you marry me."

Trying to clear her mind, Maggie drew back. "Are you talking about my doing a recording, or are we talking marriage? One has to do with my business, the other with my life."

Frustrated that she was calm when he couldn't be, Cliff dragged her back. "From now on, your life is my business."

"No." That sounded too familiar. "No, I don't want someone looking out for me, if that's what you mean. I won't take that kind of responsibility again, or that kind of guilt."

"I don't know what the hell you're talking about," Cliff exploded. "I'm telling you you're going to marry me."

"That's just it—you can't *tell* me!" She jerked away from him, and the sleepiness in her eyes had turned to fire. "Jerry told me we were getting married, and I went along because it seemed like the thing to do. He was my best friend. He'd helped me get over the death of my parents, encouraged me to write again. He wanted to take care of me." Maggie dragged a hand through her hair. "And I let him, until things started going downhill and he couldn't even take care of himself. I couldn't help him then. The pattern had been set, and I couldn't help him. Not again, Cliff. I won't be put in that glass cage again."

"This has nothing to do with your first marriage and nothing to do with cages," Cliff tossed back. "You can damn well take care of yourself, but you're going to marry me."

Her eyes narrowed into slits as she held down her own uncertain temper. "Why?"

"Because I'm telling you."

"Wrong answer." With a toss of her head, she was out of the truck and had slammed the door. "You can go cool off or go sleep it off or whatever you want," she told him coldly. "I'm going to bed." Turning on her heel, she strode up the shaky front steps to the door. As she turned the handle, she heard the sound of his truck descending the hill. *Let him go,* Maggie told herself before she could turn around and call him back. *You can't let yourself be pushed around that way.* When a man thinks he can order a woman to marry him, he deserves exactly what she'd given him, Maggie decided. A good swift kick in the ego. Imagine bringing up marriage out of the blue that way, she thought as she shoved open the front door. Marriage, not love. He dangled marriage at her as though it were a carrot at the end of a stick. She wasn't biting. If he wanted her, really wanted her, he'd have to do a hell of a lot better.

I love you. She leaned her head against the door and told herself she wouldn't cry. That's all it would've taken; that's all he'd needed to say. Understanding. No, she decided as she straightened again, they were still a long way from understanding each other.

Why wasn't the dog barking, she wondered grumpily

as she pushed the door shut again. Terrific watchdog he'd turned out to be. Annoyed, she turned toward the steps, planning on a hot bath and a long sleep, when a scent stopped her. Candle wax, Maggie thought, puzzled. Roses? Odd, she thought. Her imagination was good, but not good enough to conjure up scents. She crossed toward the living room and stopped in the doorway.

Louella sat very straight and very prim in a high-backed chair. Her hands were neatly folded in the lap of the same misty-gray dress she'd worn for dancing. Her skin was so pale that the shadows under her eyes looked like bruises. The eyes themselves seemed to stare straight through Maggie. On the table beside her there were candles burning, the tapers hardly more than stubs now, with the wax pooled heavily on the base of the holders. A vase of fresh roses sat nearby, so that the breeze through the open window carried the scent through the room.

After the first shock, Maggie tried to bring her thoughts to order. It had been obvious from the first that Louella wasn't completely well. She'd have to be handled gently, Maggie thought, and so she approached her as one might a wounded bird.

"Mrs. Morgan," she said quietly, then cautiously touched a hand to her shoulder.

"I've always liked candlelight." Louella spoke in her calm, soft voice. "So much prettier than a lamp. I'd often burn candles in the evening."

"They're lovely." Maggie kept her tone gentle as she knelt beside her. "But it's morning now."

"Yes." Louella looked blankly at the sun-filled window. "I often sit up through the night. I like the sounds. The woods make such music at night."

Perhaps if she'd thought it through, Maggie wouldn't have questioned. She would simply have led Louella out to her car and driven her home. But she didn't think it through. "Do you often come here at night, Mrs. Morgan?"

"Sometimes I'll drive," she said dreamily. "Sometimes, if the night's as clear and warm as this, I'll walk. I used to walk a great deal as a girl. Joyce used to love to toddle on the paths in the woods when she was just a baby."

Maggie moistened her lips. "Do you come back here often, Mrs. Morgan, at night?"

"I know I should stay away. Joyce has told me so all along. But—" Louella sighed, and the small, sad smile touched her mouth. "She has Stan. Such a good man— they take care of each other. That's what marriage is, you know, loving and taking care of each other."

"Yes." Helplessly, Maggie watched as Louella's hands grew agitated in her lap.

"William wasn't a loving man. He just wasn't made that way. I wanted Joyce to have a loving man, like Stan." She lapsed into silence, closing her eyes and breathing shallowly so that Maggie thought she slept. Deciding it was best to call the Agees, she started to rise, when Louella's hand closed over hers.

"I followed him here that night," she whispered. Now her eyes were intense, fully focused. Maggie's mouth went dry.

"Followed him?"

"I didn't want anything to happen. Joyce loved him so."

Maggie struggled to keep her voice low and even, her eyes steady. "You followed your husband here?"

"William was here," Louella told her. "He was here, and he had the money. I knew he was going to do something dreadful, something he'd have gotten away with because of who he was. There had to be an end to it." Her fingers tightened convulsively on Maggie's, then relaxed just as abruptly as her head fell back. "Of course, the money couldn't be buried with him. I thought, no, if they find him, they shouldn't find the money. So I hid it."

"Here," Maggie managed. "In the attic."

"In the old trunk. I forgot all about it," Louella said as fatigue washed through her voice. "Forgot until a few weeks ago, when they dug in the gully. I came and took the money out and burned it, as I should've burned it ten years ago."

Maggie looked down at the hand that lay limply on hers. It was frail, the blue veins showing sharply against the thin ivory skin. Could that hand have pulled a trigger, sending a bullet into a man? Maggie shifted her gaze to Louella's face and saw it was now serene in sleep.

What do I do? Maggie asked herself as she laid Louella's hand carefully back in her lap. Call the police? Maggie looked at the peacefully sleeping, fragile figure in the chair. No, she couldn't; she didn't have the steel for it. She'd call Joyce.

She went to the phone and asked the operator for Joyce's number. There was no answer at the Agee house. Maggie sighed and glanced over her shoulder into the living room at Louella, who was still sleeping. She hated to do it, but she had to call Lieutenant Reiker. When she couldn't get hold of him, either, she left a message with his office.

Coming back into the living room, Maggie gasped as a figure moved toward her. "Oh, you frightened me."

"Sorry." Stan looked with concern from Maggie to his mother-in-law. "I came in the back. The dog's sleeping pretty heavily in the kitchen. Looks like Louella might've given him part of a sleeping pill to keep him quiet."

"Oh." Maggie made an instinctive move toward the kitchen.

"He's all right," Stan assured her. "He'll just be a little groggy when he wakes up."

"Sheriff—Stan," she decided, hoping the lack of formality would make it easier for him. "I was just about to call you. I think Louella's been here most of the night."

"I'm sorry." He rubbed his own sleep-starved eyes. "She's been getting steadily worse since this business started. Joyce and I don't want to put her in a home."

"No." Concerned, she touched his arm. "But she told me she wanders at night, and—" Maggie broke off and circled the room. Could she tell him what Louella had said? He was her son-in-law, but he was still the sheriff. The badge and the gun he wore reminded her.

"I heard what she told you, Maggie."

She turned, her eyes filled with compassion and concern. "What should we do? She's so fragile. I can't bear to be a part of having her punished for something that happened so long ago. And yet, if she killed…" With her conscience tearing her in different directions, she turned again.

"I don't know." Stan looked at Louella while he rubbed the back of his neck. "What she told you doesn't have to be true."

"But it makes sense," Maggie insisted. "She knew about the money. If she'd hid it in the trunk, then forgotten about it, blocked it out because it reminded her—" Maggie shook her head and forced herself to continue. "Stan, it's the only explanation for the break-in here." She covered her face with her hands as her sense of right and wrong battled. "She needs help," Maggie said abruptly. "She doesn't need police or lawyers. She needs a doctor."

Relief ran over Stan's face. "She'll get one. The best one Joyce and I can find."

Shaky, uncertain, Maggie rested a hand on the table. "She's devoted to you," she murmured. "She always speaks so highly of you, of how you love Joyce. I think she'd do anything she could to keep both of you happy."

As she spoke, Maggie's gaze was drawn down to where her palm rested—on the color snapshot of Morgan and Stan, near the gully. It would all be laid to rest now, she thought as she stared down at the photo. Louella had suffered enough, been punished enough for—

Distracted, she narrowed her eyes and looked closer. Why it came to her now, Maggie would never know, but she remembered Reiker's words. "We found a ring, too, an old ring with a lot of fancy carving and three small diamond chips…Joyce Agee identified it as her father's."

But in the picture William Morgan wasn't wearing the ring. Stan Agee was.

She looked up, her eyes dry and clear with the knowledge.

He didn't have to look at the picture under her hand. He'd already seen. "You should've let it go, Maggie."

She didn't stop to think, to reason; she only reacted. In a dead run, she headed for the front door. The move was so unexpected, she was into the hall with her hand on the knob before he'd taken the first step. As the door stuck, she cursed it, cursed her own inefficiency for not having it seen to weeks before. As she started to tug a second time, Stan's hand closed over her arm.

"Don't." His voice was low and strained. "I don't want to hurt you. I have to think this through."

With her back to the door, Maggie stared at him. She was alone in the house with a murderer. Alone, she thought desperately, except for a fragile old woman who loved him enough to have shielded him for ten years. Maggie watched him rest his hand on the butt of his gun.

"We'd better sit down."

* * *

Cliff drank his second cup of coffee and wished it was bourbon. If he'd tried to make a fool of himself over a woman, he could've done no better. Drinking in the strong, bitter taste, he scowled down at the laminated counter in the café. The scent of frying eggs and sausage did nothing for his appetite.

How could he have botched it so badly? What woman in her right mind, he asked himself, would respond favorably to a shouted, angry proposal? Maggie had given him the heave-ho, and now that he'd cooled off a bit, he couldn't blame her.

Still, he wasn't one of the fancy crowd she'd run with in L.A., he reminded himself. He wasn't going to change his manners for her any more than he expected her to change for him. She'd chosen to change her life before he'd been a part of it.

Chosen, Cliff thought again, cursing himself. She'd chosen her home, and he'd never seen anyone put down roots so quickly. He shouldn't have panicked at the mention of the recording in L.A. She'd be back. The land was as important to her as it was to him. Perhaps that had been their first bond, though they both insisted they'd had no common ground.

She'd be back, Cliff told himself again. He'd been an idiot to think bullying her into marriage would assure that. Maggie wouldn't be bullied, and she was here to stay. Those were two of the reasons he loved her.

He should have told her that, he thought, pushing the unwanted coffee aside. He could have found the words to tell her he'd been in love with her for weeks and that at dawn, with the morning light spilling over her face, he'd realized it. It had taken his breath away, stolen his senses, made him weak. He could've found the words to tell her.

Straightening from the counter, he checked his watch. She'd had an hour's sleep. Cliff decided a woman didn't need any more than that for a proper proposal of marriage. He tossed the money on the counter and began to whistle.

He continued to whistle as he took the road through town, until Joyce dashed into the street and frantically hailed him.

"Oh, Cliff!"

Though he'd stopped the car in the middle of the street, he was halfway out of it as he spoke. "What is it, one of the kids?"

"No, no." Struggling for calm, Joyce gripped his arms. She, too, hadn't changed from the dance, but the hair she'd worn up was now escaping its pins and falling in clumps. "It's my mother," she managed after a moment. "She hasn't been in bed all night—and Stan, I can't find Stan anywhere."

"We'll find Louella." Cliff brushed the hair from her face as he'd done since she'd been a child. "She might have been restless and gone for a walk. With the excitement last night—"

"Cliff." Joyce gripped his arms tighter. "I think she went out to the old place. I'm dead sure of it—it wouldn't be the first time."

He thought of Maggie with a little ripple of unease. "Maggie's home," he said soothingly. "She'll look out for her."

"She's been getting worse." Joyce's breath began to shudder. "Oh, Cliff, I thought I was doing the right thing, the only thing."

"What're you talking about?"

"I lied to the police. I lied before I'd thought it through, but I know I'd do the same thing again." She pressed her fingers to her eyes briefly, then dropped them. When she looked at Cliff now, she looked at him with a surface calm that was deadly. "I know who killed my father. I've known for weeks. Mother—it seems Mother's known for ten years."

"Get in," he ordered. He was thinking of Maggie now, of Maggie alone in the house, surrounded by woods. "Tell me while we drive."

Maggie's back was stiff and straight as she sat on a low bench. Moving only her eyes, she watched Stan pace the room. She wanted to believe he wouldn't hurt her. But he'd killed once, ten years before. Now he'd have to deal with her or pay for it.

"I never wanted Joyce to sell this house." He paced to the window, then back to the center of the room. "I never wanted it. The money meant nothing to me. Her money—her father's money—never has. How could I've guessed she'd get it into her head to put it on the market when I was out of town?"

He ran a hand over his shirt and left faint streaks. He's sweating, Maggie noted. It didn't help her nerves.

"She lied to the police about the ring."

Maggie moistened her lips. "She loves you."

"She didn't know—I'd never told her all these years. Then, when I finally had to, she stood by me. A man can't ask for more than that." He paced again, so that the soles of his shoes hitting hardwood and rug were the only sounds. "I didn't murder him," Stan said flatly. When he looked at Maggie, his eyes were glazed with fatigue. "It was an accident."

She gripped that, clung to that. "Then if you go to the police and explain—"

"Explain?" Stan cut her off. "Explain that I killed a

man, buried him and drove his car into the river?" He rubbed the heels of his hands over his face. "I was only twenty," he began. "Joyce and I'd been in love for two years. Morgan had already made it clear that there couldn't be anything between us, so we saw each other in secret. When Joyce found out she was pregnant, there couldn't be any more secrets."

He leaned against the window and stared into the room. "We should've known there was something wrong when he took it so well, but we were both so relieved, both so thrilled at the idea of being married and starting a family, that we never caught on. He told us to keep it quiet for a few weeks while he arranged for the wedding."

Maggie remembered the stern face from the photograph. "But he didn't mean it."

"No, both of us were too wrapped up in each other to remember what kind of man he was." Stan kept moving in the same line, to the window, back to the center of the room, to the window again. "He said he was having trouble with groundhogs up at his old place. I was young and eager to do anything to keep on the right side of him. I told him I'd bring my shotgun one evening after work and take care of them."

He saw Maggie shudder and glance at the pistol on his hip. "It was dusk when he drove up. I didn't expect him. When he got out of the car, I remember thinking he looked like an undertaker, all in black with shiny shoes. He was carrying a little metal box that he set down on the stump of a tree near the gully. He didn't waste any time," Stan continued. "He told me outright that he'd never let a small-town nobody like me marry his daughter. He said he was going to send her away. Sweden or somewhere. She'd have the baby and give it away. He didn't expect me to keep quiet for nothing. He told me he had twenty-five thousand in the box. I was to take it and disappear."

So the twenty-five thousand had been payoff money, blackmail. Yes, she could believe that the man in the photo had thought money would ensure anything.

"I got frantic. I couldn't believe he was threatening to take away everything I'd ever wanted. He could've done it, too." Stan wiped at the sweat that beaded on his upper lip. "He would've done it without a second thought. I shouted at him. I told him he wasn't going to take Joyce and our baby away from me. I told him we'd go away, we didn't need his filthy money. He opened the cash box and showed me all those bills, as if it would tempt me. I knocked it out of his hands."

His breath was coming quickly now, heavily, as if he were reliving that moment—the anger, the despair. Maggie felt her pity well up to tangle with her fear.

"He never lost his temper. Never once. He just bent down and scooped the money back in the box. He thought I wanted more. He never understood, wasn't capable of understanding. When it got to the point where he saw I wasn't going to take the money and go away, he picked up my gun just as calmly as he'd picked up the box. I knew, as sure as I'd ever know anything, that he'd kill me where I stood and he'd get away with it. Somehow he'd get away with it. All I could think was that I'd never see Joyce again, never hold our baby. I grabbed for the gun—it went off over my shoulder. We started struggling."

He was panting now, his eyes glazed. Maggie could visualize the struggle between man and boy as clearly as if it were happening in front of her eyes. She shut them. Then she saw the scene in the film she'd scored in which overpowering need had erupted into irrevocable violence. But this was real and needed no music to spark the drama.

"He was strong—that old man was strong. I knew I'd be dead if I didn't get the gun away. Somehow—" Stan dragged both his hands up his face and into his hair. "Somehow I had it in my hands and was falling back. I'll never forget—it was like a dream, a nightmare. I was falling back, and the gun went off."

She could picture it, all too clearly. Both sympathetic and afraid, Maggie dared to speak. "But it was an accident, self-defense."

He shook his head as his hands dropped back to his side, back, she noted with a tremor, near the gun on his hip. "I was twenty, scraping pennies. I'd just killed the most important man in town, and there was twenty-five thousand dollars in a box next to his body. Who'd have believed me? Maybe I panicked, maybe I did the only sensible thing, but I buried him and his money in the gully, then sent his car into the river."

"Louella…" Maggie began.

"I didn't know she'd followed me. I guess she knew Morgan better than anyone and understood he'd never let me marry Joyce. I didn't know she'd watched everything from the woods. Maybe if I had, things would've been different. It seemed she never really came out of the shock of losing her husband—now I understand better. She'd seen it all—then, for some reason of her own, she'd dug out the cash box and hidden it in the house. I guess she was protecting me all these years."

"And Joyce?"

"She never knew." Stan shook his head and tugged at the collar of his shirt as if it were too tight. "I never told her. You have to understand. I love Joyce. I've loved her since she was a girl. There's nothing I wouldn't do for her if I could. If I'd told her everything, everything he'd threatened to do and what had happened, she might have thought—she might not have believed it was an accident. I couldn't have lived with that. For years I've done everything I could to make up for what happened in that gully. I dedicated myself to the law, to the town. I've been the best father, the best husband, I know how to be."

He picked up the color snapshot and crushed it in his hand. "That damn picture. Damn ring. I was so wired up I didn't notice I'd lost it until days afterward. My grandfather's ring." He rubbed a hand over his temple. "Ten years later it's dug up with Morgan. Do you know how I felt when I learned that Joyce had identified it as her father's? She knew," he said passionately. "She knew it was mine, but she stood behind me. She never questioned me, and when I told her everything, she never doubted me. All these years—I've lived with it all these years."

"You don't have to live with it anymore." Maggie spoke calmly, though her heart was in her throat. He was strung so tight she couldn't gauge when he might snap or what he might do. "People respect you, know you. Louella saw everything. She'd testify."

"Louella's on the edge of a complete breakdown. Who knows if she'd be capable of making a coherent sentence if all this comes out? I have to think of Joyce, of my family, of my reputation." A muscle began to jerk in his cheek as he stared at Maggie. "There's so much at stake," he whispered. "So much to protect."

She watched his hand hover over the butt of his gun.

Cliff started up the steep lane at full speed, spitting gravel. Joyce's breathless story told him one vital thing. Maggie was caught in the middle of violence and passion that had simmered underground for ten years. If it erupted today, she'd be alone—alone because he'd been a fool. As he rounded the top curve, a man stepped into the path of the car, forcing him to brake. Swearing, Cliff stormed out of the car.

"Mr. Delaney," Reiker said mildly. "Mrs. Agee."

"Where's Maggie?" Cliff demanded, and would've moved past him if Reiker hadn't stopped him with a surprisingly strong grip.

"She's inside. At the moment, she's fine. Let's keep it that way."

"I'm going up."

"Not yet." He gave Cliff a long, steely look before he turned to Joyce. "Your mother's inside, Mrs. Agee. She's fine, sleeping. Your husband's in there, too."

"Stan." Joyce looked toward the house, taking an instinctive step forward.

"I've been keeping a close eye on things. Your husband told Miss Fitzgerald everything."

Cliff's blood iced. "Damn it, why haven't you gotten her out?"

"We're going to get her out. We're going to get them all out. Quietly."

"How do you know he won't hurt her?"

"I don't—if he's pushed. I want your help, Mrs. Agee. If your husband loves you as much as he says, you're the key." He looked toward the house. "He'd have heard the car. Better let him know you're here."

Inside the house, Stan had Maggie by the arm, holding her close as he stood at the window. She could feel his muscles jumping, hear his breath whistling. As terror washed over her, she closed her eyes and thought of Cliff. If he'd come back, everything would be all right. If he came back, the nightmare would end.

"Someone's out there." Stan jerked his head toward the open window, and his free hand opened and closed on the butt of his gun. "I can't let you talk to anyone. You have to understand. I can't risk it."

"I won't." His fingers dug into her arm so that the pain kept her head clear. "Stan, I want to help you. I swear I only want to help. If you hurt me, it'll never be over."

"Ten years," he muttered, straining to see any movement outside. "Ten years and he's still trying to ruin my life. I can't let him."

"Your life will be ruined if you do anything to me." *Be logical,* Maggie told herself as waves of panic threatened to overtake her. *Be calm.* "It wouldn't be an accident this time, Stan. This time you'd be a murderer. You'd never make Joyce understand."

His fingers tightened until she had to dig her teeth into her lower lip to keep from crying out. "Joyce stood behind me."

"She loves you. She believes in you. But if you hurt me, everything would change."

She felt him tremble. The grip on her arm loosened fractionally. As Maggie watched, Joyce walked up over the rise toward the house. At first, she thought she was hallucinating; then she heard Stan's breath catch. He saw her, too.

"Stan." Joyce's hand moved on her throat, as if she could make her voice stronger. "Stan, please come out."

"I don't want you involved in this." Stan's fingers were like iron on Maggie's arm again.

"I am involved. I've always been involved. I know everything you did you did for me."

"Damn it." He pressed his face against the window glass, pounding one fist steadily against the frame. "He can't ruin everything we've built."

"No, he can't." Joyce came closer to the house, measuring each step. In all the years she'd known her husband, she'd never heard despair in his voice. "Stan, he can't touch us now. We're together. We'll always be together."

"They'll take me away from you. The law." He squeezed his eyes tighter. "I've done my best by the law."

"Everyone knows that. Stan, I'll be with you. I love you. You're everything to me, my whole life. Please, please, don't do anything I'd be ashamed of."

Maggie felt him tense as he straightened from the window. The muscle was still working in his cheek. There was a line of sweat over his lip he no longer bothered to wipe away. He stared out the window, at Joyce, then over at the gully.

"Ten years," he whispered. "But it's still not over."

His fingers worked sporadically on Maggie's arm. Numb with fear, she watched as he drew the gun out of its holster. His eyes met hers, cold, clear blue, without expression. Perhaps she would've begged for her life, but she knew, as any prey knows, that mercy comes at the hunter's whim.

His expression never changed as he set the gun down on the sill and released her arm. Maggie felt her blood begin to pump again, fast and hot. "I'm going outside," Stan said flatly, "to my wife."

Weak with relief, Maggie sank down on the piano stool. Without even the energy to weep, she buried her face in her hands.

"Oh, Maggie." Then Cliff's arms were around her, and she could feel the hard, fast beat of his heart. "That was the longest ten minutes of my life," he murmured as he began to run wild kisses over her face. "The longest."

She didn't want explanations. He was here; that was enough. "I kept telling myself you'd come. It kept me sane."

"I shouldn't have left you alone." He buried his face in her hair and drew in the scent.

She held him tighter. "I told you I could take care of myself."

He laughed, because she was in his arms and nothing had changed. "Yes, you did. It's over now." He framed her face in his hands so that he could study it. Pale, he noticed. The eyes were shadowed but steady. His Maggie was a woman who could take care of herself. "Reiker was outside, long enough to get the drift of what was going on. He's taking all three of them."

She thought of Louella's pale face, Stan's anguished eyes, Joyce's trembling voice. "They've been punished enough."

"Maybe." He ran his hands up her arms, just to assure himself she was whole and safe. "If he'd hurt you—"

"He wouldn't have." She shook her head and clung again. "He couldn't have. I want the pond, Cliff," she said fiercely. "I want you to put in the pond quickly, and I want to see the willow draping over it."

"You'll have it." He drew her back again. "And me? Will you have me, Maggie?"

She took a deep breath, letting his fingers rest on her face again. Again, she thought. She would try again and see if he understood. "Why should I?"

His brows drew together, but he managed to swallow the oath that came to mind. Instead, he kissed her, hard and long. "Because I love you."

She let out a trembling breath. She was indeed home. "That was the right answer."

* * * * *

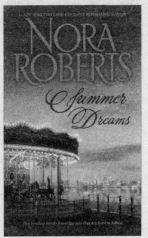

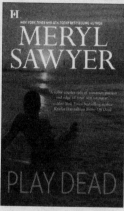

NORA ROBERTS

28587	NIGHT TALES: NIGHTSHADE & NIGHT SMOKE __ $7.99 U.S. __ $9.99 CAN.
28586	NIGHT TALES: NIGHT SHIFT & NIGHT SHADOW __ $7.99 U.S. __ $9.99 CAN.
28583	WORTH THE RISK __ $7.99 U.S. __ $9.99 CAN.
28595	WINDFALL __ $7.99 U.S. __ $8.99 CAN.
28580	THE MacKADE BROTHERS: DEVIN AND SHANE __ $7.99 U.S. __ $8.99 CAN.
28578	THE LAW OF LOVE __ $7.99 U.S. __ $8.99 CAN.
28575	THE MacKADE BROTHERS: RAFE AND JARED __ $7.99 U.S. __ $8.99 CAN.
28574	CHARMED & ENCHANTED __ $7.99 U.S. __ $7.99 CAN.
28573	LOVE BY DESIGN __ $7.99 U.S. __ $7.99 CAN.
28569	THE MacGREGOR GROOMS __ $7.99 U.S. __ $7.99 CAN.
28568	WAITING FOR NICK & CONSIDERING KATE __ $7.99 U.S. __ $7.99 CAN.
28565	TREASURES __ $7.99 U.S. __ $9.50 CAN.
28562	STARS __ $7.99 U.S. __ $9.50 CAN.

(limited quantities available)

TOTAL AMOUNT	$ _____
POSTAGE & HANDLING	$ _____
($1.00 FOR 1 BOOK, 50¢ for each additional)	
APPLICABLE TAXES*	$ _____
TOTAL PAYABLE	$ _____

(check or money order—please do not send cash)

To order, complete this form and send it, along with a check or money order for the total above, payable to Harlequin Books, to: **In the U.S.:** 3010 Walden Avenue, P.O. Box 9077, Buffalo, NY 14269-9077; **In Canada:** P.O. Box 636, Fort Erie, Ontario, L2A 5X3.

Name: _____
Address: _____ City: _____
State/Prov.: _____ Zip/Postal Code: _____
Account Number (if applicable): _____

075 CSAS

*New York residents remit applicable sales taxes.
*Canadian residents remit applicable GST and provincial taxes.

Silhouette®
Where love comes alive™

Visit Silhouette Books at www.eHarlequin.com   PSNR0410BL